The Murderou
To
Peace

By

George Donald

Also By George Donald

Billy's Run
Charlie's Promise
A Question of Balance
Natural Justice
Logan
A Ripple of Murder
A Forgotten Murder
The Seed of Fear
The Knicker-knocker
The Cornishman
A Presumption of Murder
A Straight Forward Theft
The Medal
A Decent Wee Man
Charlie's Dilemma
The Second Agenda
Though the Brightest Fell
The ADAT
A Loan with Patsy
A Thread of Murder
Harry's Back
Charlie's Recall
The Broken Woman
Mavisbank Quay
Maggie Brogan
Malinky
The Privileged Daughter
A Conflicted Revenge
Charlie's Swansong
The Rookie Suspect
No Sad Loss
Maitland
The Rule Of The Six 'P's'
The Dragon's Breath
The Murder Suspect List
The Convicted Woman
The Honest Policeman
The Man With Inner Rage
DCI Wells
Malice by Mail

This work is mine and mine alone and all characters and events mentioned, other than those clearly in the public domain, are fictitious, and any resemblance to any individual is purely coincidental.

As I likely have previously mentioned, writing crime fiction is not my profession, but my hobby and so while I recognise that it is not ideal to self-edit and self-publish one's own work, I accept that any spelling, grammatical or other mistakes are mine and mine alone.

If you should come across some errors, hopefully you'll cut me some slack, forgive such mistakes and fingers crossed, they do not interfere with the storyline.

George Donald

PROLOGUE

Apart from the very obvious of course, that being the body of the dead man lying sprawled on the linoleum floor, it seemed that the now identified deceased, James Crawford, must have loved his wee dog if any kind of a clue was the numerous photos of the Scottish Terrier that were sitting on the mantelpiece. The dog, he had been told by one of the uniform cops standing guard in the corridor outside the high-rise flat, was called Baxter and presumably named after the Glasgow Rangers famous half back.
The same cop also told him Crawford, known locally as Jimmy, was a fervent Rangers supporter. This fact seemingly was supported by several framed photos on the walls depicting Rangers players in action, as well as the Rangers scarf that was tightly wound the dead man's neck, causing his face to turn a bright shade of red and his eyes to bulge.
He couldn't help but notice too that though the body was lying face down with the deceased's face turned to one side and his trousers partially pulled down to permit the casualty surgeon to insert a thermometer, Crawford had released both his bowels and bladder. Albeit he wore a medical facemask and had attended more than a few murders, the pungent stench was far too familiar, for the overpowering smell emanating from the dead man caused him to choke back the urge to retch.
Glancing around the front room, the décor and furniture seemed to indicate it was stuck somewhere between the nineteen-seventies and -eighties, with some of the wallpaper now peeling at the edges. Raising his eyes to stare at the once white emulsion painted ceiling, his nose wrinkled when he saw it to now be a patchy light brown, almost coffee colour and most notably above where the two armchairs sat, guessing it to be the result of decades of cigarette smoking in the room, then idly wondered what the post-mortem examination would reveal about the state of the victim's lungs.

Turning his attention to the doctor kneeling on the floor by the body and similarly dressed in a baggy, all-encompassing white paper forensic suit, he watched as the doctor first removed, then glanced at the thermometer before staring up at him.

His cut-glass voice was muffled by his mask when he said, "The room's relatively warm and lividity has not set in yet, so I would conclude that he's been dead around an hour to two hours at the most. As you can probably guess, my preliminary conclusion and that," he stressed, "based on his appearance only, is the cause of death is strangulation, but then again…"

"The post-mortem will determine the cause of death," he finished for the older man.

The doctor's eyes narrowed when staring at him, he asked, "I'm sorry, but I was expecting DCI Heggerty to attend the locus. You are?"

He considered responding with, I'm bloody starving, is what I am because I've not had anything since breakfast, but instead forced a smile and replied, "DI Eddie Fairbanks, doctor. I arrived at the Division, oh," his brow creased, "just over four and a half months ago now."

"Ah, right. You're the detective who was run over by a bus, was it?"

"A Land Rover."

"Ah, yes, a Land Rover. Great vehicles," he nodded, then absent-mindedly added, "Had one myself a ways back."

With some difficulty the doctor rose to his feet on what Fairbanks presumed, if the creaking was an indication, arthritic knee joints.

"Well," he sighed as he turned to stare down at the body, "now that I've pronounced life extinct, I'll get the paperwork to you by tomorrow morning and let you get on with your job, Mr Fairbanks. Please be so kind as to pass on my regards to Bobby Heggerty, will you?"

"I'll do that doctor," he acknowledged with a nod.

The doctor was gone just a minute when DC Jackie Wilson, like the rest of the team dressed in a white forensic suit, though in Wilson's case the suit threatening to burst at the seams, stepped into the room, then angrily muttered, "Wonder why the wee dog was murdered too?"

"Here," her eyes narrowing and before he could respond, she handed him a small tube of scented hand cream, then sniffed, "My God, he must've had a curry before he died."

Fairbanks choked back his response and while he dabbed some of the cream onto his forefinger, then rubbing it across his top lip, idly considered his knowledge of Scottish criminal law and wondered; can a dog be murdered?

With Wilson by his side, he stepped towards corner of the room where the Scottish Terrier had either been flung or kicked towards and stared at the corpse, its white fur matted with dried blood.

Seconds passed before he thoughtfully nodded at the blood-stained knife lying by the dog, "The knife there seems to be part of a set from the kitchen worktop, but I'm curious why he strangled the old man and didn't use the knife."

"How do you mean?" she turned to stare at him.

"Well, the killer has brought the knife from the kitchen, so why use the scarf when he could have stabbed the victim?"

"Maybe intended using the knife just to scare the old man, but then had to use it to protect himself from the dog?"

"Possibly, yes," he sighed.

She frowned when she asked, "Who do you think he killed first, Eddie. Crawford or the wee dog?"

"I'd be guessing, Jackie, but if he's killed Crawford first then it's possible the dog has tried to intervene to save his master, so on that point, have the dog examined by the scenes of crime, particularly its mouth. If it's bitten the killer, there could be human DNA swimming about its teeth and gums and also, ensure too they take a sample of the dog's blood and hair fibres in case we find a suspect with a bite mark or the dog's blood on their clothing."

He grimly smiled when he added "In my time. I've ordered a fair few post-mortems be conducted, but never a dogs PM, so that'll be a first."

"And if the dog was killed first?" she glanced at him.

He slowly exhaled before he replied, "Then a struggle has ensued and that's resulted in Crawford being strangled, but look around you. The room seems intact and doesn't indicate any sign of a struggle and that might be because Crawford looks to be what, about five feet four or five inches? Maybe nine stone soaking wet? That and he's no spring chicken either, I'm thinking."

"He was sixty-six," she said with a frown. "The woman across the landing, she told me he celebrated his birthday a couple of months ago. That and apparently he suffered from a hacking cough and was nearly bent double these days."

She paused, then with a squint around the room, she suggested, "If there's no obvious sign of a struggle, you think maybe he knew his killer?"

Again, before he could respond, she continued, "Oh, and there doesn't appear to be any sign of damage to the front door lock and the key was in the lock on the inside. That and the attending cops told me when they arrived and got no reply to their knocking, that they just turned the handle and came in."

"What brought them here?"

"Anonymous call saying there was a disturbance in the flat."

"Anonymous call to where? The Maryhill Office or Pitt Street Control Room?"

"Don't know, but I'll find out."

"When you make the inquiry, check if there is any Call Related Data with the call. If we can get a phone number…"

He left the rest unsaid.

Turning away from the body of the dog, his interest was piqued, he asked, "The woman across the landing. What else was she able to tell you?"

"Well, he lived alone, his wife died some years previously apparently and he liked a good bevy at the weekend, but seldom drank during the week unless there was a Rangers game on Wednesday nights…"

"So, this being Tuesday," he thoughtfully interjected, "the odds are that he was sober when he was murdered."

"Probably," she nodded, then continued, "Her across the landing, she says he was a fanatical Rangers supporter, but couldn't afford to attend the games so, when there was a game on, he usually went down to one of the local pubs to watch the game on the Sky Sports."

"Any family we can notify?"

"The neighbour, she's been there for about six years she says and tells me there's a married daughter, Fiona, who lives in the city somewhere, she *thinks*, but doesn't know *why* she thinks that. Anyway, she says after the mother died a couple of years back, she hasn't seen the lassie since. Again, she's not sure, but thinks there was some kind of fallout, but doesn't know what it was about and thinks the daughter's not in touch with her father anymore. Well, he never mentions the daughter, she says."

"What about other family; sons or daughters I mean."

Wilson shook her head when she replied, "Just knows about the one lassie."

"Any contact details for the daughter or a married name, even?"

Wilson shrugged when she said, "The neighbour thinks it's McDonnell or O'Donnell or something like that, but no; she's got no contact details."

"Did she provide any information about pals or visitors?"

Wilson's face creased when she replied, "No, says she keeps herself to herself, but my guess is she's a nosey old bugger, so when the guys are doing the formal door to door interviews, I'll ensure I put myself down for her. I'm thinking she maybe knows more than she's letting on."

"Righto," he nodded then asked, "These multi-storey's, Jackie. I saw that the front door downstairs has a secure entry with buttons for the individual flats. Is there a concierge or someone like that to monitor who comes in or out?"

"I'm not sure, Eddie, but I'll find out and get back to you about that. As for the secure entrance," she sighed, "when I met you downstairs and opened the door for you, it wasn't secure because the locks buggered, so anyone can wander in or out."

"Sods Law," he shook his head, then added, "I don't think there's anything else I need to see at the minute, so you stay here with the SOCO and when they're done, see the house is secured and have a cop stand by meantime. Any issues from the shift Inspector, get in touch with me on my mobile. In the meantime, I'll head back to the office to brief the DCI with what little we know."

CHAPTER ONE: Tuesday, 19 September 2006.

Knocking on the DCI's door, Eddie Fairbanks was surprised to see that sitting at his desk, Bobby Heggerty's face was pale and he seemed to be grimacing.

"You okay, boss?"

Heggerty shook his head before he replied, "Bloody stomach is giving me gyp. The wife thinks it's an ulcer."

"And what does the doctor think?" Fairbanks face creased, but had already guessed the answer before he asked.

"Don't you start," Heggerty grumbled, then with a sigh, admitted, "Okay, I haven't actually been to the quack, but she who must be obeyed has made an appointment for me this evening, so once you brief me, I'll be away. And Eddie," he stared at the younger man, "are you sure you're okay to take this murder on? I mean, I'm not doubting your ability," he raised a defensive hand, "but after you were injured, you're only back working what, for a couple of months now? Then when you returned it was straight into the DI rank, so it's not as if you've had a lot of time to get your feet under your desk."

Fairbanks stared at Heggerty before he said, "Almost three months since I returned, but look, boss," he sat down opposite Heggerty, "if you've faith in me, then you'll know I'll do a good job. That and we both know I'll have a good team around me with plenty of experience among them."

His eyes narrowed when he stared at Heggerty and asked, "And if I'm guessing correctly, you're thinking you might be taking some sick leave?"

"Depends what the quack tells me," Heggerty almost growled at the thought, then said, "But yes, I might need to take some time off."

"Well then," Fairbanks smiled, "you'll never be further than a telephone call if I need some advice, will you?"

His eyes narrowed when he added, "Unless you're thinking that this ulcer of yours or whatever it is, is going to keep you off work for a lot longer than you anticipate."

Heggerty didn't immediately respond, but then softly exhaled when he said, "Look, Eddie, I'll share this with you in the strictest confidence. I've no idea what's going on with me, but for the past few weeks I've been passing blood in my stool."

Before a shocked Fairbanks could interrupt, he raised a hand to continue, "I know, I know, I should have done something about it sooner, but there was me like an idiot thinking it was maybe haemorrhoids or something and to my regret," he shook his head, "I never mentioned it to my Cathy. I only told her last night, so you can imagine the ear bashing she gave me and hence the doctor's appointment this evening," he grimaced.

"And rightly so," Fairbanks face creased, his expression clearly letting Heggerty know he approved of Cathy's anger, then shaking his head, asked, "Bloody *hell*, boss, what were you thinking?"

He locked eyes with his DI before he said, "There's a real likelihood if it's what we're both thinking, that maybe it's the big C, then the doctor will probably sign me off work, Eddie, and that will mean the weight of the Divisional CID will fall on your shoulders. Unless of course our new ACC (Crime) decides to appoint a temporary DCI to cover while I'm off."

"Why do I sense you don't like Mr Gardener?"

Heggerty wryly smiled when he replied, "It's not me disliking Alex Gardener, more that he and I have some personal history and leave it at that, eh?"

Seconds passed before Fairbanks said, "And I'm also sensing that Mr Gardener would be pleased to see the back of you, that if there is to be a temporary appointed DCI, you're thinking they might in fact be a replacement rather and a stand-in while you're off?"

"You've got it in one, DI Fairbanks," he continued to smile at him, then added, "If my suspicions are correct and it is the big C and *if* Gardener has his way, he'll do his damn best to influence the Force Doctor to pension me off on medical grounds. Any excuse to get rid of me."

"Well, whatever your personal history is, boss, it sounds like I'll need to be watching my step when you're away."

"Oh, aye, Eddie," he quickly nodded. "If I ever offer you any advice, it's keep a weather eye open when Alex Gardener is in the room. Sleekit doesn't even begin to describe that man, these days, and if he appoints someone to take my place, rest assured it will be one of his sycophants and they will be just as dangerous, so watch your back."

Slowly shaking his head, Fairbanks humourlessly smiled when he said, "I don't think I'll ever get used to the politics of this job."

"The sad thing is," Heggerty stared at him, "if you want to progress in the job, Eddie, you'll need to adapt to the politics. Now," he sighed, "before I head off to the doctors, what's the story about your murder? The locus is a flat in one of the multi-storey's up in Wynford Road, I'm told."

Recounting the little they had so far gleaned about the victim, Fairbanks concluded with, "I left Jackie Wilson to liaise with the SOCO and secure the locus. Once I'm done here, I'll go and organise the incident room."

"Jackie's more than capable, so a good decision. I've already got DS Considine doing that and appointed him office manager," Heggerty grunted.

Then in a quieter voice, he said, "A word to the wise, if you please. He's not the worse guy in the world, is Larry Considine, but it's no secret he likes more than a swally, Eddie. I think the term to describe him is, functioning alcoholic, but to his credit, he doesn't drink when he's working. Look," he leaned forward, "between you and me, I've looked out for Larry for some time now. He's approaching his twenty-nine years and the last thing I want is for him to lose his job and his pension because of his addiction."

"You're thinking of ACC Gardener again?"

"Exactly," he sighed, "so, if I am placed on sick leave, can you keep an eye on Larry for me?"

Eternally grateful for Heggerty's support when he arrived under a cloud at Maryhill Police Office, it was a no-brainer for Fairbanks, who nodding, replied, "Consider it done, boss."

"Good," a relieved Heggerty sat back in his chair, then said, "Now, divvying up the Department between your murder investigation and those remaining on the book, I've a couple of instructions that I'd like implemented as soon as possible."

****

When DC Jackie Wilson returned to the CID suite at Maryhill Police Office, she saw that the large room designated to handle serious crime investigation was in full swing, with the headquarters team from the Home Office Large Major Enquiry System (HOLMES) busying themselves setting up their system network while the appointed office manager, DS Considine, chivvied the Divisional civilian clerks and typists to arrange the desks and paperwork synonymous with such an investigation.

Wilson nodded at acting DC Susie Lauder to join her in the corridor, then asked, "What's going on so far?"

"Well," Lauder sighed, "our Larry's his usual tight-arse, getting up everyone's nose, but in fairness, he's getting things moving. Eddie Fairbanks is in with the DCI and I suppose they're discussing who'll be working on the murder and who'll be on the book, dealing with the day to day stuff that comes in," she huffed.

"You two," they turned to see Eddie Fairbanks crooking a finger and beckoning them to him, "the DCI wants a word."
Without waiting for a response, he turned on his heel and made his way along the corridor to Bobby Heggerty's room.
Rolling her eyes, Wilson stared at Lauder, then with a shrug, followed Fairbanks along the corridor where they saw him first knock on Heggerty's door, then usher them both inside.
When they were standing in front of him with the door closed behind them and Fairbanks standing to one side, a stony-faced Heggerty first addressed Wilson when he said, "It has come to my attention, DC Wilson, that you are vastly overqualified to be holding the rank of DC. As of today, you will assume the role of acting Detective Sergeant and while the murder investigation is being conducted, you will be responsible for the day to day running of the office, dealing with the incoming crime reports and supervising the DC's who remain on the book."
He broke into a wide smile when he added, "It's only an acting rank for the minute, Jackie, but from little acorns; well, you know the rest. Congratulations."
Stunned, she turned to stare at a smiling Fairbanks, who told her, "Needless to say, if not the boss, then I'll be on hand for any issues that might crop up, Jackie, so don't be slow in knocking on my door."
"Thanks, Eddie, I mean, eh, boss," she stuttered and to the amusement of the other three who had never before seen Jackie Wilson stuck for words.
Heggerty turned his attention to Susie Lauder when sighing, he said, "I've no need to rake over the coals about the DC we all know who was returned to uniform and posted to F Division, Susie. In short, the stupid bugger was lucky to keep his job and but for the intervention of Ma'am downstairs, who took cognisance of the fact he had a wife and two kids, he'd have been out on his ear. However, it means we're a Divisional DC down and while the usual six-month secondment period as a CID aide is not yet finished, in light of your recent performance in the acting role…"
Fairbanks saw her eyes widen and literally, her jaw drop.
"…and in agreement with Chief Superintendent Malone, as of today's date, you are hereby appointed to the rank of Detective

Constable. Congratulations, DC Lauder," he stood up from his desk to reach across and shake the open-mouthed Lauder's hand.

"First opportunity you get," he continued to smile at her, "attend at Pitt Street and have the personnel department issue you with a new warrant card, okay?"

"Yes, sir," she eagerly nodded, then added, "Thank you, thank you both," she turned to smile at Fairbanks.

"Now," Heggerty pretended to frown, "I'm a busy man, so DI Fairbanks, you'll have a murder to run while you, DS Wilson, will have the rest of the workload. Might I suggest you get yourselves out there and get to work in your new roles," he waved a hand towards the door.

In the corridor outside, Susie Lauder could hardly contain her excitement and physically resisted the urge to hug Fairbanks.

"Right," he turned to Wilson, "your first task as a DS, Jackie, and because you've been here all your service and that means you'll know better than me the strengths and weakness of the department, let's me and you take ten minutes to sit down in my office to work out who I'll have working on the murder."

"And me?" a grinning Lauder stared from one to the other.

Choking back a grin, it was Fairbanks who replied, "As your first task, DC Lauder, see if you can drum up a couple of coffees for me and the DS, if you please?"

****

Nobody took any notice of the twenty-five-year old, clean shaven young man who wearing the dark grey hoodie, had his hands in the pockets of the baggy faded jeans and who wore a black coloured New York skip cap over his short, brown hair.

Most, if not all the dozen and a half or so locals who stood quietly watching and idly chatting amongst themselves about the police presence at the tower block, had eyes only for the two uniformed police officers who stood in the forecourt at the entrance to the building.

The young man was to all intent and purpose, had anyone glanced at him, just another curious tenant or passer-by, attracted by the two marked police vehicles and the white coloured, unmarked SOCO Transit van, so nothing special that would attract any attention; least of all from the two officers.

Of course, rumours abounded about why the cops were there at the tower block in Wyndford Road, that so and so heard it was a murder; no, another interrupted, it was a drugs raid or perhaps even, the more salacious mentally crossed their fingers, a sexual thing. Maybe a rape.

Whatever the reason, the few hardy stalwarts among the crowd waited in the hope the media would attend and maybe, with a bit of luck, they'd get their face on the evening's news, even if it cost them the price of a bunch of flowers to lay down somewhere.

As the man watched, the blue and white chequered 'POLICE: DO NOT CROSS' tape gently swayed in the light breeze when he saw a heavily pregnant woman, who carried two TESCO shopping bags, approach the two officers. Then, apparently having satisfied them that indeed, she did reside in the tower block, the female officer lifted the tape to permit her entry to the forecourt of the building while the male officer gallantly took the bags from the woman then escorted her through the front doors.

Turning so that his back faced the building, the man first rubbed at his lower left leg as if to soothe the ache through the hastily applied bandage under the denim material of his jeans, while inwardly cursing the dead dog. Then standing upright, he fetched a mobile phone from the pocket of his hoodie, then pressed a pre-dialled number.

When the phone was answered, he first glanced about him for fear of being overheard, then lowered his voice when he said, "They're here. They've found him."

CHAPTER TWO.

The Divisional CID, the agreed split between murder team and those left on the book to deal with the daily crime reports, acting DS Jackie Wilson and Eddie Fairbanks finished his coffee then told her, "Bring in your guys that are in the office, Jackie, and I'll brief everyone on what we know so far."

Almost as an afterthought, he sourly added, "Which is at the minute is bugger all."

Arriving at the incident room, it was DS Larry Considine, his thick unruly, mop of red hair plastered with perspiration and his face as red as a tomato, who with a pronounced lisp due to his ill-fitting teeth, loudly called out "Right everyone, ears pinned back."

Seeing Bobby Heggerty slipping into the room at the back and wearing his overcoat, the sudden silence that followed was broken when Fairbanks began, "Our victim, James Crawford, known locally as Jimmy, sixty-six years of age, a widower and now former resident on the fourth floor of the tower block located at 151 Wynford Road, was discovered by our uniformed colleagues approximately two hours ago, apparently strangled to death. First indication is that he has been dead for no longer than four hours."

His glance around the room left nobody in doubt that the information he had just imparted remained confidential.

"Needless to say, the cause of death remains unconfirmed till after the PM. As for previous dealings with the police, the PNC has our victim recorded for a number of offences, but none in the last seven years. The offences recorded are for football Breach of the Peace, D & I and one eighteen years ago for an assault that was recorded as domestic."

One of the civilian HOLMES operators, a young woman in her early twenties, leaned towards her supervisor, a DS, to whisper, "What's a D & I?"

In the same low voice, he whispered back, "Drunk and incapable. Lifted off the street and in days gone by, let out in the early morning hours when sober, usually after paying a bail of around a fiver that was forfeited and doubled as a fine."

Fairbanks, seeing that some of the team were taking notes, paused for several seconds, then continued, "Curiously, the victim's wee dog was stabbed to death, though whether this occurred before or after Crawford's murder, we do not know."

"Bastard," someone at the back muttered, causing Fairbanks to wonder at the detective's anger at the unknown killer of a dog, while nothing had been uttered regarding Crawford's murder.

With a sigh, he said, "Yes, well, let's concentrate on the murder, shall we?"

"Sorry, boss," came the terse response.

"Now, the DCI has appointed me as the SIO for the murder, so any objections," he smiled at the team, but received no comment.

"Good. Right, the little we know about our victim is what *acting* DS Wilson…"

He stopped to permit the ragged cheer and handclapping to end, then with a smile, continued, "What acting DS Wilson gleaned from a neighbour, the little we know is that Crawford was a Rangers supporter, that he lived alone, but has a daughter, Fiona, though we have no contact information for her. Larry?"

"Boss?"

"We'll make that the team's number one priority, finding her to inform her of her father's death."

"Yes, boss," he nodded.

"Now, while DS Considine sorts out the door to door, DC Lauder, who is now appointed to the Department," he smiled again and once more patiently waited till the congratulations died down, "you and DC Smythe will obtain an Action from DS Considine and concentrate on finding the daughter, who Jackie discovered is married with the *possible* surname O'Donnell or McDonnell, but don't take that as Gospel."

"Oh, and Duke," he stared at the tall, balding and well-built Smythe, "keep an eye on Lauder. She's a tendency to go off on a tangent."

Listening at the back of the room, Heggerty smiled at the teasing laughter, thankful that Eddie Fairbanks was as he'd predicted those five months previously, a real find for his Department and not at all like his predecessor, that prat Johnny Morris, who was now languishing as a uniform Inspector in darkest Dunoon.

Catching Fairbanks eye, he gave him a quick nod then left the room to attend his appointment, confident until his return that he was leaving his Department in safe hands.

That's *if* he returns, he inwardly grimaced.

"Right," Fairbanks watched the door close behind Heggerty, "it only remains for me to say, that most of you have previously worked on serious crime investigations, so it will come as no surprise that you'll be working long hours and I will be asking things of you that might be out of your ordinary working day."

He paused then said, "We all worked on the shooting at the ASDA store and we were all involved in the hunt for that bastard, whose name I don't even want to use, who murdered our colleague, Gels McEwan. I know how hard you all worked for Bobby Heggerty and I know that you are capable of those long hours. However, I am also

aware that most of you have family commitments too, so do not ignore those commitments. If you are in need of time off to deal with personal issues, my door is open. Is that clearly understood?"
He could not know that those few words were appreciated and had come as a surprise to many of them; words that endeared him to even the most hard-bitten detectives among them and who responded to with, "Yes, boss," and the nodding of heads.
About to dismiss them to collect their door-to-door forms from Considine, he stopped when the door to the room opened to admit Tom Daly, the uniformed Constable who acted as the CID clerk and who entered with his hand raised.
"Tom?" his eyes narrowed in curiosity, knowing that the experienced Daly would not interrupt a briefing without good cause and beckoned him forward.
Daly handed him a note, then leaning forward and in a low voice, said, "I've just had the SOCO on the phone, looking for you, sir. They said to bring this to your attention immediately."
Reading the note, he turned to stare at Daly before he asked, "There's no mistake?"
"No, sir, that's what the SOCO supervisor told me."
Acutely aware the room had gone silent, Fairbanks sighed when he addressed the room to tell them, "It seems during the SOCO search of the victim's flat, they discovered a hidden recess in the bottom of a set of drawers in the victim's bedroom."
His brow furrowing, he glanced down again at the note before he added, "In the recess, they discovered a semi-automatic handgun with a box of nine millimetre bullets."
****

DC Paul 'Duke' Smythe, forty-two years of age and married with four teenage children, tossed the set of keys to Lauder and told her, "You drive, Susie, I'll need to phone the wife and let her know I'll probably be home late tonight."
"Will that be one of them, your dinner's in the dog situation then?"
He grinned when he said, "Don't let her fool you, I'm the boss in my house."
But then with a subtle shake of the head, quietly added, "When she gives me permission, that is."
"How is Shona?"
"Oh, I'd forgotten, you've met her, haven't you?"

She pulled open the driver's door, then replied, "Just the once. At Gel's funeral or rather, the purvey after it."
"Oh, she's doing fine, now that the weans are big enough to wipe their own arses and she's got herself a job."
When the large detective settled himself into the passenger seat and though she wouldn't dare comment, Lauder almost felt the saloon car tip to one side.
"How old are your kids, anyway?"
"Tim, the oldest, he's nineteen gone and at Uni," she heard the pride in his voice, "while my youngest, Sarah, she's turned thirteen and more of a handful than the other three put together."
He grunted, then added, "That lassie, she wears her school skirt like it's a wide belt. Shocking, so it is and will she listen to me or her mother?" he shook his head.
Suppressing her smile, Lauder carefully negotiated her way out of the rear yard, then replied, "Aye, kids these days, eh?"
"So," she continued, "where's Shona got herself a job?"
"Local bakery in Bearsden, just a five-minute walk from the house, so there goes the waistline," he slapped at his already expanding midriff.
"Right then," he shifted in his seat, "here's what I'm thinking. We'll speak again to the neighbour that Jackie Wilson spoke with, see if she knows of any friends or pals the daughter has and if they're local, pay them a visit. If she doesn't know, we'll call at the local health centre and check the victim's health record. It might list his next of kin or family members. How does that sound?"
"Fine by me, but the medical centre, Duke. Won't they invoke the Data Protection Act and refuse us any details?"
He glanced at her when he replied, "The man's pan bread, Susie. They can hardly protect his personal details now, can they? Besides, if they have the details of his daughter and where she can be contacted, I don't see any decent minded individual refusing to let us inform a woman that her father has died. That and," he pursed his lips, "I can be very charming and persuasive when it's called for."
"Here's hoping then," she shrugged, but inwardly had her doubts.
****
Jackie Wilson, for all her overt confidence and wisecracking with her colleagues, was still a little stunned at the unexpected acting rank thrust upon her and following Eddie Fairbanks briefing, led her eight

detectives, six male and two females, one of whom was an aide to the CID, into the general office.

"Right guys," she began in an assertive voice that hid her nervousness, for only she knew her self-assurance was as false as her girlfriends' eyelashes, "you all know me and I know all of you, so here's what I'm thinking. We're going to be undermanned while the murder investigation is on, so I'll expect you all to act like adults. Treat me fairly and I assure you, I'll reciprocate and do all I can to earn you some overtime for as long as the murder runs. However," she cast an eye about the room, "just because I'm new to being a supervisor, don't think you can make a mug out of me. You know that I'm one of the guys and that I've been round the block more than once, so I'll know when you're working and when you're skiving. Everybody clear about that?"

Nods and, "Yes, Jackie," echoed around the room, but it was Tom Daly who caught her attention when he said, "I've over a dozen CR's here waiting to be allocated, Jackie. You want me to go ahead and distribute them or do you want to do that?"

Tom Daly had been the CID clerk for over three years and was a man the detectives trusted, so Wilson made her first supervisory decision when with a smile, she replied, "Go ahead, Tom. You allocate them."

****

For all his personal issues and though he'd only known him five months, Eddie Fairbanks considered Larry Considine to be both a competent DS and incident room manager and so, calling him into the DI's room, motioned that Considine sit, then began, "You've a lot of experience running an incident room, Larry, so as a first time SIO, I'm more than happy to be guided by you."

A little taken aback at Fairbanks plain speaking, Considine nodded and took a few seconds to gather his thoughts before he replied, "Okay, boss, well, here's what I'm thinking. If you leave me to allocate the Actions as I see fit, I'll keep you apprised of anything that you should know. As the SIO and as I'm sure you're aware, your days of going out knocking on doors are gone. In short, your job is managing the investigation from that chair you're parked on, unless of course you see fit to take a turn out to conduct an interview or chase a bad guy," he smiled.

"Oh, that I might consider, if nothing other than to take a turn out of the office," Fairbanks returned his smile, then with an almost regretful sigh, added, "But for now, I'll follow the chain of command. So, here's what I'm thinking. I'll haunt the incident room, but not interfere with any decisions that you make regarding the Actions. Any decisions regarding the direction the investigation takes will be down to me. Each morning after the briefing, you and I will have a sit down to discuss the way forward. Now the rest, as they say, we'll make up as we go along. Okay with you?"

Considine peered at Fairbanks with a newfound respect, then nodding, replied, "Agreed. That sounds okay with me, boss. So, what's your first instruction?"

"Make an arrangement for the PM as soon as possible and tomorrow morning would be great, if you can work your magic."

With a soft smile, Considine replied, "Way ahead of you. When it was confirmed as a murder, I made the arrangement right away and it's at ten, tomorrow morning at the mortuary in the Southern General over in Govan. I was thinking if you're okay with it, appointing Duke Smythe and Susie Lauder as the production officers. It'll give Duke the opportunity to teach young Susie how we deal with productions in a murder investigation and," his brow creased, "I don't think she's actually attended a PM as yet. If nothing else, it'll be an experience for her," he allowed himself a grim smile.

"Agreed," Fairbanks nodded, then added, "And I have an idea about who'll accompany me as the corroborating officer. In the meantime, please create an Action to have someone attend at the SOCO office in Pitt Street and determine what information they can provide about the handgun that was discovered."

"Will do. Anything else?"

"Not at the minute, but if something comes to mind, I know where to find you."

****

It was a little after four o'clock that afternoon when seated at his desk in the DI's room, Eddie Fairbanks heard the door knock, then glancing up, saw Constable Alex Rooney standing there.

Rooney, known through the Division as Mickey, said, "I'm told you want to see me, sir?"

Fairbanks put down his pen and beckoning into the room to the chair in front of his desk, greeted him with, "How is the plainclothes squad treating you, Mickey?"

Rooney's face creased when he slowly replied, "It kind of lost its appeal after; well, you know."

Fairbanks did know, for it had been Rooney who had held the gunned down Sergeant Geraldine McEwan in his arms as she slowly bled internally to death from her wound.

"In confidence, Mickey," he held up a calming hand, "I know that the Divisional Commander made you attend the Force Medical Officer for a couple of sessions. Can I ask, how did they go? What I mean," he twisted uncomfortably in his chair, "are you okay?"

"Yes, I'm fine," Rooney's brow creased. "The doc says that the trauma of Gel's death is something that will remain with me for a very long time, but I've a good wife and a supportive family, sir, so yes, I'm doing okay, thanks for asking."

"Well, to be honest, I'm not asking out of any concern for your welfare, Mickey."

He paused for several seconds, then explained, "You know we've a murder investigation on our hands?"

"Aye, I heard about it. Some old guy in the high-rise flats over in Wynford?"

"Correct. Now, the DCI has appointed me as SIO while he's maybe taking a short leave over some health issue, so that gives me some latitude with the staff under my command. That means while you are officially a constable attached to the plainclothes squad, the squad itself comes under the remit of the CID. In effect, that makes you one of my officers."

"Sir?" Rooney's eyes narrowed.

"Look," Fairbanks shrugged, "you've impressed me, Mickey, how you handled yourself during the investigation to catch Gel's killer and, as Susie Lauder has now been appointed as a DC…"

"Good for her," Rooney interjected with a smile.

"…it leaves me short of a CID aide. I've already spoken with Ma'am downstairs and who has agreed with my decision. So, how do you feel about joining the department for a six months secondment and if it works out, possibly an appointment to the CID?"

Rooney's eyes widened when he burst out, "Yes! That would be great, sir! Yes, please!"

"Good," he smiled at Rooney's obvious enthusiasm. "Right then,

Mickey, take it as read you're starting tomorrow morning, so be suited up and in sharp here at eight and, oh," he drew a breath and grimaced, "I'm afraid you're going in at the deep end."

"Sir?"

"You'll be neighbouring me to the victim's post mortem."

****

The victim's neighbour was unable to provide any further information that might have identified the daughter, Fiona's friends or associates or even where she worked.

Glancing at his wristwatch, Paul Smythe said, "Let's mosey on down to the Maryhill Health Centre and see if we can dig up an address there."

"Mosey on down?" Lauder repeated with a smirk. "Who are you really? And I've never thought to ask. Why are you called Duke? Have you some royalty in your background or something?"

"I happen to be a big fan of *The* Duke," Smythe sniffed as he settled his bulk into the passenger seat, then added, "The great John Wayne. In fact, I've got all his DVD's."

"The cowboy actor?"

"The actor," he corrected, her, "who often played the part of a cowboy."

"My God," she stifled a grin, "and there's me thinking I should be bowing to you and pulling the forelock. And what does your wife think about this…this obsession with John Wayne?"

"Well," he wheezed, "I've got John Wayne and Shona, she's got her line-dancing at the bowling club at the weekend."

"What a pair, the two of you," Lauder giggled.

"And you, ya cheeky besom. You still going out with your reporter fella, eh, what's-his-name again?"

"Oh, aye, and it's Archie. In fact, we've moved in together. I finally persuaded him to come across to Giffnock, so he's renting out his flat in the West end and you wouldn't believe the money he's getting for it."

"Oh, I can guess," Smythe slowly shook his head. "The West End, that's where the *real* money in property is."

"Right, here we go," she pulled into a bay at the side of the red-bricked building, then switching off the engine, turned to him to say, "Okay, big man, let's see just how charming you can be."

CHAPTER THREE.

Fairbanks glanced up from his desk when the door to his office was pushed open and a man strode in.
His stomach tensed when he recognised the Assistant Chief Constable (Crime), Alex Gardener, and so respectfully rose from his desk to greet him with, "Good afternoon, sir. How can I help you?"
A handsome man who Fairbanks judged to be in his early fifties, Gardener stood an inch or two taller than Fairbanks' five feet ten, his face clean-shaven and sporting a tanned complexion, his first impression of the ACC was that he resembled a tailor's dummy. His light brown hair was neatly groomed and his white shirt with the red and blue tie contrasted with the charcoal three-piece suit, while his black shoes gleamed as though just polished.
For some inner reason that he could not explain and regardless of Bobby Heggerty's warning about the ACC, Fairbanks quickly formed the opinion that he did not like this man, not at all.
Behind Gardener stood a well-dressed man that he judged to be younger than Fairbanks's thirty-eight years by about six or seven years and whose hair was similarly light brown coloured. As tall as was Gardener, he wore a white shirt with a navy-blue tie and a navy blue, two-piece suit.
"DI Fairbanks, isn't it?" his head turned slightly to one side as Gardener stared at him.
"Yes, sir."
Waving a hand behind him, Gardener casually said, "This is my aide, DI Cameron. Now, where can I find DCI Heggerty? His office door is locked."
"The DCI is out of the office at the minute, sir, attending to a personal issue."
"And that issue is?"
"I have no idea, sir," Fairbanks politely lied.
His eyes boring into Fairbanks eyes as though trying to intimidate him, he said in the same monotone voice, "You're telling me that DCI Heggerty, the SIO in a new murder investigation, has left the office to attend to a personal issue?"

Fairbanks, too long in the tooth to be bullied, calmly replied, "No sir, you are correct when I said he has left to attend to a personal issue, but he is not the SIO in the investigation. I am. So again, sir, how may I help you?"

Though his gaze was fixed to Gardener, his peripheral vision caught the younger DI's head tilting to one side as though he did not wish to be part of this conversation.

Gardener's eyes narrowed when he stared at Fairbanks, trying to decide whether the DI was being insolent or simply curious.

Without making any attempt to sit in the chair in front of the desk, the ACC finally replied, "You may begin by explaining why an inexperienced Detective Inspector who has, if I am correct, just recently returned to duty after a life-threatening injury, been assigned as the SIO in the murder of an elderly man."

Fairbanks felt his throat tighten, but before he could respond, a woman's voice interrupted with, "Good afternoon, Mr Gardener I heard you were in the building."

It was with no small relief to Fairbanks that when all three men turned to stare at the door, they saw Chief Superintendent Liz Malone, the Divisional Commander, standing there in uniform, though without her cap, her hands politely clasped in front of her and with a warm smile on her face.

Stymied, Gardener replied, "Ah, yes, good afternoon, Ms Malone. It was my intention to pop by to see you, but I thought I'd first visit DCI Heggerty only to discover he's not here."

"No, I'm aware that the DCI is attending to a personal issue, sir, and I've just popped up to inquire of DI Fairbanks if there is any update in his murder investigation."

"Eddie?" she turned to smile at Fairbanks, who taking his cue, replied, "Early days, yet Ma'am. The team have been issued their door-to-door forms and I've a pair out trying to trace the next of kin. So far, no suspects or motive."

"Very well, keep me apprised, Mr Fairbanks," she formally replied, then continuing to smile at him, turned back to Gardener and said, "Perhaps you'll accompany me to my office, sir, where I'm certain I can persuade my clerk to rustle up some coffee."

If he gave any thought to refusing her offer, she left him no choice when she stood to one side and with her hand, motioned that he leave.

Without a backward glance, Gardener stepped through the door though to Fairbanks surprise, the young DI turned before he left to give him a fleeting smile.

When they'd gone, he slumped down into his chair and loudly sighed with relief, yet suspected that Liz Malone had not just happened to pop by for an update.

No, his eyes narrowed, she had visited him knowing that Gardener would be looking for Bobby Heggerty and out to cause trouble.

He found himself grinning and somehow, once more, just knew that again he'd dodged a bullet.

****

The stern faced, blonde-haired receptionist at the Maryhill Health Centre was an attractive thirty something, but with a voice that Lauder later opined was like someone running their nails down a blackboard.

"No," the woman's eyes narrowed and her forehead creased when she shook her head, "I cannot help you because we do not give out any patient details at all."

Lauder thought her attitude was more to do with a personal dislike of the police than actual adherence to the Data Protection Act, but was surprised when Smythe, his voice betraying his impatience, replied, "Well, *Miss*, can you fetch the practice manager for a quiet word as to why you are being so belligerent?"

"Eh, what?"

Clearly taken aback, the now red-faced and angry receptionist's eyes narrowed and her nostrils flared before she turned and disappeared through a door at behind her.

Minutes passed as the two detectives silently stared at each other, then the door re-opened to admit a woman, who seemed to be about forty years of age and was accompanied by the receptionist.

"I'm the practice manager. What exactly is the problem?" the woman addressed Smythe, though from her defensive attitude and posture, it was clear to Lauder that the receptionist had already primed her as to who the bad guys were.

He didn't immediately respond, but then calmly said, "The problem is a man has died under circumstances that are being investigated by Strathclyde Police and we are endeavouring to inform his next of kin. Unfortunately, we have no details of who and where they might be, other than it is likely a daughter. Our inquiries have led us to believe," he blatantly lied, "that the deceased was a patient at this Health Centre and so we have come to try and elicit some details that might assist us to track down the next of kin."

The manager opened her mouth, but before she could respond, Smythe raised a hand and continued, "Now, it seems to me that you are likely of an age with surviving parents or a parent, so I'll ask you. If the police were trying to contact you by *any* means available to them, about a parent being ill or worse, what would you have them do?"

Clearly taken aback, the manager glanced at the receptionist, then, her shoulders slumping, stepped forward to the desk to ask, "This gentleman who has died. What's his name and address?"

****

Chief Superintendent Liz Malone glanced up when her clerk knocked on her door to inform her, "DI Fairbanks asking if he can have a word, Ma'am?"

"Of course," she smiled and lay down her pen. "Ask him to come in."

When he entered the room, Malone motioned that he sit in one of the two chairs opposite, then asked, "What can I do for you, Eddie?"

Staring at her, he saw a woman who he guessed must be in her early fifties, but certainly looked younger and retained the figure of her youth, with her shoulder length hair, though tinged with grey, tied back into a fierce ponytail. Her uniform tunic now hung from a freestanding coat stand while her white blouse accentuated the swell of her breasts.

Liz Malone was, as many men before him had realised, still an extremely attractive woman.

Taking an inward breath, he replied, "I won't take up any of your time, Ma'am, I've just popped down to thank you for what we both know was a timely intervention with ACC Gardener."

Malone didn't immediately respond, but staring at him, she slowly smiled, then said, "Actually, you should be thanking your clerk, Tom Daly. When he saw him in the corridor Tom sensed there might be trouble, so phoned me down to let me know that Gardener was in the building, otherwise…" she shrugged.

"That," she continued, "and knowing Bobby Heggerty as I do, I must assume he gave you a heads up about our ACC?"

"He did allude to some friction between them, yes," but then raising a hand, quickly added, "Believe me, that's not why I'm here. I have no need to know what the issue is, I simply want to say thanks for saving me trying to, eh…"

"Cover your boss's, arse?" she grinned.

He returned her grin, then replied, "Something like that, yes."

"Well, as I'm in the twilight of my career, Eddie, and nothing to lose, let *me* also warn you. Watch your back with Gardener. Not a nice man, these days, though there was a time…" she shook her head and grimaced.

He rose to his feet, then nodding, replied, "Thanks, Ma'am, I think I've already become aware of that."

Making his way up the stairs to the CID suite, Fairbanks smiled as he glanced into the general office where he saw Tom Daly at his desk, his head down and reading a report.

"Tom."

"Sir?" Daly glanced up.

"Just want to say, thanks."

Daly, a long in the tooth and experienced beat man prior to being given the job as the CID clerk, liked Fairbanks.

Smiling, he nodded when he replied, "Anytime."

****

Seated at his desk, DS Larry Considine's mouth tasted like he'd been chewing a two-day-old sock and cocking his head to stare at the wall clock, saw it would be a good two hours before he could have a nip from the half bottle in his glove compartment.

"Sarge," he glanced up at the young HOLMES operator addressing him, "that's all the door to door forms for the third, fourth and fifth floors been issued. Do you want us to prepare further forms for the second and sixth floors?"

"No," he shook his head, "not till the results come in from the other floors. We can always start on them if we need to expand the door to door interviews."

His desk phone rang and lifting the receiver, heard DC Smythe tell him, "Larry, it's Duke. We've got an address for the victim's daughter, Fiona McDonnell, who lives over in Coatbridge. Craigend Drive," he added. "Do you want me and Susie to go there and give her the bad news, or does the boss want to attend himself?"

"Where are you the now, Duke?"

"Sitting outside the Maryhill Health Centre, but we'll need a decision soon. The traffic at this time of night is murder, so if we're going, let us know right away."

"Okay, I'll get back to you A S A P," he replied and ended the call. Hurrying through to the DI's room, he knocked then strode in to tell Eddie Fairbanks, "That's the Duke and Susie got an address for the daughter, boss. You want them to go ahead and break the news or do you want to go yourself?"

Fairbanks glanced at his watch then unknowingly parodying Smythe, said, "The traffic right now will be horrendous. If they're already out there, Larry, have them attend and when they obtain a statement, they've to inform her to be at the mortuary at nine-fifty, tomorrow morning, for an official identification of her father's body. Also," he frowned, "tell the Duke as subtly as he can if she had any knowledge of her father possessing a handgun."

"Will do," he nodded, but as he turned to leave, almost collided with a woman who accompanied by a man, stood to one side to permit him to pass.

Staring at the couple, Fairbanks asked, "Can I help you?"

"DI Fairbanks?" the woman smiled, then holding up her photographic warrant card, continued in a soft, Belfast brogue, "I'm DI Sadie McGhee and this is DS Norrie McCartney. We're from headquarters CID and we're wondering if we can have a quiet word?"

****

Returned to his desk, Considine dialled Smythe's mobile and relayed Fairbanks instruction, then added his own advice when he said, "If the neighbour across the landing from the victim says there might have been a fall-out between the daughter and the victim, Duke, try and elicit where she and her partner or husband where, yesterday."

"You thinking of them as suspects, Larry?"

"At the minute, pal," he sighed, "everyone's a suspect."

****

It didn't escape Fairbanks attention that while the admittedly glamorous, fair-haired and slender figure of McGhee made towards the chair in front of his desk, her neighbour, the very large and bullish McCartney, who wore a creased, three-piece brown coloured suit, a grey shirt with the top button undone and curiously, a red, white a blue striped tie that seemed to declare his love of Rangers football club, turned to close the door behind him.

Sitting back in his chair, Fairbanks studied them both before he indicated to McCartney the second chair in the room, then when the large man sat down, causing the chair to creak in protest, he said, "Headquarters CID to me usually means Special Branch. Would that be correct, DI McGhee?"

"Please, Sadie" she smiled, but he recognised it as a forced smile with no humour behind it.

He bit back a laugh then teasingly asked, "So, what can I do for the headquarters spooks?"

He saw her throat tighten at his description of them as 'spooks' before she replied, "I'm sure you won't be offended, Eddie," though he hadn't offered the use of his forename, "when I remind you that we as police officers are all bound by the Official Secrets Act."

"And you are reminding me of this, why?"

Though she continued to smile, it was the slightest of twitches in her left eye that he noticed, a hardly perceptible tic that caused him to realise she'd guessed her obvious glamour and good looks did not impress him and, he inwardly smiled, for why would they, when he had Ronnie at home.

"We've learned that you are currently investigating the murder of a man called James Crawford, that you are the SIO."

So, she want's something, he thought, then slowly nodding, said, "That's correct. I'm the SIO. Do you have some information for me…Sadie?"

She smiled again, a beguiling smile that he had no doubt had more than a few men eating out of her hand, or perhaps even disclosing secrets they shouldn't have.

"Not at this time," she shook her head, "but I understand too that during the SOCO search of his flat, they discovered a firearm, a semi-automatic handgun; a Czechoslovakian CZ 75 and a box of nine-millimetre rounds."

He stared at her and felt his stomach clenching, then with a quick, but insincere smile, said, "Excuse me for just a moment."

Rising to his feet he left the room and hurried towards the incident room.

"Larry," he bent over Considine who was at his desk, then said in a low voice, "The two guys you sent to Pitt Street to inquire about the handgun that was found. Have they got back yet?"

"Eh, no, Boss," Considine, replied. "As of twenty minutes ago, they're still waiting on confirmation of the type of weapon and likely the buggers are in the canteen. Do you want me to contact them in case there's an update?"

"Yes and I stress this, as a matter of urgency, ask them to find out who else the SOCO informed about the handgun, then let me know right away. In fact," he had an afterthought, "phone me through what they tell you."

Confused, Considine nodded as he watched Fairbanks hurry from the room.

Returned to his office, Fairbanks resumed his seat then hesitantly said, "Sorry, you mentioned a handgun, a Czechoslovakian what?"

"A CZ 75," she helpfully replied, but with a sigh.

"Ah, yes, and a box of nine-millimetre ammunition, you said," then bending his head to take a note of the make and model she described, rummaged through the papers on his desk as though seeking something.

He didn't miss the glance McGhee gave her neighbour, a glance that indicated she thought Fairbanks to be either incompetent or simply out of his depth as an SIO.

"Sorry, still trying to get my head around things, this being my first murder as the SIO," he explained with yet another smile. "Now, what can I do for you, Sadie?"

She could not know or guess he was stalling for time.

"We were wondering if at this time you have any suspects or witnesses to the murder? Unfortunately," she forestalled his question with a perfectly manicured hand, "I can't disclose our interest at this time."

Before he could respond, his desk phone rang and they heard him say, "Yes, go ahead, Larry."

Watching him, McGhee inwardly fumed that what should be a simple meet and greet with the murder's SIO was turning into a farce, dealing with this clown.

They saw him end the call, then returning the phone to the cradle, he stared at them in turn before he addressed McGhee with, "You're absolutely correct, Detective Inspector McGhee, in that a handgun was discovered at the locus of the murder, along with a box of nine millimetre bullets."

"I've already told you…" she began, but stopped dead when he raised a hand and rudely interrupted with, "Yes, I know, but what bothers me, DI McGhee, is that as the SOCO have just within the last couple of minutes identified the handgun to my guys at Pitt Street and assured them that no, SOCO have *neither* identified the make and model *nor* informed any member of any other department prior to speaking to my guys."

Seconds passed before he leaned forward across his desk and stared hard at her rapidly paling face, then asked, "So, that begs the question, how is it you come to know the make and model of the handgun before SOCO divulged that information to my officers?"

"Time to leave, Sadie," McCartney abruptly rose to his feet, then turning to Fairbanks, said, "Archie Wilmot, he's a pal of yours, DI Fairbanks. Is that correct? Going out with one of your young DC's, as I recall."

Fairbanks turned his attention to the large man then realisation dawned when he hissed, "The two bruisers from headquarters CID. The article and the photo in the paper about Martin Fraser's company winning the contract. You were one of them. It was you who attended the West End Chronicle office after Fraser was murdered and as I recall, issued a subtle threat to young Wilmot, the editor."

McCartney smiled, but neither admitting nor denying the accusation, simply replied, "Might be a helpful to your career to forget we were here, Eddie."

"Is that another threat, DS McCartney?" Fairbanks unconsciously rose to his feet, but now McGhee and McCartney were at the open door and stepping wordlessly out into the corridor.

He hadn't realised he was tense, so tense his body began to shake. What the fuck!

Slumping back down into his chair, his mind racing, he called through to Considine and told him, "Larry, come and see me. We might have a problem."

CHAPTER FOUR.

Duke Smythe and Susie Lauder found that Fiona McDonnell's house in Coatbridge's Craigend Drive was an end terraced, former local authority house that clearly, from the work completed on it had cost the occupants a lot of money.

Nor did it escape her and Smyth's notice that parked on the recently laid monoblock paved driveway was a black coloured, year-old Honda HR and a flaming red coloured, two-years old TT Coupe that suggested there was good money coming into the house.

"Two cars, suggests they're both at home, eh?" Smythe nodded at the vehicles, then rang the doorbell.

When the door was pulled open by the heavily pregnant Fiona McDonnell, her short, mousey brown hair neatly brushed and wearing a flowing, green coloured mid-calf, kaftan dress, they saw a toddler of about three years clinging to their mother's legs and staring curiously at the two detectives.

Identifying themselves, they heard a man's voice call out from upstairs, "Who's at the door, sweetheart?"

Clearly bemused as to why the CID were visiting her, she politely indicated they follow her through to the kitchen, while sending her toddler son through to the front room to continue watching the cartoons.

Calling out loudly to her husband, she cried, "It's the police. Two detectives, Patrick. Come down to the kitchen."

Both Smythe and Lauder were surprised to see that a beautiful, large extension had been added to the house to create a good-sized rear sitting room and an exceptionally large kitchen and with her own home needing some renovation, Lauder felt tempted to ask for the builder's contact details.

In a bid to ease her distress prior to delivering the bad news, Smythe glanced around the extension, then quipped, "Just how many kids are you expecting to have, Mrs McDonnell?"

She smiled then said, "After this one, Mr Smythe, he's getting the snip, though he doesn't know it yet," then with a wry grin, she added, "I'm not having a Catholic family of a dozen, for no man."

It was the joke about a Catholic family that set Smythe wondering. Indicating they sit at the kitchen table and offering them tea or coffee, they both turned when her husband entered the kitchen, seeing him to be a red-headed man of about thirty, wearing paint stained blue coloured dungarees with splashes of pink paint on his face and hands and who apologetically greeted them with, "I'm in IT and not really a painter. So, what's this about?"

Smythe turned to address Fiona then said, "Can you take a seat please, Mrs McDonnell?"

It was then as the pregnant woman slumped down into a chair that Lauder saw her face turn pale as though suddenly realising they were there with bad news.

Lifting a glass from the draining board, Lauder rinsed it then filling it with cold water that she placed in front of Fiona, she heard Smythe solemnly tell her, "I regret to inform you, Mrs McDonnell, that earlier today, your father James Crawford was discovered dead in his flat."

If either Smyth or Lauder were expecting some distress, tears or snotters, they were to be disappointed, for Fiona simply sighed, then said, "I know I'm going to sound like a right bitch, but really, he stopped being a father to me a very long time ago."

Her face pale, she turned to her husband to softly ask, "I can't feel anything about him dying, Patrick. Oh, my God," her face creased in emotional pain, "does that make me a bad person?"

He bent down beside the chair and wrapping his arms awkwardly around his wife's shoulders, stared at Smyth and Lauder in turn before he said, "Look, Jimmy was a complicated man. Let me take Fiona upstairs for a lie-down and I'll come back down and explain. Is that okay?"

"Of course," Smythe nodded, then watched her husband help her to her feet, when he added, "There's tea and coffee in those jars on the worktop. If you're having one, I'll take a black coffee and be back down in a couple of minutes."

When they'd left the kitchen, Lauder stared wordlessly at Smyth, then rising to her feet, filled the kettle and set it to boil.

Just under five minutes later, Patrick McDonnell returned to the kitchen where Lauder, handing him a coffee, asked, "Is she okay?"

He shrugged when he replied, "She's a bit embarrassed that you might think she's a heartless cow, hearing her dad's died and she's not that bothered, but believe me," he shook his head, "Jimmy Crawford wasn't cut out to be a father."

"And I gather they are…I'm sorry," Smythe grimaced, "I mean, they were estranged?"

"Oh, aye," McDonnell sighed heavily. "Literally since the day that he discovered his wee girl was seeing a Catholic, so you can imagine his anger when he found out we were having a baby together. Course, Fiona always hoped her dad would come around to accepting me, but as far as he was concerned, I was nothing but a fucking Taig. His words, not mine," he blushed.

He paused and glanced up at the ceiling, as though able to see through to the room where his wife lay, then continued, "Fiona, after her mother died and believe me," his voice became bitter, "her father gave that woman some life, so he did. Anyway, Fiona couldn't stand living with Jimmy anymore and while we intended getting married anyway, the pregnancy was the cause of us marrying that bit sooner. You know, Mr Smythe," he shook his head in disgust, "it didn't bother me that he didn't come to the wedding, but he's never," he paused and took a deep, almost angry breath, "I mean, he never even made any attempt to come and see his grandson and yes, that made me angry, but not as angry as my Fiona is."

Smyth was about to inquire about Patrick McDonnell's whereabouts the previous evening, but was stymied when McDonnell added, "Have you told his son, Peter?"

"We didn't realise he had a son. Have you got any contact details for him?" Smyth asked.

McDonnell slowly smiled, a humourless smile when he explained, "I'd have thought that was the details you guys would have. I've never actually met him, but I know that Peter's in the jail. He's serving life for murder."

****

Still bristling after the detectives from Special Branch had gone, Eddie Fairbanks fetched his mobile from his coat pocket and dialled the number for his partner, Ronnie Masters.

Ronnie, a thirty-five-years-old former international model with a chequered past and now the owner and manager of a bespoke boutique, located in the Merchant City area of Glasgow city centre, was in the back-room office of her shop and smiled when she saw who was calling.

"Love of my life," she warmly greeted him in her husky voice, then with a smile, added, "You're working late, so put your dinner in the oven?"

"God, you know me so well," he grinned at the phone. "I've landed a murder, my very first as the SIO."

"SIO?"

"Sorry, Senior Investigating Officer. The guy in charge who gets the kudos if I solve it and the slap on the back of the head if I don't."

Her eyes narrowed in curiosity when she asked, "Not that I'm not pleased for you, but isn't it usually your boss, Bobby Heggerty, who deals with the murders?"

"Aye," he sighed, "you're right, but there's a story there, sweetheart, so I'll explain when I get in tonight."

"Any idea when that might be?"

She picked up on his hesitation, then before he could respond, she added, "It doesn't matter what the time is. I'll be up waiting and Eddie. Be safe. Please."

He couldn't help but smile when he replied, "I know you still worry about me, sweetheart, and I will. I promise and Ronnie. Thanks for being so understanding."

When the call had ended, she sat staring at the glass window of her office that faced out into the brightly lit stockroom, wondering that her life had changed so dramatically in the last five months.

Her modelling career had ended dramatically in a resounding disaster that just over two years earlier, not only saw her become addicted to both drugs and alcohol, but following a conviction in New York for possession of drugs, she was deported from the US for life.

Of course, the media in both the US and the UK then tore her life apart and following a disastrous marriage to a man in London that lasted just a matter of weeks and who after pillaging most of her savings, was himself convicted of fraud.

Returning to her native Glasgow, divorced with what little savings she salvaged from her account, a broken and addicted woman in the depths of despair, she turned to her younger sister, Gill.

Her heart beat a little faster when she thought of her sister Gill, who at that time had been dating Eddie Fairbanks, a recently promoted Detective Sergeant.

To her own surprise and what Ronnie could not admit, meeting the kind and thoughtful Eddie, for her it was love at first sight.

She unconsciously smiled and her face reddened when she recalled the first time she had tried to seduce him, an abject failure that still haunted her; she, a drunken, drugged woman stripping off and groping at him while he had stepped back to reject her.

His horror that she did so caused her in turn to angrily lash out at him.
And yet, she smiled, even though she was humiliated and embarrassed, Eddie had been kind; recognising her pain and covering her weeping, naked body as she lay distraught on the floor of her flat and promising never to mention it to Gill.
And he didn't.
It was that foolish, stupid act that drove her to seek help for her addictions and there followed an unrequited love she kept hidden for those two years it took to get her life back on track.
Even though she had not known it then, that humiliating few moments was the beginning of her salvation, starting with her first step when she joined the Alcoholic Anonymous programme. With the help of a woman called Anne, herself a recovering alcoholic who was to become a close friend, she fought and finally beat her addictions, though the first to admit that even today, temptation had never gone away.
On her road to recovery, the few savings that remained from her successful life enabled her to open a boutique providing bespoke women's clothing for Glasgow's wealthier customers and regardless of her very public downfall, such was her fame as a model the clientele soon flocked to her shop.
But then Gill, who she loved dearly, but who was promiscuous and unfaithful behind Eddie's back, pretended he was the father to a pregnancy that she ruthlessly terminated.
In a petulant, unforgiving rage and angry at her sister, Gill left for a job with her bank in England somewhere and who continued to refuse to acknowledge Ronnie's phone messages and letters.
And it was then, Ronnie shivered at the memory; she thought she'd lost him forever.
Her thoughts turned to his neighbour at the time, the young acting detective, Susie Lauder, who she later learned cajoled him into realising that yes, Ronnie really did love him.
She frowned, recalling that awful day when once more she'd thought she'd lost him when the murderer he was pursuing, Terry Clancy, now serving a lengthy sentence, had tried to kill Eddie.
She took a deep breath and shaking her head, she thought; why am I going over all this again?
I know he loves me as I love him.

"And that's final," she heard herself say and smiled at her reflection in the mirror.

"Miss Masters?" she heard her name called by her deputy manager, Laura.

"That's a customer seeking some *personal* attention from you. A regular," Laura smiled at her with upraised eyebrows, the unspoken caution that the customer was a difficulty.

****

Fairbanks glanced up when Larry Considine appeared at the door and said, "That's Duke and Susie back from breaking the bad news, boss, if you want to come through to hear what they've got to say."

"What about the rest of the team, Larry? It's," he glanced at his wristwatch, "almost five, so if anyone's hanging around, chase them till tomorrow morning, then you bring Duke and Susie through here where it's quieter."

Two minutes later, Considine was followed into the DI's room by Smythe, who carried a wooden chair, and Lauder, who carried two mugs of coffee.

When they were all seated, Fairbanks sat back in his chair and glancing at them in turn, asked, "Who's got the story?"

"Me, Boss," Smythe nodded then began.

"Fiona McDonnell, married to Patrick and residing with him and their three-year-old son in Craigend Street in Coatbridge. She's heavily pregnant and though I never asked, I'm guessing due to pop any day now."

"Pop?" Lauder could barely restrain her laughter.

When Smythe turned to frown at her, Fairbanks, pokerfaced, said, "Go on."

"Nice young couple and he's in IT and from the sounds of it, I'm guessing he's pretty good at what he does because he teaches, too. As for them being suspects," his brow furrowed when he shook his head, "she can barely lift her weight let alone strangle her father. He says that last night, he was delivering a lecture to some students at Coatbridge College, so that shouldn't be hard to verify, though my gut's telling me it's true."

He paused then continued, "When we broke the news about her father," he took a short breath, "she wasn't really that upset, says that she and him have been estranged for some time and the victim, he'd never even met his grandson and she's certain he didn't even know where they live. Now before I continue," he turned to Lauder, "Susie's going to make an inquiry on the PNC. It seems that the victim has a son, Thomas William Crawford, who's currently serving time at Her Majesty's Pleasure for murder, sometime in two thousand and one; April, she thinks."

He took a breath then his glance at Lauder caused Fairbanks to ask, "What?"

"According to Patrick McDonnell, our victim used to boast about his son murdering a Catholic, that it was one less Taig to worry about." Several seconds of stunned silence followed, broken when at a nod from Fairbanks, Lauder left the room, then he asked, "Was the daughter able to tell us anything about her father? Who might have wished him dead?"

"And there's the rub," Smythe sighed. "If I recall correctly at the briefing, you told us, that the victim was on the PNC for a football breach of the peace, a D & I and a domestic assault some years ago, I think you said?"

"Yeah, that's correct," Fairbanks nodded.

Smythe's eyes narrowed when he asked, "Nothing of interest in his antecedent history?"

"Nothing that I recall. Why?"

"Well, according to his daughter," he shook his head, "in the late seventies, early eighties, our victim was a card carrying member of the British National Party and involved in a number of disturbances and on one occasion she recalls, even travelled down to London to participate in a demonstration that resulted in some rioting that went on. She remembers it because it was on all the news channels."

Staring at Smythe, Fairbanks could feel the blood drain from his face when he asked, "Did she share anything else?"

"Before she walked out on her father, it seems his right-wing allegiance was transferred to a local Loyalist group that supported the Ulster Defence Association. Some mob of bampots that hung about in a pub over in the east end of the city."

"Jeez," Considine shook his head. "This is two-thousand and six. I thought all that nonsense was finished after the Good Friday Agreement in, when was it again…"

"Nineteen-ninety-eight, but it didn't take effect until the next year," Fairbanks interjected then explained with a smile, "I watched a documentary on the BBC about it last week. Go on, Duke."

The door opened to admit Lauder who carried two printout sheets that she handed to Fairbanks, before resuming her seat.

"That one," she pointed to a sheet of paper, "is for the victim, boss, and clearly, it definitely omits any antecedent history about his right-wing support. Why, I have not a clue," she shook her head.

"The second page is for his son. Right enough, Thomas, aged twenty-one at the time, was sentenced in April, two thousand and one for murdering a Celtic fan in a pub in the city centre. That's all the info the PNC has, but tomorrow, I'll contact Crown Office and try to find out more."

"I'll issue an Action for that, Susie," Considine nodded to her.

Rubbing wearily at his forehead, Fairbanks then sat forward and told Considine, "Larry, I want you to issue a second Action, to Duke." Then turning to the large man, he continued, "I want you to visit Pitt Street tomorrow and find out if you can from whatever department monitors the PNC, why our victim's antecedent history is no longer recorded on the PNC."

"Hang on, boss," Smythe raised a questioning hand, "you think it was recorded, but it's been deleted?"

He didn't immediately respond, but then nodding to both Smythe and Lauder, he grimly smiled when he said, "Guys, thanks for you hard work today, so get yourselves home and we'll see you in the morning."

A little taken aback at their abrupt dismissal, Smythe glanced at Lauder and they left the room.

When the door was closed behind them, Fairbanks turned to Considine, then said, "I had an interesting visit this afternoon from the Special Branch."

****

Mark Mathieson, then aged sixteen years of age, had enlisted as a junior soldier at the Army Apprentice College in Chepstow in Wales.

Twenty-four years later, married with two grown children and having attained the rank of Staff-Sergeant, Mathieson found himself honourably discharged, but acutely aware there wasn't a lot of jobs going for forty-year-old armourers, schooled in all types of weapons, no matter how proficient they might be at their trade.

Over the next eighteen months, working at a series of low-income jobs in his native Ripon in Yorkshire and with the University fees for his oldest daughter, Clare, on the horizon, Mathieson had become increasingly disenchanted with civilian life and once more longed for the comradery and security of the army.

Arriving home one evening in October, nineteen ninety-nine, his wife Lily, curiously animated, placed a folded form in front of him as he sat waiting for his dinner.

"What's this, then?" he stared curiously at the form, then at his wife.

"My sister in Glasgow, she sent it down; thought it might interest you," Lily unconsciously held her breath.

Mathieson stared at the form, then again at Lilly before he said, "The police? Really?"

"Read it, you numpty," she placed a reassuring hand on his shoulder, then explained, "It's an advert for the police Scenes of Crime Department. They're looking to recruit someone with an advanced technical knowledge of firearms for their Ballistics Department and Mark, that's you!"

He turned to stare up at her, then slowly replied, "But it's in Glasgow."

Impatiently, she cast a hand around the small, dining room before she replied, "We rent this place, Mark. It would be no problem upping sticks and moving and besides, in the meantime we could stay with my sister. She's got a four-bedroom house and there's only her and her husband, so we look for a place up there when we're back on our feet."

Squeezing his shoulder, she encouragingly continued, "This is *you*, sweetheart, it's what you loved doing in the army, what you were trained for."

"What about Clare? She's due to start at Bristol Uni. How can we leave her? Then there's our Jason."

"Mark!" she shook her head. "Jason still can't find a job down here. He's a better chance finding one in a big city like Glasgow and you know my sis loves him to bits. And as for our Clare. Whether she's at Bristol or not, we'd still have to travel to visit her and it will be just as easy catching a train from Glasgow as it is from down the road in Harrogate."

"Lily," he grimaced when he slowly shook his head, "I don't know, love."

Seven years later and sat at his work bench in the SOCO Department at Pitt Street, Mathieson thanked a God he visited every Sunday at his Baptist church for his wife's persistence that he'd fill in the application form.

Now, he couldn't be happier, particularly as the five years of court attendances had well passed and thus qualified him as an expert trial witness.

Taking a breath, he stared again at the black enamelled semi-automatic handgun, a Czechoslovakian CZ 75. He hadn't seen many of these before and glancing at the paperwork, saw it had been discovered by his SOCO colleagues at a murder locus and in a hidden recess beneath a set of drawers.

The box of nine-millimetre bullets was pretty easy to identify and unfortunate though it was, easily available on any black or illegal market, though strictly controlled for legal Section One firearms certificate holders. Shaking his head, it had always eluded him why any human being would use hollow point to shoot someone, inwardly grimacing at the memory of bodies he had seen struck by these particularly vicious bullets.

Lifting his mug, he sipped at the cooling coffee, then again turned his attention to the handgun, and seeing that no attempt had been made to file off the serial number, but that meant nothing anyway. Since the turmoil when the country split in 1992 to becomes the states of the Czech Republic and Slovakia, the registration of the locally made Czechoslovakian weapons had literally dissolved and there was no way any of them could now be tracked.

The weapon, again according to the SOCO paperwork, had already been printed with just the deceased's fingerprints discovered on both the handgun and the box of bullets, yet Mathieson's habit and training was to continue to use nitrile gloves when handling weapons he inspected.

Yet, there was something about the gun that he couldn't quite figure out, something that irked him.

Turning it over and over, his eyes narrowed when he stared at the retaining bolt that held the moulded grips together; grips that covered and hid the skeletal frame of the handle of the gun.

What he now saw and had taken his attention was the tiniest sliver of enamelled black paint missing at the cut in the retaining bolt.

His curiosity aroused, he placed the barrel of the gun into his bench vice, then drawing a powerful desk magnifying glass towards him, switched on the bright, attached light of the magnifying glass. The magnification confirmed his suspicions. A tiny, almost minuscule piece of the black enamelled paint had been scraped from the cut on the bolt, suggesting to Mathieson that at some time, a screwdriver had been used to unscrew the bolt.

Softly exhaling, he lifted a screwdriver from the rack on the bench then inserted it into the cut. As he turned the screwdriver, the grips on either side of the handle loosened and his stomach tensed for Mathieson feared finding what he suspected.

His throat dry, he gently removed one side of the grip and his shoulders slumped.

Though a serving soldier for twenty-four years, Mathieson's Baptist upbringing had remained with him and he was not a man given to using expletives.

Nevertheless, when he saw what was inside the skeletal frame of the handle, he sat back in his chair and unable to stop himself, he quietly muttered, "Oh, for fuck's sake!"

CHAPTER FIVE: Wednesday, 20 September 2006.

Leaving the flat in Watson Street, Eddie Fairbanks climbed into his dark blue coloured Ford Focus, then before switching on the engine, sat for a couple of minutes contemplating how in the preceding five months or so, his life had so dramatically changed.

He could not help but smile when he thought of Ronnie, his partner and now the love of his life.

His eyes narrowed when he glanced up at the old building where her flat was located and thought back to those weeks where she had devoted her days and nights caring for him after he had been discharged from hospital.

How she had politely refused to give herself to him until she was absolutely certain that he was; well, that he really did love her.

And he did.

Wholeheartedly.

Their joint decision that he move in with Ronnie, prior to refurbishing his own flat in the Queens Park area of the city and selling it was, as far as Fairbanks was concerned, a no-brainer.

And those last months, both returning to work in his new role as a Detective Inspector and learning to live with Ronnie, had been both exciting and if he was truthful, a little daunting too.

She in her mid-thirties and he is his late thirties, they had mutually agreed that there were certain concerns where they'd be set in their ways and decided that if anything one of them did something that was annoying to the other, they'd point it out so that it didn't become an issue.

So far, he smiled again, things were working out and continued smiling when he thought of their nights together, for Ronnie wasn't just a beautiful woman, but very athletic too.

Starting the engine, his thoughts turned to what might be waiting at the office for him, then glancing in the rear-view mirror, pulled smoothly away from the kerb.

****

Already at his desk that morning, Larry Considine reached into his desk drawer and withdrew the packet of paracetamol.

Popping two from the blister pack, he threw them back then swallowed a deep mouthful of coffee.

With a sigh he thought again about last night's argument, his wife Sheila once more berating him and insisting…no, demanding, he visit the doctor and finally, her usual threat that she would leave him if he didn't do something about his drinking.

But they both knew she wouldn't leave, she'd not give up the thirty-one years she'd invested in both him and his pension and lump sum that was due to him in just under nineteen months.

The children, all three flown the coop some years previously, the sad fact he had come to accept was that the and Sheila now lived under the same roof, but had their separate lives, their own bedrooms and shared nothing other than the meals she cooked.

But even that had dwindled because of the hours he kept and with her nights out at her clubs and charity functions, he was often bringing home takeaways.

And, as she stoically reminded him, all because he preferred alcohol to her.

His thoughts were disturbed when the door opened and a cheery Duke Smythe entered to greet him with, "Morning, Larry."

"Morning, Duke," he forced a smile then a sudden thought struck him.

"Drag up a chair, Duke, I'd like a quiet word."
When he was seated, Smythe's eyes narrowed when he asked, "What's up?"
"Am I right in recalling that one of your pals in the bowling club, he's a Branch guy?"
"Aye, and you're asking why?"
"How tight are you with him?"
"Well, we're neighbours in the club competitions and the matches and the wives get on well, too."
"So, if you were to ask him something, he could keep it to himself?"
"Ask him what, Larry?" Smythe's suspicions were now apparent.
"Eddie Fairbanks had a visit yesterday from two of the SB. A DI McGhee and a DS McCartney. I'd think it might be advantageous to us to know something about them."
"Is this to do with the murder investigation and why me and young Susie were asked to leave his office yesterday, so you two could have a private word?"
"That's for Eddie to share, Duke, but it's me that's asking."
Smyth slowly nodded, then said, "I'll give my pal a ring and I'm to tell him what? That it's strictly confidential?"
"*Extremely* confidential," stressed Considine.
Glancing at his wristwatch, Smyth said, "Okay then, it's a bit early to phone him, but I'll get it done and I'm assuming there's no Action for me asking?"
Considine, his head still thumping, managed a smile before he said, "Strictly off the book, as they say."
****

On her way to work that morning, Susie Lauder dropped off her partner, Archie Wilmot, the editor, sole reporter and owner of the West End Chronicle, a free newspaper that survived on advertising. However, due to its comprehensive reporting on the gun battle at the Maryhill Asda and the murder of Sergeant Geraldine McEwan, the paper had quickly become a local source of information and much envied by the larger tabloids who on many occasions, tried to persuade Wilmot to sell or at least become a franchise accountable to the tabloids.

But all to no avail.

With a tacit nod from the head of Maryhill CID and particularly when they sought information about local crimes, a *quid pro quo* arrangement existed that permitted Lauder to provide Wilmot with titbits that were completely unattributable and would not reflect back on either her personally or Strathclyde Police.

Waving cheerio to Wilmot as he trotted off southwards in Byres Road, Lauder's attention turned to the unusual dismissal by Eddie Fairbanks yesterday evening, when she and Duke Smyth were asked to leave the room.

It just wasn't like Eddie, but with a sigh, she knew that the Eddie she had neighboured during the poison pen letter investigation was now DI Fairbanks, the SIO in an on-going murder investigation. While she still trusted and respected him, she had to accept he had stepped up a rank and therefore, with more responsibilities, was less likely to share with a very junior DC all that was going on in the investigation.

Still, she smiled, while DI Fairbanks was definitely the boss at work, she was pleased that regardless of the difference in their rank, he had insisted she and Archie would remain social friends with him and Ronnie, a woman who Lauder not just liked, but openly admired.

Her thoughts turned to Ronnie Masters and she found herself smiling.

It wasn't the first time she wondered that such a beautiful woman, a former international model no less, who had fallen from such a great height yet, with all those odds stacked against her, had beaten her demons and turned her life around to become a successful businesswoman and now considered Lauder to be a close friend.

Such was her thoughts that with a start, Lauder was turning into the rear yards at Maryhill Police Office and guiltily wondering that she'd driven there almost on autopilot.

Getting out of her car, she heard her name being called and turning, saw the Divisional Commander, Liz Malone, a civilian jacket over her police shirt and tie, waving at her.

"Ma'am," Lauder strode towards her, surprised when Malone extended her hand then said, "I didn't get the opportunity yesterday to congratulate you, Susie, on your appointment to the CID. Well done and I expect good things from you in the future. Mind you," Malone grinned, "you've only got about four weeks or thereabouts to impress me, because after that I really won't care when I'm sunning myself in the Costa Brava."

Walking together towards the rear door of the building, Lauder asked, "You're really going then, Ma'am?"

Malone stopped and when Lauder turned towards her, she softly smiled when she replied, "In a little over four weeks, that'll be just over thirty-two years I'll have been a cop, Susie. In that time, I served in uniform for almost fifteen of those years and the rest in CID. I've seen the best of humanity and the most depraved of it too. I've been personally responsible or helped put some very bad people behind bars, some of them for life. In my own private life," she sighed, "I loved a man who cheated on me, yet discovered as the years passed, I wasn't the wife he really wanted, so I've come to forgive him. While we were together, I gave birth to four of his children of whom three survived and, thank God, are all doing well as adults and who so far," she smiled, "have presented me with four grandkids. I'm in my early-fifties and believe me, I'm starting to feel it in my knees and hips so yes, I'll be going because who knows, I might still have a life waiting for me."

"Now," her face creased when she stared at Lauder, she quietly said, "why am I sharing this with you? Well, let me first say that I know you can keep a confidence, so regardless of the difference in our ranks, as one woman to another I have to tell you that working as a police officer can be a satisfying and rewarding career, but it is *not* without its pitfalls."

She paused as she continued to stare at the younger woman, then continued, "For one, the glass ceiling I faced as a young cop is slowly and surely splintering, but it has not as yet fully gone away. While many men now accept women to be integral members of the Force and as professional as them, that's not to say there isn't male colleagues out there who will consider you as less competent, simply because you *are* a woman. Any promotion you might be awarded in the future will be scrutinised by such male colleagues far deeper than if a man were awarded the same promotion. By that I mean there are those who will question your promotion and they'll wonder; who is her wire or who does she know to be promoted? What favour is being done or what boss is she romantically involved with to *be* promoted? That sort of *drivel*," she almost spat out the word.

Taking a deep breath, Malone stared hard at her when she said, "My generation had our difficulties being accepted by not just the bosses, but also by the rank and file, Susie, but though we've overcome many obstacles, there are still barriers to be broken down and it's young, female officers like yourself who have to carry the mantle, now that us old codgers are all on the point of retirement," she suddenly smiled.

She couldn't explain why, but after such a simple and yet emotive statement from the older woman, Lauder could feel herself welling up and had to physically restrain herself from hugging Malone, who recognising the younger woman was becoming a little emotional, reached out with her hand, then rubbed gently at Lauder's arm when she brusquely said, "Right, Susie, get yourself up to the CID and suite and make us old codgers proud by showing them what you can do."

With that, Malone pulled open the rear door, then stepping through into the dimly lit corridor beyond, strode off and out of sight.

Still standing in the rear yard, Lauder took a deep breath, then wiping at her eyes with the sleeve of her jacket, softly exhaled before pulling open the closing door.

****

Pushing open the door to the incident room and though he thought he'd be one of the first to arrive, Eddie Fairbanks was a little embarrassed to find that most if not all of the team were already present and inwardly promising himself he'd do better tomorrow morning.

"Morning, boss," Larry Considine greeted him, then said, "The DCI requested when you get in you give him a phone call at home," before handing Fairbanks a scrap of paper with Heggerty's home number scrawled on it.

"I'll do that after the briefing," he nodded at Considine, then asked, "Anything in during the night?"

"I spoke with the FSO who manned the telephone, but nothing," Considine shook his head.

"What about the door to door. Anything turn up?"

"Nothing so far," Considine again shook his head, then added, "But it's early days though."

And what am I going to brief the team about, Fairbanks eyes narrowed at the thought, then he said, "I've appointed Mickey Rooney from the plainclothes squad as an acting DC, Larry, and he'll come with me to corroborate the PM, so I expect we'll leave here about nine-thirty, if you can keep a set of keys aside for me."

"Will do, boss."

They both turned as Mickey Rooney stepped into the incident room, his face flushed and feeling a little self-conscious in his navy blue, two-piece suit.

Turning to Considine, Fairbanks smiled when he said, "I'll let you bring Mickey up to speed with what little we have while I try to find something to say that will motivate the team," then nodding at Rooney with a smile as he passed him, returned to the DI's room.

****

It was Bobby Heggerty's wife, Catherine, who answered Fairbanks phone, then heard her loudly calling out, "Bobby, its Eddie at your office."

Almost immediately her voice lowered when she hurriedly whispered, "Eddie, please don't get him stressed. He didn't get good news yesterday."

Taken aback, Fairbanks waited the few seconds for Heggerty to lift the phone then said, "Morning, boss, you're looking for me?"

"Morning, Eddie, just checking in to let you know the bloody doctor has given me a sick line for three weeks and all because he thinks I've to undergo some tests."

"So, he's wrong, you don't need the tests?"

"What?"

"Well," Fairbanks drawled, "I'd imagine these tests you're talking about cost the NHS a fair few bob, but you obviously think they're not necessary, that the doctor's got it all wrong."

Seconds passed before a stunned Heggerty slowly replied, "Oh, I get it now. Reverse psychology. You're letting me know that you agree with the doctor and you think that yes, I do need the tests."

"It's not important what I think, boss, what's important is that you listen to what a professional is telling you. I mean, you're a DCI and if you were to offer advice to a probationary cop who has an issue, would you give that probationary cop the benefit of your experience or let him or her make the decision regarding that issue based on *their* experience in the job?"

He heard Heggerty sigh, then humourlessly laugh before he said, "You and the wife. Are you two colluding against me or what?"

"I think what you *mean* to say is are we concerned that you take things easy and let the medical professionals decide what's best for you?"

He listened to Heggerty slowly exhale, then rudely ask him, "Okay, DI Fairbanks, you've made your point. So, what's happening?"
Smiling at the handset, he replied, "As far as the murder is concerned, regretfully no new information about any suspects; however, what *is* interesting is that the SOCO discovered a hidden recess in a set of drawers that contained a handgun. The gun's currently with SOCO as we speak. That and I'm needing some advice, boss. You got a couple of minutes to hear me out?"
"Eddie," Heggerty sighed again, "I've got nothing *but* minutes, so go ahead."
Fairbanks related the visit of ACC Gardener and the timeous intervention of Chief Superintendent Malone, who he later thanked and who like Heggerty, told him to watch his back.
"But that's not really what I need advice about," he continued then described the visit of the two Special Branch officers.
"The name Sadie McGhee means nothing to me, but I do recall a DC called Norrie McCartney, though that was years ago and who if I remember correctly, worked in one of the city Divisions. Big guy, handy with his fists when dealing with suspects, as I recall, though I've no idea where he went. However, that all said, it's not unusual for some detectives to disappear into the Special Branch for the rest of their career."
"Anyway," he continued, "it's highly suspicious they knew about the make and model of the handgun before you did and the very fact they're sniffing about your murder investigation," he paused as though in thought.
"My advice," he began again, "is record everything about them. Times of visits, what's said and yes continue to take Larry Considine into your confidence. On that point, how is Larry doing?"
"No complaints, boss, and he's got his finger on the button as we speak."
"Good. Right, anything else I should know?"
"I've appointed Mickey Rooney as the acting DC to replace Susie Lauder and he's coming with me," he glanced at his wristwatch, "in twenty minutes, to the PM."
"Good choice. Mickey needs this because I think he's probably still trying to get over Gels McEwan's murder. Now, Eddie, remember that I'm only a phone call away if you need me for advice or even to come into the office for anything."

"Aye," Fairbanks voice dripped with good-humoured sarcasm when he replied, "Like I'm going to risk my health asking you to come into Maryhill when your wife knows fine well you should be resting at home? Like *that's* going to happen."

He heard Heggerty laugh, who then replied, "Good luck, Eddie. You've a good team about you, so for what it's worth and regardless of their junior ranks, I've always found it's useful to listen and use their experience too."

When the call had ended, Fairbanks sat back in his chair and gave some thought to just how seriously the doctor considered Bobby Heggerty's symptoms to be.

****

"Mickey," he turned when Larry Considine called him, "grab these keys and remind the boss, he'd better watch his time for getting to Govan for the PM."

"Right, Larry, I mean Sarge," he took the keys from the DS's hand.

Considine stifled a smile at Rooney's awkward seriousness and watched as the younger man left the incident room.

"Larry," he turned when Duke Smythe leaned across his desk, then quietly said, "I've made that phone call you asked about and my mate couldn't speak, but he'll get back to me sometime today or tomorrow. If it's today, do you want the story or will I wait till the boss gets back from the PM?"

Curious though he was, Considine's eyes narrowed when he replied in the same low voice, "Might as well hang fire until Eddie's returned. No point in double handling."

****

Flattered, but ignoring the good-natured, wolf-whistles from the half dozen workers clad in yellow safety helmets and Hi-Viz jackets, working at unloading their equipment from a flatbed truck prior to commencing repairs on the nearby Albion Street junction, Ronnie Masters, her shoulder length raven coloured hair fashionably bundled on top of her head and dressed in a white blouse and knee length, burgundy coloured business suit, walked on.

Unusually a little late opening her boutique on the Merchant City's Bell Street, she smiled at her deputy manager, Laura, who stood patiently waiting, then turned when she heard a man call out, "Miss Masters?"

The man she saw to be about her height of five feet nine inches and

in his mid-twenties, with gelled, collar length dark brown hair and dressed casually in a white striped NIKE shoes, charcoal coloured jeans, grey coloured polo shirt and a dark brown leather bomber jacket.
Over his shoulder he carried what to Ronnie seemed to be an expensive brown leather shoulder bag.
In those first few seconds and used to men ogling her or probing her body with their eyes, to her surprise when he didn't, she surprised herself when her first inclination was that he was gay.
Extending his hand, with a smile he introduced himself as, "Anthony Harper. Tony," he beamed. "I wonder if I might have a word?"
Glancing at the pokerfaced Laura, she suspected the older woman was leaving the doorstep solicitation for Ronnie to deal with.
Pushing open the now unlocked front door and followed by Laura and Harper, she entered the shop.
Switching on the overhead lights, she turned to him and with a forced smiled, asked, "How may I help you, Mr Harper?"
"Please, Tony," he returned her smile, then said, "I'm the chief features editor with a monthly magazine called Life & Fashion Management, based in Edinburgh, and it was suggested by one of our contributors that we contact you to inquire if you are available to be interviewed? We're relatively new to the fashion industry and have published for a little over the preceding twelve months now, but so far mainly in the Lothian area and concentrating on Scottish fashion and businesses."
He continued to smile when in a rush to impress her, he continued, "However, due to our extraordinary success in the last year, we're branching out nationally and hoping to compete with some of the better-known and for the minute, more popular publications."
Before she could interrupt and conscious Laura was hovering nearby, he continued at a rush, "My editor, Charity Dawson, she feels that an interview and cover photo-shoot with Ronnie Masters, who has previously graced the covers of Vogue and Harper's Bazaar, would go a long way to introduce Life and Fashion Management to the West of Scotland."
Bending modestly at the knees to lift the mail from the floor behind the door, then turning to watch Laura visually check the shop to ensure all was well, Ronnie felt herself blush at the now unaccustomed praise, then stood upright before she curiously

replied, "I'm not familiar with your magazine, Tony. Do you have a copy with you that I can peruse?"

"Ah, yes, as it happens, I do," he continued to widely smile, then fetching a magazine from his shoulder bag, handed it to her.

She glanced at the glossy magazine cover, immediately impressed by its professional layout, then turned to greet her two young shop assistants who entered behind Harper, both of whom stared curiously at him before making their way through to the rear stock room to leave off their coats and handbags.

To Ronnie, her intuitive suspicions about his gender choice seemed to be confirmed when Harper paid no heed to either of the extremely attractive young women.

Continuing to smile, she politely told him, "You've caught me rather wrong-footed, Tony, so perhaps you can leave this magazine with me and, eh, if you have a business card?"

Hardly able to contain his relief that he wasn't being shown the door, he drew a wallet from the shoulder bag and presented her with a card, telling her, "Both my office and mobile number are on there, Miss Masters, and I'm in Glasgow for the next couple of days catching up with a friend, so should you require more information?" He left it hanging for her to respond with, "I'll be in touch when I've given it some thought."

When the door had closed behind him, Laura joined her and suggested, "Not that we really need more publicity for the shop, but I don't supposed it would do any harm to draw in some more customers."

Ronnie had come to trust Laura's business acumen and her brow ceased when she sighed, "I suppose you're right, but we have a substantial and regular clientele as it is. Do we really need more business? I mean, a national feature on Ronnie Masters, the once famous international model turned bad could do more harm than good. It might even resurrect the memories of my drug and alcoholism issues and that *certainly* would put a dampener on some of the business."

"However," she continued with an impish grin, "I won't pretend the thought of once more being in front of a camera and on the cover of a magazine isn't provoking some interest…"

"Look," Laura suddenly took charge by holding her elbow and began to steer her towards the rear door to the stock-room, "it's quiet

at the minute, so get yourself away into your office with that magazine and I'll bring you a cuppa. Take some time to yourself, Miss Masters then before you make any kind of decision, have a wee chat this evening with Eddie. You know he only wants the best for you and he's the person you're better mulling this over with."
With a resigned smile, she nodded and made her way towards the stock-room door.
****
Already informed that the deceased's daughter, Fiona McDonnell, was heavily pregnant, Eddie Fairbanks had no problem identifying the young woman who sat with her husband, Patrick, in the mortuary waiting room at Govan's Southern General Hospital.
Introducing himself, he started by offering his condolences, but was interrupted when Fiona raised a hand and with a shake of her head, told him, "Thank you and I know you're being kind, but there's no need, Mr Fairbanks. My father was not a nice man and to be frank, I'm only here today because Patrick," she turned to glance at her husband and to lay a hand on his arm.
"He thinks that if I say goodbye to my father, it will give me some sort of closure."
"Well," Fairbanks nodded, "DC Rooney here will speak with the mortuary attendant, Mrs McDonnell, and find out if your father is ready for you to view."
Rooney returned some minutes later accompanied by a young woman in her early thirties and with a nod at Fairbanks, the McDonnell's and the detectives followed the mortuary attendant to a viewing room.
Watching Fiona McDonnell, Fairbanks saw her staring pale-faced at the body of her father, then after several seconds, wordlessly turning away to be accompanied by her husband to the corridor outside the room.
Joining her there, Fairbanks asked, "Can you confirm the man you saw is indeed your father, James Crawford?"
"Yes," she quietly replied, then asked, "If there's nothing else, I'd like to leave."
"Ah, of course, but before you go, I have one more question for you, Mrs McDonnell."
Her brow creased when she stared at him.

"Your brother, Peter. I understand he's currently serving life for murder. Have you recently been in contact with him or do you have any kind of relationship with Peter?"

He watched her glance at her husband, then shaking her head, she replied in a calm voice, "I have no brother, Mr Fairbanks. As far as me and my family are concerned, the man who was my father's son died the day he stabbed a young lad to death, just because the lad was wearing a Celtic top."

With that she turned away and holding her husband's arm, he watched them slowly make their way to the exit doors.

His concentration was broken when Rooney, standing beside him, quietly remarked, "Unbelievable, boss, that even in this so-called enlightened age, no matter what they call the god they worship, people are still arguing and killing each other because of religion."

"Aye, Mickey," he ruefully shook his head, "we never learn, do we?"

****

Duke Smythe and Susie Lauder were waiting patiently for them within the examination room to where discreetly, the mortuary attendant had now moved the body of James Crawford.

The examining pathologist, a man only slightly known to Fairbanks, formally greeted him, then immediately commenced the autopsy. With a subtle glance at Lauder and aware it was her first post mortem examination, Fairbanks noticed a slight sheen beneath her nose and covering her upper lip, guessing Smythe had suggested she apply a smear of scented hand cream to avert the nausea caused by the strong body and formaldehyde odours that hung in the air. Throughout the procedure, he also saw Smythe stand close to Lauder, readying himself and obviously concerned that the sight of the dismemberment of the body might cause her to faint.

However, what he couldn't anticipate was that his neighbour was made of sterner stuff and fascinated by the medical dissection of a human body, actually took a step forward to closely watch the pathologist carry out his grim task.

Quickly and professionally, the pathologist completed his examination, then turning to the DI, said, "My conclusion, Mr Fairbanks, is that this gentleman is typical of most residents his age who reside in the west of Scotland, where we all suffer from a damp climate that in due course, leads to the onset of arthritis."

He paused then lifting one of the deceased's hands, stared at the hand when he continued, "Mr Crawford, as you can see from the misshapen fingers and knuckles, is indicating multiple areas of arthritis and wear and tear in his hands and particularly his fingers, his knees and hips too, though as I say, that is to be expected of a man his age. That aside, he had no obvious serious health issues that I can determine other than heavy scarring to his lungs through what I can only surmise was caused by him being a heavy smoker. Therefore, I base my conclusion that his death was as a result of being strangled," he used a forefinger to point to the neck area, "with the damage being mainly to the vertebral compartment and the obvious swelling on the neck that indicates a ligature was applied to the deceased's throat. That in turn has quite literally and in layman's terms, denied the deceased the ability to breathe. Therefore, without doubt," he turned to Fairbanks, "your victim was indeed murdered."

"One question, sir, if I may," Fairbanks brow furrowed.

"In your opinion, given that Mr Crawford's hands are notably arthritic, is it possible he would be able to hold, aim and fire a modern semi-automatic handgun?"

The pathologist was taken by surprise, then sighed when he said, "I suppose it is possible, but in my considered opinion, he'd need to have used both hands to hold and aim such a gun and while I am not myself a firearms enthusiast, I do believe there is a certain strength that is required to pull a trigger while aiming a handgun; perhaps two or three pounds. So no, and again I stress it is my opinion only, Mr Crawford it is an unlikely he was capable of holding and using such a handgun that you describe."

Thanking the pathologist, Fairbanks turned to Smythe to tell him, "You and Susie collect what productions you need, Duke, then after you've delivered your samples to the Forensic Department at Pitt Street we'll see you back at Maryhill."

With a nod to Rooney and again thanking the pathologist and the mortuary attendant, they left the building to return to their car.

CHAPTER SIX.

Seated at her desk in the small office located in the stockroom, Ronnie Masters finished flicking through the Life & Fashion Management magazine and found herself smiling for if she were totally honest, she was more than a little excited at the thought of a fashion shoot.

However, her face creased, she wouldn't make any decision till she had spoken with Eddie and though she instinctively knew he would support her, again gave thought to the possible adverse publicity her past such might arouse if such an article was to be published in an apparently popular magazine.

Still, she wryly smiled again when she thought, it *would* be nice to once more see her image on the cover of a fashion magazine.

"Miss Masters," she turned to see Laura bearing down on her and no matter how many times she had told her deputy manager, who described herself as old school, Laura still insisted on calling her boss, 'Miss Masters.'

"Don't tell me," she raised a hand, then adopting a deep, Northern English accent, comically said, "trouble at the mill."

Even the formidable Laura, a former senior supervisor with the M&S company, smiled at that, then visibly relaxing, said, "Not quite that bad, but we've a customer returning a ball gown with stitching that *seems* to have mysteriously come undone. Though," Laura raised one eyebrow in a clear indication of her thoughts on the claim, "I have my own reservations about how that has occurred."

Ronnie raised *both* her eyebrows and trusting Laura's impeccable instincts, asked, "You think it's deliberate?"

"The customer is suggesting she return the gown; however, I couldn't help but notice it is visibly stained and has quite obviously been worn," then her voice dripped with sarcasm when she added, "and she's seeking a full refund."

"Oh," Ronnie wryly smiled, "one of *those* returns."

It hadn't been the first time the scam had been tried at the shop and certainly wouldn't be the last, she knew, so taking a deep breath, she adopted a professional smile and followed Laura from the stockroom to meet or more likely, confront the customer.

****

Acting DS Jackie Wilson sat alongside the CID clerk, Tom Daly, who was at his desk and sipped at the coffee she had made them both.

"It's going to be a slow couple of days till things get back to normal," she sighed.

"How do you mean?" he turned to her.

"Well, you've been here long enough to know, Tom, that when there's a murder investigation, a lot of the lowlifes keep their heads down for a few days in case they get a pull from us. Once they know they're not going to be pulled, they revert back to their wicked ways and the crime reports jump back to their usual numbers."

"Aye, Jackie," he laid down his mug, "so if there's a couple of days respite, that'll give you the opportunity to catch up on some of your paperwork."

"Hey," she pretended to scowl when she huffily said, "I'm always up to date with my paperwork, so don't start on me."

"Maybe your *own* paperwork," he pointedly stared at her, "but you're the acting supervisor in charge of a team, so now you're going to be checking their paperwork too, aren't you?"

She slowly exhaled before she replied, "Why do you have to be so bloody sensible, Constable Daly, and by the way, why have *you* never asked to join the Department?"

He patronised her with a wide smile before he replied, "Because I'm a real police officer, not one of you suits swanning around and pretending you're Columbo or Starsky and Hutch."

"Columbo? Starsky and Hutch?" she stared wide-eyed at him before she added, "Tom, you really need to get yourself a colour television and come into the twenty-first century, pal."

Further debate ended when the door to the general office was knocked then opened by a man with an English accent, who stepped into the room to say, "I've been sent up from downstairs by a constable at the bar. I'm looking for Detective Inspector Fairbanks?"

Rising to her feet, she said, "I'm DS Wilson, sir, can I ask what it's about?"

The man fumbled in his inside jacket pocket, then producing a laminated Force Support Officer identity card, he said, "My name's Mark Mathieson. I work at Pitt Street in the Ballistics Section of the SOCO. Mr Fairbanks, please?"

Sensing that Mathieson was a little nervous, Wilson also sensed too that he was not about to divulge to her why he needed to speak with Eddie Fairbanks, and so she smiled, "While Tom here gets you a tea or coffee, Mr Mathieson, I'll find out where DI Fairbanks is at the

minute."
****

Seated at his desk, Larry Considine was disappointed the door to door statements produced not an iota of useful information, though in general, the victim's flat being located in a high rise building, the majority of those residents interviewed had never met nor had any knowledge of their fourth floor neighbour. Those few who did reside on the fourth floor only knew Crawford as a man who kept to himself, occasionally sharing a lift where he would nod a greeting, but if they were being truthful, never engaged any of them in conversation. Even the nosey woman across the landing, who had initially been interviewed by Jackie Wilson, provided only the most basic information and knew nothing of any visitors or friends he might have had.

The one positive result from the SOCO examination of the locus, quite apart from the discovery of the firearm, was that following the post mortem examination of the dog, it was ascertained the dog had indeed been stabbed to death and human blood been discovered in its mouth. However, an examination of the DNA extracted from the blood did not disclose any suspect currently registered on the DNA database.

As for the Rangers scarf used to throttle the victim and aside from Crawford's own DNA, skin cells that were presumed to be the killers, were discovered on the scarf.

DNA extracted from the cells was then confirmed to be a match for the DNA discovered in the dog's mouth.

"And all that tells us is the killer murdered Crawford and killed the wee dog too," sighed Considine.

"But if there is human blood in the dog's mouth, Larry, then at least we know we're looking for a killer with a bite mark somewhere on his body," remarked DC Jaya Bhan, a thirty-one-years old, five foot, eight-inch Glasgow born woman of Indian parentage and three years as a CID officer from her ten years on the Force.

Bhan, single and constantly ribbed by her colleagues for living with her parents, had endured much racial slur and abuse during her service, but quick-witted and with an indomitable sense of humour, was usually quick to turn the tables on her abuser and judged to be one of the funniest detectives in the Department. Reliable and extremely competent, Bhan had recently passed her second examination and was on the cusp of being promoted to uniformed sergeant, but had made it clear during her annual assessments if she was to be promoted, then it must be to the CID or she'd insist on remaining where she was.

Close friends with Jackie Wilson and Wilson's live-in partner, Debbie, the trio were frequent social cronies and often hit the bright lights of the city together. However, while the very attractive Bahn was heterosexual, she was forever complaining that on their nights out together, she'd no chance of getting a man due to the constant vetting of any would-be suitors by her bodyguarding pals.

Now, staring down at Considine, she asked, "You're an old guy, Larry, what does the law say about us making suspects take their shirts and trousers off to check them for a dog bite?"

"Who you calling an old guy," his eyes narrowed and brow creased in pretend anger, then he grinned, when he added, "We can only do that, Jaya if we've detained or arrested them. We can ask, of course, but if the suspect is a ned he's hardly likely to comply, is he?"

"No, I suppose not," she shook her head, then said, "How many floors do you think the boss will want us to continue checking on the door to door?"

"Why do you ask?"

"Because," she sighed, "the bloody lift's not working and have you any idea what it's like doing the door to door and going up and down all them stairs? I don't fancy climbing twenty storeys' only to find the residents are at work or out shopping."

He grinned when he replied, "If nothing else, it'll keep you fit."

"Larry, Larry," she softly exhaled, then slowly shook her head at him when she said, "Look at me. With a body like mine, do you really think I need to keep fit?"

"Then how come you can't get a boyfriend?" he teased.

"Two words; Jackie and Debbie," she shook her head again.

They both turned when the door to the incident room opened to admit Eddie Fairbanks and Mickey Rooney.

Striding towards Considine's desk, Fairbanks asked, "Anything doing?"

"No, other than SOCO resulting the examination of the dog. It seems there was human blood in its mouth, but the DNA that the Forensics extracted from the blood isn't on their database."

"Good to know at least we've got some kind of a result," he nodded, but then Considine added, "That and there's a guy from the SOCO Ballistics waiting to see you; a Mr Mathieson. He's in the general office being minded by Tom Daly."

Fairbanks face creased with curiosity when he asked, "Did he say why he's here?"

"Nope," Considine shook his head. "Only that he wants to speak to you personally."

Nodding, Fairbanks said, "Larry, let me read the synopsis file of what little we know so far and if you're not busy, come along in five minutes. Mickey, when Larry gives you the nod, fetch him Mr Mathieson and bring him to my office."

Turning back to Considine, he added, "If he's from SOCO, then as you're my deputy, Larry, whatever this guy has to say, I want you to hear it as well."

****

In his office in the Command Suite at police headquarters in Pitt Street, ACC (Crime) Alex Gardener, seated behind his desk, stared up at his aide and said, "Regardless of what Chief Superintendent Malone told us, DI Cameron, I rather suspect that to use the old Glasgow vernacular, she has sold us a dummy. DCI Heggerty was not at his office yesterday for a good reason and to appoint an inexperienced DI to manage what seems to be a who-dunnit murder? Well," he pouted his lower lip when he shook his head, "I am not happy, not happy at all."

You never are anyway, thought Cameron, but politely replied, "From what I hear of DI Fairbanks, sir, he sounds to be a very competent officer. As I'm sure you will recall," and he hated himself for sounding so patronising, "Mr Miller, on the day he was appointed to the role of acting Deputy Chief Constable and you assumed charge of the CID, sir, he did tell us that he was most impressed by DI Fairbanks detection of the man who not only was charged with the murder, but…"

He got no further, for Gardener interrupted by slapping a hand onto the table when he snapped, "There is nothing wrong with my recollection of that day, DI Cameron, and yes, I do recall that Mr Miller did have good things to say about Fairbanks. However, I am now the Assistant Chief Constable in charge of Strathclyde Police CID…"

And more's the pity, thought Cameron.

"…and it is me that Fairbanks will have to impress. And further," to Cameron's surprise, Gardener actually growled, "I am *not* happy that a mere DI is to act as the SIO in any murder investigation in my area of jurisdiction. Now," he leaned forward and stared at the younger man, "this is what I want you to find out."

****

The reading of the synopsis for the murder of James Crawford took less than a minute, for the file was woefully thin.

A dejected Eddie Fairbanks sat back in his chair and tightly closed his eyes when he wondered, how the hell can I motivate a team with this, then tossed the cardboard file down onto the desk.

Minutes later, his door was knocked and he irritably called out, "Come in."

Mickey Rooney pushed open the door and said, "Mr Mathieson, sir," then stood to one side to permit the SOCO man to enter.

Directly behind Mathieson, Larry Considine arrived then nodding at Rooney, entered and closed the door behind him.

A little apprehensively, Mathieson stared from one to the other, then asked, "DI Fairbanks?"

"That's me," he introduced himself, surprised when realising and though it didn't really matter, that no-one thought to mention Mathieson was an Englishman with a strong Yorkshire accent. Indicating the two chairs in front of his desk, he added, "This is DS Considine. He's acting as my deputy in the murder investigation. Now, Mr Mathieson, you've asked to speak with me?"

However, Mathieson stood where he was then said, "With respect and no offence intended, DI Fairbanks, but can we speak privately?"

"Does what you have to say concern the murder investigation, Mr Mathieson?"

Hesitantly, he replied, "Yes, sir, it does."

"Then as DS Considine is my deputy, he must be party to everything that concerns the investigation. Does that concern you?" his eyes narrowed.

It was apparent to both detectives that Mathieson was clearly uneasy, though for the life of him, Fairbanks could not fathom why.

Seconds passed, then, as if making a sudden decision, Mathieson unconsciously nodded and sat down.

Licking nervously at his lips, Mathieson began, "What I have to disclose is, well, something I had to share with my line manager, but no-one else is party to the information. In fact, it was my line manager who suggested I do not share this information with anyone other than the SIO," then staring at Fairbanks, he pointedly added, "You."

He glanced at Considine then when he stared back at Fairbanks, he said, "I probably wouldn't even have come to see you, DI Fairbanks, but my good friend at the SOCO Department, Davy McKinnon…"

"Davy in the Handwriting Section?" he interrupted.

"Yes, sir," he nodded, "that's him. Davy told me you are a man who could be trusted, but I didn't even share with him what I'm about to disclose."

Fairbanks took a deep breath then leaning forward, his hands clasped on the desk, he said, "I believe you told DS Wilson you work in the Ballistics Section at SOCO. Can I assume then that this concerns something to do with the handgun discovered at the victims flat?"

They watched Mathieson take another deep breath, then nodding, he said, "For your information, DI Fairbanks, I'm a former regular army soldier. Twenty-three years with the Colours and over seven years working for Strathclyde Police in the Ballistics Section."

"So it's fair to say you've acquired a fair modicum of experience," Fairbanks smiled at him in an effort to relax the nervous Mathieson.

He was rewarded with a soft smile, then Mathieson continued, "First, might I inform you gentlemen," he stared from one to the other, "that as a member of the armed forces, I was and still am a signatory to the Official Secrets Act, so please respect what I have to tell you and this it is not for general dissemination."

"As are we both," Fairbanks nodded at him, "so rest assured, Mr Mathieson, this conversation is for our ears only."

"Thank you," the relief in his voice was evident.

"Right, my job in the army was working as an armourer, everything from small arms to larger calibre weapons that included not just NATO weapons, but Soviet armaments too, as well as the weapons of the Soviet's satellite countries. The point is," he sat forward, a little more animated now having begun his story, "I have a wide and varied experience of weapons sir. How they work, how to repair them, disable them even and also, how weapons can be used as surveillance tools."

"Sorry," Fairbanks confusion showed on his face. "You said,

surveillance tools?"

"And that's why I'm here," Mathieson sat back in his chair.

Fairbanks glanced at an equally confused Considine before he said, "Go on."

"Well, sir, during my service, like most soldiers who served from nineteen sixty-nine through to nineteen-ninety-eight, I served in the army's Operation Banner, the Troubles, as they came to be called, over in the Province. Of course, being an armourer, my tours thankfully," he sighed, "was usually base bound, repairing weapons or examining and destroying seized weapons from both the republican and Loyalist organisations."

They watched Mathieson nervously swallow, then he continued, "One of my jobs was assisting the Security Forces or the SF as they were known…"

"You mean the army?" Considine interrupted.

"The army, the RUC, God bless them, and of course, the Security Services or as they're more popularly known, Box or MI5."

"Assisting them, how?" this from Fairbanks who realised his stomach was knotting when he immediately recalled the visit from the Special Branch.

"Have you ever heard the word, 'dicking'?"

"Sounds vaguely rude," smiled Considine.

"Well, rude or not," Mathieson shrugged, "it was a word coined to describe attaching a surveillance device to a weapon."

"For what purpose?" asked Fairbanks.

"Let me give you a hypothetical situation. If a weapon or let's say, a cache of weapons was discovered by the SF and the terrorist organisation suspected of controlling the weapons were unaware of them being discovered, the SF would often plant a tracking device into the weapons and thus be able to tell when the weapons were being moved. Then when the tracking device was seen to be moving, they had several options; following it to its destination, ambushing those involved at the location where the cache was discovered or anyone who had arrived to transport the weapons."

"Like a listening a device, you mean?" asked Considine.

"I'm not a technician, DS Considine," he slowly shook his head, "but in my limited experience, I'm more inclined to believe it was a tracking device that detected movement rather than sound, though of course if the circumstances were right, the SF would occasionally place listening devices around the location to forewarn of any noise approaching the cache."

He paused to lick at his lips, then continued, "Back in the day, I think because these devices were so small, there was a limit to their range. That said," he shrugged, "in those few short years, technology has moved on. I mean, for example, in the last decade look at the development of mobile phones."

"Point taken," Considine nodded.

"And now to the point, you are here why?" Fairbanks interjected.

Mathieson took a short breath and exhaled before he replied, "When I inspected the handgun discovered at your victim's flat, Mr Fairbanks, the Czechoslovakian made CZ 75, at this point, I have to inform you I am satisfied the weapon has not been fired in the recent past."

He shuffled in his seat and with his right hand, reached into his jacket pocket and withdrew a small, brown envelope.

He took a sharp breath before he continued

"When I was checking over the handgun," he said again, "I took off the handgrip and discovered this."

Opening the flap of the small envelope, he reached across to the desk then slowly tipped the envelope to one side and from which a small electronic device fell out onto the brown folder that lay on the desktop.

"What the hell is that?" Considine rose from his chair to get a better look.

"I have absolutely no idea, but in my opinion," Mathieson wheezed, "and only if I'm correct, it's a tracking device. Though to be frank," he continued with a grimace, "it's a lot smaller and seems to be a lot more sophisticated than anything I've ever seen or used back in the Province. And again," he repeated, "It's *only* my opinion."

Stunned, Fairbanks stared first at the device, then at Mathieson before he asked, "Is it live?"

"I have absolutely no idea," he shook his head, "but as it was hidden in the firearm, I would suggest that part of its construction is a miniature battery with a lengthy life."

Reaching into the inside pocket of his jacket, he fetched out a ball point pen, then said, "Do you see that small and very thin wire sticking out? That there," he used the pen nib to point at it.

Both Fairbanks and Considine peered at the half inch silver coloured wire.

"I think that's maybe the aerial," Mathieson muttered.

"So, right now it could be giving off a signal?"

"I'd suggest probably yes, rather than possibly," Mathieson agreed with a shrug.

"What kind of range would a thing like that have; in your opinion, I mean," asked Fairbanks.

"Back in the day, the devices I worked with were usually effective for no more than two miles at best, so usually there was a mobile control vehicle, usually operated by vetted personnel from the Royal Corps of Signals, who tracked the 'dicked' weapons. However, like I said, with the advances in technology these days," he shrugged, "you could be looking at a far greater distance."

"Then," Considine sat back down in his chair, "whoever is monitoring it, if indeed they are monitoring it, will likely believe it's still sending a signal from within the handgun…"

"And they'll think the handgun is here at Maryhill office, rather than within the productions safe at the Ballistics Section in Pitt Street?" Fairbanks unconsciously nodded.

"Likely, yes," Mathieson agreed again.

"If I might ask, Mr Mathieson," Fairbanks stared at him with suspicion, "you decided to inform me about this thing, but why didn't you simply leave it inside the weapon and ignore it? Surely that would have been a lot simpler for you?"

"Maybe," Mathieson nodded in understanding, then taking a breath and with a hint of pride in his voice, he added, "but I wouldn't have been doing my job, DI Fairbanks, and I like to think that in all my years working with weapons, I've never been anything but professional."

Several seconds of silence passed before Fairbanks asked, "And what's your thoughts about who might have placed this device in the weapon?"

"That's a question I'll leave for you and Mr Considine to answer, but whoever they are, my guess is that they too are professionals and for whatever reason they've 'dicked' this weapon, it's because they want to know where it was going and for what purpose it was to be used."

"Well," Fairbanks exhaled through pursed lips and watching as Mathieson slid the device back into the brown envelope, reached across the desk to take the envelope from him, then continued, "You've certainly given us something to think about, Mr Mathieson, and all I can do is thank you. Needless to say, this remains between us three and you can report to your line supervisor that you have indeed been very helpful."

Rising to his feet, Mathieson nodded when he replied, "I rather think that what I've actually given you is a headache, DI Fairbanks. But good luck and if I can assist in any other way, you know where to find me."

When Mathieson had left the room and closed the door behind him, it was Considine who said, "And now we know why the Branch visited you. They want their gun back."

"You think it was them that, what he said, dicked this handgun?"

"No doubt about it," Considine nodded, then continued, "and it also offers an explanation as to why there was nothing in the victim's antecedent history about his leanings towards the right wing or support for a Loyalist organisation. They've amended his PNC entry."

"Which begs the question and we're assuming they *are* responsible; why did the branch give a gun to an old man like Crawford, in the first place?"

"Maybe the gun wasn't for him."

Picking up on Considine's inference, Fairbanks nodded when he suggested, "He was the middle man? The courier?"

"Sounds like it to me, yes," Considine nodded.

They sat in silence, each with his own thoughts, then the silence was broken when Fairbanks said, "Then we've another question to be asked. Who was to be the recipient of the weapon and why?"

Staring at him, Considine raised a hand, then warned him, "Before you go off on one, I have to tell you that I was as curious as you as to why the Branch visited you. So, knowing Duke Smythe has a pal in their Department, a guy he bowls with, I asked him to make some discreet inquiry about this DI McGhee and her pal, DS McCartney."

"Well, in light of Mathieson's visit and what we now know, Larry, I don't think that was such a bad idea. If Duke does have some info about that pair, bring him to see me."

Rising from his chair, Considine nodded, "Will do, boss."

****

The Special Branch offices located in police headquarters in Pitt Street, occupied almost a quarter of the first floor on the south side of the enormous red-bricked building.

Within the SB suite were a number of offices occupied by separate Departments that included Covert Surveillance, Source Handling, Intelligence Desks, Research as well as a number of Departments dealing with other matters.

One office, that was employed in clandestine work and where the staff was managed by an affiliated agency, had restricted access where regular SB staff were not permitted to enter.

In this windowless office, no larger than the combined space of two front rooms of an average home and where the security door was accessed by a digital lock whose combination was known to no more than a handful of people, a technician, wearing muffling headphones, sat on a swivel chair facing an array of electronic equipment. His open-necked shirt, the sleeves rolled up to his forearms, wafted slightly from the cool breeze emitted by the large fan in the corner, whose main function was to regulate the room temperature and ensure the sophisticated and extremely expensive equipment that occupied a full desk, did not overheat.

Without turning, his concentration fully focused on the three linked screens in front of him, he beckoned forward the woman standing behind him, then pointing at a digital map on the left-hand screen, he said, "The device is indicating that the gun has been moved to this location."

His hand resting slightly on a mouse, he clicked on the right-hand screen to drag the high-resolution map from that screen to the centre screen, then expanded the map.

Continuing, he said, "According to the readout, the gun is now located and is motionless at," he leaned forward and narrowed his eyes to read the buildings name and location, "in Maryhill police office."

He paused and eyes narrowing again, used the mouse to cancel the map featured on the centre screen and replaced it with the building schematics of Maryhill police office, before he added, "It looks like it's in an office on the first floor. Just there," and unwittingly pointed to the room where Eddie Fairbanks was currently seated behind his desk.

CHAPTER SEVEN: Thursday, 21 September 2006.

Arriving at her shop that morning, a quietly excited Ronnie Masters greeted her deputy manager, Laura, with the good news.
Unlocking the front door, she grinned, "I had a long chat yesterday evening with Eddie and he's agreed that I should go ahead with the fashion shoot for the Life & Fashion Management article. That said," her brow creased, "he was so wrapped up thinking about his latest investigation, I think half of what I told him went right over his head."
"He's a man, so you have to allow for selective hearing," Laura returned her grin with a wry smile, then removing her coat, asked, "Will the shoot take place here or where?"
"I really have no idea," Ronnie frowned. "I've still to confirm with that young fellow, Harper, if the shoot's still on. I mean they might have changed their mind."
"And why would they, Miss Masters," Laura tut-tutted with a shake of her head, then taking a step backwards, critically examined her boss and said, "Look at you. Even coming to work and dressed as you are, with your beauty and your style, how could they not want you to grace the cover of their magazine?"
Finding herself blushing, she replied, "Laura, you know all the right things to say and when to say them. Now, let me get the kettle on while you set up the tills."
****
Across the city, seated by Larry Considine's desk in the incident room within Maryhill Police Office, Eddie Fairbanks was more than disappointed that no further information had come in through the night about the murder of James Crawford.
"You look dead beat," remarked Considine, who squinting at the DI, was himself feeling the effects of a goodly part of a bottle of Glenfiddich the night before.
With a shake of his head and fighting a yawn, Fairbanks admitted he had little sleep and that the information passed by the Ballistics FSO, Mark Mathieson, had kept him awake.

Rising to his feet, he slowly exhaled when he said, "I'll give it ten minutes to collect my thoughts, then I'll come back for the morning briefing. Oh, first things first, though, when Duke Smythe arrives and if he's got anything to tell us, bring him along."

"Boss," Considine acknowledged with a nod.

Striding along the corridor, Fairbanks pushed open the door to the DI's room and removing his suit jacket, stepped across to hang it on the hook on the wall.

Turning, his eyes narrowed when he noticed some wood chips and the broken drawer lock on the floor beneath the desk.

Moving closer to the desk, he sighed when he saw the splintered wood and the top drawer forced open, but pushed closed again.

He didn't need to open the drawer to know the device within was gone.

Lifting his desk phone, he dialled the internal number for Considine and quietly said, "Can you come along to my office, Larry. We have another problem."

****

"This is getting bloody outrageous," snarled Considine, bent down on one knee as he examined the forced drawer. "Anything else missing?"

"Nothing, as far as I can tell," Fairbanks ruefully shook his head, then added, "I'm as much to blame. I should have hidden the bloody thing before I left last night, but it never occurred to me the Branch would come and steal the device back."

Considine's eyes narrowed when he suggested, "They probably weren't here to steal the device, boss, they probably thought they were coming to reacquire the gun. That and if the device had given off a signal where it was located, then no matter where you hid it, they'd know its location."

Seconds of silence was broken when Considine, rising to his feet, sat with his backside against the desk, then asked, "Are you intending letting Bobby Heggerty know about this?"

"No," Fairbanks replied a little more sharply that he intended, then apologetically added, "Sorry, Larry, but no, I'm not telling him."

Before he could explain, Considine asked, "Is it because he's ill?"

"You know about that?"

"I do now," he sighed then quickly added, "Look, you're not giving away a confidence. Me and Bobby go back a long way, so I knew there was something up and let's face it, these last couple of months he's not been himself, has he?"

Slowly nodding, Fairbanks said, "I'm not sure what's wrong with him, but if he does decide to share it, then I'm sure given your lengthy relationship, it will be to you."

"So, returning to this problem we have," Considine's face creased. "We'll need to bring it to the attention of some management or other. We can't keep something like this quiet for too long," he waved a hand at the forced drawer.

"You're right, of course," Fairbanks nodded, then added, "I have an idea about that."

****

Carrying the brown cardboard file beneath his arm, DI Iain Cameron pushed open the door that admitted entry to the Command Suite at Pitt Street and hated himself for what he was about to do.

A reluctant appointment to be ACC Alex Gardener's aide, Cameron's Glasgow's Kelvindale Councillor uncle believed he was doing him a good turn when at a Police and Fire Committee event, he spoke to Gardener about his University graduate nephew. Cameron, who had attained the rank of DS and was happy at Dumbarton CID, eight months later found himself summoned to Pitt Street by Gardener, who sensing a valuable future contact in the Police and Fire Committee, a Councillor who would now owe him a favour, arranged for Cameron's promotion to Detective Inspector. Now here he was, three months later and no more than a gopher, fetching and carrying for a man for whom he had little respect.

His latest chore and he despaired of the task set him, was to search the personnel file of DI Edward Fairbanks and find anything that would permit the ACC to legitimately question DCI Heggerty's decision to appoint Fairbanks as the murder SIO; anything that would indicate either Heggerty's poor judgement call or the DI's lack of experience and his capability to manage a murder investigation.

Fortunately, aside from an incident some six months previously when the then DS Fairbanks had been involved in a physical altercation with a Detective Inspector, his file indicated his aptitude and commitment to the Force had been excellent. What was more fortunate and pleased Cameron no end, was that a note had been inserted into the file just months previously from the then acting, now appointed Deputy Chief Constable, Charles Miller, commending Fairbanks for his tenacious and exemplary conduct in hunting down a prolific poison pen author, who was also charged with murder.

In Cameron's humble opinion, as he pushed open the door into Gardener's outer office, there was nothing the ACC could do to justifiably remove Fairbanks from the investigation, but then his hand raised to knock on the inner door, he hesitated as a thought struck him.

After visiting Maryhill Police Office, on the return journey to Pitt Street an angry Gardener had made a huge issue about the unavailability of the DCI, Bobby Heggerty.

His eyes narrowing with sudden insight, Cameron realised it wasn't Fairbanks the ACC was gunning for.

It was the DCI and he was seeking to discredit Fairbanks in an attempt to somehow damage Heggerty.

Conniving bastard, he grimaced then taking a breath to compose himself, he knocked on the door.

****

DC Duke Smythe beckoned that Larry Considine follow him into the corridor where ensuring it was empty, quietly said, "I had a word last night with my mate at the bowling practise. Do you want to hear it yourself or…"

Considine stopped him with a raised hand then said, "Follow me." Leading him to the DI's room, he knocked on the door then pushing it open, said, "Duke's here, boss."

Once they were settled in the two chairs Smythe began, "My mate, he's been with the Branch for almost ten years, now and what he doesn't know isn't worth knowing."

His eyes narrowing, he asked, "I assume what I'm about to tell you, boss, won't get back to the Branch? I don't want my mate…"

Fairbanks interrupted when he replied, "Duke, this is purely for me and Larry, so no fear, okay?"

"Right, boss," he sighed, then said, "This guy, DS Norrie McCartney, is by all accounts a right bad bastard. Works in what my mate says is the dirty tricks mob. When I asked what that is, he says whatever McCartney gets up to and by the way, my mate says that *is* rumoured to be quite a lot, there's never going to be any come-back on him. Apparently he's handy with his fists and where there's a problem with their sources, he's the man they send to sort it out and never an backlash."

"When you say sort it out, did your mate…?"

"I asked him what that means, to sort it out, and he says, everything from threats to families, beatings and occasionally punters finding themselves up in court for everything from theft to kiddy porn on their computers."

"What! Special Branch are…?"

"Hang on, boss, that's the rub," this time, it was Smythe who raising his hand, quickly interrupted.

"Officially McCartney *is* Special Branch, but my mate says it's the mob from down in London who pull his strings, that the Branch have been trying to get shot of McCartney for years, but they have to tug the forelock to their, what he called," he shrugged, "their spook cousins, and that McCartney, he's definitely working for that mob in Thames House, in London."

"Thames House?" Considine turned to glance quizzingly at Fairbanks, who softly said, "The Security Service, Box or MI5 or whatever name they choose to use."

"As for the DI, this woman McGhee," Smyth continued.

"She's a high flyer who transferred to Strathclyde Police as a DI about five months ago from the PSNI over in the Province, and straight into the Branch. My mate," his face ceased, "he says she's an unknown quantity at the minute. He's seen her about the office, but she never engages in conversation other than with officers of her rank or the bosses and it's her who runs the dirty tricks mob. That said he's of the opinion too that McCartney is her lapdog and where you find her, he's at her heel. One thing about her, though," he grimaced, "my mate heard from a bowling pal that he has in the PSNI Special Branch, that apparently she got out of the Province ahead of the posse, that whatever problem she caused the PSNI, it was the Thames House mob who arranged her transfer to Glasgow. That's only a rumour though, boss; just what my mate's heard."

"Suggesting then that her strings too are also pulled by them," Fairbanks brow knitted then asked, "Anything else?"

"That's all I've got, boss," Smyth exhaled.

"And that's plenty, Duke, so thank you," Fairbanks acknowledged him with a nod as the large man stood up and left the room, pulling the door closed behind him.

"What you thinking?" he stared at Considine.
He watched the older man's brow furrow before he replied, "I'm thinking that this isn't a straight forward murder. I'm thinking that our victim was a patsy and that we've got ourselves involved in the Security Services plan to murder someone with the gun that's locked up in the safe in Pitt Street. And I'm also thinking…" he paused and licked at his dry lips, "if *we're* not careful, we could find ourselves being set up too."

****

Wearily facing yet another door, DC Jaya Bhan, her clipboard held in her hand, regretted that last cup of coffee while wondering where the hell she could go for a pee, knocked on the door with no nameplate on the sixth floor of the high rise building, then heard a croaky female voice call out, "Who is it?"

"Strathclyde Police," she shouted back then waited for several seconds before the door creaked open, though not fully open due to the attached security chain inside.

A wrinkled face with grey hair peered out through the crack in the door, then the same voice suspiciously said, "I thought you said you were the polis?"

"I am," Bahn, her warrant card round her neck on a plastic card holder, held out the laminated card for the woman to examine, then cringed at the smell that seeped out from the flat.

The woman's eyes narrowed when she peered at the card then said, "But you're a Paki, hen. I didn't know the polis hired Paki's these days."

Biting back her retort, Bahn slowly replied, "*Actually*, I've Indian parents, but I'm Glasgow born and bred, missus. Now, can I ask you some questions?"

"Is this about the polis who were hanging about the bottom of the flats on Tuesday?"

"Ah, yes, it is," Bahn acidly replied, already deciding that the elderly woman was not going to be of any use.

"Do you need to come in? I'm not used to visitors, you know."

"It would be helpful, yes," Bahn forced a smile, eager to get this door-to-door interview done and dusted.

"Are you okay about cats?"

"Cats?"

"You're not allergic, are you? That woman the social sent me last month to do the cleaning. She said she couldn't come in because she was allergic. I think she was at the madam, that she just didn't want to do her job, bloody layabout she was. And she looked like a Paki too."

"I'm not a …" Bahn started, then thought, why do I bother, inwardly agreeing that the unknown social carer obviously made a wise decision, avoiding this bloody old racist.

That, thought Bahn, and she was probably put off too by the awful smell escaping through the crack in the door.

Forcing another a smile, she politely said, "No, you're all right. I'm not allergic."

"Okay then, you can come in," the woman slowly replied with a suspicious look on her face.

Glancing along the corridor to where her neighbour, DC Brian Saunders, was at a door speaking with another resident, she gave him a subtle shake of her head just as the door in front of Bahn closed, then she heard the rattling of the security chain before the door was fully pulled open.

And that's when the smell really hit her.

God almighty, she thought and almost reeled backwards at the pong of not just *a* cat but several cats, some of whom stared at her from the hallway within as they meowed their welcome.

Her eyes watering and choking back the urge to spit out a mouthful of phlegm, Bahn cautiously stepped onto the visibly soiled carpeted floor, only to be warned by the occupant, "Mind where you step, hen, these cats of mine aren't fussy where they piddle or shit."

The elderly, hunchbacked wizened woman with straggly grey hair who wore a faded pink dressing gown and bright red lipstick that was also smeared on her obviously false, yellowing teeth, beckoned Bahn follow her to the dimly lit front room where the detective saw the raggedy curtains were clumsily pulled together.

Curiously though, also seeing a pair of what seemed to be powerful, black coloured binoculars with a brown, leather strap, sitting on the dusty window ledge.

To Bahn's horror, the room was occupied by a dozen or more cats who sat or lay on the various items of furniture, though her estimation didn't include the half dozen who trailed the woman and Bahn from the hallway and insisted on rubbing up against the younger woman's lower legs.

Trying to breathe through her mouth, Bahn stuttered, "Can I ask you name, please?"

"It's Margaret Thompson. Miss Thompson," she added with a smile that would have terrified young children, then said, "Would you not like to sit down, hen?"

Glancing at the stained settee and couch and armchairs where rested several of the cats, Bahn weakly shook her head when she lied, "No, you're all right. I've been sitting all day, so it's nice to stand for a wee while."

"Now," she quickly added, "if you hadn't heard, a Mr James Crawford who resided on the fourth floor, was discovered dead on Tuesday in his flat. I regret to say Mr Crawford was murdered. Did you know the man or hear about the murder?"

"Murder?" the older woman frowned. "No, hen, I didn't hear about it because you see, I don't get many visitors."

I'm not surprised, thought Bahn, but then Thompson shook her head and said, "Tuesday? Funny you should say that."

"Funny? How do you mean, Miss Thompson?"

"Well," Thompson startled when seemingly from nowhere, a ginger cat leapt into her arms, then idly stroking at the purring cat, her eyes narrowed when she said, "I remember seeing the commotion outside, all them polis cars and vans arriving, you know? Not that I'm nosey, you understand," she sniffed with righteous indignation that anyone might even consider such a thing, while tactfully ignoring the binoculars on the window ledge, "but I was keeking out of my window there and I wondered why he was standing there all that time before the polis came. Then he just stood there all that time the polis was hanging about."

Unconscious of it happening, it seemed to Bahn that the awful smell and the mewing of the cats had faded as the old, familiar sense of something important about to happen raced through her body.

Her total focus now centred on Thompson, she asked, "You say him, Miss Thompson. Is this individual someone you know?"

"I don't *know* him, hen, but he's been hanging around here before, that I do know. Down at the bottom of the flats, watching the comings and goings, you know? All Monday, I mean."

"All Monday?" Bahn unconsciously repeated, then muttered, "The day before the murder." Staring thoughtfully at the old woman, she softly asked, "Miss Thompson, just how much about this man do you recall?"

CHAPTER EIGHT.

Eddie Fairbanks lifted the desk phone to hear Larry Considine tell him, "That's Jaya Bahn just returned to the office, boss, and she's got something that might be useful. Do you want me to bring her through or do you…"
He interrupted with, "Bring Jaya along here, Larry."
A minute later, with both Considine and Bahn seated in front of Fairbanks, she began, "It was on the door to door, boss, up on the sixth floor; a Margaret Thompson, aged seventy-six who lives alone. Well, her and her twenty odd cats, I mean."
"What? Cats? Twenty of them?"
"At least, and by the way, if you intend having her revisited, I'd recommend a Forensic suit and a facemask," Bahn shuddered at the memory.
"Anyway, she didn't know the deceased and had no knowledge of the murder, but when I spoke with her, she recalls seeing a male hanging around the flats on Monday and was of the opinion he might have been, her words, watching the comings and goings."
Now into her story, Bahn leaned forward when she continued, "On Tuesday, when the uniform were swarming about and set up the cordon on the entrance to the forecourt of the flats, Thompson was at her window and saw the same man hanging around, before the cops arrived and said he remained there for most of the time the cordon was in place. Just watching what was going on, Thompson said."
Her face creased when she quickly added, "Oh, and Thompson also said he used a mobile phone at least once and *believes* he was the same male she saw on Monday."
Fairbanks sat back in his chair, his brow knitting when he asked, "Don't suppose she recognised this man or knows him?"
"No," Bahn shook her head, but added, "Though she did give me a fairly decent description."
Glancing at her clipboard, she continued, "On Tuesday when she saw him, Thompson reckoned him to be about mid-twenties, average

height and wearing a grey coloured hooded top, denims and he'd brown hair under a black skipped cap with lettering on the front, but she didn't know what the letters were."

"Wait a minute," Considine stared suspiciously at her, "all this from a woman in her seventies looking out of a window on the sixth floor of a high rise?"

"Aye," Bahn smiled, "but a woman who uses a pair of high powered binoculars she keeps by the front window to peer down at her neighbours. I tried the binoculars when I was there, boss," she turned to Fairbanks, "and I was able to read the reggie numbers of vehicles down in the car park below."

Then still smiling, she added with a smirk, "Not that she's nosey or anything. But that's not the most interesting thing about this man she said she watched."

"What's that then?" asked Fairbanks.

She slowly smiled when she said, "Thompson watched him walking away from the flats and she's definite, boss. She says he was limping on his left leg."

"The dog," Considine snapped a glance at Fairbanks, who nodding, said, "What's the odds on there being CCTV cameras on the high-rise buildings, Larry?"

"The council tried installing them a couple of years ago, to cut down on disorder in the area, but the local neds vandalised them because they didn't want to be identified."

"Bugger," Fairbanks muttered, then said, "Right, our priority is tracing this man who is the only suspect we've got so far if only to eliminate him from the investigation. Larry, you've got a description, so find out what cops were on the cordon on Tuesday and I want each of them interviewed to see if they recall anyone like this man's description standing at the cordon."

"I'll get onto that right now," he replied, then left the room.

"Jaya," Fairbanks turned to her, "in your opinion, just how reliable is this witness; her eyesight and, being the age she is, her memory too?"

"She's a right old bugger, boss; a racist to boot, but in her case it's more of a generation thing."

"Generation thing?" he was confused.

"Aye, her birth year was nineteen-thirty, so old people like her have never really caught up with the politically correct decade and she

thinks all us brown skinned people are the same; she thinks we're all Paki's, I mean, just come over on the boat from the sub-continent." Fairbanks suppressed his grin, then raising a hand, he apologised with, "I'm sorry, Jaya, I'm not really laughing or anything, but I can only imagine how you dealt with that."
He wasn't prepared for her response when she shrugged and replied, "To be honest, boss, I didn't bother trying to even argue with her. The thing is too, when she called me a Paki, I'm convinced she genuinely never thought of herself as being offensive, just that she's likely lived through those decades when it was deemed to be an acceptable term to call someone by that derogatory name. After all," she shrugged again, "she's an old woman and she's not going to change now, is she?"
"I suppose not, no," he shook his head then asked again, "And how would you rate her as a witness?"
"Definitely not someone I'd put in the witness box, not unless you had her hosed down and disinfected," she grimaced, "but as an informant, I think what she saw is absolutely spot on. For all her age, she's still sharp as a tack; sharp enough to tell me that the guy she saw, he was definitely on his own and didn't interact with the other rubberneckers. Oh, that's my expression, not hers. That and he stayed as far away from the uniforms without actually losing sight of what was going on."
"So, when we try to trace him, you're confident we can go with her description of the man she saw?"
"Yes, boss, I am," she vigorously nodded.
"Anything else to tell me?"
She stared at him, then with a sigh, stood up and walked around his desk, then to his surprise, she bent close to him and gingerly asked, "Be honest and tell me the truth, boss. Do I smell of cats?"
****

DCI Bobby Heggerty sat with his wife on the uncomfortable, plastic tubular chairs in the waiting room on the second floor of the Beatson West of Scotland Cancer Centre, located in the west end of the city and adjacent to Gartnavel Hospital.
"That's nearly twenty minutes over your appointment time," she whispered to him, her left hand nervously beating a tune on her knee.
He turned in his chair to softly smile at her, then replied, "Cathy, we're in no rush to go anywhere fast, sweetheart, because I'm off

work and you've taken the day off too. We don't know what's happening in there," he nodded towards the closed door, then added, "Someone could be in there right now, getting the worse news of their life, so let's be a little patient, eh?"

She reached out to tightly grasp his hand when she said, "Sorry, Bobby, it's just that, well, it's just…"

But she couldn't finish, for her throat tightened and she had to take a deep breath to compose herself.

"Mr Heggerty?"

As one, they both startled when his name was called by a young, smiling nurse who standing in the doorway, beckoned them forward. Rising to his feet, his wife also arose and continuing to tightly hold his hand when he turned to glance at her, she said, "We're a couple, Bobby Heggerty, so no matter what the news is, I'm not letting you go in there alone."

He turned to stare quizzingly at the nurse, who smiling again, nodded when she said, "That's fine, Mr Heggerty. If you'd like to follow me, please?"

****

Glancing at the wall clock, Duke Smythe and Susie Lauder were called forward by Larry Considine, who providing them with a description of a possible suspect, instructed them to quickly nip downstairs to the uniform Inspector's room and request that he hold back his officers from commencing their late shift while the two detectives had a word with them.

Now making their way down the stairwell, Lauder asked, "What's the odds on the description of the woman Thompson saw is our man?"

"Aye, like it's going to be that easy," he sighed, then pulling open the heavy fire door in the corridor that led to the muster room, added, "We'll not interview them separately, Susie, but collectively. If any of them have noticed this man, they might recall saying something to one or the other, so we'll treat them as a group. Okay with you?"

"Agreed," she nodded and held open the door to the muster room to permit Smythe pass her by.

As it happened, the Inspector was at the wooden dais, just concluding the reading of the Daily Briefing Register to his shift and turned when he saw the detectives enter the room.

With one eyebrow raised at the interruption, he was more than happy to hand the dais over to the large man when Smythe explained their purpose.

Asking which officers who were in attendance at the locus at the time the victim was discovered, it transpired that allowing for comfort and refreshment breaks during the time the cordon was in operation, a total of seven officers had been involved in monitoring the cordon.

Nodding that the remainder could depart to their beats, the shift Inspector remained standing in a corner of the room when Smythe explained about the presence of the man described by the witness, Margaret Thompson.

He was surprised when almost immediately, a young probationary constable not known to him by name, hesitantly raised a hand to say, "I think I saw the man you're talking about."

Before Smythe could elicit any further information, the young woman turned to her neighbour, a long in the tooth constable called John Cooper, and almost immediately, Smythe's hopes were dashed when he heard her say, "That's the guy I thought was really suspicious. Do you remember him?"

He watched Cooper purse his lips then slowly shake his head when he replied, "No, I don't recall seeing him."

"You must remember, John, I told you about him," she persisted, her face expressing her confusion, but Cooper raised a hand and almost angrily replied, "I *told* you, I don't recall seeing anyone like that."

She turned with a pleading glance at Smythe, who stoney-faced, addressed the room when he called out, "Anyone else recall seeing a man fitting that description?"

He watched shaking heads and heard mumbled, "No, sorry," from the remaining five constables, then turning to the Inspector, he said, "Thank you, sir. Now, if we can we have a quick word with constable, eh…"

"Alice Redwood," the Inspector grimaced, but Smythe knew that his annoyance was not directed at the trainee, but at the older cop, Cooper.

"Alice," the Inspector turned to her, "take as long as the detectives need you then come and see me in my office when you're done."

When the door had closed behind the Inspector and the constables, Smythe nodded at Redwood and Lauder that the three sit on the vacated chairs, then grimly smiled at the flushed face of the young woman when he said, "I'm sorry, but we haven't crossed paths yet, so I'm Duke and this is Susie. Alice, is it?"

"Yes, sir," she nodded, only for Smythe to smile when he said, "No need for that, Alice, we're constables too, just with a fancier title. Now, how long you been in the polis?"

"Eh, a little over three months."

"So still finding your feet, eh?"

"Yes," she continued to blush.

Sitting quietly watching them both, Lauder realised that her neighbour was trying to calm the nervous young woman, who seemed clearly confused at John Cooper's denial of her claim she had pointed out the suspicious man.

It was then an embarrassed Redwood insisted, "I didn't make this up, honestly. I *did* mention the guy to John, but he said the guy was just rubber-necking like the rest of them."

"Alice," Lauder interrupted with a raised hand, "I had the misfortune to neighbour John Cooper during part of my probationary period and for what it's worth, here's an example of your neighbour."

She took a quick breath then continued, "We were walking on Maryhill Road having just started nightshift and heading back to the office because he'd forgotten his notebook when we saw a rammy outside a pub at the corner of Shakespeare Street; maybe half a dozen guys punching and kicking among themselves. I was in the job, what, six or seven weeks?" she shrugged.

"Anyway," she leaned forward and with a shake of her head, said, "The neds in the rammy hadn't noticed us and when Cooper dragged me into the doorway of a tenement close and peeked out towards where the neds were fighting, I got my baton out and myself prepared for a brawl. Then, as I'm readying myself to leave the close and head towards the fight and wade in, Cooper turns to me and tells me, 'It's okay, they've gone.' Well," she shook her head and exhaled, "I'm left wondering, was he protecting me or is he just a lazy, shiftless git who doesn't want to get involved in anything. Needless to say, as the days passed, that's what I realised. Cooper is a right Pontius Pilate; he'll wash his hands of anything that means him getting involved."

She paused then stared at Redwood when she added, "So, when you say you mentioned this guy you were suspicious of and Cooper says

you didn't tell him, who do you think we're going to believe?"
They watched as Redwood visibly relaxed, then nodding, she quietly sighed, "I was beginning to wonder if it was me."
"This guy you saw," Smythe turned to subtly nod his appreciation of Lauder's tale, then his eyes narrowed when he turned back to Redwood to ask, "What can you tell us about him?"
****
While her two part time assistants attended to the three women who were in the shop, a regular customer and a mother and daughter seeking gowns for a forthcoming wedding, Ronnie Masters sidled up to her deputy manager, Laura, to excitedly tell her, "I phoned that guy, Tony Harper, and he says he's still in Glasgow and can pop by this afternoon to discuss the photoshoot."
Laura thoughtfully smiled when she replied, "Well, I've been thinking about this photoshoot and I'm of the opinion that you wear some of our own range; it's free advertising and after the photoshoot, we can organise a sale here in the shop and sell the clothes," she used her forefingers to make italics in the air, "as worn by Ronnie Masters, International Model. On that point," her brow furrowed, "I assume you will; be getting a commission for the photoshoot?"
Bemused, Ronnie stared at her before she replied, "You know, I never thought to ask, but I suppose so. I was so caught up thinking about a return to modelling it never occurred to me to ask, but as he's coming here this afternoon, I'll have a list of questions ready for him."
Her face expressed her uncertainty when she continued, "Believe it or not, Laura, but in all the years I was modelling, I've never actually had the opportunity to choose what I wore. I suppose the reality was I simply saw myself as a clotheshorse and left the decisions to the designers and the customers. That said though, it would be nice to have a say in what I wear and I like your idea of selling the clothes I've worn, though of course I'd drop the price as really, they'd been worn and so will be second-hand."
Her brow knitted when she added, "Maybe we could drum up some business if we were to auction those clothes for sale, the proceeds to a charity. How does that sound?"
"Yes," Laura slowly drawled, "and maybe organise our own photoshoot with the newspapers covering the event when the auction takes place. Perhaps even hire the City Halls across the road and

have an entry charge to cover the cost of the hire?"

Ronnie widely smiled when she laid a hand on Laura's shoulder to tell her, "I love that idea. Now who do we know who could present such a show and act as an auctioneer? That and what local charity would we support?"

"Hold your horses, Miss Masters, but aren't we getting a little ahead of ourselves?" Laura cautioned her.

"Let's get your photoshoot arranged first, then we'll start discussing our venture into hiring halls and auctioneering."

"You're right, of course you are," Ronnie sighed then added, "I was getting carried away there, but that said, if this afternoon goes well, I think we can start planning for what sounds to be a great idea. And who knows," she pretended to pout, "maybe this time the media will be a little kinder to me."

****

Once more Andrew Collins again mentally cursed the dog that had bitten him.

He'd changed the dressing on his lower left leg several times and swallowed as many aspirin as was safe, yet the leg still ached like buggery.

Now wearing grey coloured trousers, patent black shoes, a maroon coloured polo shirt and a black quilted jacket, he painfully climbed the tenement stairs in the red sandstone building in Dennistoun's Finlay Drive.

Taking a deep breath as he paused on the half landing, he hoped the tight bandage he had applied would not leak, for the bite had worryingly wounded him far more than he could cope with.

However, though he had considered the idea, attending at a hospital A&E was completely out of the question.

Stopping outside the black painted door that bore four small screw holes where the nameplate had been removed, he rang the bell and waited as patiently as he could, hoping that on this his third visit, he'd be offered a seat.

He was about to ring the bell a second time when the door was snatched open by a man a little over twice his age and two inches shorter that Collins five feet nine, wearing a sky-blue coloured shirt, navy blue knitted and tightly knotted tie, a navy-blue three-piece suit and highly polished black shoes. His hair was a patchwork of stringy, grey hair and combed across his head to hide the Alopecia.

Staring suspiciously at Collins, the man snapped at him, "Were you followed?"

"No, sir," Collins instinctively snapped to attention.

Seconds passed, then staring past the young man, he ushered Collins through the door, telling him, "Come in, quickly."

When the door was closed, Collins limped after the older man through to the front room where the overhead light burned brightly and the curtains were fully drawn.

The only furniture in the room was the same small folding table the man used as a desk with just the single folding chair beneath it and a second folding chair placed against a wall.

On the wall above the fireplace hung a large, white flag with a red cross within which was stitched the red Hand of Ulster in the centre of the cross and in the top left-hand corner of the flag, was woven in black, the letters UDA.

The Ulster Defence Association, a vigilante organisation formed in September 1971 that united a number of para-military Loyalist groups under the one banner during the Troubles that split Northern Ireland into two halves; the Catholic Republican's and the Loyalist Protestants.

During these Troubles the UDA and its many splinter groups fought bitterly with the sworn enemy of the United Kingdom, the Irish Republican Army, and were believed to be responsible for more than four hundred murders; the victims being predominantly members of the Catholic faith. The majority of these murders were randomly carried out and justified as so-called revenge killings for the actions of the IRA; more commonly known locally to the Northern Irish Catholics as the 'RA'.

In an attempt to prevent their organisation being prohibited, the UDA killers operated under the alias the Ulster Freedom Fighters (UFF) and who in 1973, were proscribed as a terrorist organisation by the UK Government.

Throughout their short history, one problem faced by the UDA was that unlike their nemesis, the IRA, the UDA were often infiltrated by undercover members of the Royal Ulster Constabulary and Security Services, who by bribery, promises of immunity for crimes committed or witness protection in foreign lands and numerous other inducements, were able to use the information provided by their

Loyalist agents to thwart many operations planned by the Loyalist terrorist groups.

Infighting was another serious issue for the Loyalist organisations and many of their members were murdered by fellow Loyalists operating within the umbrella group.

One such group, albeit fellow Loyalists but politically opposed to the UDA, were the Ulster Volunteer Force (UVF), who because the UDA members chosen uniform was the fur-trimmed hooded Parka jacket, ridiculed them with the nickname, 'The Wombles.'

However, in 1992, the UK Government finally had enough of the UDA as an organisation and so they too were proscribed.

That, however, did not mean the representatives of the UK Government ceased all contact with the UDA and recent history revealed the Government continued to conduct secret and clandestine meetings with an overall view to ending the conflict.

Throughout the Troubles, one of the worrying concerns of the UK Government was the UDA's affiliation with some Neo-Nazi groups within the UK Mainland, predominately the extreme right-wing Combat 18 Group, the British National Party (BNP) and the National Front (NF).

Of course, regardless of which Loyalist group an individual belonged to, internal security was paramount and both the initiation to join and serve with any of these groups was taken rather seriously.

It therefore should not have been a surprise to Andrew Collins when his host, the fifty-years old, self-styled Commandant of the Glasgow Battalion of the newly formed Friends of Ulster Loyalists (FUL) demanded that Collins be strip searched.

"What the fuck…" was all he managed before being struck down from behind and forced to the linoleum floor of the front room by two masked men.

His face pushed against the unforgiving floor, he gasped as the heavier of the men, his knee in Collins back, held him down while the second, slighter built man, tore off his jacket then running his hands across Collins body, finally grunted, "He's clean, sir."

"Let him up," instructed the Commandant, who then indicating the second folding chair, said, "Sit."

With the two masked men standing menacingly behind him, Collins slumped down into the chair that was brought from the wall to face the seated Commandant, who waving a forefinger at the two men, said, "Leave us."

When the door had closed behind them, he turned to Collins and snapped, "Tell me. Everything."

Nervously licking his lips, Collins began, "Like you instructed, sir, I went to the flat to collect it, but the old guy, he started asking me all sorts of questions and then…"

"What kind of questions?" the Commandant interrupted, hands flat on the table when he leaned forward to menacingly stare at him.

Gulping, Collins replied, "He wanted to know what it was to be used for and who was going to use it. I tried to scare him with a knife and told him to shut up, that it was none of his business that he was only holding it for…"

But the Commandant interrupted with, "And how did he respond to that, Volunteer Collins? That he was to be told nothing?"

"Eh," his face expressed his surprise, "well, I couldn't tell him anything even if I wanted to, sir. I mean, I don't know, do I? I mean," he shrugged, "you haven't told me anything yet."

The Commandant sat back and continuing to stare at him, slowly nodded when he asked, "And is that when you decided to kill him, *because* he was asking questions?"

Collins, now conscious that the pain in his left leg was almost beyond suffering, both legs were shaking when his throat tight, he stuttered, "Yes, sir, I strangled him with the scarf he was wearing because you told me I'd to kill him after…"

He almost choked when the bile collected in his throat as he thought back to what he had done, then forced himself to continue, "I was to tell him nothing and then, when I'd got it, the gun I mean, that he was to be, you know," he swallowed and grimaced at the memory of choking Crawford to death.

Catching his breath, his voice almost a whisper, he quickly added, "Anyway, but that's what you said I'd to do, wasn't it?"

"But you didn't get the gun, did you," the commandant again hissed at him, "so why didn't you obtain it *before* you strangled him?" the Commandant hissed.

"I thought I'd find it in the flat."

"But you didn't?"

There was no way he intended admitting that after using the knife he'd threatened Crawford with to stab the wee bastard of a dog, he was going to spend any time searching that smelly, bloody flat, particularly after the old man had shit himself.

So, his head drooping, he hesitatingly whispered, "No, sir."

The Commandant continued to stare at him, then loudly sighed, "So, now we have to acquire a second weapon before we can progress our mission and all because you acted prematurely and without thought."

"I'm sorry, sir."

"Sorry doesn't really help though, does it?" he sarcastically sneered at Collins.

There was no way to respond to that, so Collins wisely kept his mouth shut and stared at the table between the Commandant's hands.

"In here," he called loudly for the two masked men to return to the room, then stared thoughtfully at the distraught younger man.

"Tell me, Volunteer Collins, now that you've murdered the man who procured the gun for us, how do you propose we acquire a replacement firearm?"

Collins brow knitted when he slowly shook his head for he had not a bloody clue, and so he replied, "I'm not really sure, sir."

The Commandant grunted, then stared for several seconds at Collins before he said "It is fortunate for you, Volunteer Collins, that we have several friends in this city who are as like-minded as are we. I am certain those friends will provide us with what we need, but my question is; are you up for the mission that I will set you?"

Thank God, he thought, I'm getting a second chance, then eagerly nodding, replied, "Yes, sir, one hundred per cent."

The Commandant stared at him before he softly said, "Good. For Queen and Country, Volunteer Collins."

The pain in his leg for those few seconds ignored, Collins rose to his feet and shuffling into a semblance of attention, his spine straightened when he repeated, "For Queen and Country."

CHAPTER NINE.

Seated in his office with Larry Considine, Eddie Fairbanks said, "I want someone to visit Barlinnie prison, and interview the son, Peter. Even though he's inside, he might have an idea what his father was

up to these days and maybe even who would want him dead."
"Other than every Irish republican in the city?" smiled Considine.
"Well, if nothing else," Fairbanks wryly grinned, "it would narrow the list of suspects to just about forty thousand Celtic supporters."
"Aye, but how many of those forty thousand are walking about with a bitemark on their leg?"
He glanced up when his door was knocked to see Duke Smythe and Susie Lauder striding in.
"Got a minute, Boss?" asked Smythe.
"I have if you've anything worth reporting," his eyes narrowed.
The pair didn't bother sitting down, but Smythe replied, "Spoke to the shift like you said and a young probationer, a lassie called Alice Redwood, saw what sounds to be the same guy the old woman spotted from her window."
"Ms Thompson," Considine reminded him.
"Aye, her," Smythe nodded.
"According to Redwood, the guy was there for most of the time she was manning the cordon and she was suspicious of him, so suspicious she pointed him out to her neighbour, John Cooper."
Fairbanks turned when Considine muttered, "Aw, shit."
"What am I missing?" he asked the DS.
"John Cooper," Considine shook his head. "The worst excuse for a cop I've ever met. Why the hell they use him as a tutor cop, God alone knows. He's the laziest sod I think I've ever come across in my…"
"Anyway," Smythe quickly interrupted with a glance at Considine. "Cooper wasn't interested, so the lassie didn't approach the guy, but watched him walk off and like the woman Thompson said, the guy limped away on his left leg."
Fairbanks rubbed wearily at his forehead when he icily remarked, "So, if this cop, Cooper, if he'd listened to his neighbour, we might have at the very *least* had the suspects name and address, if not actually arrested him?"
Considine, Smythe and Lauder remained silent, conscious that Fairbanks was building up to an anger, but it was Smythe who broke the silence when he quietly said, "In fairness to Redwood, boss, she's only three months under her belt, so likely didn't have the confidence to act without her neighbours permission."

Fairbanks moodily stared at him before he replied, "Don't worry, Duke, I'm not angry at the probationer, but this Constable Cooper. He's on shift at the minute?"

"Ah, yes, boss; likely out on the beat with Redwood."

"Thank you, both," he nodded in turn at Smythe and Lauder, then told Considine, "Go ahead and make an arrangement for two of the team to attend at Barlinnie. If you're looking for me, I'm going down to see the Chief Super and might be a while."

****

Bobby Heggerty and his wife had found a bright and airy, but quiet coffee shop in a side street just off the row of shops on Great Western Road, near to the major junction of Anniesland Cross.

Staring at her husband, Cathy Heggerty could not recall ever seeing him as dejected as he now was.

Reaching across the narrow table, she placed her hand gently upon his, then said, "You heard what the consultant said, Bobby. Until they perform a colonoscopy and retrieve a sample of the lining from your colon so that they can perform a biopsy, we can't be sure it's cancer."

Neither noticed the cheery woman who arrived at their table to ask, "Can I get you anything else?"

Glancing from one to the other, some sixth sense told the woman that she had inadvertently interrupted a tense situation and so, taking a breath, she added, "Look, if you need anything, just shout. Take your time."

Forcing a smile to acknowledge the woman, Cathy then exhaled.

"To be honest, hen," Heggerty sombrely replied with a shake of his head, "after he told me it could be cancer, I never heard half of what he said."

Her hand still across the table, she gently squeezed his hand before she said, "Well I for one won't believe its cancer till they confirm it, so why should we worry about something that isn't there?"

He wryly smiled at her when he replied, "My Cathy, ever the optimist. Never wonder why I love you, hen."

She took a deep breath when releasing her grip, she forced herself to curtly respond with, "Yes, I *am* an optimist, Bobby Heggerty, and that is why I will not permit you to feel sorry for yourself."

"Me? Feeling sorry for myself," he feigned a hurt expression.

On this occasion, her smile was genuine when she said, "If you think for one minute that after all the years we've been together that I would permit you to leave me alone, then you have another thing coming. It doesn't matter what they find when they perform the colonoscopy. Like I told you back in the hospital, we're a team and whatever is wrong with you, we'll face it together. Got it?"

"Got it," he grinned at her.

****

Briefed by Larry Considine, DC's Jaya Bahn and her neighbour, Brian Saunders, first telephoned the Procurator Fiscal's Office to request written permission to the Governor of HMP Barlinnie, for them to visit and interview Peter Crawford, serving life imprisonment for the murder of an innocent man simply because his victim wore a Celtic football top that to his killer, indicated the man must be a Catholic.

Their request relayed, Bahn and Saunders drove the short distance across the city to the PF's office in Ballater Street in the newly revitalised Gorbals, where the document was waiting to be collected at the commissionaire's desk by the front door.

Now on the road to the prison in the Ruchazie area of the city, Bahn, the senior of the two detectives, suggested that Saunders take the lead in the interview.

"And why?" her neighbour, driving, risked a glance at her.

"According to the PNC and his antecedent history," she slowly replied, "Peter Crawford is twenty-seven years of age and prior to the murder, had already accrued a number of arrests including three for domestic assault against his partner."

She shook her head when she muttered, "These days, with the assistance available to them, why do women feel they have to continue to live with some *bastard* like that?"

"Anyway," she continued with a sigh, "that to me suggests he's either a chauvinist or a misogynist, maybe both and certainly with a prejudice against women, so it's unlikely he'll see me as a police officer, but more as a woman and therefore have both contempt and feel superior to me. That and likely the colour of my *ever* so soft skin will prejudice him too."

"Ooh," he grinned cheekily at her, "who knew our Jaya was a militant feminist?"

"Cut that out," she snapped back, "you know I'm only telling it like it is. Abusive men like him need castrated and if that makes me a feminist, so be it."

Softly, he said, "You know I'm joking, Jaya, and yes," eyes on the road, he nodded, "I agree with you, but castration? Ouch! And what about women who abuse their men *and* we both know that happens too."

"They must have been provoked," she smiled.

"Anyway," she quickly continued before he could protest, "knowing what his opinion of women is, the chances of him disclosing anything will be a lot better if he were speaking with a man and you're the nearest thing to a man I've got at the minute," she pouted at him.

"Okay," he ignored the jibe when he slowly drawled, "then what's our line of approach? Sympathise with his loss or treat him like the bigoted bastard he undoubtedly is?"

Her face creased when she gave the question some thought, then replied, "I think if you were to be as open with him as you can, inform him we have not a clue who murdered his father. Maybe," she shrugged, "even suggest that though he might hate us, without his assistance we've little hope of finding the killer."

His concentration still on the road, he smiled when with curiosity, he asked, "You're saying we should bond with him?"

Nodding, her eyes creased when she responded with, "I know you don't smoke, Brian, but why don't we stop at the shops on Smithycroft Road, just around the corner from the prison and buy some fags?"

****

Stepping past the secretary who held open the door to the Chief Superintendent's office, Liz Malone smiled at Eddie Fairbanks, then indicating he sit down opposite, said, "So, what can I do for you?"

"I've a bit of an issue that I need to discuss with you, Ma'am, but I'm here to seek advice *only*," he emphasised, "not for you to take any action. Also, I don't want to burden my DCI because frankly, I think he's got enough going on at the minute."

Her tunic hanging from a hook on the wall behind her desk and wearing her uniform blouse and black clip-on tie and her hair lying loosely on her shoulders, Fairbanks could not but again notice Malone looked a lot younger than her years and idly wondered if the thought of her forthcoming retiral date had somehow perked her up.

"Eddie, firstly, you are correct coming to me rather than Bobby Heggerty and I agree. He's not in a good place right now to offer any kind of advice or support. Now, you have my undivided attention," she crossed her arms and stared at him.

He began with the discovery of the firearm in his murder victim's flat, then the visit of the Special Branch officers who seemed to be aware of the make and model of the firearm before it had formally and correctly been reported to him, the murder investigation's SIO. When he recounted the visit of the SOCO Ballistics expert, Mark Mathieson, Malone wordlessly uncrossed her arms then leaned forward with her forearms on her desk, listening intently when he related Mathieson's discovery of the device within the firearm.

As he continued, he admitted his foolishness in leaving the device within a locked drawer in his desk and his anger that morning, discovering the drawer broken open and the device gone.

His narrative finished, he took a breath then said, "To be honest, Ma'am, I'm at my wits end," he shrugged, "wondering whether I should confront DI McGhee and her neighbour or what?"

She didn't immediately respond, other than to sit back in her chair, then clasping both hands together, first deeply inhaled, then slowly exhaled.

Almost a silent minute passed before she said, "In my career that included time serving in the SB, I have never known them to participate in any break-in to a police office, but that said, I was never party to all the things the Branch got up to."

She paused before she continued, "From what you told me, have you shared any of this with DCI Heggerty?"

"Only up to the visit of the SB, Ma'am, but while the DCI hasn't shared what's wrong with him and I'm *not* asking," he stared meaningfully at her, "I thought it best not to inform him about my desk getting screwed. The last thing I want to do is put pressure on him to come back when he's not ready," he grimaced when he added, "or so I'm guessing."

"Wise decision," she nodded, then continued, "I do understand why you come to seek my advice, Eddie, but the fact is," she raised a hand towards him and he could see she was trying to contain her anger, "though you had the best intentions not to involve me, you have unwittingly included me in your investigation. Now that I *am* aware of what has occurred, I cannot in good faith ignore the fact that the desk of one of my senior officers within *my* police station was broken into and that a piece of crucial evidence in a murder investigation was removed and *possibly* by members of Strathclyde Police."

He watched her rub at her forehead before she continued, "Like it or not, we have a serious situation on our hands and I have no need to ask, for like you, I believe that from what you have told me it seems likely the firearm discovered in your victims flat was supplied to him by the Branch."

"Yes, Ma'am," he slowly nodded, "that was my conclusion."

"Is there anything your investigation has turned up to suggest why Crawford was given the gun?"

"No Ma'am, nothing. Or rather, nothing yet."

"Okay," she slowly nodded, then asked, "Is there anything to suggest it was Crawford who might have been tasked to use the gun?"

His face creased and he hesitated slightly before he replied, "It's my opinion and I stress, only my opinion, that Crawford was probably holding the gun for someone. He was the middleman, if you will."

"Why do you think that?"

"Okay," he sat forward as he stared at her, "his antecedent history disclosed some violence in his past, but not for many years. That and physically, he wasn't a well man, slightly built and," he shrugged, "according to the pathologist, he suffered badly from arthritis in both his fingers and his hands. Though I'm no expert, that would probably make it difficult to wield a handgun that I'm told weighs about two and a half pounds; in essence, it would be like him trying to hold something slightly heavier than a bag of sugar, aim then fire it."

"So," her brow knitted in thought, "a third party?"

"I believe so, yes Ma'am," he sighed.

"You think the killer might be this third party?"

Shaking his head, he slowly replied, "At this time and without any evidence, I really have no idea."

"What's your next step?"

"Well, we have a vague description of a man seen outside the locus standing apart from the usual rubberneckers, so we'll need to try and trace him to either treat him as a suspect or eliminate him from our inquiries."

"How did you come by this description?"

"An elderly witness on the sixth floor, but later corroborated by one of our own probationary constables, a young lassie called Alice Redwood."

He stared at her when he soberly added, "And about that, Ma'am."

****

Seated at his desk, Larry Considine was desperate for a drink.

No, not just desperate, frantic to ease the pain in his gut that could only be satisfied by a large swallow from the half bottle of the fiery Glenfiddich that right now, called to him from the glove compartment in his car downstairs.

"You okay, Sarge?" the young HOLMES operator stared curiously at him.

"Eh, aye, I'm okay just a touch of wind. I think I'll take a turn around the back yard to try and ease it," he forced a smile, then turned when the door opened to admit, of all people, Alex *bloody* Gardener!

The ACC strode into the room, followed by his aide, the young DI, and ignored the curious glances of the HOLMES staff.

"Ah, DS Considine," he made straight for him. "One of the very men I came to see."

Almost theatrically, Gardener stooped low over Considine's desk and took a long, drawn out sniff, then said, "You seem to smell of spearmint."

"I find chewing gum keeps me concentrated," Considine dully replied, inwardly thanking God that Gardener hadn't arrived ten minutes later when likely he'd have smelled the bevy from the DS.

"Mr Heggerty doesn't seem to be in his office and nor does DI Fairbanks. Where exactly are they?"

"I have no idea where Mr Heggerty is, sir, only that I understand he is taking some personal time."

"Personal time," Gardener repeated in a voice that rippled with disgust, then asked, "And DI Fairbanks?"

"Ah, I do know where *he* is, sir," Considine confidently smiled, knowing he was irritating the ACC.

"And where would that be?" Gardener scowled at him.

"He's currently downstairs with the Divisional Commander, sir."

Standing upright, Gardener stared at the DS with undisguised loathing then turning on his heel to stride towards the door, he snapped at his DI, "With me."

Considine glanced at the young DI only to see him subtly smile, then wink at the DS.
When the door had closed behind them, he wondered; what the hell was that about?
****
The thing that always struck DC Bahn on the rare occasions she visited HMP Barlinnie, was the overpowering and combined smell of cooked food and sweat that seemed not just to irritate the nostrils, but permeate right through to her skin.
Wrinkling her nose, she promised herself when she returned home that evening, a long and scented bath and wouldn't wear her suit again till it had been through the drycleaners.
Escorted from the Reception Area by a sullen prison officer who barely acknowledged their presence, she and her neighbour, Brian Saunders, were led through several dull green and black painted corridors to the D Wing where the A Category prisoners were held; those convicted of serious violent crimes that included murder, armed robbery and rape.
At one of many doors they passed through that were unlocked then re-locked behind them, the prison officer said, "Wait here. I'll find out if your man has been brought to the interview room yet."
Two minutes later, they were beckoned into yet another corridor where a second and more affable prison guard stood outside a small room and who with a smile, nodded that they enter, telling them, "He's not cuffed so watch yourselves. I'll be right outside if he kicks off."
Entering the brightly lit room, the walls painted in the same dull green and black, they saw Peter Crawford already seated across the desk.
Dressed in the regulation prison shirt and trousers, Bahn's first impression of the twenty-seven years old Crawford was his shaved head and the many black ink tattoos that covered not just his arms and hands, but his head, neck and of particular interest, was the swastika tattooed on his right cheek.
Introducing them, Saunders was immediately ignored when Crawford smiled then stared at Bahn and to her surprise, said in a falsetto voice, "You like my Ink, then?"
"Wonderful," she dryly replied, then added, "Must have hurt like hell, that one on your face."

"Pain is just a figment of your imagination," he sneered at her, then as Bahn had correctly anticipated, turned to Saunders to ask, "What you and the Paki bird wanting with me, then?"
Of course, she realised he was goading her, as did Saunders, and it was with great effort that Bahn refrained from reaching across the desk and slapping Crawford in the mouth, so merely waited for her neighbour to commence the interview.
Nodding to Bahn that they sit down, Saunders replied, "Our condolences on the death of your father."
The saw Crawford's eyes narrow before he finally asked, "Is this a wind-up?"
"No, Peter, it's not," Saunders softly replied, unconsciously being applauded by Bahn who thought, well done, neighbour; good use of his forename.
Crawford bit at his lower lip, then his face a sneer, he said, "You've not come here to offer your condolences, so what is it you really want?"
"To catch you father's killer. Look," Saunders hurried on, "you hate us, I know that, but you've heard of the old saying, 'my friend, the enemy of my enemy,' haven't you?"
"Never heard of it, no," he shook his head.
Saunders sighed when he explained, "What I'm trying to tell you, Peter, is that we have a common goal. Finding the person who murdered your father and you should consider working with us to achieve that goal."
Don't overthink it, Brian, using fancy words on this clown, thought Bahn who inwardly resisted the urge to take over the interview.
Fetching the unopened packet of cigarettes from his jacket pocket, Saunders made a show of opening them, aware that Crawford's eyes were greedily watching him, then to both the detectives surprise, he burst out laughing when he sneered, "Not that old chestnut, thinking you can bribe me with fags. Oh, and another thing, what you idiots don't now is that I hated that old bastard and whoever done him in; well, he did me a huge favour because it saved me killing him when I get out of this shithole. Now, are you pair finished? I've a game of snooker booked and I'm already late for it."
His face red, Saunders returned the pack to his pocket, then turning to glance at Bahn, heard Crawford asked, "What happens to Baxter, now?"

"Baxter?"

"Aye the wee Scotty. The old sod was watching him for me while I'm in here."

Saunders again glanced at Bahn who seized the initiative to ask, "The wee white Scotty dog. It's your dog?"

"Aye, Baxter, he's mine."

"Were you fond of him, Peter?"

"Course I am," he stared at her, confusion evident on his face when he asked, "Wait a minute, what do you mean *was* I fond of him?"

"Well, I'm sorry to inform you the dog was killed because we think he was trying to protect your father when he was murdered."

Stunned, they saw his shoulders slump and his eyes tear up when he gasped, "Baxter. He's dead?"

Though it pained her to do so, she forced herself to sound sympathetic when nodding, she replied, "Yes, the individual who killed your father also killed your wee dog, Peter, and that's why we're trying to find out who it was."

Saunders inwardly startled when he saw Crawford's hands clench into fists and prepared himself to defend both Bahn and himself, but then heard the now distraught prisoner sob, "Nobody told me he was dead," he hissed through gritted teeth.

"That wee dog, he never hurt anyone in his life. He was the friendliest wee bugger you ever met."

Tears now rolling down his cheeks, he stared from one to the other when he snarled, "What's the chances of you catching the *bastard* that murdered my Baxter!"

"Not good, unless you help us," her eyes narrowing, she quickly replied.

"And if you get him, he'll probably end up in here, won't he?"

"Oh, aye," she agreed with a nod, knowing full well what was on Crawford's mind.

Glancing at the door as though fearing he might be overheard, he stared at Bahn when he said, "I only know what I'm hearing from the other cons."

CHAPTER TEN.

Unaware that ACC Alex Gardener was prowling the CID suite looking for him, Eddie Fairbanks, deciding to take a five-minute break to himself without being disturbed, had taken off to sit in his car in the rear yard to make a couple of personal phone calls.

His first call took Bobby Heggerty by surprise, who said, "That's me and the wife just returned home, Eddie, and we're still in the car in the driveway. What's happening at the office?"

"More to the point, boss, what's happening to you? How you feeling?"

"Oh, so, so," Heggerty glanced guiltily at his wife.

"I've been for a consultation and I'm to be admitted to the Beatson on Monday, for some tests. The twenty-fifth, I think it is."

Fairbanks startled, for the Beatson was widely known as the centre of excellence dealing with cancer patients, but he said nothing, other than, "Well, you're not missing much here. I'm not that forward with my investigation, but like you told me, if I get stuck, I'll give you a phone."

Before Heggerty could respond, Fairbanks quickly added, "That all said, you concentrate on yourself at the minute and give your wife my regards."

"I heard that and thank you, Eddie," he heard Cathy Heggerty respond.

The brief call ended, Fairbanks sat pondering what Heggerty had told him, then with a sigh, pressed the button to call Ronnie Masters.

"Hi, darling," her deep and very sexy voice greeted him. "You calling from your office?"

"Actually," he glanced about him, "I'm in the car in the back yard for a bit of privacy. Sitting here, I'll have no-one hammering on my door," he smiled, then with a resigned sigh, explained, "Bobby Heggerty didn't just leave me a murder to investigate. You wouldn't believe the paperwork that he has to deal with in just one day."

"Oh, can I call you back, Eddie? I have Tony Dawson, the reporter from the magazine with me right now. We're discussing the photo-shoot."

"And I hope to hear all about it when I get home tonight," he smiled at her excitement.

"Do you know when that will be?"

"Sorry, sweetheart," he shook his head. "Right now, I'm chasing my tail, so shall I bring something in?"

"No," she quickly replied. "I'll have something quick and ready to go when you arrive, so do not rush. Just come home, safe," she sighed in his ear.

It was as he was returning the phone to his jacket pocket he saw the rear security door open, then ACC Gardener and his aide, DI Cameron, step out and walk towards a large, black coloured and very shiny saloon vehicle.

It was only then that Fairbanks noticed the civilian driver, most of who were retired Traffic Department cops, folding a newspaper as the duo approached the vehicle and correctly guessed it to be a staff car.

For some curious reason that even he couldn't explain, he forced himself back into the seat and slumping down, watched as Cameron held open the rear door for Gardener, before getting into the front seat.

Seconds later, as the vehicle passed him by, he saw Gardener's head down as though reading something and to his surprise, Cameron smiling at him.

What the hell, was his first thought, then getting out of his Ford Focus, made his way to the rear door of the office.

****

Standing outside the Divisional Commander's door, Constable John Cooper unconsciously pulling to adjust his uncomfortable body armour, he asked his Inspector, "Do you have any idea what this is about?"

"Not a clue," the Inspector sighed, but didn't add that after the CID had spoken with the young probationer, Alice Redwood, he himself had a quiet word with her and had a feeling that Liz Malone had been informed of Cooper's dismissal of Redwood's suspicion about a man she'd seen at the locus of the murder.

Maybe, Cooper sourly reflected, it had been a mistake to deny seeing the guy limping away.

Knocking on the door and both men wearing their caps, they entered when Malone loudly called out, "Come."

Seeing her seated behind her desk and wearing not just her uniform tunic, but her cap too, the Inspector thought, oh, bugger, this isn't going to be pretty, then formally greeted her with, "Constable Cooper, Ma'am, as you instructed. Do you wish me to remain?"

Standing beside him, he could almost sense the foreboding from the lazy bastard, and watched while Malone stared pokerfaced at Cooper before she said, "Remain please."

She paused for several seconds, her eyes boring into Cooper's, then barked, "I am in receipt of a formal complaint from the CID, Constable Cooper, about your lack of action at the locus of the murder they are currently investigating."

"Ma'am?" he replied, feigning surprise while inwardly promising himself he'd see to that wee bitch Redwood, first chance he got. Seeing Malone's right hand resting on a brown manila coloured file, it was then that the Inspector recognised it to be a personnel file and presumed it to be Cooper's.

"I am also told," Malone continued, "that when probationary Constable Redwood brought to your attention a man she believed to be acting suspiciously at the locus of the murder, you ignored her suspicions and when the CID quizzed your shift, seeking information, you denied even seeing such a man."

Pretending outrage that he should be questioned like some scruffy wee ned he barked, "That's a fucking lie! There wasn't anyone like that! She's making it up to impress those bastards upstairs!"

"Constable Cooper!" the Inspector rounded on him and was about to say more, but stopped when Malone calmly raised her hand and said, "So, you are telling the Inspector and I that there was no such individuals standing there, that Constable Redwood, albeit she says she *physically* pointed the man out to you, your stance is that she is lying?"

"Absolutely," he sneered, then added, "And besides, it's her word against mine and I'm a cop with thirteen years' service now, while she's hardly able to wipe her own arse! So, *Ma'am*," he confidently leered at Malone, who as he stared at her considered her to be just another *bitch* who lay flat on her back to get where she is, "it's down to credibility, isn't it?"

"Constable Cooper," the Inspector angrily laid a hand firmly on his arm, "you are totally out of order!"

Yet again, Malone raised her palm towards them both, then softly smiled when she said, "You know, Constable Cooper, if it *were* a case of credibility, your word against that of Redwood's, some would admit you to be correct, that your thirteen years would serve you well against Constable Redwoods three months service."

When she paused, then stared hard at him, Cooper had a faint

sensation that something was wrong, that Malone…no, he inwardly decided, he *was* right. It was that bitch's word against his.
And as for Malone, she couldn't do a thing without proof.
But then her smile gave way to a deadpan expression when she continued, "Unfortunately for you, Constable Cooper, the CID have a witness who also saw the individual you have just alleged was not there. In fact, part of the description of this individual provided by both the CID's witness and Constable Redwood corroborates each other; an individual who the CID now believe might be a significant suspect in the murder investigation."
She didn't bother listening to his outburst, as once more he again vilified the young Redwood and hissing that he was being set up, but during his rant, she slammed the flat of her hand onto her desk, then snapped, "Constable Cooper! Be quiet!"
A tense silence fell, broken when Malone lifted the personnel file from her desk, then waving it at Cooper, told him, "I have reviewed your performance appraisals over the preceding years, Constable Cooper, and I find them to be appallingly poor. How you have managed to evade being found out, I am uncertain, but now you *are* found out, I am sending a recommendation to the Deputy Chief Constable that you face a disciplinary board."
She paused once more to allow the threat to sink in and watching his face pale, she continued, "You will be charged under the Police Scotland Act of 1967 that you did fail to properly carry out your duty, as well as maligning a colleague and lying about such failure."
She stopped, then drawing herself to sit bolt upright in her chair, she quietly said, "For now, you are suspended from duty and will make yourself available to attend a disciplinary board to defend yourself against those charges. In the meantime," she turned to address the stunned Inspector, "please remove Constable Cooper from my office, have him surrender his warrant card and notebook, then escort him from Maryhill police office. You might also wish to apprise him of the facilities offered him by the Police Federation should he wish to raise a defence against the allegations. Thank you."
The Inspector took her 'Thank you' to be their dismissal and wordlessly nodded at Cooper, who clearly shocked, stumbled from the room.

When the door closed behind them, Liz Malone sat back in her chair then removing her cap, placed it upon the desk and slowly exhaled through pursed lips.

She glanced up when her secretary, June, pushed open the door, a cup and saucer carefully carried in her hand and who said, "Thought you might be needing this, Ma'am."

"Yes, thanks, just a pity it's not gin," she lopsidedly grinned.

****

"He didn't find you, then? ACC Gardener," Larry Considine asked Fairbanks, who shaking his head, grinned, "I didn't know he was looking for me, but I was in my motor making a couple of calls, when I saw him and the DI…"

"DI Cameron," Considine at last recalled the name and curiously aware that the earlier craving for a pull at the half bottle in his glove compartment seemed to have waned.

"I saw them coming out the back door into the yard. Funny thing was when they were driving away Cameron was in the front seat. He definitely saw me and smiled when they passed by."

"Aye," Considine's brow wrinkled, "he winked at me when he was leaving the incident room, almost like he was…I don't know," he shrugged, "not happy about following Gardener around."

In a low voice, Fairbanks said "Look, Larry, I know that you and the boss have been pals for a long time now and I don't want it to sound like I'm being nosey, but Gardener seems to have it in for him. Is it personal or did they cross swords in the job?"

"You've not met Bobby's wife, Cathy, have you?"

"Eh, no."

Considine smiled when he continued, "Believe me when I tell you, Cathy is a right good-looking woman nowadays, but my God, you should have seen her when she was younger. Turn any man's head, she could. Anyway," he coughed a little to hide his own embarrassment when recalling how once-upon-a-time, he himself had fancied Cathy Heggerty.

"I'm sure that Bobby wouldn't disagree with me when I tell you that he wasn't any more than an average looking guy, nothing special I mean; not like Alex Gardener, who was a right handsome bugger and a smart dresser too. And," he sighed, "dare I say it, he wasn't a bad guy either, back then."

He paused as though trying to recall the details, then said, "The two of them were in the CID in Stewart Street at the time, Bobby a DC and Gardener a DS, waiting for a DI position to become available. They weren't neighbours, or anything, but as I recall in the Department at that time, the DCI was a good guy and we all got on together reasonably well. Then Gardener met Cathy and I think it was about six, maybe seven months later, they were engaged."

"Oh, oh," Fairbanks grimaced, "I think I know where this is going."

Considine smiled when nodding, he replied, "Aye, as I recall they were at a party when Gardener introduced his fiancée to Bobby. *Big* mistake, *huge* mistake on his part," Considine cheerfully grinned, then added, "The upshot was that Cathy broke off the engagement with Gardener and as the say, the rest is history. And can I just add that a happier couple would be hard to find."

"So, in short, that's why Gardener has it in for the boss?"

"I reckon so and if my memory serves me correctly, about that time when I was also a DC, Gardener's temper got worse and he'd go off on one without any provocation. I put it down to him feeling humiliated and embarrassed that she'd dumped him for Bobby, so watch yourself; anyone who associates with Bobby is fair game to that resentful git."

"You're not the first to warn me about him," sighed Fairbanks, who then asked, "Anything to report?"

"Nothing other than Jaya Bahn and Brian Saunders phoned to say they're on their way back from the prison."

"Soon as they arrive," he replied with a nod, "bring them along to my office."

****

ACC Alex Gardener arrived at Police Headquarters in Pitt Street and was seething.

Exiting the staff car at the front entrance, he stamped through the door held open by the commissionaire, who wisely avoided any eye contact, angry that not only had he failed to find Heggerty or his DI, but was still clueless as to why the DCI had not returned to duty. What made him even angrier was that Heggerty's immediate line manager was his Divisional Chief Superintendent, so as long as Malone knew why he was off, the ACC had no real authority to question her about it.

That said, even his attempt to again speak with Liz Malone was thwarted by her secretary who had calmly but firmly informed him that the Chief Superintendent was not to be disturbed, that she was currently dealing with a discipline issue.

Unfortunately, and though he was an ACC, even he knew that it was not proper to interrupt such proceedings.

Striding through the corridor in the Command Suite to his office, he stopped dead then turning to his aide, he snarled, "Head back to Maryhill. Find that DI Fairbanks and learn what you can about the murder investigation. If you doubt or suspect that the proper procedures are not being carried out, report it back to me immediately."

Without waiting for a response, he turned then entering his outer office, slammed the door behind him.

Iain Cameron knew that what Gardener instructed him to do would be better suited to the Detective Superintendent in charge of the north side of the city's CID Divisions, who had clout by virtue of his rank, but for some reason unknown to him, Gardener wanted to keep his outrage at Heggerty and Fairbanks quiet.

But what was the reason, he continued to wonder, though did harbour a suspicion whatever it was driving Gardener crazy was very personal.

Staring for several seconds at the closed door, with a sigh he turned to make his way downstairs to where his car was parked in the underground garage.

What Gardener could not suspect was that Cameron had no intention of visiting Maryhill Police Office.

No, he smiled to himself, sod Gardener.

He'd visit that nice wee café out in Bearsden him and his girlfriend used and treat himself to one of those delicious cakes and a latte and while he was there, he'd compose a story to tell the ACC when he returned to Pitt Street.

****

Neighboured with the quiet, but competent Constable Harry Fortescue, Alice Redwood wondered at the Inspector's sudden decision to drag John Cooper off the street then send her out to meet with Harry.

"And you have no idea what's going on?" a curious Fortescue asked.

"No, no idea whatsoever," she pursed her lower lip and shook her head.

"Maybe it's just a wee temporary change of neighbour, let you see a different attitude to the job," he suggested, but idly thought the nervous young woman seemed relieved to be away from that lazy prat Cooper, probably the most unpopular man on the shift, if not the whole of Maryhill police office.

Aged twenty-eight, Fortescue had been a cop for five years and with an interest in cars and all things mechanical, harboured an ambition to join the Traffic Division.

"Right," he suddenly turned to her, "if you're up for it, we've a call to make up in Duncruin Street. It's a follow-up to a domestic assault where the husband was lifted for smacking his missus around, then barred from going near the house. Let's just check that he's keeping to the bail conditions and if we're nice about it, we'll maybe get a cuppa," he grinned.

A sudden and curious feeling overtook Redwood, a strange yet satisfying sense that for the first time since returning from Tulliallan Police Training College in Fife, she was actually looking forward to walking the beat and all because Harry Fortescue was treating her with some respect.

However, little did she know or suspect that her tutor cop, John Cooper, was at that time being suspended and blaming his downfall on the young, twenty-two-years old Redwood.

****

All three seated in front of Eddie Fairbanks desk, it was Jaya Bahn who began with, "Brian commenced the interview, boss, and to be frank, it seemed that he was about to beat his flat forehead against a wall."

"What do you mean, my flat forehead?" Saunders turned towards her.

"And how did the interview go?" smiled Fairbanks.

"Well, let me describe Peter Crawford," she exhaled.

"A chauvinistic, right-wing racist, multi- tattooed, Nazi supporting fascist who I suspect likes hurting women when the fancy takes him."

"Really? That's quite a description, Jaya, but don't hold back. Tell us what you really think," he continued to smile.

"Seen his likes before, boss," she huffed, "and of course me being a Paki," she used her forefingers as italics, "I see them every day in my working life too."

"And there was me thinking you were from an Indian family."
"I am," she sighed, "but like the advert says, one colour covers it all."
"Oh, right," he choked back a laugh, then asked, "What was the result of the interview? Did you learn anything at all?"
"We did, but first let me tell you this. Quite frankly, Peter Crawford couldn't give a shit about his father being murdered. It seems they had quite an acrimonious relationship that ended when his father apparently stepped back from fascism and decided that maybe Catholics weren't the evil bastards he'd been drumming into his son for all those years."
"Now that we didn't know or suspect that," mused Fairbanks, then asked, "Would that be anything to do with him having a Catholic son-in-law?"
"More to do with him having a new grandson and another Catholic baby on the way," she sighed.
"According to Peter, his father had recently written him a letter informing him that James was considering contacting his daughter to try and make some peace with her in an effort to see the wee grandson."
"I take it that didn't set well with Peter?" this from Considine.
"Not at all," she shook her head, then continued, "You might be interested to know that when he was first told by the prison Chaplain about the death of his father and that arrangements would be made for him to attend the funeral service, he categorically refused; apparently told the Chaplain he wasn't in the least interested in attending any traitor's funeral. That said," she sighed, "one of the prison officers told me he's changed his mind about that because it'll give Crawford an away day from the jail."
Fairbanks glanced at Considine, who shaking his head, muttered, "Religion, the cause of more death and acrimony than any other reason."
His brow furrowed, he asked Bahn, "But you did learn something?"
"To be honest," she glanced at Saunders, "me and Brian were about to give it up when he asked Brian about the wee dog, Baxter."
"The dog?" Fairbanks face expressed his confusion.
"It seems, boss, that the dog was being cared for by our victim, but Peter was the owner and he loved the dog. So much so when we told him about it being killed, that we assumed it died because it tried to

protect his father, he was completely distraught and angry, *so* angry he decided to help us with what little he knows and only because if it helps us catch the dog's killer. He's not actually interested in us arresting his father's killer, but believes if we do, the killer, assuming he's male, will end up in the jai beside Crawford who he inferred can exact his own revenge."

"For the dog, mind you," she shook her head, "not his father."

Fairbanks eyes widened when he asked, "And what does he know, Jaya?"

"He told us that some months ago, he'd heard from one of the cons in the jail that his father had become entangled with a new Loyalist group that has been formed in Glasgow."

She took her notebook from her handbag then read out, "The Glasgow Battalion of the Friends of Ulster Loyalists, with the acronym, F-U-L. Apparently they are some sort of support group for the UDA over in Northern Ireland and have contacts with them."

Fairbanks couldn't help himself and flashed a glance at Considine, who as subtly as he dared, shook his head.

"Did he provide any further information about this group, where they meet, how many there might be?"

"Only that the way he described them, they sound like they are some sort of procurement group, my words, not his and believe me, that is not the sort of word that moron would know how to use," her lip curled.

She sighed before she continued, "He's of the *opinion*, not fact, boss, that it's their job to obtain weapons and any kind of armaments that might assist the UDA. As for where they meet, he could only surmise that because of his father's past history supporting the Loyalists, James was either approached in a pub or at the football match, but if I recall you briefing us, he didn't have the money these days to go to the matches. Is that right?"

"That's what his neighbour told us, yes," Fairbanks nodded, then asked, "What about names of any of this group?"

They watched her shake her head when she again sighed, "The man in charge of this group is called the Commandant. Peter said there can't be any more than a dozen, maybe even less, who are involved with this group. We tried to persuade him for more information or the name of the other prisoner who told him about his father and this group, but Peter wouldn't grass him in, making the point if we

interview the other con, Peter might end up with a shiv in his ribs for grassing the guy in. Oh, one other thing. They don't refer to themselves as a group, but as a *unit* like they're some sort of military outfit," she couldn't help herself from sneering.
She paused and her eyes narrowed when she added, "What he did tell us and what to us seems quite logical is that the more members this unit has, the less secure they must be."
Her brow furrowed when she added, "He says that years ago, when he was eighteen or nineteen, he joined a UDA support group in the Dennistoun area; can collecting and fundraising karaoke nights in the Rangers supporters' pubs, that sort of stuff, but the group numbered several dozen and trying to keep secrets was a joke and that's why after a few months, they folded. In short," she shrugged, "what he was saying is the smaller the group, the tighter the security will be, which will make it more difficult for our colleagues in the Special Branch to infiltrate them."
Larry Considine, who leaning forward in his chair, asked, "Do you believe that what he told you is true?"
It was Saunders who shrugging, replied, "He could have been pulling our chain, Larry, but to be honest, both Jaya and I saw him literally spitting teeth and we believe he was that angry about the wee dog, he'd have admitted who Bible John was, if he'd known."
"There is one further thing," she stared pokerfaced at Fairbanks. "He had a request to make of us, boss."
"And that is?"
She raised her perfectly shaped eyebrows when she said, "He wants us to give the dog a Christian burial."
****

When alone with Fairbanks in the DI's room, Larry Considine discussed the day's events and they agreed that their victims alleged link with this mysterious unit, the Friends of Ulster Loyalists, must be connected to the SB providing James Crawford with the handgun.
"But one gun?" Considine shook his head. "Not that I'm any kind of expert, but after what went on in Northern Ireland for all those years, the place must be awash with all sorts of military hardware. Why then give Crawford just the one gun?"
"Again," Fairbanks eyes narrowed, "I'm thinking that the gun was to be given to a third party, but for what reason? And that," he glanced at his wristwatch and stifled a yawn, "is the question for tomorrow.

Right now, I think after we've briefed the team about the little we know, we'll call it a day and resume in the morning."

"But we'll continue to keep the SB's visit between us? I'm asking because, not if, but *when* those buggers learn we know about Crawford's association with this Ulster support mob, they'll be here sticking their noses into our investigation."

"For now, yes, we'll keep their visit between us," Fairbanks replied, then rising to his feet, added, "but that doesn't mean we can't commence our own inquiries into this FUL unit."

His shoulders slumped and he wearily shook his head when he said, "Listen to me. I feel by using their acronym I'm giving them some legitimacy as a unit when in reality they're nothing but bigoted thugs."

"Then as you so rightly say, let's call them what they are," Considine smiled. "Thugs who if we get this right, we'll have the pleasure of giving them the jail."

****

Fifteen minutes from the end of their shift and strolling slowly through the slight fall of rain back to Maryhill Police Office, Constable's Harry Fortescue and Alice Redwood discussed their career ambitions within the police; he disclosing his interest in joining the Traffic Division while Redwood confessed she was far too recent in the Force to make any kind of decision and wanted nothing more than to survive her probationary period.

Handing over their personal radios at the uniform bar, she shyly told him, "Thanks for today. I feel that was the first time that I really enjoyed being on the beat."

Before he could respond, a shift colleague passing by said in a low voice and with some satisfaction, "Did you heard about that wanker, John Cooper? He's been suspended pending a disciplinary hearing at Pitt Street."

Redwood's eyes widened, but before either she or Fortescue could ask why, the constable's head bowed as he hurried on and when she turned, she saw the shift Inspector approaching and who asked, "How did today go, Alice?"

"It went well, sir," she hesitatingly glanced at Fortescue.

"And did Harry here manage to teach you anything new?"

"Actually, quite a lot sir," she gushed.

"He showed me things like how to mark a door and…"

But the Inspector interrupted her when he held up a hand, then with a smile, said, "Well, no doubt you've already heard about Constable Cooper, so take it as read this layabout," he nodded with a grin towards Fortescue, "is your new tutor."

His grin continued when he asked Fortescue, "You okay with that, Harry?"

"Yes, sir, happy to be a tutor," he grinned back.

Neither the Inspector nor Fortescue could imagine the relief that surged through the young woman who visibly relaxed, excited at the news she would no longer have to suffer the sullen and sarcastic Cooper nor would they ever know that in the recent weeks, she had even contemplated resigning rather than bear anymore of Cooper's arrogance.

Ten minutes later, her body armour, utility belt and sundry items stored away in the women's locker room, Redwood waved a cheery, "Bye," to both her fellow female constables, then headed through the office to the backdoor and her car parked in the rear yard.

A smile on her face, she decided that she'd not be cooking this evening when she returned to her one room flat in Albion Gate, just off the High Street, but she'd grab a pizza and celebrate with the remainder of the bottle of white wine in the fridge.

Moving towards her car, so intent was she in keeping her head down from the fall of rain and groping in her jacket pocket for her car keys, she didn't see nor was aware of the figure in dark clothing who running at her, slammed into her then grabbing at her head, battered it against the wall of the building.

Dazed and too stunned to call out for help, Redwood could feel the blood running down from her forehead before she fell to the ground where her assailant began to kick her about the body.

Losing consciousness, she thought she heard a scream, but was unaware it was she who was screaming, then passed into unconsciousness.

CHAPTER ELEVEN: Friday 22 September 2006.

Turning off the shower, Fairbanks saw the en-suite door pulled open, then Ronnie popped her head in to tell him with a grin, "Breakfast in five, so get a move on."

He smiled and once more wondered what he had done to deserve a woman like Ronnie, who loved him with a passion he had never before experienced and who he loved in return.

Getting dressed, he critically examined himself in the tilting mirror in the bedroom, then made his way through to the kitchen where Ronnie, wearing a knee length, emerald green coloured robe that tightly pulled about her waist, left little to the imagination and who was serving bacon, potato scones and fried eggs onto a dinner plate. Sitting himself down, he stared in awe at the raven-haired beauty, then told her, "I can't believe that you're up at this time of the morning making me breakfast. You could have had another hour in bed, you know."

"What," she smiled at him, "let my man go to work without something in his stomach? What kind of woman do you think I am, DI Fairbanks?"

He reached out to grab gently at her wrist, then pulling her towards him to sit on his lap, he replied with a grin, "If last night was anything to go by, a really shameless one."

She squealed in delight when grabbing his face in both her hands, she kissed him on the lips then said, "If I'm shameless it's because you excite me, then you wear me out so I'm no good to any other man. It's just you, Eddie, and it's because I love you."

He smiled then stroking back a lock of hair that had fallen across her eyes, he felt the emotion catch in his throat before he softly told her, "Then loving you, darling, that makes me the luckiest man in the world."

He watched her take a deep breath and admired the swell of her breasts before she pushed up onto her feet, then said, "Eat up or you'll be late."

"Yes, ma'am," he pursed his lips then turned when his mobile phone beeped an incoming text message.

Opening the phone, he saw it to be from Larry Considine then read: *Incident at the office. Obliged if you can get in ASAP. Call from car when you're on your way.*

His brow furrowed in curiosity and slurping back a mouthful of coffee, said, "Sorry, sweetheart, I need to go now."

Shaking his head, he added, "No idea what's happening, but seems I'm wanted."

Wordlessly, she hurried from the kitchen, only to return seconds later and holding his overcoat, her arms stretched wide to help him into it.

Grabbing her, he sloppily kissed her on the lips, then heard her say, "If what's happened has already happened, killing yourself getting there won't change anything."

He grinned widely at her wisdom, then kissed her again before hurrying from the flat to his car in the roadway downstairs.

****

She'd been there all night, ever since the phone call had come and now Chief Superintendent Liz Malone, her hair fiercely tied back into a ponytail and wearing a slate coloured roll neck sweater, blue coloured, shaping slim jeans and black, leather ankle boots, anxiously paced the corridor of the Gartnavel Hospital casualty ward, her eyes betraying her weariness.

Sitting on an uncomfortable tubular plastic chair that not just hurt his back, but bothered his haemorrhoids too, the weary night shift uniformed Inspector once more suggested, "Liz, you're *really* doing my head in. Can you not take a seat? You'll wear yourself out."

"I'll sit when I know more," she snapped back, then almost immediately added, "Sorry, Paddy, but you know what I'm like."

Inspector Paddy Brogan, one of the few junior ranks permitted in private moments to be familiar with his Divisional Commander, did indeed know what Malone was like, for he had known her since they were rookie cops together. Shaking his head, he said, "I'll away and get us another coffee or if I can find a shop open, how about a bacon roll?"

"No, I'm too uptight to eat," she waved a hand, then softly smiled, "but a coffee will be fine."

Minutes later and still pacing the corridor, she turned when one of the two fire doors was pushed open and saw Eddie Fairbanks striding towards her.

"Ma'am," he nodded at her then said, "I got a text message this morning, then on the way to the office I phoned Larry Considine who updated me about what happened. How is she?"

Malone shook her head when she replied, "They're talking about taking her over to the Neuro Ward at the Southern General Hospital in Govan. Her head took a serious knock and they're worried that…" She stopped to take a deep breath to compose herself then slowly exhaling, her eyes tearing, she continued, "They're worried there might be some neurological damage."

She sighed when she added "Her parents are at her bedside right now, poor souls. I can only imagine what they're going through."

"Any suspect?"

"Oh, aye, Eddie, there's a suspect," she snarled through gritted teeth, then detailed her interview the previous afternoon with John Cooper and her strong suspicion that it was he, who refusing to accept that he had done any wrong, blamed his neighbour for his own ineptitude as well as accusing her of lying.

"Any witnesses or evidence to the assault?"

Malone wryly smiled when she replied, "He's a cop, Eddie, albeit a poor excuse for one, so no; no witnesses or any evidence as to his guilt."

She softly exhaled when she added, "That's not to say I won't be going after the bastard!"

He stared at her, shocked at how furious she was and realised that even with her experience and her senior rank, right then at that moment Liz Malone was an emotional wreck on the verge of losing control.

Staring at her, he worried about her paying Cooper a visit and guessed the likely outcome would be the disgruntled cop transported to a hospital and a case against him that would never stand-up in court and might even result in Malone herself being arrested.

And so, he said, "There's nothing I can do here, Ma'am, so I suggest that I return to the office and if need be, I'll put the murder investigation on hold, at least for today. I'll concentrate my team on finding something, anything, that can indicate who assaulted this lassie."

His voice faltered, then he said instead, "I mean, Alice."

Staring at her pale face, he took a breath, thinking carefully of what he intended saying, then his mouth suddenly dry, he slowly told her, "I can see how hard this is for you, Ma'am, but I wouldn't be doing my job if I didn't warn you. No matter how much you suspect Cooper of being responsible, you have to let me do my job and that means you staying away from him."

He stared meaningfully into her eyes when he carefully added, "Do I make myself clear?"

Her head slightly tilted upwards, as though staring at the ceiling and clearly embarrassed at such a show of emotion in front of a junior officer, she couldn't trust herself to speak and nodded her agreement. Choking back her tears and her voice almost a whisper, she stared him in the eye with a fierce expression, then shook her head and said, "I can't lose another young cop, Eddie. I lost young Gels McEwan to that murderous bastard who shot her. I can't lose this young lassie too. You need to get him, Eddie. You need to make sure he doesn't get away with this."

Then almost as an afterthought, her eyes narrowed when she growled, "Whatever it takes."

A chill run through him for he realised what her inference was, that Malone was urging him that, within or outwith the legality of the law, John Cooper had to answer for what he had done.

There was nothing he could say to console her and so simply reached out to stroke gently at her arm, then turned to make his way along the corridor.

En-route to his car parked outside, he dialled the direct number for the incident room, then told Larry Considine, "Keep the team there for now, Larry. We've an attempted murder that for the time being, takes priority over our investigation."

****

The team were assembled and patiently waiting when Fairbanks arrived at Maryhill CID suite and removing his overcoat as he stepped into the incident room, he scanned the faces and immediately sensed the tension and the hostility.

It was Larry Considine who standing behind his desk greeted him with, "The words out boss. They know it was that bastard, John Cooper."

Joining Considine at his desk, Fairbanks again swept his gaze around the room, seeing the anger in their eyes, their furrowed brows and their clenched jaws, then holding up his hand and as calmly as he dared, he said, "Is there any evidence that Cooper assaulted Alice Redwood?"

To his surprise, it was Brian Saunders who replied, "Unfortunately, at the minute there's no evidence, boss, simply a suspicion that because of him being suspended and him, well, *being* him," he grimaced, "the guys here want to go after him."

Fairbanks could see heads turning towards Saunders, frowning at his statement and so he quickly nodded, then said, "Thank you, Brian."

Turning to address the room, he continued in a flat voice, "I do not have to remind anyone here that first and foremost we are police officers and are duty bound to operate within the law."

He paused to let it sink in then said, "We are also detectives and we do not apply the law unless we have evidence to present to the Procurator Fiscal and no matter that we suspect *any* individual, suspicion is *not* evidence."

He paused again to clear his throat, Liz Malone's words still resonating in his head, *'Whatever it takes.'*

Then once more, he continued, "I am as angry as clearly are you all that one of our colleagues, a young probationer, has been seriously injured in a brutal attack within the yard of our own police office, but we serve her no justice if we do not conduct ourselves and our investigation as *professional* police officers. Is that clear?"

The muttered, "Aye, boss," and nodding of heads seemed to indicate his warning was accepted or so he hoped, then said, "Now, as likely you are already aware, I am suspending the murder investigation for one day only to enable us to find the culprit who assaulted Alice Redwood. So, ladies and gentlemen, I want your best effort to find me some evidence. Right, for your information, I have spoken with the Divisional Commander, who is in attendance at Gartnavel, and who informed me that it is likely Alice will be moved to the Neurological Ward at the Southern General, in Govan. As updates arrive, you will be kept informed."

Turning to Considine, he nodded, "Now, give Larry and I ten minutes to sort out who is doing what and one more word of caution, ladies and gentlemen. When we arrest our suspect as I am certain we will, the suspect will be treated with kid gloves for I do not want to risk losing a case because of any allegation that we…" he paused and drew a short breath, seeking the correct word, then said, "manhandled our suspect."

His eyes roamed the room to ensure everyone had correctly heard, then he said, "In the meantime, grab yourselves a cuppa or a coffee while Larry and I sort out what's to be done."

With a nod that Considine follow him, they left the room.

****

In the front bedroom within a semi-detached house in Southlea Avenue, in the Orchard Park area of the city, the man known as the Commandant, dressed and prepared to leave for his office.

From downstairs, he could hear the sound of his wife rattling around in the kitchen and sighing, knotted his tie.

Lifting his wallet and car keys from the dresser, he made his way downstairs to find her still in her grubby nightdress and carrying a mug through to the front room, where the television loudly blared and the two hosts of a popular morning show prattled on about some drivel that in his opinion, interested only bored housewives or idiots.

"You off then?" she said over her shoulder as she slumped down into the well-worn settee, her eyes fixed longingly on the well-groomed and smarmy BBC presenter with the dazzling, toothy smile, a cigarette smouldering between the forefinger and middle finger of her right hand.

He hated her smoking in the house, but she ignored his regular complaints, calling him an old woman and reminding him it was one of the few pleasures she had left in life because he was such a useless, soulless bastard who never took her anywhere.

"I've a meeting tonight," he lightly said, expecting her usual complaint, but if she heard, she didn't acknowledge him, then grabbing his rain jacket from the stand in the hallway, made his way out to the car parked in the driveway.

He stood for several seconds, staring into oblivion, wondering once more how he had ended up with this life; a woman who no longer interested him and who in turn, thought him to be an abject failure, an opinion she freely and often expressed.

Unlocking the door to the six-year-old black coloured Vauxhall Astra, his thoughts turned to the evening's meeting.

He didn't immediately start the engine, but sat for several seconds, reflecting once more on how he had come to be the Commandant of the recently formed, Friends of Ulster Loyalists.

In the meantime, the meeting would once more be held in the flat in Finlay Drive, one of the many properties that was on his estate agency's books and with little chance of being seen sold in this austerity ridden era; a safe if temporary place to gather the few members of the FUL about him.

Eight members actually, but one he deliberately kept separated from the others and what he liked to term, for operational reasons.
He smiled at that, believing it made him sound very military.
His bony chest swelled with pride when he thought back to that heady day when his hand on the one, true bible, the King James version, and with a backdrop of masked men holding an array of automatic weapons and colourful banners, he swore his allegiance in the smoky back room of the Loyalist club that was located just off the Shankill Road in Belfast.
His oath, spoken with gusto, that come what may he would be true and loyal to the cause, that he would form a unit dedicated to serving the Crown, supporting Unionism and carrying out, without failure, all missions, instruction and commands issued by the Inner Council of the Ulster Defence Association.
He unconsciously smiled, committing to memory the list of names of trusted Loyalists who over the period of four months, he first identified, then befriended before recruiting to his new unit.
Then, when satisfied that all were in place, the telephone call that informed him to expect a package that was to be delivered to the Finlay Drive flat.
And when that package arrived, his initial confusion that what it contained was to be their first mission as a unit would be so publicly astounding.
Starting the engine, he reversed out of the driveway, but continued to reflect on how he had come to Loyalism.
His family had always been supporters of the Crown and brought up as Glasgow Protestants, it was inevitable that he supported the Rangers football club, the sworn rivals of the Irish Republican supported Celtic.
His father, an authoritarian member of the Church of Scotland, a man who believed in corporal punishment for his sons and who regularly used his leather belt to instil discipline, had literally beat his support for the Crown into his three sons; a support that followed the Commandant into adult life, whereas his brothers left home in their teens, never again to be in contact with him nor their parents.
As time passed, his support for the Crown and the Royal family increased and the shooting and bombing atrocities of the IRA only served to strengthen his resolve to somehow pay back the murders of decent Protestant people.

Health issues and his cursed alopecia denied him the opportunity to enlist in the armed forces, but did not prevent him from garnering support for the Loyalist organisations who in Glasgow, were mainly found in the pubs and clubs in the Dennistoun area of the city.

It was to these premises that he volunteered his services; charity can collecting on behalf of the Loyalist prisoners behind the wire, raising funds for the widows and orphans murdered by the republican terrorists and a number of other initiatives that moved money across the Irish Sea.

And all beneath the police radar.

Or so he believed.

His management of a Glasgow estate agency, part of a UK wide group, soon came to the attention of the leadership of the UDA, who in time recruited him to covertly provide them with the keys and access to empty Glasgow flats where, ignoring the conditions of the Good Friday Agreement in 1998, the UDA could make use of the properties to secrete weapons being shipped to the Province and on occasion, to accommodate individuals being hunted by the police and the Security Services.

Then, just over five months previously, came the call to Belfast where following his initiation into the UDA, he partied, was feted and provided with all he might desire.

He still blushed at the memory of the busty, middle-aged, dyed blonde woman who was tasked to both provide board and sexually entertain him at night, though he never knew her real name.

Of course, as far as Cecilia his wife was concerned, it was a boring, three-day business visit, and she would neither learn of the woman, Queenie, nor the five hundred pounds in cash given to him for 'unexpected expenses.'

Turning onto Thornliebank Road, he suddenly frowned, for the hiccup that was the murder of Jimmy Crawford leapt into his mind. The last thing he and his unit needed was any police interest and he fervently hoped that blundering idiot, Collins, had not left anything that might enable the police to identify him.

He recalled the exact moment he had authorised Collins to kill Crawford, the exact words he had used.

'When you obtain the gun, you must dispose of Crawford,' was how he had phrased it.

It was something of a thrill, he wasn't afraid to admit it to himself, that as the Commandant, he could order the murder of another individual.

To have the power of life and death, to be able to order another individual to take a life; he suddenly found himself smiling.

But this new instruction, their first mission as a unit, closed typed on a single sheet of paper with dates, names and location and the aftermath of what was his unit's first and really important operation.

In his mind, he had practised for hours going over the briefing he would give his Volunteers; what their exact instructions would be.

He suddenly felt chilled when he recalled what was being asked of him - of them - and knew that if they succeeded, as he confidently and undoubtedly knew they will, every police agency in the UK and the Security Services too, will be set to hunt them down.

****

It was the acting DS, Jackie Wilson, who had been sent to the control room to examine the external CCTV footage for the time that Alice Redwood had entered the rear yard and it was she, closely watching the monitor in the control room, who saw the hooded figure dressed in dark clothing run from a corner of the darkness and out of sight of the CCTV camera covering that area of the yard.

Five minutes later, stood in front of Eddie Fairbanks and Larry Considine, she breathlessly said, "I'm in no doubt, boss, whoever that individual is," she pulled a face, "he knew what coverage the camera has and the way he ran, I'm also in no doubt it's a man. Also, knowing how skinny that wee lassie is," the sixteen stone Wilson shook her head, "the way he run at her, he'd have bowled her over with no problem at all."

"No sound on the disc?"

"No," she shook her head, "vision only."

"And there's nothing on the cameras located at the front of the building?"

"Again, the individual responsible," her voice oozed sarcasm, "seemingly knows where the coverage is."

While the DI and DS processed her information, she asked, "Any word from the hospital?"

"Only that Alice has been taken over to the Neuro," Fairbanks sighed, "but I intend taking a turn over there this afternoon."

"I'll arrange a whip-round from that bunch of tight-fisted buggers out there," she nodded in the general direction of the incident room, "and see that you get a bunch of flowers to take with you."

"Thanks, Jackie, and yes," he grimaced, "while like you I'm confident it's Cooper you were looking at, it's the same old story."

"I know," she held up her hand, "we work with the evidence."

"One more thing, before you go," he said and saw her stop at the door, then turn to glance at him.

"Strictly speaking, because I'm continuing as the SIO for the murder, the attempted murder of Alice Redwood should be dealt with by you and your guys as part of your remit for dealing with incoming crime reports. Yes," he held up his hand, "I know I've been all over this since I got in, but how would you feel about you being the SIO for the attempted murder investigation?"

She stared thoughtfully at him, then narrow-eyed, she responded, "I'd be pleased to deal with it, boss, and thank you."

When she'd left the room, Considine said, "For what it's worth, that was a good decision. Jackie's well capable of dealing with the attempted murder."

"I just hope I'm not overloading her," Fairbanks brow furrowed.

It was then Considine asked, "Given any more thought as to why the ACC was looking for you yesterday?"

"No idea at all," he replied, then rose from his chair and walked to close his office door.

Returning to his chair, he sighed when he said, "Don't go off on one, Larry, but did you have a heavy bevy last night?"

Taken aback, Considine could feel his throat tightening when he replied, "Why do you ask?"

"Because your eyes are like piss holes in the snow and you're reeking of spearmint chewing gum."

He held up his hand, palm forwards, when he quickly added, "While I don't want to get involved in your personal issues, you have to know that if Gardener comes back, if he can't find me, you're his next port of call and we both know he's out to get the DCI, so that puts me *an*d you in the firing line as well. For your sake Larry, don't be offering yourself up as an easy target for him."

Considine blinked, recalling the previous day when anxious for a nip from his half-bottle, he had almost left to fetch it from his car just as the ACC walked into the incident room.

With a resigned sigh, he stared at Fairbanks before he asked, "I take it Bobby Heggerty had a word with you?"

"He did, yes, and you have to know, he's worried about you, that you'll get caught and done for the bevy and with so little time left to serve before you retire."

Considine slowly shook his head, then said, "You're right, of course, and with the short time I *do* have left to serve, I know just how vulnerable I am, Eddie."

His shoulders slumped when he added, "But believe me, I've tried to cut down the drink, but I'm an alcoholic and that's all there is to it."

Fairbanks felt a lump in his throat when he made his decision, then said, "My partner, Ronnie. Ronnie Masters," he smiled as her image jumped into his thoughts. "I'm certain you must recall the headlines about her, a few years ago. International model and junkie. Thrown out of America. It was all over the news," he shrugged.

A little embarrassed, Considine nodded that yes, he did remember.

"Well, in confidence, let me share this with you. Every day Ronnie wakes up, every *single* day, Larry, she knows it will be a struggle, that she is still an alcoholic, still a junkie and every *single* day she fights against the desire, knowing that one slip up, one taste of wine or any alcoholic drink, could set her back to her old ways. If she has a headache, she copes with it because she fears that any over the counter medicine could initiate her craving for something stronger. Every - *single* -day."

He paused, then with a shake of his head, he quietly continued, "Ronnie is without doubt the strongest individual I know. I'm one of life's fortunate people, Larry, because the drink and the gambling has never really interested me and I've never been drawn to using so-called recreational drugs either. But when I'm with her, the woman that yes," he nodded, "I'm crazy about and love more than life itself, I can't help but wonder," he shook his head when he groaned, "How the hell does she cope?"

He grimly smiled when he continued, "Well, she does cope, but she will be the first to admit, she doesn't do it alone. Even though she hasn't touched drink or drugs for over two years, she continues to attend regular AA meetings, even counsels some new members who attend and also continues being counselled herself by Anne, a woman who helped her take the first step on the road to recovery."

He stopped to take a breath, then smiled, "I'm sorry, this is sounding like a lecture, but what I'm trying to say is, you have a successful career behind you with just a short way to go till you can retire."
He shook his head when he continued "Don't risk your pension and your commutation by coming to work smelling of the bevy. And," his face creased with a smile, "if you should ever *consider* seeking some help for yourself, I happen to know a good woman you can speak with."
Considine stared thoughtfully at him, then with a long sigh, simply replied, "Thanks, Eddie, I'll give it some thought."
Further conversation was halted when the door was knocked, then pushed open by Susie Lauder who, followed into the room by Duke Smythe, excitedly grinned when she said, "We might have a breakthrough about Alice Redwood's assailant."

CHAPTER TWELVE.

Aware that ACC Alex Gardener was always at his desk no later than seven-thirty each working day, DI Iain Cameron never failed to be in attendance for the arrival of his boss, a fact that irritated his live-in girlfriend, Jill, who frequently complained that she was never ready to be woken each morning at such an early hour.
He gave a brief thought to Jill, who in the recent past had been seeking any opportunity to argue with him, and suspected was looking for any reason, any excuse to end their eighteen-month relationship.
"Morning, sir," he politely greeted Gardener when the ACC pushed open the door to the outer office, then handing him that morning's newspapers and the Force twenty-four-hour crime synopsis, asked, "Coffee, sir?"
Without turning as he strode to the door of the inner office, Gardener replied, "With me."
Softly shaking his head at the ACC's lack of courtesy, Cameron followed Gardener through to the office where after sitting down, he asked the younger man, "Yesterday, how did you get on at Maryhill?"
Still standing, he stared poker-faced at Gardener when he lied,

"Unfortunately, DCI Heggerty still wasn't in his office and as far as I could ascertain, remains on personal leave."

"And his stand-in, DI, Fairbanks?"

"Truth be told, sir, DI Fairbanks was engaged in a lengthy briefing about the murder investigation and I didn't think it appropriate to intervene. That and I formed the opinion you wouldn't want anyone to suspect that you had a keen interest in DCI Heggerty's whereabouts, so I took my leave."

Cameron knew that Gardener would be suspicious of his story, yet would not be able to contradict it without actually checking himself and mentally crossed his fingers that the ACC would be reluctant to do so.

Staring at Cameron for several seconds, the DI could see the doubt in his eyes, but finally he sighed, then said, "I'll have that coffee now, thank you," and glanced down at his desk with an unspoken dismissal of Cameron.

Closing the door behind him, Cameron greeted Gardener's arriving secretary, who in a low voice, asked, "What kind of mood is he in this morning?"

He grinned when he replied, "Same old, same old. I'm off to the canteen to fetch coffee. Pot of tea?"

"Yes, please, Iain," she smiled and thought not for the first time, this young man is wasted here running after that pompous arse.

****

Chief Superintendent Liz Malone, having returned home to shower and now wearing her uniform, arrived at her office a little after midday, to be greeted by her secretary, June, who grimly told her, "I've known you long enough now, Ma'am, to tell you that you look awful. Go and sit at your desk and I'll bring you and Mr Miller coffee."

"Mr Miller?"

Jean unconsciously lowered her voice when she replied, "He's waiting for you in your office. He's been here all morning, but instructed me not to contact you, that he'd deal with any urgent business that came in."

She glanced at the closed door, then her voice still lowered, asked, "Has he been upstairs to the CID?"

"No Ma'am, just told me that it's an unofficial visit that he'd fill in because he'd been told you were at the hospital all night. And that begs the question," the matronly woman, a police employee for over thirty-eight years, then asked, "Why aren't you at home in your bed?"

"Oh, don't you start," Malone pretended to chide her, then with a warm gesture lightly squeezed the older woman's arm, nodded and taking a deep breath to compose herself, pushed open the door to her inner office.

Deputy Chief Constable Charlie Miller seated behind her desk and leafing through some paperwork, rose to his feet to greet her with, "Liz. I didn't think you'd be coming in today."

"And why ever not? Am I that old I can't handle a nightshift anymore?"

He stepped out from behind the desk and smiling, said, "I'm the Deputy, I'm permitted to worry about my staff and I know that you worry about your guys too, so cut me some slack, eh?"

"Okay, Charlie, and of course you're correct. I'm knackered," she sighed, then slumped down into her chair while he occupied the chair in front of her desk.

"Any word yet?" he softly asked.

"No," she shook her head. "I phoned her father just before I left the house, but he could hardly speak, other than to say she's at the Neuro and being attended to."

"I gather from what I'm told she's young, twenty-two or three?"

"Twenty-two," she nodded.

"A fighter?"

"I bloody hope so," she replied with some feeling.

Some seconds of silence descended on the room, she deep in thought and he idly scratching at the faint scar on his right cheek.

The silence was broken when he said, "Digressing completely. Any word from Bobby Heggerty?"

"Again, I called him last night but he was sleeping, so I spoke to his wife, Cathy. This coming Monday, he's booked in at the Beatson for a colonoscopy, so we'll know more when the result of that is known."

"Ouch," Miller's face creased at the mention of the procedure.

"Ouch, indeed," she softly exhaled.

"Did Cathy happen to mention if he's up for a visit?"

"I'm popping by on Sunday. You're welcome to accompany me," she offered.

"I'll see how I'm fixed, but if I can I will."

"And with Bobby off sick, how is Eddie Fairbanks getting on as the SIO in the murder investigation?"

She stared blankly at him, then softly said, "Now, there's a story."

****

With the two part-time assistants minding the shop front, Ronnie Masters and her deputy, Laura, were having a coffee break in the small office and discussing Ronnie's photo-shoot, due for the Saturday morning within the prestigious Central Hotel in Gordon Street.

Ronnie asked, "With so little notice because their magazine issue comes out on Tuesday, I'm thinking of closing the shop on Saturday."

"Oh, is there any need for that? I mean I'll be here with the girls."

"Ah, but what I'm thinking," Ronnie smiled, "is giving the girls a paid day off while you accompany me as my dresser to the photo-shoot. If you're okay with that?"

Surprised, Laura's face lit up and clasping a hand to her chest, she eagerly nodded when she gasped, "Oh, yes, Miss Masters, I'd love that. Me, on a photo-shoot with a famous international model."

"*Former* international model and these days, more *infamous* than famous," Ronnie grinned at her, then hesitantly asked, "Would you mind remaining behind this evening after we close so that we can pick out a dozen or so outfits for the photo-shoot? I'd really like your advice on what I should wear."

"You want *me* to advise you? Oh, you needn't ask," she waved a hand as though Ronnie were being foolish. "Of course, I'd be *thrilled* to be so involved."

"Then it's settled, Laura. Me and you together on our first photo-shoot."

****

"It was actually Susie's idea," Smythe gallantly began, then turned to her and nodded that she should take up the story.

Grinning from ear to ear, she said, "It occurred to us, me I mean," she added with a glance at Smythe, "that whoever attacked Alice must have either entered the rear yard on foot or if he came by car…"

Smythe raised a hand to interrupt, then said, "John Cooper lives over in Friarton Road in Muirend on the south side of the city…"

"So, he would drive here when he's at his work?" Considine chipped in.

"Exactly," Smythe agreed then nodded at Lauder to continue.

Giving him a sour look, she turned to Fairbanks to tell him, "We figured that knowing the area as he does, Cooper would park his car away from the building here and come in on foot, but he'd want his car parked where it would not be noticed by anyone who could recognise it."

"Among other cars?" Fairbanks suggested.

"Yes," she could hardly contain her excitement, "and the nearest place where there's a lot of cars at that time of the evening is McDonald's on Maryhill Road at the corner with Ruchill Street, about six hundred yards down the road from here."

"Please tell me McDonald's have CCTV coverage in their car park?" Fairbanks felt his chest tense.

"Oh, aye, they do," her grin was now plastered all over her face. "We checked both their cameras and seized their discs. Both cameras, recording from separate angles, clearly show John Cooper, who we both recognised and who was wearing dark clothing, arriving in the car park twenty-five minutes before Alice was attacked. Then three or four minutes after we believe she was attacked, Cooper, wearing the same dark clothing, runs into the car park and gets into his white coloured Proton saloon before he takes off at speed and almost collides with a parked car."

His mind racing and mentally crossing his fingers, Fairbanks asked, "Did you happen to check the CCTV to find out if he was a customer at the McDonald's?"

"We did," she replied with a note of triumph in her voice, then added, "We checked both the internal CCTV cameras that covers the entrance door and the serving counter for thirty minutes each way, from the time when he was recorded arriving in the car park until he left and we are happy to report there is no evidence of him entering the takeaway."

"And that's not all, boss," Smythe broke in with a smug voice.

"More good news, I hope?"

"What Cooper obviously hasn't realised is that when he was running down the Maryhill Road on the north side of the street, there is a CCTV camera located on the corner wall of the shopping centre that is supposed to monitor the side door on the west corner of the building. However, the camera has a wide angle, I think they call it, and catches some of the Maryhill Road on the opposite side, right next to McDonald's."

It was then Fairbanks allowed himself to smile when he asked, "The camera caught him running towards McDonald's from the direction of the office here?"

"Not just that," Smythe glanced at Lauder, "but he's stuffing something into the pocket of what we think is a dark coloured hoodie, maybe a balaclava or something like that."

"And given the blood loss that Alice suffered, if we find it we could be looking at some Forensic evidence?"

"Yes, boss," Smythe soberly nodded.

Glancing at Considine, who couldn't help but smile, Fairbanks turned to Smythe and Lauder then grimly said, "Well done, guys, now find Jackie Wilson. Jackie is the SIO in Alice Redwood's investigation and after you've apprised her of your information, go with her and get Cooper."

****

Bobby Heggerty was having a bad day.

His early morning bowel movement had produced yet more dark blood and the pain in his gut was more than just irritating, in turn causing him to be irritable. That and he felt guilty about being off work and even more so for Cathy had had enough and snapped at him, "Right, get yourself showered and dressed. We're going out for a walk."

"It's raining," he bleated, only for her to quickly respond, "And skin's waterproof, so don't give me any of that patter, Robert Heggerty. Just get yourself into some clothes and waterproofs. We're going to the Botanic Gardens for a walk to try and shake you out of the doldrums, you old misery guts, you."

He couldn't help but grin at her anger then quietly retorted, "Well, if I'm needing cheering up, Cathy, you're going about it the right way. How's about some food down in Byres Road?"

"Now that's the Bobby Heggerty I know," she visibly relaxed, then smiled at him.

****

Unlike many of the individuals with whom he would later associate no-one could honestly say that Andrew Collins had a difficult childhood, that his upbringing was the reason that turned him towards Loyalist terrorism. In fact, Andrew had a decent and relatively affluent background.

Born to parents who doted on him, Andrew was what is referred to in the medical circles as a menopause baby. His mother, Anita, being forty-four years of age when she delivered him, her only child, simply believed that after several miscarriages and two still born babies, never for a minute thought she would become a mother.

As for his father Joseph - *never* Joe - he was a little older at forty-eight.

A respected manager in a small engineering works in the Shettleston area of the city, a church elder and fervent Rangers supporter, Joseph, a true Christian, did not for one minute condone or agree with the then Rangers policy of never signing a Catholic player.

"Stupid rule and it limits our ability to sign quality players," he was often heard to remark to his fellow golfers at the club.

Having resigned himself to being a childless father, Joseph's whole outlook on life changed dramatically at the birth of Andrew.

Overcome with joy, he set out to make his son's life as contented and fruitful as possible, spending every free moment with Andrew and his equally adoring wife.

Raised in their comfortable bungalow home in Teawell Road in the Newton Mearns area of the city, the baby Andrew was surrounded by love and the best clothes and toys money could buy and hardly a week passed but some new outfit or toy landed on his bed.

Initially a pupil at the local primary school, then on to Hill Park Secondary School, Andrew was an average looking child who was a moderate student, neither overly bright nor dim witted.

In fact, he could at best be described as boringly ordinary.

However, the one thing that his parents, Joseph and Anita, could not provide for him was friends, for Andrew, who often felt suffocated by his parent's attention, was a loner by nature; a sorrowful fact that was not picked up by the school teaching nor guidance staff.

Like most if not all young men and some women who were born and raised in Glasgow or thereabouts, traditionally they followed the football team supported by their family and Andrew was no different.

Aged ten, Joseph proudly presented his son with his very own season ticket for Ibrox stadium.

The first home game that Andrew attended, Rangers against Hibernian, his team run out winners and for the first time in his young life, Andrew Collins felt a sense of belonging; a part of something huge that at his tender age, he neither understood nor could explain his excitement. In spirit, he had also just acquired thousands upon thousands of new friends and when at the final blow of the ref's whistle, Joseph watched his son literally dance in the aisle at the Rangers victory and felt a surge of pride that Andrew was following in his father's footsteps.

However, what Joseph could not know was that young Andrew really couldn't give a fig about the result. What mattered to him was the deep sense of being part of the chanting, Union Flag waving, patriotic British and very demonstrative crowd.

As the years passed and he continued to attend the games with his father, Andrew listened to the bravado of the Rangers supporters who in song, deemed it their duty to defend the Crown against all-comers and in particular, the nasty and vicious Irish Republicans from the other side of the city and who were represented by Celtic Football Club.

Added to this was Andrew's ritual of watching the news broadcasts that almost nightly reported murders and bomb atrocities carried out by the IRA, who claimed they represented the Catholic minority in Northern Ireland, whereas Loyalist attributed acts of violence were, in Andrew's young mind, justifiable and in defence of the Crown. And so, slowly but surely, a deeply rooted hatred took hold of his soul and aged just twenty-two, after barely managing to graduate from Strathclyde University with an associate degree in Economics, he decided that it was his own patriotic duty to serve in some manner, the Crown.

Without his parent's knowledge, Andrew began visiting the pro-Loyalist pubs that were to be found in the Dennistoun area of the city.

Wearing the obligatory Rangers football top and his red, white and blue supporters' scarf, something that he would only don after he left the family home, Andrew was at first treated with suspicion by the regular customers of these venues, then as time passed, became an accepted face and to his unbridled joy, was even back-slapped and called by name.

As for the football, when Collins senior decided that he was getting a little old for attending the matches and surrendered his season ticket, Andrew continued his visits and now with his father staying at home and lost in the crowd of like-minded supporters, he was able to curse and vehemently use expletives that would shock his parents, while loudly giving vent to his hatred of all things Catholic; but more specifically, Irish republicanism.

As time passed and now a regular at the Rangers pubs in the east end of the city, he met the man who was at that time the co-ordinator for the charity can-collectors, the man who was later to become his Commandant; the man introduced to him as Arthur Denholm.

What really interested Denholm was after speaking with Andrew Collins, he learned the younger man had never for any reason come to the attention of the police and so he mentally noted him as worthy of Denholm's future attention.

But then in February 2006, quite suddenly and without any warning, Andrew's father Joseph suffered a fatal heart attack.

Devastated, Andrew concentrated the next two months consoling his distraught mother and apart from attending at his workplace, literally fell off the grid; so much so, that Arthur Denholm took the risky decision to contact the younger man to confirm that Andrew was still a committed Loyalist.

Learning of his bereavement, a solicitous Denholm, with ingratiating words and generous praise for Andrew's commitment to the Crown, finally decided to recruit him as a member of the newly formed Friends Ulster of Loyalists.

Again, as time passed and now employed as a junior supervisor within an insurance call centre located in an industrial estate in a Hamilton suburb, Collins began to meet regularly with Denholm, both within the pubs and then finally, at a number of city centre flats where he earnestly convinced Denholm of his commitment to the Loyalist cause.

It was in one of these flats that Collins swore that oath that tied him to the Friends of Ulster Loyalist group and where he now became known as Volunteer Collins.

Then, after receiving his instructions from the UDA high command, Denholm instinctively knew who he would choose to carry out the collection of the firearm and the murder of Jimmy Crawford; a necessary killing to prevent Crawford from ever being associated by the police with the forthcoming mission.

Nor was Denholm to know that killing Jimmy Crawford did not in any manner psychologically or in any other way truly affect the committed Andrew Collins or could not possibly perceive that that Collins was in fact, an undiagnosed sociopath.

CHAPTER THIRTEEN.

DC's Duke Smythe and Susie Lauder, travelling in the second CID vehicle behind acting DS Jackie Wilson and the CID aide, Mickey Rooney, arrived outside the council-built tenement building in Friarton Road in the Muirend area of the city. Parking in two empty bays directly opposite the local primary school, Wilson got out of the car and stared up at the council-built flats with their verandas to the front of the building that seemed to have recently undergone re-roughcasting, then remarked to Rooney, "I don't know why, but I never thought Cooper would be a council tenant. I thought most police properties were gone for years, that cops these days would have bought their houses."

"He might have done," Rooney replied. "Some of those windows are replacements, so I'm guessing they're privately owned now."

Rooney then added with a nod, "White Proton parked there, Jackie. Seems like he might be at home."

She turned when Smythe and Lauder joined them, then the big man asked, "How do you want to play this, Jackie? Straight arrest or what?"

"No," she shook her head, "We'll Section 14 him and if he's agreeable, we'll search his flat. If not, you two stand by the flat while Mickey and I obtain a search warrant and remember, if we do get in to search it, we're looking for a dark coloured hoodie."

Making their way into the common close and turning into each veranda to check the names on the door, it was on the second floor of the building where entering the veranda, Lauder stepped over two children's bikes then saw the name 'COOPER' on the door.

When Wilson knocked on the white painted wooden door, it was opened seconds later by a heavy-set, woman in her late thirties, wearing a loose fitting, dark blue coloured, knee length maternity dress whose shoulder length fair hair was lying loosely on her shoulders and whose eyes seemed to Wilson to carry the weight of the world.

"Mrs Cooper," she asked then inwardly angry at the sight of the bruise under the woman's left eye that was now turning yellow, continued, "I'm Jackie Wilson from Maryhill CID. Is your husband at home?"

The woman nodded, then lowering her head, stepped to one side to permit them to enter, quietly whispering as she did, "What's he done?"

Wilson stopped, then in the same low voice, replied, "We think he's seriously assaulted one of our colleagues. A young lassie."

Two children, a boy aged four and a girl a year older clutching her brother's hand, silently appeared behind their mother and stared at the four detectives, then heard their mother whisper, "He's in the living room."

Nodding that they follow, Wilson strode along the hallway and entering the living room, saw Cooper, barefooted and dressed in a white T shirt and a pair of black coloured jogging pants, seated on an armchair and watching a horse racing event on the television, but who turned and when seeing them, hissed, "What the *fuck* is this!"

It was Wilson, who watching him leap to his feet replied in a monotone voice, "John Cooper, I am detaining you under Section 14 of the Criminal Procedure (Scotland) Act of nineteen-ninety-five that you are suspected of attempting to murder Constable Alice Redwood."

"Who the fuck are you to come into my home…" his fists bunching, he took an aggressive step towards her, but sensing Smythe at her back, Wilson calmly replied, "I'm not a young innocent lassie, Cooper, so one more step and I will *seriously* hurt you. Understood?"

She watched his face turn pale, then over her shoulder and in the same monotone voice, told Smythe, "Handcuff this piece of *shit* and take him down to the car. I'll join you back at Maryhill."

"Okay, Boss," she heard Smythe respond.

When Smythe and Susie Lauder had left the room with a still belligerent Cooper, Mickey Rooney asked her, "You okay, Jackie?"

Her chest tight, it was all she could do to reply, "I've always hated bullies, Mickey, but worse than that, bullies who assault women." She took another deep breath then turning, exhaled when she softly asked, "Where's his wife?"

"I put them into a bedroom so the weans wouldn't see their father getting arrested."

Nodding, she replied, "Let's have a word with her."

Fetching Rose Cooper from the bedroom, Rooney brought her to the living room while the children remained playing.

Seeing how nervous she was, Wilson forced a smile then said, "Maybe you should sit down, Mrs Cooper. Again, my name is Jackie, Jackie Wilson and this is Mickey Rooney. It's Rose, isn't it? Can I call you Rose?"

"Aye, of course," she nodded, yet too embarrassed to meet Wilson's eye.

Glancing at them in turn as she sat down on the settee, Rose, her hands wrestling in her lap, asked, "Is it really serious, what he's done?"

Before she answered that question, Wilson pointed to the bruised eye and said, "I take it that was him, then?"

Unconsciously raising a forefinger to brush lightly at the bruising, she first choked back her reply, then nodded when she said, "Last week. I forgot to bring him in some lager."

"And him hitting you, is that a regular thing?"

Tears sprung to Rose's eyes when again nodding, she spluttered, "Only when he's annoyed at me and yes, that's pretty regular."

Wilson choked back her rage as Rooney, seeing how angry she was, quietly asked, "How far on are you, Mrs Cooper?"

"Just over seven months now, but that's why he's always angry, these days. He didn't want any more kids and blames me for getting pregnant."

Then, before either of the two could say more, Rose asked again, "What's he done?"

Wilson, now composed, told her, "Did he tell you he's been suspended?"

"No," she shook her head, "just said he was taking time off that was owed to him."

"Can you tell me where he was late last night?"

"Out," she shrugged, "but he never tells me anything about where he goes and to be honest, Jackie, the further away from me and the kids, the better, so I don't ask anymore. It's not worth a sore face."

She began to cry and again asked, "This lassie's he's hurt. Was it a prisoner?"

"Why do you think she was a prisoner?"

Rose's face fell when she explained, "He's always bumming about slapping prisoners around and how tough he is, that all the neds in Maryhill are scared of him."

"No, she wasn't a prisoner," Wilson shook her head as Rooney bent towards Rose to hand her a white, folded handkerchief.

"It was a young probationer that he thinks complained against him."

Rose gasped when she said, "Is she going to be okay?"

Wilson took a slow breath before she replied, "We hope so, but she's critical at the minute. We suspect that late yesterday evening he attempted to murder a young female colleague at the office who had just finished her shift. She's currently within the Neurological Ward at the Southern General Hospital in Govan."

Rose reached a hand towards her mouth and her body began to shake.

"Look," Wilson reached towards her, "is there anybody we can call for you? A relative, maybe?"

They watched as Rose began to hyperventilate and it was Rooney, a former paramedic prior to joining the police, who snapped at Wilson, "Go and fetch a glass of water, Jackie, and find me a paper bag if you can."

While Wilson left the room, Rooney knelt down in front of Rose, then taking both her hands in his, began to softly encourage her to breathe calmly through her nose and out her mouth.

It didn't help any that just then, the children being curious as to what was going on entered the room and seeing their mother in distress, began to wail.

Then the girl, seeing Rooney holding their mother's hand, wrongly assumed him to be the cause of Rose's distress and taking a run at him, jumped onto his back.

Hearing the uproar, Wilson returned to the room with a glass of water and an empty brown paper bag that once contained bread rolls to see the small boy with his hands on his head and screaming, Rose continuing to hyperventilate and the little girl on Rooney's back and pounding at his head with her small fists.

As later that afternoon, she told a packed incident room, "Honest, you couldn't make it up and poor Mickey, he's trying to calm the mother while being assaulted by a five-year-old, two stone Mike Tyson."

The team turned to a grinning Rooney who could do no more than shrug and shake his head.

"So, how is Mrs Cooper?" asked Eddie Fairbanks.

"She's fine now, boss, but we had her GP attend before we left just to ensure that she was okay and that's why we were a bit later getting back to the office."

"That's not a problem, Jackie, and you said you brought back some productions?"

"Aye," she nodded. "Mrs Cooper, Rose, she was more than helpful and particularly when we said if we get a conviction, he'll be going away for a very long time."

Almost as one, the team turned when the door to the incident room was pushed open to admit the Divisional Commander, Liz Malone, who waving a hand, said, "Sorry to interrupt, but I'm hearing good news, that you have a suspect in custody for the assault on Alice Redwood."

"Yes, Ma'am, John Cooper has been detained and is currently downstairs waiting to be interviewed by Jackie and Duke Smythe," Fairbanks nodded meaningfully at her.

Then with a smile, he added, "And all down to the good work by DC's Smythe and Lauder and the rest of the team. Jackie here," he nodded at her, "was just about to inform us that the wife of the suspect, Mrs Cooper, has provided Jackie with what seems to be Forensic evidence. Jackie?" he turned to her.

Clearing her throat, she began, "When we explained the reason for his detention, Ma'am, she told us that he had been out late last night in his vehicle and dressed in dark clothes which when he returned, he told her to wash. However, because it was a darks wash and she hadn't enough to fill the machine, she hadn't yet got around to it."

She nodded at the brown paper bags on a desk, then continued, "There's a pair of black jogging pants, a black fleece and most significantly, a black balaclava. I'm no expert, but there's staining on both the fleece and the balaclava that could be blood. There's also staining on the training shoes that are grey coloured and I am *convinced* it's blood. Mickey and Susie are about to take the productions to the Forensic Lab at Pitt Street to get them tested against Alice's blood…"

"And if there's any issues at the lab, use my name to expedite the tests and tell them it's time critical," Malone butted in.

"Ma'am," Wilson nodded gratefully at her.

"And Mrs Cooper. Wasn't she upset her husband is detained?"

Shrugging, Wilson replied, "Mrs Cooper is currently sporting a bruised eye where her husband used her as a punchbag. That and she's seven months pregnant, so Mickey and I," she glanced at Rooney, "are of the opinion she's happy to see the back of him and hopefully for a number of years."

"Oh," was all Malone could respond with, then with a wide smile, said, "Thank you, all of you and now I'll let you get on. DI Fairbanks?" she raised her eyebrows at him then followed by him, left the room.

In the corridor outside, she sighed, "I was on to the hospital earlier. Still no change. I intend visiting the Neuro around five this evening if…"

"Yes, ma'am," he interrupted with a nod, "I'll be happy to accompany you."

"If nothing else," her brow creased, "we should have good news for her parents about her assailant."

Agreeing he would be at her office at five o'clock, he watched her walk off, then decided to phone Ronnie to tell her it would be yet another late night home.

****

Her jet black, collar length hair fashionably styled, Arlene McCandlish stared into the wardrobe mirror and mindful of the upcoming interview, once again checked her make-up, for the media television cameras were not overly kind to a woman in her mid-forties who though considered to be very attractive and who regularly worked out, was acutely conscious of the extra half a stone that her five feet five inch frame currently supported.

Tugging at the navy blue coloured pleated suit jacket, then at the knee-length charcoal grey skirt, she realised the pencil skirt was a bad choice, but had gone along with it simply because her sister had suggested she must seem to be business-like when dealing with the TV reporters.

Glancing out of her mid-terraced, first floor bedroom window to the children's playpark across the road, the railings painted an almost obligatory red, white and blue, her attention turned to the black, Mercedes saloon car parked outside her front gate with the two minders who awaiting her, sat in the front seats, then softly sighed. Johnny and Axel were decent enough lads, but if brains were Semtex, those two wouldn't have enough to blow open a packet of crisps, for peace treaty or not, if the 'RA or whatever name they used these days really wanted to kill her, then even carrying their legally licensed firearms, McCandlish knew there was no way those two muppets could prevent it.

Yet even during this supposed time of peace the minders were necessary, simply because who she was…or rather, who she once had been.

But she softly smiled, knowing she was being overly harsh, for both Axel and Jimmy were volunteers, men prepared to put themselves at risk to keep her safe; bullet-catchers, Jimmy had recently joked.

She took a couple of minutes watching the children at play; Protestants all, hand on heart she could say and reasonably guessed it was unlikely any of them had ever played with a Catholic child.

And that, her eyes narrowed, must change.

Born into a fiercely Belfast Unionist family, McCandlish's father had been a stalwart of the Orange Order, a man whose religious beliefs had come second to his hatred of all things Catholic and Republican; a sentiment he had passed on to his sons and only daughter.

Much revered by his fellow Orangemen, Thomas Cavanagh was a shining beacon of Loyalism and steadfast supporter of the Crown, a founding member of his local brigade of the UDA and because of his outspoken beliefs, an early target for the IRA.

Such was the hatred Cavanagh had for all Catholics, his two sons and daughter, Arlene, followed their father's teachings, only for his older son to also be a victim of gun violence, for one dark, winter night, when leaving a Loyalist shebeen, he too had been gunned down.

Cavanagh's younger son, enraged by his father and brother's assassinations, took up arms against his Catholic neighbours and lasted a little longer than did his sibling, for joining the Ulster Volunteer Force, he was reputedly involved in the murders of a number innocent Catholic's before himself being caught in an exchange of fire with fellow Loyalists, whose political views completely differed to those of the younger Cavanagh.

And that left Arlene.

Joining the Association of Loyal Orangewomen of Ireland as a teenager and helped by her father's reputation and stature amongst the Orange Order, Arlene soon rose to prominence in the Associations hierarchy.

As the years rolled by and she saw her father and both brothers murdered, Arlene's hatred for republicanism and the very thought of uniting Protestant Northern Ireland with their southern countrymen in the Free State, repulsed her and she grew even more fervently Loyalist.

Aged twenty-eight, Arlene was two years married to John McCandlish, a leading member of the UDA when she herself was formally recruited into the ranks of the organisation.

Within a year, she was organising and planning armed operations against the IRA, who soon recognised that they were up against a clever and resourceful individual.

And those armed operations she planned more often than not, resulted in the death of Catholic Republicans involved in their struggle or as they described it, their 'Cause' against the security forces.

During those heady days, two attempts on her life were thwarted; on the first occasion, when travelling from the Shankhill Road towards her home, her car was rammed, but the IRA assassin who leapt from the stolen vehicle to shoot her with his nine millimetre Browning semi-automatic handgun, cursed when the weapon jammed, and so she survived.

On the second occasion, when attending a Loyalist rally, a Kalashnikov spraying bullets from a passing hi-jacked taxi killed two women beside her, while McCandlish suffered nothing more than skint knees after Axel, her new minder back then, pushed her to the ground to avoid the murderous stream.

And so, through the years, the tit for tat murders continued until the day, just months before the Good Friday Agreement, she suffered her greatest loss; the death of her beloved husband, John.

It was a day that was to change Arlene McCandlish's life for ever, a day that she experienced what she later come to recognise as her epiphany.

Standing almost perfectly still, staring out of the window of her bedroom, she was able to intensely recall that day with such clarity; the day that John had waved her cheerio, the day that he and his two minders had visited the Shankhill Community Centre where he was to meet with his fellow Belfast Brigade leaders for a covert conference to once more discuss the forthcoming Agreement.

They had never discovered who his killer was, though of course the IRA accepted responsibility, but there were always doubts about the veracity of the 'RA's claim.

In truth, Arlene suspected an opposing Loyalist faction who mistrusted John's belief in a peaceful solution to the conflict, but a suspicion that that time she dared not disclose for fear of igniting yet another internal feud.

Her eyes narrowed at the memory of her and her minders making their way on foot to join John, having earlier agreed that they would attend a safe pub on the Lisburn Road for a meal and a drink after he had concluded his meeting.

Just a few hundred yards from the Shankhill Road, they had heard the shots and her heart had almost stopped, instinctively knowing it was her John who was the target.

Even now, she could not recall running the distance, but arriving there and pushing her way through the knot of people who were being held back by a passing army patrol, all standing shocked and open-mouthed.

John, lying on his back, his jacket and shirt torn open and to her amazement, a priest, a Catholic priest, bent over him as he tried to resuscitate him by mouth.

On her knees hovering over John, an elderly nun, bareheaded and her hands red with arterial blood, using her Wimple as a makeshift bandage to stem the flow of blood.

A second nun, young and sobbing and somehow guessing she was John's wife, reaching for her to hold tightly her and whispering to console her, though so many years had now passed and try as she might, she could not recall what the nun had said.

The sirens signalling the arrival of both the RUC and the ambulance, she being thrust by her minders into the back with John on a

stretcher and seeing the priest, bloodstained and pale-faced, making the sign of the cross as the ambulance doors closed.
He didn't make it to the Royal Victoria Hospital.
The young doctor who climbed in the back, shaking her head and pronouncing him dead.
Even today, the rest remains a blur.
She took a deep breath and sighed.
Catholic's, she slowly shook her head and eventually smiled.
You just never know with them.
It was that act of mercy, an elderly man and an equally elderly woman, regardless of religion, who didn't ask a dying man which foot he kicked with, but who made the decision to try and save his life; it was that act of mercy that decided her that things must change; had to change.
The country, her country and their country, *our* country, she quietly smiled, could no longer afford to be at war because of a religious divide.
And if she were to make changes, no matter that there had been a Peace Agreement, the old bigotries remained and so she must stay where she was and work that change from inside the Inner Council of the UDA.
Almost nine years had passed since she lost her husband and difficult though it had been, she had convinced many of the hawks within the organisation, if not to actually agree with her, to at least listen to what she had to say.
Slowly, one senior figure at a time, she convinced the more malleable members of the Council that discussion was essential and she *was* making progress, albeit slowly, towards a peaceful solution with the old enemy, the IRA. And, if the clandestine meeting that was to be held on the forthcoming Tuesday in a neutral venue with her Republican counterparts were to be a success, she needed to be on top of her game.
If she were truly honest, she looked forward to the trip and the couple of days being feted by the local Loyalist supporters that possibly might include a visit to Ibrox to see her favourite team play, for curiously, Arlene McCandlish had never before travelled to Glasgow.

****

Ronnie Masters was having second thoughts about three of the outfits she and her deputy manager, Laura, had chosen for the following day's photo-shoot at the Central Hotel.
Calling Laura through to the backroom where the dozen outfits, each within a nylon garment carrier, were hung on a portable rail.
After ten minutes discussion, Laura removed two of the garments and with Ronnie's agreement, replaced them with alternative outfits.
"Right," Ronnie sighed, "that seems to be that issue settled, so make-up. What's your thoughts?"
"I was hoping to surprise you on the day," Laura smiled, "but you recall my niece, Gemma, who's currently on her second year at college studying hair and beauty? Well, Gemma has agreed to come along on Saturday morning and if you're okay with it, she'll attend to your hair and your make-up. The only thing she asks is if you will consent to her photographing you when she's done so that she can add the photos to her portfolio."
"Of course," Ronnie grinned widely, then added, "and we'll request that her name is added to the article as, say, 'Make-up and Hair by Gemma.' How does that sound?"
"Oh, she'd love that," Laura enthused, then said, "Digressing completely, how is your man getting on? I heard it on the radio about that poor young police officer that was attacked in the police station in Maryhill. I take it that's something Eddie is investigating?"
"Yes," Ronnie sighed, "he was in charge, though he doesn't really talk much about his work when he gets in; sometimes because he doesn't want to distress me and other times, he's too tired from a long day."
"So," Laura smiled benignly, "a thoughtful man?"
"Very," she agreed with her own happy nod.
"And can I just add, I have never seen you…" she paused then squinting at Ronnie, said, "I suppose the words I'm looking for is, so content."
She found herself blushing at Laura's kind words then taking a breath, replied, "And to be honest, I didn't believe I could ever be happier."
But what Ronnie couldn't know was that her deputy manager suspected Ronnie's happiness was a lot more than just being with Eddie.

****

As agreed, Eddie Fairbanks met with Liz Malone at her office before travelling together in a CID car driven by him, to the Neuro Ward at the Sothern General Hospital.

Along the way, Malone, wearing a knee-length, navy blue overcoat over her uniform tunic, frequently yawned, causing Fairbanks to remark, "You really should be going home, Ma'am."

"To what, worry there instead of worrying here?" she curtly replied, then almost immediately, sighed and said, "Sorry, Eddie, it's been a long day."

"And a long night, from what I heard."

She smiled when she said, "The burden of command and likely, if your career takes off like I hope it will, you'll be in my shoes one day," then frowned when she added, "But hopefully not under these circumstances."

En-route to the hospital, his mobile phone buzzed and awkwardly, fetched it from his jacket pocket before handing it to Malone.

"DI Fairbank's phone," he heard her say, then add, "Hold on, Larry, it's Liz Malone here. I'm putting you on speaker."

She fumbled with the phone, muttering under her breath, then said, "Okay, Larry, go ahead."

"Ma'am," he heard Considine say, then continue, "Jackie Wilson is just back from interviewing Cooper. The bad news is he kept his mouth shut and refused to even acknowledge his name. Jackie says even the duty solicitor tried to encourage him to plead his innocence rather than say nothing, but he simply refused to speak at all."

"That's the bad news," Malone sighed, "So, *is* there good news?"

They could imagine the wide grin on Considine's face when he disclosed, "The Forensics pulled out all the stops for us. They have confirmed it is Alice Redwood's blood on the fleece, the balaclava, the jogging pants and most significantly, his training shoes. That and the photos SOCO took of the bruises on her torso…" he paused, catching his breath, then said, "match the underside of the trainers where he *stamped* on her."

His eyes on the road, Fairbanks, more calmly than he felt, asked, "Can I assume that this information arrived when the interview had concluded?"

"It did, yes, boss."

Seconds passed before he said, "Have Jackie contact Cooper's solicitor and apprise him of that information. Give him the opportunity, if he wishes, to bring this information to his client's attention and if he does, ask if he wants us to re-interview his client to give Cooper the opportunity to deny the evidence. I want everything to be seen to be done in fairness to Cooper, to give him a chance to explain why her blood is on his clothes. Treat him with kid gloves, yeah?"
"Will do, boss, and can you give us an update when you get to the hospital?"
"I'll see to that, Larry," Malone replied for them both.
Arriving at the hospital, Fairbanks found a parking bay close to the entrance of the building and travelling in the lift they exited on the sixth floor.
By chance in the corridor, they bumped into Ariana Nabavi, the attractive, forty-four-year old consultant neurosurgeon, who wore a brightly coloured hijab and hospital scrubs.
Nabavi, a refugee from her native Iran, months before had been responsible for treating the then injured Fairbanks.
With a wide smile and to his surprise, she hugged him, then said in her faultless if slightly accented English, "Eddie, so good to see you well."
But then her face clouded over when glancing at Malone, she continued, "The young police officer. You are here for her?"
He nodded, then introduced Malone who formally shook hands and asked, "Is there any news?"
"I regret that there is no good news, but no bad news either," she quickly added.
"My colleague is responsible for the young woman's care and he has decided that while she remains unconscious, he will continue to keep her sedated and will not perform any surgery at this time. Scans seem to indicate a small blood clot that, Allah willing, might just disperse and he is of the opinion that while she remains sedated, he can monitor any movement of the clot and if he is correct, there is a likelihood she might recover without the need for an invasive procedure."
"Is that your opinion, too?" Malone asked.
She softly smiled when she quietly replied, "My colleague, he did ask my opinion and I concurred."

Before they could comment further, Nabavi said, "Perhaps you might wish to meet with the young woman's parents?" then without waiting for a response, turned and led them to a waiting room further along the corridor.

When Malone entered the room, Nabavi laid a hand on Fairbanks arm to hold him back, then when the door closed behind Malone, she peered into his eyes when she said, "And you, Eddie, no headaches or any loss of vision since we last spoke?"

Taken aback by her dark-eyed and intense stare, he involuntarily blushed when he shook his head, then replied, "No, nothing."

"Good," she smiled then added, "Please thank Ronnie for the beautiful business suit she had delivered to me. I am so very grateful and of course, being a former model, she has an eye that ensured it fits perfectly."

He hadn't known of Ronnie's kind gift to Nabavi, but was further surprised when she continued, "My partner and I are due soon to travel to Leeds for a Neurological Convention, so I intend bring her to meet Ronnie where we will both choose suits for our visit there."

He mentally kicked himself for his insensitivity, for it was out before he could help himself when he blustered, "Her?"

To his relief, Nabavi smiled when she nodded then replied, "And that, Eddie, is why I came to the UK as a refugee from my own, intolerant culture."

"Now," she nodded at the closed door, "Do not let me keep you, but do ensure that you tell Ronnie I will be seeing her very soon."

Feeling like a fool, he watched the attractive and graceful Nabavi walk off, then pushed open the door to the waiting room.

.. FOURTEEN: Saturday 23 September 2006.

Chief Superintendent Liz Malone didn't normally work the weekends unless there was some critical reason for her being in her office, the assault on Constable Redwood certainly being one of those reasons.

So, when she arrived that Saturday morning at her office and found Larry Considine standing with her secretary, June, who suspiciously had also decided to come to work and both with a mug of coffee in their hands.

"Morning," she greeted them, then staring curiously at Considine, asked, "You waiting to see me, Larry?"

"Yes, Ma'am," he smiled at her, then glancing at June, who was also smiling, he said, "I was in the office five minutes when I received a telephone call from the hospital. Alice Redwood regained consciousness and though still a little dazed, the woman I spoke with, a Miss, eh," he grimaced, "I'm sorry, I think she said her name was Nirvana or something."

"You mean Nabavi?" Malone suggested with a soft smile, her heart beating a little faster with the good news.

"Aye, that's her," he nodded. "Says she knows Eddie Fairbanks. Anyway, she says to tell you that she and the consultant treating Alice are very optimistic about a full recovery and that she's already informed Alice's parents."

To her surprise, Malone felt herself become a little light-headed and though she couldn't explain it, fought the emotion that come upon her, though was unable to prevent her eyes tearing up.

"Look at me," she joked, "I'm just a sentimental old git."

Taking a deep breath, she pushed open the door to her office, then said to her secretary, "When you're done with yours, June, maybe fetch me a mug too, please and eh, thanks for coming in today."

"And with what's been happening, why wouldn't I be here, Ma'am," she smiled at her boss.

In the privacy of her office and seated behind her desk, Malone used a tissue to wipe at her eyes, then taking a deep breath, dialled the internal number for the Deputy Chief Constable's office at Pitt Street, knowing that Charlie Miller would already be at his desk.

It was his secretary, Ellen, who curiously was also in her office on a Saturday and who answered her call, then said, "He's at his desk, but on the line to the Chief at the minute, Miss Malone. I'll get him to…no, wait, he's finished his call. I'm putting you through now."

Seconds later, Miller greeted her, then said, "I hope this is good news."

Relating Larry Considine's information, she heard Miller sigh with relief then he said, "You concentrate on catching up with what is happening at Maryhill, Liz. I'll pop by the hospital later, when I get a minute, and speak with the lassie if she's awake. Right now, I need to inform the Chief of your update, but thanks again for letting me know. I really am so relieved that we're not going through this again after…well, you know."

When the call had finished and as if on cue, the door was pushed open by June who brought in Malone's coffee, then laying it down onto the desk, hesitantly said, "DS Considine told me they've charged that man, Constable Cooper, with attempting to murder young Alice Redwood?"

"Aye, he's appearing this morning at a special sitting in the Sheriff Court, June, so likely once the media get a hold of the story, there will be a lot of telephone calls you'll need to field."

June smiled when she replied, "Not the first time, Ma'am, now drink your coffee and take five minutes to yourself before you start the day."

When the door closed and not for the first time, it reminded Malone that when she did retire, she would go with June's mobile phone number listed in her 'Favourites' directory.

****

On the first floor of the insurance call-centre building located in the Hamilton International Park, wearing a headset with the lead trailing down his chest and slowly limping between the desks where the predominantly young employees manned their telephone consoles, Andrew Collins, the team's immediate supervisor, occasionally nodded when one of them would catch his eyes, but right then his thoughts were elsewhere.

Since strangling the man in the flat, the man the Commandant said had to die because he was a direct link to the Friends of Ulster Loyalists, Collins had not slept well, not that it had anything to do with bad dreams.

No, Collins sleeplessness was due to the wound on his left leg and was worrying him, for none of the over the counter creams or anti-inflammatory gels had soothed the now infected leg.

He had awoken that morning feeling hot and sickly, his skin and pallor unusually pale and his father's old glass thermometer indicating his temperature was well above normal.

That and his mother's insistence that he take the day off work and visit the doctor hadn't helped his temper, for unusually he found himself shouting at her not to fuss.

No way would he attend at the doctor, for the dog bite had turned an ugly, swollen and discoloured red and paranoia or not, he had no way of knowing if the police had issued some sort of lookout for a man suffering a dog bite.

"Andrew," he heard his name called and turned to see his manager staring at him, a woman older by fifteen years and her face expressing her concern; a cheerless woman he believed past her prime and whose job he coveted.

"You don't look so good, honey, I think you'd better consider going home."

"I'm fine," he replied a little sharper than he intended, then waving a hand at her, forced a smile when he added, "Just a touch of the cold, I think."

"Yes, well, that's all it might be," she sniffed, "but a cold is an infectious virus, so I don't want you to be the cause of more of the team taking time off and," she stepped a little closer when she lowered her voice to confide, "you know this lot. They'll use any excuse to avoid coming into work."

"Maybe you're right," he nodded, then said, "I'll take the rest of the weekend in bed with hot drinks and be here bright and early on Monday."

"I'll see you then," she herself forced a smile, for though he couldn't know it, Andrew Collins was not a man she liked and though she had no complaint about his work ethos, privately she considered him to be a devious individual who, for some curious reason she couldn't explain, caused her to wonder why she would think that.

Collecting his jacket, shoulder bag and car keys from the locker room, Collins made his way from the first floor of the building downstairs to the ground floor, then pulling opening the security door that led to the large car park at the rear, he stopped and thought himself about to faint.

Grabbing at the lengthy steel handle on the heavy door, he stood for several seconds, gasping as he drew a deep breath and his body shaking as his heart thumped in his chest.

Exhaling, he tightly closed his eyes then licking at his dry lips, forced himself to be calm.

Now almost a full minute had passed and feeling a little better, he pulled open the door and made is way in the bright sunshine towards

his racing green coloured Mini Clubman, a gift from his parents when he passed his driving test some four years earlier.
Starting the engine, he focused on the route to the car park exit, a little surprised that his vision was slight blurred.
Turning out from the car park then onto the Technology Road, he drove on the roundabout towards Hillhouse Road, braking at the junction of the red traffic light, but then once more felt himself about to faint, then slumping over the steering wheel, was unconscious when his vehicle slowly rolled forward to smoothly collide with a gentle bump at the rear of the stationary van in front.

****

Concluding his short briefing and reporting the good news about Alice Redwood, Eddie Fairbanks motioned that Larry Considine and Jackie Wilson join him in his office.

Wilson, who was in daily attendance at the briefings, in turn would brief her team that continued to deal with the day to day reported crime.

When all three were seated, Fairbanks told them, "I'm grateful for the efforts that went into arresting John Cooper yesterday. Jackie," he turned to her, then asked, "I assume you have submitted your case to the PF?"

"Done and dusted, boss," she nodded at him, then added, "It'll be myself and with your permission, Duke Smythe from your own team, who will take Cooper to the Sheriff Court. I had him detained here at Maryhill rather than have the prisoner transport company take him this morning. That way I can keep him under our supervision and hand him directly to the police court officers who'll ensure he goes into solitary confinement until his appearance. That way he won't be able to allege that we put him in with the rank and file prisoners to be assaulted because he's a cop. Or soon to be ex-cop," she wryly smirked.

"Good decision," Fairbanks agreed. "Now, how about the crime reports coming in? Any issues there I need to know about?"

"All under control," she raised her palm towards him, pleased that there was nothing so far that challenged her while she was in the acting rank.

"Fair enough," he turned to Considine to ask, "Right Larry, I'm stuck about how to progress our investigation. Any ideas?"

"Well," he cleared his throat, "it seems to me our main focus should be identifying this suspect, the man seen at the locus by Redwood and our civvy witness. I've had Actions out looking at any CCTV cameras in the area to try and locate one that might have captured him about the time he was seen walking off, but regretfully," he shook his head, "nothing so far. That's not to say he might have left on foot, then got into a car, so if that's happened, we're stymied."

"We know he was limping," Fairbanks leaned forward, his elbows on the desk, "and we know the dog has presumably bit our killer, so two and two might make five, but my gut tells me he's definitely our guy, though why he hung about after the murder, I have no idea." He paused for several seconds, then thoughtfully continued, "The dog bite. If the bite has been deep enough to cause him to go away limping, is it possible that he might have required some medical aid? I'm thinking can we check the casualty wards of the local hospitals to see if anyone has turned up to have a dog bite attended to."

"I'll get some Actions raised for that, boss, and I'll have someone go through the phone and include local medical practices too."

"Problem there I think," they turned to see Wilson grimacing, who then said, "Of course it depends who the team might talk to at the hospital's and medical centres, but these days," she shook her head while sighing at the same time, "too many receptionists I've encountered fall back on the Data Protection Act and refuse details without the patients permission."

"Good point," Fairbanks conceded, then added, "though regardless or not, they'd have to have a good reason to deny that a patient attended with a dog bite without actually giving out the patients details. Try anyway, Larry, and make the point that whoever has the Actions to tread warily when asking for the information."

"Boss," he acknowledged with a nod.

His brow furrowed when a thought occurred, then said, "I don't suppose it would do any harm either to have an urgent entry onto the PNC for the Daily Briefing Registers, asking Divisions to let their cops know if they come across or have any information about anyone who they come into contact with and who is suffering from a dog bite to the left leg."

"I'll see it gets done," Considine nodded.

"Oh, and one more thing," Fairbanks eyes narrowed, "our witness, Margaret Thompson. I know she's old and while Jaya Bahn reported Thompson used binoculars to spot our suspect, I'd like Jaya to return and to witness Thompson using the binoculars. Have one of the team stand where she saw the suspect standing and have Thompson describe whoever you use as a test subject, as best as she can. I'd like Jaya to record what Thompson tells her in a statement because there's no doubt if it comes to court and we put Thompson on the stand, a defence lawyer will undoubtedly question if she's watching from six floors up in a high-rise building, both her eyesight and cognition."

Pursing his lips, Considine nodded, "Good idea. It might add some credibility to Thompson's statement, her being seventy-six."

"Right, anything else?" he asked, glancing at them in turn.

When both shook their heads, he asked Considine to remain behind, then when Wilson had left the room, closing the door behind her, he said, "I'm thinking we should invite DI McGhee from the SB here for a meeting and put it to her about the gun and the tracking device. We both know that she probably has information about our victim and I'm also in no doubt, she'll either be aware who might have murdered him or at least have her suspicions. What's your thoughts on that?"

Considine stared at him before he replied, "You do know she'll deny any knowledge of the murder, the gun or about screwing your desk to recover the device?"

"That's a given," Fairbanks sighed, then added, "but it just might put her on the spot if we suggest we intend making a formal complaint to the Professional Standards Unit."

"What about the Ballistics guy, Mathieson. Won't it put him on her radar if we confront McGhee about what we know? I mean she's bound to realise that he's the guy who found it and hasn't officially reported it. Might even use the Official Secrets Act to put pressure on him to force him to deny he knows anything about the device and where does that leave us then?"

"Good point," Fairbanks slowly responded, then exhaling, said, "I'm also thinking about asking Liz Malone to be present when McGhee arrives and the reason for that is I'm a DI, you're a DS, so I don't expect her to be intimidated by us, regardless what we think we know or can prove. *However*," he stressed the word, "if a Chief Superintendent is present and is aware of what we know, McGhee might think twice about withholding information in an ongoing murder investigation."

Fairbanks eyes narrowed in thought, causing Considine to ask, "What?"

"The first time they visited me, McGhee made a comment that has since had me thinking. When I asked if she had information for me about Jimmy Crawford's murder, she said, 'Not at this time.' Now, I kind of wondered what she meant then, but thinking about it, I think what she was telling me was that she *did* have some information, but wasn't able to disclose it."

Considine grimaced when he said, "I agree with you about having Liz Malone present, boss, but Chief Superintendent or not, if McGhee invokes the Official Secrets Act, she might just keep her mouth shut and we're no further forward. Other than letting her know that we are aware of the Branch's interest in our victim. That and we also know they screwed your desk, though of course we won't be able to prove that," he shook his head.

Slowly nodding, Fairbanks at last replied, "Of course, you're correct, Larry, but," he reached for his desk phone and grinned, "if nothing else, why don't we invite her anyway and see if we can shake things up a little?"

"You think she'll come?"

"She's bound to be eager to find out what if anything we know, but better than that," he dialled the internal number for the Pitt Street telephone switchboard and continued to grin when he added, "she's a woman and it'll be killing her not to know."

****

Completed in 1883 by the Caledonian Railway Company as the then Central Station Hotel, the building, located in Glasgow city centre's Gordon Street and towering over the railway station below, has seen many changes in its life.

The Hotel initially became famous when in nineteen-twenty-seven, John Logie Baird, the acknowledged father of today's modern television, transmitted the world's first long distance television pictures directly to the Hotel.

In its heyday the Hotel famously hosted such guests as the then future President of the United States, John F Kennedy, the Beatles, the UK's World War II Prime Minister, Winston Churchill, the Rolling Stones, the famous American actor and dancer, Gene Kelly and other such notable actors, like Cary Grant. In nineteen thirty-two, the comedians Laurel and Hardy, who were regular guests at

the Hotel, caused a near riot among their fans and during the crush when both were mobbed by adoring admirers, both had their pockets picked and Laurel had his wristwatch stolen.
And this famous venue was now to be the location for the photo-shoot starring the former international model, Ronnie Masters.
As agreed, Ronnie and her deputy, Laura, met with the Life & Fashion Management photo-shoot crew at eleven o'clock that Saturday morning within the splendid and opulent function room of the Grand Central Hotel in Glasgow's Gordon Street.
Greeted by an enthusiastic Tony Harper, who arranged for Ronnie's outfits to be taken to a booked suite in the adjoining corridor, he then shepherded them towards a tall, slim woman in her late fifties with bright orange coloured curly hair and thick-lensed, rainbow coloured framed spectacles.
Wearing a loose fitting and, Ronnie guessed, extremely expensive multi-coloured kaftan, Harper introduced the woman as Charity Dawson, the magazine's editor.
If Harper was enthusiastic, Dawson was literally hyper that Ronnie had agreed to the photo-shoot and in a high-pitched voice, gushed like a schoolgirl, informing Ronnie and Laura that the photo-shoot was a real coup for the flourishing magazine.
"And your stylist, she's already here and in the room we've allocated for you to change in," Dawson gushed once more, then her brow knitting, added, "though she does seem to be rather young for such an important event."
Though yet to meet Gemma and to Laura's relief, Ronnie confidently replied, "But very competent, I assure you."
While Ronnie and Laura inspected the suite where the photoshoot was to occur, the crew set up under the critical supervision Tony Harper and a Hotel employee, a young attractive woman who identified herself as a deputy manager and who took a few minutes watching them flitting about to ensure everything went smoothly.
Satisfied that the crew seemed to be as professional as any he had previously worked with, Harper led the two women to the booked room where Gemma awaited them.
Quite obviously nervous when her aunt and Ronnie entered the room, Gemma was clearly a little intimidated by the beautiful and once famous model, but then taken aback when with a subtle wink,

Ronnie said, "Gemma. How nice to see you again," then hugged the young woman to her.

Satisfied that for the minute, all was well, Harper left them alone, telling Ronnie, "I'll send someone to let you know when we're ready to shoot."

Smiling at Gemma, then arm in arm with her as she slowly escorted her to the dressing table where the young woman had set out her kit, Ronnie told her, "Don't be nervous. Think of me as one of your fellow students at your college, who's getting their hair and make-up done for a nominal fee. Is that how they still work it?" her face creased in a wide grin.

"Yes," Gemma bashfully grinned then taking a deep breath, said, "Okay, I'm ready."

****

While her paramedic colleague worked on the patient, the ambulance driver, who blue-lighted Andrew Collins to the Accident and Emergency Department at Hairmyres Hospital in East Kilbride, had radioed ahead that their unconscious patient was suffering breathlessness, had an extremely high temperature and in his semi-conscious state, was talking in his stupor, but slurring his words. That and while there was no apparent smell of alcohol, they didn't rule out the use of an illegal substance which might have also accounted for his fast heartbeat, body tremors and unusually pale pallor.

"No," she replied to the question as she raced along the Queensway, now just minutes from the hospital, "no apparent injuries connected with the RTA collision."

"He's fitting!" her colleague shouted from the rear of the ambulance, then she relayed that information too.

Their arrival in the ambulance in the covered bay at the entrance to the A&E was met by a doctor, a nurse and two porters wheeling a trolley who rushed Collins through the doors to an examination room.

Perhaps it was a sign of the times as well as both the symptoms and appearance of the patient, but whatever was going through the young, almost exhausted and newly qualified doctor's head was for a later discussion, for her first thought and comment was, "It looks like he's on something."

That initial suspicion took root and as she later admitted, it was what caused her to believe her patient was suffering from some sort of overdose or reaction to an illegal drug.
In the cubicle, the experienced Staff Nurse said, "Right, let's get him undressed."
With the assistance of a burly porter, they quickly began to remove Collin's clothes, cutting off his trousers and shirt, rather than trying to manoeuvre his unconscious body and it was when they drew down his trousers, they saw the store-bought bandage wrapped around his lower left leg.
"What the hell?" the doctor muttered then using surgical scissors to cut away the bandage, she physically recoiled at the ghastly wound and the putrefying odour coming from it.
"It's some sort of a bite wound," the experienced Staff Nurse helpfully suggested, then turning, exclaimed, "He's starting to fit again!"
The doctor reached behind her for the syringe that she intended using, but the nurse loudly called out, "We need the paddles!"
However, no electric shock treatment was necessary for minutes later and to the doctor's consternation, Andrew Collins gave a gentle sigh and died without regaining consciousness.

CHAPTER FOURTEEN.

Constance McKenzie had suffered her own pain when some fifteen years previously when after a spending a Saturday afternoon shopping downtown for an outfit for her sister to wear to a friend's birthday party, both her parents and younger sister had been standing in a queue, chatting away while waiting for a bus to take them from Belfast city centre their home at Vara Drive.
McKenzie's sister, aged just sixteen, was excited at the prospect of that evening's night out where a young man in her sixth year had already intimated that he liked her, a secret she shared with her older sibling, but not her parents for fear they might not then permit her to attend the party.
It was unfortunate that bombs, do not discriminate when they detonate and so with three other innocent bystanders, all six in the

bus queue were killed when a nearby vehicle, its boot loaded with an improvised explosive device or IED as they had come to be known, detonated and sent its parcel of nails, screws, nuts and bolts at tremendous speed to shred flesh and bone.

The car, a Ford Fiesta stolen days before the detonation, been illegally parked nearby on double yellow lines and loaded with what the security forces later assessed to be one hundred and sixty pounds of ANFO, a home-made explosive that had in turn been initiated by a couple of pounds of military grade Semtex.

The bomb killed not just McKenzie's family and the three others, but injured and maimed another thirteen passers-by, some of whom also lost limbs.

Within minutes of the bomb going off and using a telephoned code word, responsibility for the explosion was claimed by the Irish Republican Army who, and regardless of their denial, it was also later established failed to send any kind of warning of their intent.

Once the shock of losing her family had subsided, the murder of her parents and only sibling had driven the previously mild-mannered McKenzie to seek revenge against those responsible and the only way she considered she could achieve such revenge was to join the organisation that she believed truly fought the IRA; the Ulster Defence Association.

Once initiated into the organisation, her involvement commenced as a courier, carrying messages back and forth between various groups and members, for no-one, least of all a designated terrorist organisation, trusted the telephone or even the commercially bought radios that were so easily intercepted by the security forces.

And so, it was down to women such as McKenzie and on occasion, children, to secrete written coded messages and instructions in their clothing, usually carried in their undergarments, to be delivered not just in Belfast, but throughout the Province.

McKenzie, then employed working in a local fish and chip shop that involved lunchtime or late evening work and dependent on her shifts, enabled her to spend the mornings and afternoons employed in couriering; however, once she was established as a trustworthy member of the organisation, her duties were stepped up to include the transportation of munitions and on occasion, explosives.

Though McKenzie often volunteered for more risky work such as targeting Catholics, her handler only used her on one occasion that unfortunately for her, quickly went sour.

Late one Friday night after she finished work, her handler collected McKenzie from the chip shop and explained that an unexpected opportunity had arisen to murder a prominent Sinn Fein member who the handler had learned was due to arrive at an address in a predominantly republican area of the city. There being no one else available, he pressed her, was she willing to take the job on?

An excited McKenzie immediately agreed and was handed a .455 Webley revolver that unknown to her, dated back to the First World War.

She was surprised at how heavy the revolver was for when loaded with six bullets in the cylinder, it weighed just under two and a half pounds.

Driven to the location, her nerves kicked in when just minutes from Glenpark Street, situated within a deeply republican housing estate and where she was to be dropped off at rear garden door in the street, she was told to watch for the arrival of a white coloured Ford Escort. The target, her handler told her, was the passenger who alighted from the vehicle.

Her body shaking with excitement and in those few minutes driving to the location, given a rudimentary explanation of how to hold, then fire the revolver, it didn't help that she needed to pee.

Confident that her hatred of all things republican would see her achieve her aim of killing the target, McKenzie stood at the garden gate and in the shadow of a brick wall while noting that common to all the inner-city streets where the army and the RUC patrolled, most if not all the street lights had been vandalised to permit the shadowy movement of terrorist gunmen and the security forces alike.

Some fifteen minutes later and as she had been briefed, the Escort arrived, but sat for several minutes with the driver and the front seat passenger apparently talking.

But then the passenger door opened and a woman alighted.

McKenzie, initially surprised, wondered why her handler hadn't said or perhaps, hadn't known the target was female, but then as the Escort drove off and the woman stood to wave cheerio, McKenzie stepped out of the shadows.

Unfortunately, never having held a handgun previously and thus unaware of what would occur when she pulled the trigger, McKenzie held the heavy weapon in her right hand and, with her left hand supporting the right hand and too close to her face, closed her left eye and sighted along the six-inch barrel.

Her mouth to dry to even shout out and from a distance of eight metres, she sighted the target along the barrel, then pulled the trigger.

As the shot was fired, not only did the weapon's kickback take her by complete surprise, but the hammer struck her on the right cheekbone with such force it lacerated the skin and stunned, she missed her target.

Ignoring the sudden pain, she fired off a second shot at the panicked woman, but again jerked the trigger, missed and watched as the woman run through a rear garden door, slamming it behind her.

Dazed and now bleeding profusely, McKenzie then turned as her handler screeched his vehicle alongside to scream, "Get in!"

Scrambling into the rear passenger seat, she listened to her handler cursing her for her failure, then minutes later dropped her at the casualty department of the Royal Victoria Hospital with the instruction she tell staff she had been attacked in the street.

A bandage pressed to her wound, the attending casualty surgeon, a middle-aged doctor who through the Troubles had dealt with all manner of injuries, ranging from severe 'so-called' punishment beatings to gunshot wounds, shrapnel injuries as well as burns inflicted from petrol bombs, almost immediately recognised the lie and could even smell the gunpowder residue on her face.

Sighing at the weeping McKenzie, he told her, "I'm not interested in how you came by this laceration, young lady, but you have to know I can only stitch the wound and likely as not, you'll require plastic surgery if you're to be your old beautiful self again."

Embarrassed and humiliated at her failure to kill the Sinn Fein woman, her snappy response was, "Just fix it."

And he did, with stitches that closed the ragged tear in her skin, but didn't quite hide the two-inch scar that resulted on her right cheek.

Within a week and continuing her cover story, McKenzie returned to both her job in the chippy and working for her handler who decided that as she wasn't quite up to killing Catholics, returned her to couriering and supplying the operational teams with their munitions.

Throwing herself into her clandestine task, as time passed so also the risk of arrest heightened and to her misfortune, two years prior to the Good Friday Agreement and one evening in a pub in County Antrim, tasked with delivering three handguns to an active service member of the UDA, she was betrayed and apprehended.

After trial, McKenzie was sentenced to eight years in prison.

It was to her good fortune that just two years into her sentence and under the terms of the Agreement, McKenzie was released, but found herself jobless, homeless and with the war against the republicans officially over, without any direction in her life.

Upon being discharged from prison, McKenzie's first accommodation was in a Belfast women's hostel where thievery and violence was an everyday occurrence.

Bitter and without direction, every morning when she stared into a mirror, her prominently scarred face reflected to remind her of her abject failure that night.

But then Arlene McCandlish stepped in.

As a senior figure in the UDA, McCandlish knew of McKenzie and her history.

It was some weeks after learning of her release from prison that thanks to the intervention of McCandlish with the local community housing association, McKenzie, discovering that her former parental home in Vara Drive had become vacant and was telephoned by McCandlish who gave her the good news; she was now the new tenant.

It was also at that time McCandlish, who had begun to solicit support among the UDA's hawks for her peace initiative with the republicans, sensed that one day and in the not too distant future, they might indeed begin to live in peace with their Catholic neighbours.

Her good fortune continued when McCandlish and with her ever-growing popularity among the Loyalist community, realised she needed a trusted assistant to deal with administration matters and offered McKenzie the job.

And so, after serving two years of deprivation in HM Prison Armagh, McKenzie assumed the role of McCandlish's personal assistant and took to the job with an enthusiastic passion.

Now McCandlish's trusted assistant, McKenzie had her own desk located in the small commercial unit off the Shankill Road, that was officially designated as the Lanark Way Community Initiative, but in reality, was Arlene McCandlish's headquarters.

Peering at the paperwork in front of her, McKenzie studied the travel, accommodation and contact details of their visit to Glasgow the following Monday, the twenty-fifth of September.

The Stena Line ferry booked and the tickets for McCandlish, her two minders and McKenzie already purchased, she was satisfied that with the arrangements made, there was nothing left for her to attend to and sat back in her chair with as satisfied smile.

****

Eddie Fairbanks call was put through to the Special Branch general office where a male simply confirmed the extension number, but didn't disclose his name.

"DI Fairbanks at Maryhill," he dryly said. "I'd like to speak with DI McGhee, please."

After a few seconds paused, the man replied, "Can I have your extension number, please sir, and I'll have someone phone you back."

With a smile, Fairbanks provided the details, then told Considine, "Not only wouldn't the bugger give me *his* name, but he didn't even confirm they *have* a DI McGhee."

"Paranoia is infectious," Considine grinned. "Duke Smythe told me that when his pal in the Branch is at the bowling club, he always checks under his car before he drives off home. Thinks he's important enough for the IRA to blow him up."

"Right," Fairbanks shook his head when he rose to his feet, "I'd better pop down and see Ma'am to ask if she's willing to sit in when and if, DI McGhee arrives."

However, before he reached the door, his desk phone rang and with a glance at Considine, lifted the receiver.

"DI Fairbanks."

Considine watched him nod, then repeat, "Okay, four o'clock here at my office. See you then."

Smiling, he told the DS, "She's coming."

****

The consultant, a kindly man who could see that the young doctor was overly concerned that she had somehow failed to spot how seriously ill the patient had been, grimly smiled when he told her, "Looking at the wound that does *not* seem to have been professionally treated and from the description of his symptom, I'd opine that the severity of the wound has caused septicaemia and in turn triggered the Sepsis that has set in. In short," his thick eyebrows joined when he sighed, "I'm thinking, though a post mortem will need to be conducted, there is little you could have done in the short time between his collapse and his demise."

Turning to the Staff Nurse who stood silently at the cubicle's closed curtain, he said, "It seems to be an obvious bite mark and that worries me. I would suggest that we should contact the local police office to report this young man's death just in case or for any reason, there should be some requirement for a FAI."

"Sorry," the experienced Staff Nurse stared curiously at him. "A what?"

"A Fatal Accident Inquiry," then patiently explained, "When there is an unexplainable death, albeit we do suspect Sepsis, we must report the circumstances to the police who will investigate the circumstances of how this young man came to be bitten and who in turn, will inform the Procurator Fiscal of the death. If the PF so decides, a hearing will be held at the Sheriff Court."

"The FAI?" the Staff Nurse repeated.

"Exactly," he softly smiled, then added, "Now, Staff, if you will please contact the local police office and it will also be proper and helpful if they are the ones who will inform this young man's next of kin of his demise."

****

Lying in bed, her parents seated by her side, the room awash with baskets of flowers and cards from well-wishers, Constable Alice Redwood, her head still bandaged and her face grazed on the left side after she was so brutally pushed against the wall, stared at the large, bulky man with the scar on his right cheek who pushed open the door and entered with a smile.

"Hope I'm not interrupting?" he stared from Redwood to her parents, then extending his hand to her father, said, "Charlie Miller, I'm a colleague of your daughter."

"Oh, right, you're from Maryhill?" her father half-rose from his chair while her mother smiled at Miller.

"Actually, I'm based at Pitt Street, but these days I seem to spend quite a bit of time there."

Turning to Redwood, he continued to smile when he asked, "I'm hearing you're well on the mend, Alice?"

With just three months in the job, the young woman didn't really recognise or know who the tall man was and though his face was vaguely familiar, she stared a little uncertainly at him, then took a guess when she hesitantly asked, "You're a boss, I mean, a senior officer, aren't you, sir?"

"Well, only when I'm at work, Alice," he smiled at her.

"When I'm at home, my wife Sadie's in charge and to set your mind at ease, I'm the Deputy Chief Constable and I'm here to both see you're okay and find out if you're needing anything and also to tell you, the Chief sends his best wishes."

He could see the surprise register on her face and quickly held up his hand when he added, "But that still makes us colleagues and that's why I'm here to see how you're getting on and to tell you that we really need you back at work. So," he adopted a serious expression, then gruffly said, "When can we expect you to return to work, Constable Redwood?"

Taken aback by his straight forward question, she gulped, then stuttered, "I'm hoping to get out of here soon, sir."

"Well," his voice a little softer, he teasingly smiled, "not until you're fit and ready, young lady. It's my instruction that once you're discharged from here, you *will* take some sick leave and maybe even pay a visit to the Occupational Treatment Centre at Auchterarder. When you're up there, I assure you, they'll look after you. Understood?"

Turning to her parents, he continued to pretend to be gruff when he added, "Any nonsense from her about coming straight back when she's not ready, give me a phone at police headquarters. We need excellent officers like your daughter in the service and I don't want her coming back too soon."

With a cheery wave, he winked at Redwood then took his leave and left the room.

In the corridor outside, he fetched his mobile phone from his pocket and as he walked to the lift, dialled Liz Malone.

When she answered his call, he said, "It's me. I've just left. Her folks are still with her and she's definitely on the mend, but after the trauma of what she went through," he entered the lift when the doors opened, then turning, continued, "I think we should consider some

counselling, so I'll leave that to you to organise, Liz."
When the call ended, he exited the lift on the ground floor then making his way to the parked staff car, got into the front passenger seat and told the driver, a retired Traffic Department Sergeant, "Back to the factory, please, Ernie."
****

The duty Sergeant at East Kilbride Police Office strode into the locker room, then addressing the two constables standing there, said, "That was Hairmyres A&E on the phone. Seems they've a sudden death there and they want the polis to attend because they're not happy with how the guy died. When you get there, speak with the consultant on duty at the casualty."
Constable Chris Rae, a cheerful thirty-one-year old fair-haired bachelor and his divorced neighbour, Rachel Best, an attractive thirty-two-year old with short, mousey auburn hair, reached into their lockers to grab at their stab-proof vests, caps and utility belts before heading downstairs to the car park.
Neighbours for nine months, the pair were, as they thought, secretly dating and had even gone as far as discussing moving in together; however, while believing themselves to being as discreet as possible, they were while totally unaware that their shift sergeant, a man in the twilight of his career, knew of their relationship.
However, he judged them both to be good cops and had made the decision that provided it didn't interfere with the running of his shift, they were entitled to a private life.
With Best driving, they were soon at the A&E where Rae, the senior cop by two years, led the way to the nurses' station.
Learning the consultant and the doctor were both attending to an emergency patient and thus unavailable, it was left to the Staff Nurse who leading the pair to the cubicle where the body remained, told them, "The ambulance crew brought his bag with him from the car that he was in. An RTA I think it was. That and his wallet seems to identify him as Andrew Collins, though I'm sure you guys will confirm it."
Pulling at the closed curtain to the cubicle, she held it back to permit them to enter.
"And what's made the Consultant suspicious?" Rae asked.
Lifting the white sheet that covered the body, the nurse replied, "That."

Staring at the wound, Best took an involuntary step back while Rae cringed, his expression changing to one of revulsion when he said, "Bloody hell, that must've been hurting before he died."
"The PM will confirm it, but the consultant is pretty certain that he's contracted septicaemia and it's turned into full blown Sepsis."
"Sepsis? What is that anyway and is that what's causing that God awful smell, too?" Best's eyes narrowed when she asked.
"Yes, and simply put," the nurse lowered the sheet, "it's blood poisoning. He's obviously not sought treatment for the bite and it's become infected; so much so that the infection had gone too far and there was nothing we could do for him when he arrived here."
"Phew, what a way to go," Rae shook his head, then said, "This is a bit above my pay grade to make a decision. Is there a phone I can use? I'll need to bring our CID here, if the buggers answer their radio that is, this being Saturday and the Old Firm are playing," he sighed.
"Wait a minute, Chris," his neighbour, her eyes narrowing when she held up a hand and suspicion in her voice.
Turning to the Staff Nurse, she asked, "Is that *definitely* a bite mark of some sort?"
"We thinks so, yes, but what made kind of animal bit him, we can't say."
"Chris, it's his left leg!" she could hardly contain her excitement. "It was in the DBR this afternoon when we started our shift! The Maryhill CID, I think it is! They're investigating a murder and they're looking for a suspect with a bite mark to the left leg!"
****

The door knocked then was pushed open by Duke Smythe, who pokerfaced, said, "Your visitors are here, boss."
DI Sadie McGhee, her fair hair again tied back in a ponytail and wearing a skirted, emerald green suit and white blouse while her neighbour, DS Norrie McCartney, was dressed exactly as Fairbanks remembered from their first meeting; a creased, chocolate brown coloured three-piece suit, grey shirt and what looked suspiciously like a Rangers tie.
If the pair thought they were meeting just with Eddie Fairbanks, their surprise showed in their expressions when they saw both Larry Considine sitting on a chair to the left of Fairbanks desk, while in

full uniform, Chief Superintendent Liz Malone sat on a chair to the right of the desk.

When the Special Branch officers stared at the trio, it was Malone who opened the conversation when with a fixed smile, she politely told McGhee's neighbour, "You may return to the general office along the corridor, DS McCartney, and wait there. If we need you, we'll call you."

Glancing first at McGhee, he turned to stare malevolently at Malone when he growled, "I don't think that's a good idea, Ma'am."

In a voice that projected boredom, she calmly said, "I really don't give a monkey's shit what you think, DS McCartney, but I *am* a senior officer and I have issued you with an instruction. Now, get out."

The large man's eyes betraying his hostility, Fairbanks thought for a brief second that McCartney was about to bark a response to Malone, but instead, took a deep breath then wordlessly left the room, petulantly leaving the door wide open.

With an audible sigh, Considine rose from his chair and striding across the room, closed the door while Fairbanks motioned to McGhee that she sits down in the chair in front of his desk.

"Is this some sort of interview?" she refused to glance at either Malone or Considine.

"If you're asking if I intend interviewing you about your knowledge and dealings with my murder victim, James Crawford, then yes, I suppose it is," he responded with a gentle smile.

She stared him in the eye then with a smile, almost lazily replied, "I'm afraid that any information I might or might not have about your murder victim, DI Fairbanks, is covered by the Official Secrets and…"

But she got no further, for Malone, rolling her eyes, interrupted with, "Oh, for heaven's sake, not *that* old chestnut again!"

As they turned to stare at her she fetched a mobile phone from her tunic pocket and sighing, pressed a number before lifting the phone to her ear.

Then they heard her say, "Callum? It's me. It's as I was telling you. Yes, yes," she involuntarily nodded, then handing the phone to McGhee, told her, "Your boss wants a word."

Fairbanks saw McGhee's face pale and her head bobbing when she replied, "Yes, sir, I understand. Yes, when I get back," she nodded, then added, "Yes, sir, I'll call you."

Ending the call she returned the phone to Malone, who rising to her feet, stared down at her when she said, "This isn't some television thriller, DI McGhee, this is a complicated murder investigation, so you will divulge *everything* and *anything* that DI Fairbanks needs to know and believe me," she maintained eye contact when she stooped to emphasise, "I find out you have *not* fully cooperated, then you could be looking at a charge of attempting to pervert the course of justice and while I have no idea how that is handled in Northern Irish courts, over here, you'll be looking at jail time. Is that *clearly* understood?"

Her face now chalk white, and struggling to swallow, McGhee could only nod.

Without another word or a backward glance, Malone left the room, closing the door behind her.

As Considine later related, "Jesus! Liz Malone was bloody impressive and the atmosphere in the room was so tense, it could have been cut with a knife."

However, before Eddie Fairbanks commenced his questioning of McGhee, the door was knocked, then pushed open by Jaya Bahn, who gasped, "Sorry, boss, but I need to speak urgently with you." She glanced at the figure of McGhee, who she didn't recognise, before she added, "Here, in the corridor. Now," she stared at him.

He turned to glance at Considine, then as one, both men rose to their feet to step through the door.

"Hell, Jaya," Fairbanks irately grimaced when pulling the door over behind him, he shook his head.

"That's the worse time ever you could have knocked on my door. So, what's so urgent?"

"We've just had a phone call from Hairmyres Hospital in East Kilbride, from a Constable Best.

"And?"

"Best says a patient was admitted this afternoon with an infected bite to the lower left leg, a guy called Andrew Collins."

He could feel his chest tighten at this sudden break, then said, "Has he detained Collins?"

He saw her face fall when she quietly added, "Best's a she, but unfortunately boss, Collins has died. Some infection called Sepsis, they think."

CHAPTER FIFTEEN.

Her head still buzzing at the conclusion of the photoshoot, Ronnie Masters, ably assisted by Laura and Gemma, was changing from the last outfit into her travelling clothes when the door was knocked, then opened by Charity Dawson, who cheerfully called out, "Only me."

Striding into the room, her hands flat against her bosom, Dawson grinned from ear to ear when she gushed, "That was fantastic! I've been to many a photoshoot, Ronnie, but your experience, your advice and your poise made *all* the difference to the camerawork. Congratulations, my dear, and dare I say," she peered myopically at her, "you're back!"

Her forehead creased or, as Laura later cattily remarked, as far as the Botox might permit it to crease, when she asked Ronnie, "I assume that Tony has already made the financial arrangements clear?"

"Yes," Ronnie smiled, then said, "and they are perfectly satisfactory. However, I have both a request and a proposition for you, Charity. Firstly," she glanced at Gemma, "I'd be grateful if Gemma's details could be added to your feature as the stylist."

"Yes, no problem with that, I'll have Tony note Gemma's details," Dawson nodded, then asked, "And your proposition?"

"If your article receives a positive response, then in aid of a charity still to be decided, Laura and I," she glanced at the older woman, "intend auctioning off all the outfits I displayed today at a fashion parade, hopefully at an event still to be confirmed, but within the Fruit Market in the Merchant City. We would offer your magazine the advertising rights and for us, it would be a tremendous boost if you might consider…"

"Of course, of course," Dawson interrupted with a grin while she slapped her hands together, already envisaging the publicity for the magazine to again have Ronnie Masters once more involved in a photoshoot.

"We'd love to cover that sort of event and we'd also be most willing to assist with the advertising and coordinating the arrangements with you."

"Then I look forward to hearing from you," Ronnie extended her hand, but was taken aback when Dawson chose instead to tightly hug her.

Over Dawson's shoulder's she saw Laura biting her lower lip then raising her eyes to the ceiling.

When Dawson had left the room and they were packing up the garments, it was Gemma who said, "When I was watching the photo shoot Miss Masters…"

"Don't you start," she interrupted with a smile, then added, "I'm not having you *and* your auntie both calling me Miss Masters. It's Ronnie, okay?"

With a happy grin, Gemma nodded then said again, "When I was watching the photoshoot, that guy Harper, I heard him asking if you'd brought a swimsuit. Was he just being weird? You know," her eyes narrowed and she blushed when she stared meaningfully at Ronnie, "him wanting to see you in a swimsuit or is that normal for photoshoots, the models wearing swimsuits?"

She didn't bother explaining her strong suspicion that Harper was gay and likely not interested in seeing her in a swimsuit, other than for the photoshoot, but instead replied, "On occasion, models do wear swimsuits, but usually at a pool, though I'm not certain if this hotel has a pool. Anyway," she felt her face flush, "I'm not really ready for a bathing suit at the minute."

Nor did she miss the curious glance that Laura gave her.

****

Leaving Larry Considine to deal with the discovery of the body of a possible suspect at Hairmyres Hospital, Fairbanks returned to the room to deal with the matter in hand.

Resuming his seat at his desk, he forced a smile when he said, "James Crawford."

"What was that all about?" McGhee cocked her head back at the door.

There seemed little point in lying, so he replied, "A body in an East Kilbride hospital that might have some bearing on the murder investigation. Again, James Crawford?"

He wasn't certain, but saw again the very slight tic in her left eye before she formally replied, "I have one request to make of you, DI Fairbanks."

"I hardly think you're in a position to make such requests, DI McGhee, but go on."

"Anything that I divulge is for your information and not to be divulged to your team. Yes," she nodded, "I understand there is information I can share with you, but regardless of what Ma'am said, some of that information remains subject to the Official Secrets Act."

"I understand and again, mindful of what Ma'am said, I'll decide what my team can and can't be told."

She stared at him, but he couldn't be sure whether her expression was dislike or was she thinking him to be naive?

Then she began again, "Without prejudice, I have to inform you that Special Branch know very little about James Crawford's recent activities, other than his past support for the Ulster Loyalists."

"And what of the details of such support for extreme right-wing organisations that you deleted from his record on the PNC? That and you supplied him with a firearm."

He watched her chest rise when she took a deep breath, then nodding, she audibly sighed and said, "Just over six weeks ago, Crawford arrived as a walk-in to police headquarters."

"A walk-in?"

"He arrived at the Pitt Street front door and asked to speak with a Branch officer; nobody in particular, just someone from the Branch. One of the guys from the general office brought him upstairs to an interview room where Crawford offered to provide some information about a new Loyalist group."

"I can't imagine that anyone and particularly someone with Crawford's past history with the police, would simply volunteer information without wanting something in return. So, what was he wanting from you?"

"Difficult though it might be for someone like you to believe," her face creased with derision, "it seems that Crawford had become a grandfather and his daughter is apparently married to a Taig…" she paused, then corrected herself, "I mean, a Catholic."

Licking nervously at her lower lip, she continued, "Now, it's no great secret but in Belfast, a union between a couple of the two faiths is not only frowned upon, but actively discouraged and as I'm certain you are aware, in certain areas in *this* city, such a belief continues. As for Crawford, I don't know," she shrugged, "perhaps he was looking at his own mortality, but he told us he wanted a reconciliation with his daughter and thought by coming to us with his information, he could somehow renew the bond with, eh," her eyes narrowed, "I forget her name," she flippantly waved a hand. "Anyway, his daughter."

"But how would that help him?"

Her lips parted in a smile that Fairbanks thought to be completely false when she replied, "He asked that we provide him with a document that stated he was a changed man, that he no longer had any religious bias. Utter tosh, of course, that we would condone such a proposal, but in exchange for his information and for the sake of a typed letter, we were quite happy to agree."

I'm sure you were, he thought, but said, "And did Crawford happen to intimate how he come by this information about this new group?"

She paused as though reluctant to continue, but then said, "His story was that a friend of his, though he blankly refused to provide the friend's name," she shook her head, "told Crawford that this new group, the Friends of Ulster Loyalists, were seeking to acquire a handgun. Also, we don't know enough to assess if Crawford's informant is a member of this group."

"Did you have previous knowledge of this group?"

"No, and we still weren't able corroborate its existence, so Crawford's information remained that; simply information, not confirmed intelligence. At least not until three weeks ago."

"What happened then?"

"We received word from our colleagues in the PSNI in Belfast that such a group does exist, that they purport to be a support group funding and aiding the UDA. Other than that, we have no information about their numbers, locations or who their contacts in Belfast might be."

"The UDA?" his face expressed his surprise. "I thought that lot were finished after the Good Friday Agreement?"

She wryly smiled, a smile that he took to mean, 'don't be foolish.' "No," she said at last, "the UDA continue to function, though on a low key and intelligence, again from Belfast and corroborated by the Security Service, suggests that currently there is some inner turmoil, that a good number of them want peace with the hierarchy of the IRA who, we also hear, have a number within their senior figures who seek a peace agreement without the involvement of the UK

Government. In short, it seems the doves are hovering over the hawks who are finding themselves in the minority."

Several seconds of silence followed while he digested this information, then he asked, "Why did Crawford want a firearm?"

"The short answer again is, we don't know and unfortunately, neither did he."

His brow knitted when he softly replied, "We did suspect that he might be a middleman."

He stared at her when he asked, "And that's why you bugged the firearm, to find out where it might be going and why?"

"Correct," she nodded.

"How did Crawford make contact with this group, the, ah…" he pretended no previous knowledge of them.

"The Friends of Ulster Loyalists," she reminded him, then her expression indicating she was apparently satisfied that she was disclosing new information to Fairbanks, she continued, "The PSNI instructed one of their sources to drop Crawford's name to a Loyalist they strongly suspect of being in touch with the new group, suggesting Crawford to be a man who could procure munitions. Two weeks ago, Crawford informed us he'd received a telephone call on his landline from a man who didn't give his name, but identified himself as the Commandant of this new group. Described him as not young, but thought him to sound between forty and sixty years of age and who said he'd heard that Crawford could obtain a handgun."

"I'm guessing you either had Crawford's telephone monitored or did a billing to check his incomings calls?"

"Correct again, DI Fairbanks, to both," she smiled.

"We have a recording of the call and of course, the man's voice, but the Call Related Data failed to disclose an incoming number and the billing simply confirmed the call was made from a pub phone; predictably, one of the pubs in the east end of the city that is frequented by Loyalist supporters and Rangers football fans."

"And no CCTV in the pub?"

"None that we have access to, no," she sighed.

His face creased when he formally asked, "DI McGhee, I have three questions for you. Do you have any idea at all who might have murdered Crawford or indeed, why he was murdered at all and for what purpose he was procuring the handgun for the group?"

"One, I have no idea at all who killed Crawford and two," she held up the palm of her hand towards him, "please note this is only my own opinion?"

"And that is?"

"Well, you can imagine the security in these groups and organisations is paramount, so I can only assume that if whatever the group are planning, if it goes sideways, Crawford would be able to identify who collected the firearm from him and that in turn…"

"Might lead us to this man, the Commandant," he quietly interrupted.

Her eyes narrowed when, her voice curious, she said, "What makes you think it wasn't this guy, the Commandant, who murdered Crawford?"

He sighed deeply when he replied, "We have the description of a suspect who is said to be in his twenties. You said this Commandant is aged between forty and sixty, so that seems to rule him out."

"Oh, and are you willing to share any information you have about this suspect?"

"Really?" he stared at her. "You interfere with my investigation, screw my drawer here to recover your device," he slapped a hand down onto the desktop, "and have the *gall* to ask me share my information with you?"

"Then perhaps in future you will consider that we might share what we know?" she lopsidedly smiled.

"Not if I have to come asking for it," he shook his head. "If you were to agree to volunteer your information, I might consider reciprocating, but that takes me on to my third question.

"What do you think this group are planning?"

"Truthfully," she maintained eye contact with him, "I have no idea."

After several seconds of staring at each other, he broke their eye contact, then said, "Well, unless there is anything else you can tell me, I believe your boss is at Pitt Street, waiting for a word with you."

He saw the faintest slump of her shoulders, then she said, "We're not the enemy, Eddie. We were acting in good faith, trying to maintain the security of our operation."

He softly smiled when he replied, "But you got caught out and that's certainly not been helpful to either of us."

Rising to her feet, she smoothed at the front of her skirt then with a smile, said, "If we need to exchange information, why don't we consider doing it in a pub somewhere?"

He recognised the suggestion for what it was, but he had a beautiful woman waiting for him at home and attractive though McGhee might be, she could never compare to Ronnie.

Slowly nodding, he replied, "Thank you, but I believe we should continue to remain professional, so any future meetings will either be at Pitt Street or here. And Sadie, don't forget to collect your ape on the way out."

Her eyes flashed in anger, but forcing a tight smile, she turned and left the room.

****

Arriving at the A&E entrance at Hairmyres Hospital, Duke Smythe told Susie Lauder, driving, that the car park was usually mobbed and suggested while he contacted the two uniformed cops, she find a parking space.

Striding through the entrance doors into the A&E, he saw a uniformed cop waiting and identifying himself, the cop replied, "I'm Chris Rae. My neighbour, Rachel, she's with the body in the cubicle."

His brow furrowed when Rae asked, "Am I correct in thinking you want us to seize the body?"

"That's right, yes," Smythe nodded. "We think this guy Collins might have been a suspect we're looking for, so the SOCO are on their way here now to obtain samples of his blood and DNA from the wound to confirm or not if the bite is a dog bite. Do you have his clothing and personal effects and fingers crossed, a mobile phone maybe?"

"They're in the cubicle and can I remind you," the young cop grimaced, "that we haven't yet informed his family of his death."

"They'll find out when we arrive to turn his house over," Smythe wryly grinned, then seeing Lauder enter through the doors, beckoned her over.

When she joined them, Smythe told Rae, "Right, Chris, let's have a look at our suspect."

****

Calling Larry Considine into his office, Eddie Fairbanks first asked, "What's the story from the hospital?"

"I've sent Duke Smythe and Susie Lauder to seize the body. The

SOCO have been dispatched to attend from Pitt Street and I've also asked them, after they've attended to the body, to make themselves available to go with Duke and Susie to the suspect's house to turn it over."

"What about a search warrant for the address?"

"I've got Jaya Bahn attending to that and she's on her way to collect the warrant from the duty Fiscal at her home in Baillieston, then she'll attend at the duty Sheriff's house in Dumbreck for a signature. It being Saturday and the Old Firm playing at Hampden, though, it's likely she'll have problems with the traffic, so I've told Duke to wait near the house and not go in till Jaya arrives. Her neighbour, Brian Saunders, and the aide, Mickey Rooney, are in the incident room waiting on the call from Duke to go and assist in the search."

"They'll leave from here and rendezvous with Duke and Susie at the suspect's home address that the cops at the hospital have provided as," he glanced down at his notepad, "Teawell Road in Newton Mearns, over in the south side."

He paused for breath, then reading again from his notes, continued, "And just in case whoever is in the house might want to kick off, I've alerted the local sergeant at Giffnock Police Office to help out with some uniform back-up."

"How did we come by Collins home address?"

"The cop, a Constable Rae, sounds a solid young guy. He did a PNC check on Collins vehicle that he crashed when he passed out and it's registered to him at that address. Rae also telephoned to say Collins had a wallet on him that contained a security pass in his name for a local insurance company, apparently just a few hundred yards from the RTA. They think he was driving away from his place of work when he crashed the car."

"Good work, Larry, and I don't underestimate your ability coordinating all this."

He was rewarded by a red-faced Considine who replied, "No problem, boss. How did you get on with McGhee?"

"Now, there's a story," Fairbanks shook his head, then thoughtfully said, "She provided me with some information, but I have a feeling she's both holding back and only told me what she wants me to hear. Without anything to contradict her as a liar, I could only listen, but that said, some of which she did tell me corroborates what we already know and in particular about this Loyalist group and their leader, this man called the Commandant."

He glanced at Considine when he added, "But let's me and you grab a coffee, because the telling of it might take some time."

****

In the car returning to Pitt Street, Sadie McGhee still angrily stung from Fairbanks declining her offer to meet socially with her, for the good-looking woman that she knew herself to be, she wasn't used to getting knock-backs from men.

DS Norrie McCartney broke into her thoughts when he asked her, "Did you tell him about the meeting?"

"Course I didn't," she snapped back. "I'm not that stupid. I've given him enough to corroborate what he probably already knows, just enough to convince him that we're on the level; no more, so I don't think we'll have any more trouble from him. It's what we might have to tell our boss, I'm worried about," she scowled.

"Well, that's something, anyway," he moodily replied, then added with a sneer, "As for Callum Fraser? He'll not want the waters getting muddied, so take it from me, don't be worrying about him. He'll just take whatever we choose to tell him as gospel. What about the gun? Are we getting it back?"

"Not at the minute," she frowned, "and besides, it's a production in Fairbanks case and it's no longer of any use to us if the Ballistics have tested it, is it? If we were to use it, who do you think they'd come looking for?"

"What about the Commandant? Has he identified him, did he say?"

She frowned before she shrugged, "I got the feeling he didn't know about the FUL or the Commandant, but there's no way of knowing if that information will help him now."

"No matter," McCartney smirked. "Even if Fairbanks does know now, it's too late for him to do anything about it. The operation is all set to go."

Her eyes narrowed in thought when she wondered, how the hell did I get landed with this stupid bugger. Admittedly good at what he does, terrorising anyone we need to work for us or for running errands, but thinking for himself? He has completely underestimated how smart Eddie Fairbanks seems to be.

She inwardly sighed then snatching a glance at him, she said, "We still need to supply them with a gun. Can you get another one?"

He didn't immediately respond, but then slowly replied, "Stand on me, Sadie, that won't be a problem."

CHAPTER SIXTEEN.

DC Jaya Bahn was both tired and stressed out of her box because of the Saturday evening traffic that was twice as heavy due to the football crowd exiting Hampden Park, for not only was she bursting for a pee, but the supercilious attitude of that *cow* of a Depute Fiscal she'd collected the warrant from didn't help either.
She took a deep breath and fought to compose herself when she knocked on the large, and imposing Victorian dwelling where the duty Sheriff resided.
The door was opened by a matronly, blonde-haired woman who staring at Bahn, softly smiled then said, "You must be the detective that we received the call about. Is that right?"
"Yes, Ma'am," Bahn forced a smile, her nose twitching at the smell of cooked food and her stomach reminding her she'd had nothing since breakfast.
"Come away in, my dear," the woman, beckoned her forward, then her eyebrows arching, she said, "Goodness, dear, you look all in. Do you have time for a cup of tea?"
Taken aback by the woman's unexpected kindness, Bahn shook her head when she replied, "I regret not, Ma'am. The warrant I'm to get signed is time critical; however," she lowered her voice when her face wrinkled, "if I might use your loo?"
"Here," the woman reached for the paperwork held by Bahn, then smiled, "I used to work as a court official before that lout of a husband of mine made a good woman of me, as they say. So, you away into the cloakroom there," she waved a hand at a closed door, "and I'll wake him from his nap."
In the surprisingly spacious cloakroom toilet, it occurred to Bahn that she should not have handed the warrant application to the Sheriff's wife, for protocol was she was too formally swear in front of him that the information contained in the application was true. With a frustrated sigh at her schoolgirl error, she quickly finished her toilet then washing her hands, dashed from the loo to find the Sheriff

and his wife stood in the hallway, waiting for her.

With his glasses perched on his nose and wearing what to Bahn looked like a ragged grey coloured cardigan, green corduroy trousers she would not have used as rags and slippers with his big toe peeking out from the right one, the silver-haired sheriff stared at her when he asked, "DC Bahn, is it? Didn't I see you in my court earlier this year?"

"Ah, yes, Milord," a sudden sense of misgiving overtook her.

"At the beginning of the year, I think it was. A serious domestic assault where the husband battered his wife and then she skelped him…I mean, when she struck her husband over the head with a frying pan."

"And if memory serves me correctly," his eyes narrowed when he slowly replied, "you were in attendance when the affray was on going?"

Her stomach fell when nodding, then it was as if she was back in his court when she replied, "That's correct, Milord. I'd answered the call on my radio from nearby the locus and had to baton the man after he knocked his wife to the floor, then attacked me."

"And again, as I recall," he beat with a forefinger at his chin and his brow furrowed with recollection, "you said in evidence that twenty of his stitches were attributed to you?"

She gulped when again she nodded and thought oh hell, this isn't going well.

To her astonishment, the Sheriff turned to his wife, then gleefully said, "See, I told you I recognised the name. This is the young woman I was telling you about. Whacked the bugger for six and into unconsciousness, so she did!"

Turning to Bahn, he grinned, "And I've waited for some time to tell you this, DC Bahn; well done, lass," he vigorously nodded. "If ever a man deserved a beating, that *bastard* most certainly did!"

"Archie! Language," his wife chided him.

With a wide grin, he handed the signed warrant to a stunned Bahn, then she was even more taken aback when leading her to the door, his wife pressed a plastic travel mug into her hand and a sandwich wrapped in tinfoil, telling her, "Coffee and I hope you take milk and I've put a wee spoonful of sugar in too, dear. I hope I'm not insulting your religion, but the sandwich is sliced ham and mayonnaise, if you're okay with that?"

Surprised, Bahn stuttered, "Right now, Ma'am, I'm that hungry I'd eat a monkey dipped in fat."

Outside, making her way to the car, a suddenly rejuvenated Bahn found herself smiling and all thought of the heavy traffic and sarcastic Fiscal now gone, slipping in to the driver's seat she first took a much-needed sip of the coffee before starting the engine.

****

Excited that the day had gone so well, Ronnie Masters would not take no for an answer and sitting her deputy, Laura, and the young stylist, Gemma, down onto the couch, insisted they stay for pizza and a glass of wine.

"And while I'm still buzzing," she lifted her phone to text Eddie Fairbanks that they had visitors and asking, did he have a time for returning home, requesting he bring in some vino while she would order the delivery of the pizza.

In his office with Larry Considine, Fairbanks read the text and smiled, then returned a text explaining that he had an on-going issue at work, but would call when he was returning home, only to read the returning text asked him to bring Susie Lauder with him, that Ronnie would contact her partner, Archie Wilmot, and have him come to the flat.

Laying the mobile phone back down onto his desk, he sighed, "This is the part that I hate. Having someone else do what I really want to do myself; get out there and chase the bad guys."

"That's what rank's all about though, Eddie," Considine decided that a little less formality was okay when they were alone. "You're on the up and up and before you know it, you'll be managing all the time from a desk. I'm sorry to remind you," he smiled, "but your days as a door to door investigator are over."

"Anyway, digressing completely, Larry, and on a personal not, if you don't mind me asking; how are you doing?"

Considine frowned when he said, "To be honest, I had a bit of a shakeup last night. I went into the cupboard and fetched out a bottle of Whyte and Mackay; not my favourite, but when you get to be an alcoholic, sometimes beggars aren't all choosers, if you get my drift."

He paused and slowly shaking his head, continued, "I reached into the cupboard for a glass when my missus walked into the kitchen, took one look at what I was doing, then very quietly told me that if I poured myself a whisky, *one* whisky, mind you, she was packing a case and gone."

He sighed when he added, "Then she said she would ensure that the kids…kids," he smiled. They're, twenty-six and twenty-four. Anyway, she said the kids would side with her and I'd not see them again."

"Sounds like a loving blackmail, if there is such a thing."

"Aye, maybe, but the thing is, Eddie, I didn't pour that whisky. Can you believe that?" he shook his head as though the very notion surprised himself.

"As much as I needed that *fucking* drink, I did *not* pour that whisky." He drew a deep breath then said, "By this time of the day, I would have been down at my car and fetched out that half bottle that's in the glove compartment, but curiously, this is the first day in as long as I remember that I *haven't* visited my car."

"So, how do you feel now?"

"How do I feel?" he wryly smiled.

"Truthfully? My guts are churning, my nerves are shredded and I'm barely holding it together, but I just know that if I take one sip of whisky, just one sip, I'll feel *so* much better."

"Then," Fairbanks eyes narrowed, "why don't you take that one sip, Larry?"

Seconds passed before he softly responded with, "Because that one sip would cost me dearly and I'm not talking about my pension or commutation. I'm talking about my family and some things are more precious and valuable than my addiction."

They sat in silence for minutes, each with his own thoughts, then Fairbanks said, "You do know that the offer to meet my Ronnie still stands?"

Slowly nodding, Considine took a painful swallow, then replied, "When and where, I'll make myself available."

It was then they both startled when the desk phone rang.

"DI Fairbanks."

"Boss, Duke Smythe. Is Larry with you?"

"He's here, Duke," Fairbanks pressed the speaker button on the phone, then said, "Go ahead."

"We're in and no need for the warrant after all and with Mrs Collins permission, I'm on the house landline."

He paused then continued, "Collins lived with his widowed mother.

Lovely home and according to her, he's the perfect son. No siblings and needless to say, the poor woman is distraught, so I've asked Susie to contact her GP and he's agreed to come out to see to her. Anyway, it seems too she had an idea her son had an injury to his leg, but of course had no idea how severe the injury was. In fact, she admitted he was quite evasive about it and even shouted at her not to bother him about it."

Fairbanks had a bad feeling about this, that they'd got the wrong man, then asked, "Any indication of his affiliation to any organisation or support for one?"

Though Smythe thought it an odd question, he didn't ask why Fairbanks was so curious, but replied, "Other than he seems to have been a regular attender at Ibrox and he's got Rangers Football Club posters on his bedroom wall, nothing that seems to link him to Loyalism, if that's what you're wanting to know?"

"It is," Fairbanks admitted then heard Mickey Rooney's voice in the background when he called out, "Duke, come and a have a look at this."

A full minute passed, before Smythe returned to the phone, then his voice expressing his curiosity, said, "Something a wee bit odd there, boss."

"Odd how?"

"Well," Smythe drawled, "for a mad Rangers supporter as he seemed to have been, Mickey's found a plastic bag stuffed at the bottom of his wardrobe."

Smythe paused, then sighed, "I'll ask his mother to see if she knows anything about it, but curiously, Collins has what looks like a brand new, three-hole black balaclava and a brand new, still in its wrapper, Celtic football top."

****

Pushing open the front door to the office in the Lanark Way Community Initiative building, Arlene McCandlish, turned to tell her two minders, Axel and Johnny, to go grab themselves a cuppa, then smiled at her assistant, Constance McKenzie.

"I'm sorry to have dragged you out on a Saturday," she shrugged then slumped down into the chair in front of McKenzie's desk. "I'm sure you must have had other things to tend to instead of running after me."

"What?" McKenzie dryly grinned at her, "you mean, the washing and ironing and trying to sort out that wee plot of garden at the front of the house? No, thank you. I think I'd rather be here."

She thoughtfully glanced at McCandlish when she asked, "How did the interview go?"

McCandlish shrugged again when she replied, "Just the usual questions. Can you confirm you are still a senior member of the UDA? No," she made a face. "Have you any information about the whereabouts of the missing who were allegedly murdered by the UDA during the Troubles? No," she sighed with a shake of her head. "Can you confirm the UDA have in fact surrendered all their weapons? Yes, of course," then smiled when she added, "As if they'll believe that one."

"But nothing contentious? Nothing about the meeting in Glasgow?"

"Fortunately it seems that the word isn't out, so no; security is still tight about that," she shook her head. "No questions about Glasgow."

"And on that point," she continued, "I assume the tickets are all booked and arrangements confirmed?"

"Yes," McKenzie nodded. "On Monday, early morning passage has been booked on the ferry to Cairnryan. I've also booked our tickets for the return on the evening ferry on Wednesday."

It was no secret that in the years following the Good Friday Agreement, security at the arrival and departure ports to the UK's mainland had lapsed and was now more a perfunctory issue, handled primarily by basic wage security teams, than a serious lookout for travellers flagged on the Security Services watch-list.

And so, McKenzie continued, "You, me and the lads and I will be travelling over in a black coloured Ford Mondeo estate car I've hired for us as a party of four family members heading over to Glasgow for a wedding. Albeit we'll be accommodated by our supporters over there, I've taken the precaution of booking rooms at the Premier Inn, just off George Square, in our false names in case we're asked where we're staying. Needless to say, I've paid a deposit, but we won't be using the hotel. I've also hired the Mondeo under an alias, though from a sympathiser's company who knows not to ask too many questions. As far as security is concerned, at the minute I'm the only one who has all the details. I thought it better that way so there's no leaks or any accidental giving out information."

"And you have arranged false identities for the four of us?"

"All done," McKenzie smiled with a nod, then said, "The only hiccup is that the boys won't be able to take their sidearms with them, so we'll be travelling without armed protection."

"Well, God willing," McCandlish's brow creased, "if security remains tight, then we shouldn't need armed protection."

"Don't worry," McKenzie reassured her with a nod, "I've got it all sewn up."

****

With the return to Maryhill Police Office of Duke Smythe and his team, Eddie Fairbanks decided to have quick de-brief of the whole team together, then telling them as much as they needed to know, that their victim was a known Loyalist supporter who apparently was somehow connected with a new Loyalist group, the Friends of Ulster Loyalists; that it was assessed Crawford was holding the firearm to be collected by an unidentified third party and that the collection had been arranged on the telephone by a man also yet to be identified.

Was it the same individual?

Nothing to confirm that other than it now seemed likely the man on the phone, thought to be at least forty years of age or older, and the suspected killer, Andrew Collins, did not appear to be the same individual.

Then, about to dismiss them for a ten o'clock return the following morning, the phone on Larry Considine's desk rang.

Pausing to permit the DS to answer the call, Fairbanks eyes narrowed when Considine held up his hand for the room's attention, then nodding, they heard him say, "Yes, grateful thanks."

Replacing the handset, he stared poker-faced at Fairbanks, then said, "That was the duty scientist calling from the Forensics at Pitt Street."

"She's aware of our investigation being time critical and so expeditated the examination of the blood and DNA that SOCO collected from Andrew Collins body."

He slowly grinned when he added, "It's a match for the samples taken from the dog's mouth."

The muted cheer that went around the room, slowly died when a relieved Fairbanks held up his hand to say, "Okay, I know, we've now identified our killer, but we've still a lot of work to do, guys. We don't know why Jimmy Crawford was murdered or who sent Collins to kill him. That and could it be Collins who Crawford was holding the gun for? That and why was Collins, a season ticket holder at Ibrox, in possession of a bag containing a balaclava and a Celtic top, his own teams' nemesis?"

"Duke," he singled out the big man. "Did Collins happen to have a mobile phone?"

"Have it with us and bagged as a production, boss. It's security locked, but I'll get it to the Techies tomorrow, see if they can unlock it."

"If they can't," said a DC's voice to laughter, "I know a guy."

Grateful for the team's good humour and brought on by the killer's identification, Fairbanks held up a hand for quiet then slowly glanced around the room before he continued, "Much as I would like to tell you that this murder investigation is concluded, I regret that it has not. In fact, ladies and gentlemen, it seems we are about to delve into the world of Irish terrorism."

He paused to gather his thoughts, then continued, "With the discovery of our killer, a number of inquiries have arisen, not least for what purpose the gun was to be used, by whom and when. Andrew Collins?" he pursed his lips when he shrugged.

"Perhaps, but if so, who is the man assessed to be aged between forty and sixty years of age who contacted Crawford from a Loyalist pub in the east end to arrange the pick-up of the weapon."

He saw Jaya Bahn's hand raised and said, "Yes, Jaya?"

"Do we *now* know who provided our victim with the gun, sir?"

He slowly exhaled, then deciding not to lie, nodded when he replied, "Yes, we do, Jaya, but at the minute, I'd prefer to keep that information between myself and DS Considine."

He had no doubt that the team knew exactly to whom he was referring, but was pleased that none of them pursued the issue. Then, as if by way of explanation for his intransigence, he said, "Look, I hate having to ask you to work in the dark, but there are certain matters that at the minute must remain confidential. However, that said, you are all bright and intelligent police officers…"

"Except Duke Smythe," came a voice from the back.

To laughter, he replied, "That's a bit harsh, even if it's true."

When the banter had calmed down, he smiled when he said, "I appreciate your support and the fact you might feel you're working with one hand tied behind your back, but I promise you; when I know the whole story, you'll know the whole story, so until tomorrow, ladies and gentleman. Thank you."

As the team dispersed, it was then he saw Bobby Heggerty, wearing a green oilskin jacket and denim trousers with a brown coloured flat cap on his head, standing just within the doorway.

Heggerty was smiling and patting arms and shoulders as the team greeted him when leaving the room and when the room was clear with just Fairbanks and Considine left, he approached and with a grim smile, said, "Thought I'd pop by for a visit. So, Eddie, what have I missed?"

****

Driving her car to the Merchant City, Archie Wilmot had been surprised when Susie had phoned to say she didn't need picked up, that Eddie Fairbanks was giving her a lift and he was to meet her at Ronnie Masters flat.

Wilmot, the owner, editor, chief and sole reporter as well as the general dogsbody, as he often described himself, of the free newspaper, the West End Chronicle, assumed that they were to have dinner or something at the flat.

These days they often socialised with Eddie and Ronnie, a couple he had become extremely fond of since he and Susie had become themselves become a couple.

If truth be told though, he was a little in awe of the beautiful Ronnie, not because *of* her beauty, but having once been an international model who graced the covers of so many prestigious magazines, then having so spectacularly fallen from grace, she had risen like a phoenix. Her widely reported drug and alcohol addictions, her brief imprisonment in New York and the media frenzy that resulted after her humiliating return to London; yet she survived and having beaten her addictions, was the owner of her own bespoke boutique and now a successful businesswoman.

Yes, there was a lot to admire about that woman and though he wouldn't admit to it, sometimes wondered if Ronnie might agree to an interview with him for his own paper.

As for Eddie, since his days as a cub reporter working in Birmingham, Wilmot's dealings with the West Midlands force had caused him to mistrust the police. Yet during his initial dealings with the then Detective Sergeant Fairbanks, he soon come to realise he had tarred all cops with the same brush, for never before he had so quickly developed a liking and trust for another man.

Then there was Susie, he involuntarily smiled, for cop or not, she was *definitely* the one.

He'd often wondered about Eddie and Ronnie's relationship, a relationship Susie had intimated was initially very acrimonious, but to see them together now, he often hoped that both he and Susie's feelings for each other would be as open and as strong as was theirs.

Stopping the car in a bay outside the building where Ronnie's flat was located, Wilmot switched off the engine, then sat for several minutes, gathering his thoughts.

It had been less than six months since he had been dating Susie, yet already he was checking out engagement rings on the web and wondered if it was too soon?

Curiously, and to his own surprise, his next thought was, maybe I should speak to Eddie about it.

Getting out of the car, he glanced up at the building then fetching a bunch of flowers and a bottle of prosecco from the boot, made his way to the front security door.

****

They were in Fairbanks car and en-route to Ronnie's flat before Susie Lauder said, "Couldn't help notice that the boss turned up at the end of the briefing."

"Yeah, and thanks for hanging on for that ten minutes, Susie. He just popped by on his way to collect a carry-out for him and his missus and to collect something from his desk," he glanced at her and smiled.

Yet close friend that Susie had become, he couldn't share with her that Bobby Heggerty had really visited to inform his DI that on Monday, he was attending the Beatson for a colonoscopy and likely wouldn't be returning for at least a week; if ever, he had dryly added.

That and he had elicited a promise that the following day, Fairbanks would meet Heggerty at the café located within the Botanic Gardens to update him on what was happening in the murder investigation.

"But the gardens?" he had asked, only for Heggerty to shrug and reply, "If Cathy finds out I've come into the office, she'll literally have my balls for earrings, so aye, the gardens and you being a DI now, you're paying," Heggerty had grinned.

Turning to glance at her to change the subject, he teased, "You and Archie?"

"What about me and Archie," she had narrowed her eyes, knowing fine well what he was implying.

"You know he's the one for you, don't you?"

"What, like *I* knew Ronnie was the one for you? Who do you think you are, Fairbanks? Me?"

"Oh, no" he grinned, "I'm many things, Susie, but I do *not* have your female intuition."

What Susie Lauder didn't know was that Eddie Fairbanks considered his younger friend and junior rank to be not just one of his brightest staff, but one of the most intuitive detectives he had ever worked with, and so his brow creased when he said, "And on that subject. You know that I trust your instinct, Susie, and you've not let me down yet, so what do you make of the balaclava and Celtic top that was found in Andrew Collins bedroom? I mean, it's a complete contradiction, isn't it? Him apparently being a season ticket holder at Ibrox and all?"

"Well," she slowly drawled as her brow furrowed in thought, "to be honest, I've been wracking my brains about that, Eddie, and I've narrowed it down to one of two explanations."

She took a soft breath then exhaled, "The balaclava. That's at complete odds with anything else we found in his wardrobe. Woollen tammy's yes, skip caps, yes, but a brand new, label still attached to it, three-hole balaclava?"

She slowly nodded when she added, "You already know what I'm thinking. That it was to be used as a disguise."

"And the Celtic top?"

"Well, as regards the first explanation, Duke asked his mother if she knew of any Celtic supporting friends he had, but curiously, she didn't and even went so far as to tell us how quiet he was, that he kept himself to himself and other than football matches or the occasional evenings out himself for a pint, didn't socialise much. A very attentive young man to his mother, was how she described him."

"So the Celtic top wasn't a possible gift, say for a workmate or someone?"

"Apparently not, but Duke suggested to Larry Considine to organise an Action for someone to attend tomorrow at the call centre where

Collins worked over in Hamilton to ask about any pals he might have there."

"On a Sunday?"

"It's a seven day, twenty-four hour insurance company. You know," her face creased, "a modern day sweat shop; a huge aircraft hangar like building and minimum wage staff?"

"Right," he nodded, "and the second explanation?"

She turned to stare at him and took a deep breath when she said, "Again a disguise. What I think is called a false flag. Collins was going to wear the balaclava to hide his face, which means he intended getting away with whatever he planned. And wearing the Celtic top? Maybe it was his intention of having anyone who saw him believe he was a Celtic supporter. And," her brow furrowed, "because you said in your briefing this is likely now an Irish terrorism issue."

She paused to give it a few seconds thought, then unconsciously chewing at the inside of her mouth, she continued, "I'm thinking the Celtic top by definition would make any eye witnesses assume him to be a Celtic supporter or, if we're talking Irish terrorism, an Irish Republican supporter."

His mind reeling and with sudden recollection of the discovery of the handgun, he then softly muttered, "And if there had to be witnesses to whatever Collins was planning, it would suggest it's to be a public incident."

He turned swiftly to glance at her when he hissed, "Jesus, Susie, are you suggesting Collins planned to publicly murder someone, commit some kind of assassination?"

Wordlessly, she pouted when she shrugged that it was one possibility, but it was enough to start him thinking.

He slapped one hand against the steering wheel when he added, "Which begs the questions of when, where, who and why?"

CHAPTER SEVENTEEN: Sunday 24 September 2006.

Throughout what was intended to be a relaxing celebration of her successful photo shoot Ronnie Masters sensed the tension that existed when Eddie arrived with Susie, and with as much courtesy and decorum as she could muster, had ended the evening a little after ten.

When their guests had left, it was Eddie who quickly apologised when he'd said, "Sorry, I can't discuss what's going on, but just when Susie and I were in the car coming back to the flat, she came up with a suggestion that means though we've identified our killer, it's probably just the start of what's going to be a lengthy investigation."

Though he realised she was a little disappointed that the night had been a little edgier than she'd anticipated, he had smiled when throwing her arms about his neck, she had saucily replied, "I think I know how you can make it up to me."

"Gladly," he'd hugged her tightly before grimacing, "But only if you don't mind me finishing the last of the pizza. I'm famished."

****

He was awake before seven that Sunday morning, hearing first the gentle pitter-patter of rain on the bedroom window, but surprised then to hear Ronnie already in the en-suite and startled when through the partially closed door, he heard her retching.

Jumping up from the bed, he hurried through to the well-lit room to see her wearing her nightie, kneeling with one hand on the toilet bowl and the other holding back her hair, her face chalk-white and her body shaking as the nausea swept over her.

"Ronnie," he knelt beside her, seeing her discharge the yellowy bile into the bowl, then held her tightly to him.

"Sorry," she gasped as her body again heaved, then taking a deep sigh, she half-turned to sit on the tiled floor, too embarrassed to look at him because she realised the violent retching had caused her to pee herself.

Grabbing at a hand towel from a stack on the utility unit, he gently wiped at her mouth when smiling, she sighed, "I'm so sorry, Eddie, I had hoped you wouldn't see me like this."

"See you like...what?" stunned, his eyes widened when he asked, "You've been sick before?"

A cold chilling fear coursed through his body, but he didn't give her time to respond when he pressed on, "Ronnie, are you ill? Tell me! Please!"

She stared him in the eye then shaking her head, she softly replied, "No, Eddie, not ill."

"Then what…" he stopped, his eyes locked on hers with a growing suspicion.

"Wait a minute, are you…I mean, you're not…" he daren't even form the words, but just stared at her and saw her shoulders slump when she replied, "Yes. I'm pregnant. About six weeks, I think. Maybe seven?"

She swallowed the nausea and fought back the urge to again heave, while subtly sliding the hand towel beneath her bottom.

"Me," she tried to wryly smile, but coughed and swallowed the phlegm that again threatened to erupt from her, "who because of my addictions, never thought I'd ever have a baby. Well, that what my New York doctor told me anyway," her voice tailed off with a caustic sigh.

In those few heartbeats that seemed to last for minutes, they both experienced differing emotions; Ronnie, fearful that her news would evoke in him the memory of being lied to and cheated by her sister, Gill, while in those short seconds, his heart thumping in his chest, she could not know that he was vainly trying to compose the words that expressed his complete joy.

Staring at his expressionless face, a cold hand gripped Ronnie's heart, but it was then to her surprise, she saw his jaw quite literally drop and he suddenly grinned when he heard himself say, "Ronnie Masters, will you marry me?"

****

Arthur Denholm, the man known to the Friends of Ulster Loyalists as the Commandant, was an anxious man.

Sent by his lazy sod of a wife to collect milk and bread from the Spar on Thornliebank Road, a woman too idle to get off her arse and do the shopping, not for the first time it crossed his mind to have one of his volunteers do him a personal favour and bury her body on Eaglesham Moor.

His thoughts returned to the worrying lack of contact from Andrew Collins, the man personally groomed by him to carry out the important mission bestowed upon the fledgling FUL; to his knowledge, the first time the Inner Council had designated such an operation to a group not based in the Province.

Parking the car that quiet Sunday morning on the main road outside the shop, he fetched the burner phone from the glove compartment, then opening it, was dismayed to see no new calls or text message.

Drumming his fingers nervously on the steering wheel, he decided if he hadn't heard from Collins by lunchtime, he'd ring his phone and if there was no answer, he'd have to assume the worse.

But maybe, just maybe, if Collins was working today, his brow creased, then decision made he opened the burner phone.

Minutes later and still unable to speak with Collins, he sat pensively mulling over in his mind of all the dark reasons why the younger man had not been in touch.

Suddenly, during those few minutes, his previous unwavering belief and resolve in his comrades across the Irish Sea failed him. If somehow Collins been compromised and if that *was* so, it would mean phoning the phone number that the member of the Belfast inner council had given to him as the local contact; a phone number that he was warned against writing down.

The unnamed contact who would either tell him to continue with the plan as it were, to make alternative arrangement's or worst-case scenario, to stand-down.

But Denholm knew if he was ordered to stand-down, there would be consequences, for the member of the Inner Council had made it quite clear that so important was the mission, failure was not an option.

A cold dread passed through him and his stomach churned for he knew too that to protect the integrity of the operation, just as Jimmy Crawford had to be silenced, it was not beyond the realm of possibility the Inner Council member might decide, so too should he.
****

Driving to Maryhill Police Office that morning, Susie Lauder thought again of Ronnie's polite, but firm ending of the evening and knew there was definitely something going on.

She had no qualms that their relationship was on an even keel; God, she thought, you only have to see the way that he looks at Ronnie and she him, to know they're meant for each other.

Her thoughts turned to Eddie Fairbanks and she wondered at the trust he placed in her.

Yes, she acknowledged they'd had a good working relationship during the poison pen investigation that resulted in a murder, and she'd be forever grateful that he, an experienced DS had often sought and acted upon her advice and instinct.

But this latest murder and the death of the suspect Andrew Collins, coupled with her suggestion that Collins was involved in the preparation of some sort of false flag murder. Was she adding two and two together and coming up with five?

Yet Eddie was no fool for she was certain that though he hadn't said, he'd likely himself arrived at the same conclusion.

No matter, it was gratifying that though he was now a DI and she a DC, he retained the ability to listen to and take from his team the best of their ideas.

It was then another thought struck her.

Her eyes narrowed and she took a deep breath, then unconsciously stepped down a little harder on the accelerator, for she was eager to get to the office and share that thought.

****

Still stunned by the news he was to become a father and even more so that Ronnie had said yes to his marriage proposal, Eddie Fairbanks phoned the incident room from the flat, confident that Larry Considine would already be at his desk.

"Morning, Larry, Eddie here. Listen, my apologies, I'm going to be about half an hour late this morning and I'll explain when I see you. Keep the team at the office till I get there. Oh, and I've spoken with Ronnie. She says if you're okay after our discussion and you still want to have a chat with her, to come by about twelve. One other thing, she's intending asking a friend to come by who she implicitly trusts, so she says to let you know that you're not being ambushed. Anyway, as far as I'm concerned," he smiled at the phone, "you're okay to leave for the meeting and you're not indispensable, so I'm sure we'll get by without you for the rest of the day. Okay?"

"Okay, Eddie, and thanks," Considine breathed a heavy sigh.

After ending the call, he returned to the kitchen where Ronnie, wearing her dressing robe was clearing away the breakfast dishes. Wrapping his arms around her waist, he suddenly jerked back and stared wide-eyed at her stomach, but she laughed then said, "It won't hurt the baby just because you're giving me a tight hug."

"Oh, my God, Ronnie, I can't tell you how happy I am," he widely grinned.

"Nor me," she placed her hands on his cheeks and drawing him to her, kissed him fiercely on the lips.

"Have you…I mean…"

"Told anyone? No," she shook her head, then said, "So far it's just between you, me and the Clearblue pregnancy test, but I have a

sneaking suspicion that my deputy, Laura, has already guessed, so now that my fiancé…" she stopped and giggled. "It sounds funny, me saying that, but I love the sound of it."
Taking a deep breath, she continued "So now that my *fiancé* knows, I'd better make an appointment with my GP for a referral to…"
Her brow wrinkled, when she added, "You know, for all that I'm a woman of thirty-five, I have no idea how to go about having a baby, who I should talk with or what."
"Well, we'll learn together and believe me, I am *so* looking forward to making plans with you and for our baby," he smiled, then eyes narrowing and his face creasing, asked, "How's the nausea?"
She shrugged when she suggested, "I think it's a morning thing only because I've been well during the rest of the day."
"I can't believe that I haven't noticed you being sick," he apologetically sighed.
"Because I've been careful in case…" she hesitated, worried her explanation might somehow tempt fate, "In case it didn't work out. The pregnancy, I mean."
Seconds passed, then before he could respond, she said, "That and to be honest and do not ask me to explain it," she held the palm of her hand towards him, when she grimaced, "The last week, I've had a curious urge to eat liquorice."
He stared bemused at the small, black square in her hand before he asked, "You like liquorice?"
"Not really," she grimaced when she shook her head, "but I think I'm having a craving; so, if you happen to be passing a sweetie shop?"
"Liquorice. Got it," he nodded then kissing her, said, "Time I was off. Any, eh, issues, anything at all, phone me."
He had gone from the flat just a few minutes when Ronnie decided to sit with another cup of tea, then reflected on her relationship with Eddie.
It was no surprise to her that she had never been happier, that her turbulent history was now a thing of the past. A successful woman with her own business and now, not only was she having the baby she never believed she could conceive, but with the man who loved her as she loved him.
She smiled as she sipped at her tea and unconsciously patted at her stomach, then thought, for once her life was on the up and having no

doubt of Eddie's love for her, what could go possibly wrong?
****

Bobby Heggerty completely understood his wife Cathy's anxiety for his health and the apprehension that the colonoscopy procedure the following day could bring the worse of news, but he was becoming a little irritated at her claustrophobic monitoring of him.

"But if you're going to the Kelvingrove Park for a walk, why wouldn't you want me to come with you?"

He sighed when a little more brittle than he intended, he said, "Look, I love you dearly, but I need some time on my own. Is that too much to ask?"

Stung by his response, she shied away, the hurt evident on her face, then reaching for her, took her by the arms and said, "Look, to be honest, I'm going to the café to meet with Eddie Fairbanks, my DI." He quickly held up his hand when he continued, "I'm not getting involved in any investigations, I promise you, but you've heard me talk about Eddie. He's a good one, that young guy, and I've left him in the lurch with a murder investigation and the Department to run. That and he's got that bugger Alex Gardener sticking his nose in to try and find out why I'm not at my desk."

"Alex Gardener?" she stared at him, her expression one of confusion.

He didn't immediately respond, knowing he'd creaked open the lid of a can of worms, then softly explained, "Ever since you dumped him, he's been looking for any excuse to get one over on me."

"What? I can't believe that…" she raised her hand to her mouth as her eyes widened, "You can't mean because of me! Why didn't you tell me about this?"

"*Because* you chose me," he smiled at her, "and for what it's worth, while I know I'm punching above my weight, I still think you made the best choice."

She stared at him, her eyes glazing over with unshed tears and gently stroked at his cheek when she replied, "Yes I did make the best choice, but I'm shocked that Alex would carry a grudge all these years."

"If I were him," he continued to smile at her, "I think I'd still be hurting too, if you'd chosen him."

Her lips quivered as she continued to stroke at his cheek, then slowly nodding, said, "Go and meet your DI, but I'm dropping you off at the café and I'll be picking you up, no matter how long your meeting goes on. That's *not* negotiable, Bobby."

"Okay," he nodded, "and I'll bring you back a cream cake."

****

Yawning widely and wishing she were still at home in bed and not on shift at police headquarters, the duty technician took off her wet rain jacket, then carrying it by the collar along the corridor, stopped and listened.

Yes, there it was again, a phone ringing, a mobile phone and it was coming from the locked cupboard that served as the production room, where phones seized in major investigations were stored.

As far as the technician knew, there was only one phoned seized that was to be unlocked and that was from the on-going Maryhill murder investigation.

Hurrying to the supervisor's office, she saw her boss at his desk, then said, "Quick, you got the key to the production room."

"Eh, morning and yes. Why?" his eyes narrowed.

"I'm sure I heard a phone ringing and there's only one in the cupboard at the minute."

Fumbling in his desk, the supervisor handed her the Chubb key and watched her race off.

Following her to the cupboard at a more sedate pace that his age and girth would permit, the supervisor saw her standing by the open door, now wearing nitrile gloves, her ear to the phone from which a lengthy piece of string and a production label trailed, and listening intently.

"Sod it," he heard her mutter then he asked, "What?"

She slowly shook her head when she sighed, "I missed the call, but there was a message left. A man's voice asking…no," she her eyebrows knit, "not asking; telling volunteer Collins to contact the Commandant, immediately."

The supervisor sighed when he said, "I think you'd better give Larry Considine a phone at Maryhill to let him know what you heard and after you do that, prioritise unlocking that phone. We'll need the calling number to try and obtain a name and address."

****

Upon his arrival at the rear yard of Maryhill Police Office, he had to sit for a few minutes in his car to again take in Ronnie's news.

Happy as he had been when she broke the news, the more thought he gave to her pregnancy and what it would mean to them as a couple, the more anxious he became.

His worries and doubts resulted from his fear that Ronnie, relating what she read and being thirty-six years of age when she delivered the baby, admitted she would be more at risk than a younger mother and he knew that he could not risk losing this woman.

But what was the option; to trust to fate or…he took a deep breath at the shocking thought, terminating the pregnancy?

No, he unconsciously shook his head that was *definitely* not an option.

He could not know that his fears were those experienced by most fathers whose wife or partner was a woman of mature years and with a sickening feeling in the pit of his stomach, realised that come hell or high water, no matter the outcome, he and Ronnie would see the pregnancy through. He wryly smiled when, he remembered back in the day in uniform and about to go through a door to tackle a violent wife-beater, a much older and wiser neighbour drawing his baton, before telling him, "Prepare for the worst, Eddie, but hope for the best."

Minutes later he opened the door to the incident room and, as he had instructed, the team were all present and patiently waiting on the mornings briefing.

However, his attention was drawn to Larry Considine who beckoned to him, then related the information from the technician at Pitt Street.

"I know the supervisor," Considine intimated. "He's a good guy and he's instructed his techie work on the phone to try and unlock it for the calling number."

"I'm a bit of a technophobe when it comes to mobiles," Fairbanks, frowned.

"How was she able to hear the recorded message without the phone being unlocked?"

"I asked that too. Apparently when a call comes in, as you know you don't need to unlock the phone to respond to it and just as the lassie hit the green button to respond to the call, though the caller had just finished speaking, for some reason even the supervisor can't explain, she got through to the voicemail and picked up the message that had just been recorded. It might have been an anomaly," Considine shrugged, "but it's worked in our favour."

"The Commandant. The man who apparently is running this local Loyalist group, the Friends of Ulster Loyalists," Fairbanks pondered. All thoughts of his cheerful news now pushed to the back of his mind, he stared at the DS before he made a decision, then said, "Unless you've any reason for me not to divulge the whole story?" Considine knew exactly what he meant, so nodding, he said, "If the team are warned about sharing what we tell them, then I think they should be warned about what and who we might be up against. That," he grimaced, "and if there's already been one firearm involved…"

He left the rest unsaid, for they were both conscious of the devastation to the Department's morale caused by the murder of their colleague, Geraldine McEwan, and it was absolutely correct that their colleagues be aware there might be the possibility of a further threat to life.

"Fair enough," Fairbanks nodded, then loudly clapping his hands, he called out, "Right, guys and gals, here's what is happening. But first, who remembers when they joined the polis, they signed the Official Secrets Act?"

CHAPTER EIGHTEEN.

DC Jaya Bahn and her neighbour, DC Brian Saunders, decided that on the road to the call centre where Andrew Collins had been employed, they'd catch some breakfast en-route.

Stopping at the Tim Horton's located just two minutes from the call centre, they collected coffee's and sandwiches that they devoured in the car before heading to the building.

"You know we'll be breaking the news about his death, too?" she told Saunders.

"Hadn't thought about that, but I don't suppose it will be like breaking the news to a family."

"He might have close friends there, so we'll play it by ear," she said.

Arriving at the building's security gate, Saunders lowered the driver's window to inform the security guard through the speaker box who they were and requested they be met by the duty manager at the front door.

Two minutes later and parked in a visitor's bay, they were met by a woman Bahn thought to be about fifty years of age, who wearing a black trouser business suit, her greying hair tied up in a bun and who introduced herself as Sam Cready, the duty manager.

Leading them to a small interview room and once they were seated, Bahn broke the news of Collins death to a visibly shocked Cready, then asked, "Given the number of staff you must employ here, was he well known to you?"

Swallowing with difficulty, she removed her glasses to dab at her tearstained eyes with a handkerchief before she replied, "Only as one of the junior supervisors. One of the staff mentioned yesterday that they thought it was his car involved in a bump just down the road. Is that what killed him? The accident?"

"We don't think so, but a post mortem will establish the cause of death."

"So," she took a deep breath, "how can we help you, DC Bahn?"

She and Saunders had already discussed how they would approach the subject of determining if Collins had any friends within the building and in particular, Celtic fans.

And so, she said, "Due to the curious nature of his death and," she quickly held up her hand, "not that we believe it to be suspicious, but we'd like to speak to any of his friends who might have noticed a difference in his recent behaviour. How he was feeling, that sort of thing?"

"Well, funny you should ask that," Cready began, "I thought he wasn't looking well yesterday and when I asked him," she again dabbed at her tearstained eyes, "he said he thought he was coming down with the cold, so I suggested he go home."

"And was he someone who had many friends in the building?"

She stared strangely at Bahn before she sighed, then in a low voice as though fearing being overheard, she said, "I certainly have no wish to speak ill of the dead, but Andrew? He was a curious sort of young man. Good at his job and that's why we promoted him to a supervisory position, but not the friendliest of people."

"Can we speak to his team, please?"

"Ah, yes," she hesitated before she asked, "But can I ask if this will take long?"

With a forced smile, Bahn replied, "As long as it takes to obtain the information we need."

Leaving the interview room, Cready led along a corridor, then up a wide, metallic stairway, their feet nosily ringing out as Saunders wondered, what kind of racket would this make with a couple of dozen people leaving at the same time.

Pushing open a door in the corridor on the first floor, Cready led them out onto a spacious gallery that towered above the floor below and where Bahn and Saunders could see the ground floor was divided into different areas, each area sub-divided into units where, Bahn estimated, at least a hundred people were at desks, most of whom wore headphones.

Seeing her expression, Cready explained, "We're the primary call centre for the company, so all calls, both UK and international, are routed through here. Now," she gestured towards a similar set-up on the gallery, where a couple of dozen people were at desks and again, most wearing headsets, "this is where Andrew worked and those eight over there, they're his team. If you wait here, I'll have them sign off their systems and you can speak with them either as a group, or if you want to speak to them individually, you can use the two interview rooms downstairs."

Bahn saw no benefit in taking time to conduct them downstairs to interview them individually, so instead suggested, "Perhaps we can speak with them in the corridor, as a group and dare I say, it's a little quieter there too."

"I'll bring them to you," Cready nodded, pleased that this wouldn't take her staff off the phones for long.

Minutes later, the door from the corridor opened to admit Cready, who led the eight workers out into the corridor, then turning, explained, "These are detectives from Maryhill. I'm afraid they have some sad news to impart."

The eight young men and women turned to stare at her and Saunders, the oldest, Bahn guessed, no more than in his late twenties and guessing most were probably students working part-time, then she said, "I'm sorry to have to inform you that yesterday afternoon, your colleague, Andrew Collins, died at Hairmyres Hospital."

The silence the greeted the news was broken when a young woman asked, "Was it the crash? We heard he'd crashed his car."

"Ah, no. The cause of Andrew's death has not been confirmed, but a post mortem examination is to be held."

It was the man, the oldest looking of the group and likely because of his full beard and lengthy ponytail, who then asked, "You're CID. Was he killed?"

"No," Bahn smiled, "it's not a murder. We're simply trying to find out if anyone who knew him has any suspicions as to him being unwell. Anything at all."

She couldn't fail to notice the glances between them nor the fact that none of them seemed particularly upset at the news of Collins death. "Were any of you a close friend of Andrew's?"

A young, redheaded man, no more than twenty-one or twenty-two, she thought, who stood at the back of the group and who sniggered, "Did he have any friends?"

Before she could respond, those around him cast reproving looks with one woman sneering, "Don't be a prick, Eric. The guy's dead." Shrugging, Eric added, "What? I'm only saying what everyone's thinking. The guy was a crabbit bugger, always finding fault and picking on Esther, there," he nodded towards a heavy-set young woman in her mid-twenties, her head downcast and blushing furiously.

"So, he wasn't popular, then?" Bahn directed her question at Eric.

"I didn't like him," he defensively replied, then continued, "When we were on the floor, he used to pick us up if we received a call on our mobiles, but it didn't stop him using his."

"On the floor means at their desks," Cready quietly explained.

"I think I got that," Bahn forced another smile, then asked Eric, "Did he have *any* friends here at the company?"

"Not to my knowledge," he glanced around the group, but nobody spoke up and several heads were turned down, staring at their feet.

"Curious question I know," she smiled reassuringly at them as she cast a glance around the group, "but do any of you know if Andrew had a friend here in the building who was a Celtic supporter?"

The knitted brows and creased faces that stared back told her what she wanted to know, so was about to thank Cready when the young woman Esther, said, "I don't know if it was a friend, but someone was looking for him yesterday morning, then again in the afternoon, but he'd already left by then," her voice trailed off and faded as though she realised she should have kept her mouth shut.

"Can I ask how you know this?"

Biting at her lower lip, Esther replied, "He was at the loo when the first call came into his desk phone, that was early in the shift, so I answered it and a man asked for him, then when I said Andrew was unavailable right then, he told me to get Andrew to phone him. Then he hung up on me. He was very rude, too," she sullenly added.
Fighting the urge to take the young woman to an interview room and grill her properly, she calmly smiled when she asked, "Did the man leave his name, who Andrew was to phone, I mean?"
"No," Esther shook her head, "just said Andrew would know who to call."
"Must've been a Ghostbuster," the same young man called Eric quipped, but nobody laughed or even smiled, though two of the women shook their heads at his insensitivity.
Ignoring him, Bahn asked Esther, "Do you know if Andrew made that call?"
"He didn't," her lips quivered and her eyes teared up.
"How do you know that?"
Seconds passed before Esther sniffed, then glancing guiltily at Cready, she muttered, "I forgot to tell him."
Bahn thought if Collins bullied Esther, it's more likely she deliberately didn't bother telling Collins and was now feeling guilty about it.
"Oh," was all Bahn said, then asked, "But the man phoned back later, you said."
"After Mrs Cready sent him home, yes," she turned to the manager as though to seek some sort of support.
"And it was you who again answered his desk phone?"
"Yes. It was the same man, but very angry and," her voice now low and on the verge of tears, she sobbed, "he swore at me."
The tense silence was broken when a thoughtful Bahn asked, "Mrs Cready. I'm surmising that in the event of a complaint or such thing, your company will record all incoming calls, so I'm guessing, too, you have call related data?"
****

Arthur Denholm decided that he'd be better calling from his car than at home where his wife, Cecilia, might overhear, and so drove a short distance from his house before stopping.
Parking in the nearby Orchard Park Drive, he readied himself for a moment, then dialled the number.

The gruff voiced man with a grating Glasgow accent answered his call with, "Is there a problem?"

Taking a deep breath and conscious that his body was shaking, Denholm replied, "It's the Commandant," he tried to inject some authority into his voice, then continued, "I can't contact my volunteer. He isn't answering his mobile."

"And why is that a problem?"

He gulped, all confidence gone by the man's own authoritarian voice, then stammered, "He's the one, the volunteer I mean, who was to find another…you know, a thing."

"A thing?" The man's voice oozed sarcasm.

Denholm tightly closed his eyes and wondered, why was he so afraid of a voice, yet incredibly, he *was* afraid.

"My volunteer, if he's to successfully carry out his mission, he'll need another one, a thing I mean, but he's gone AWOL."

He liked that word, AWOL; made him sound military.

"AWOL," the man sneeringly repeated, then sighed heavily when he added, "and you need another *thing*, do you?"

He knew he was being baited, teased even, but the voice quite literally had the power of life and death over him, so biting back a retort, he hissed, "Yes. Can you help?"

There was a silent pause of several seconds that seemed overly long to the anxious Denholm who thought the call had been cut off. Finally, the man replied, "Eastwood Old Cemetery on Thornliebank Road. "You know where I'm talking about?"

"Ah, yes, I do, it's up by…"

"A rubbish bin on the left before you go through the gate," the man abruptly interrupted. "Tonight, at midnight. A plastic bag with your *thing* in it lying behind the bin," his voice was undeniably sarcastic. "Do *not* arrive too early or too late. Midnight. Got that?"

"Yes," he breathed a sigh of relief.

"And one more thing," the gruff voice interrupted his thoughts. "No more chances. Get it done and get it done right. The success of your *mission*," the voice sneered at the word, "depends on your leadership and we know what happens to leaders who fail. They fall on their sword, don't they, *Commandant*?"

His heart almost stopped at the overt threat to his own life and nodding furiously, he snapped back, "Of course," but by then the man did not hear for he had ended the call.

Sitting back in the driver's seat, Denholm exhaled with relief.
The operation was still a go, but now he had to assume that for some reason, Collins was unavailable and so as a matter of urgency, he needed to find another volunteer.
His mind was in a whirl, for already dismissing Collins, he gave thought to the few number of volunteers who might be capable of completing the mission, then in that heartbeat, his thoughts settled on the one Volunteer he had kept apart from the rest of the unit.
The one Volunteer whose loyalty was beyond question.
He felt calmer that having made his decision, he would begin by having the Volunteer accompany him to collect the gun because he certainly wasn't going himself.
If the worst came to the very worst, no way would he ever incriminate himself by having anything to do with a firearm.
****

Pressing the red button on the mobile that was yet another burner phone, DS Norrie McCartney, returned the phone to his desk drawer, then turned to his boss, DI Sadie McGhee, and said, "You heard?"
"Yes. Where did you obtain the shooter?"
He smiled when he recalled, "Same place as the one Fairbanks team's nabbed. Nine, maybe ten years ago we hit a house down in Auchenleck in Ayrshire. The place is riddled with Loyalist supporters in the part of the country. We'd had word from the RUC that an arms shipment was being moved from a house down there via the Stranraer ferry, to Belfast. Made three arrests and recovered an assortment of high and low velocity weapons, one of which was a snub-nosed Smith & Weston revolver with six rounds in the chamber and," he grinned. "I was in charge of the productions that were seized and I *forgot* to log a few in the register. The Smith & Wesson has seen better days and wouldn't fetch a fiver on eBay, but," he smirked, "I thought that like the others, one day it might come in handy. All Denholm's man needs is to get close enough, because there's no skill required to use it."
Making a fist with the forefinger extended and the thumb up, he added, "All he has to do is point and pull the trigger."
"Good thinking," she slowly drawled, then leaning forward onto the desk, added, "I'll give our lords and masters a phone call to update them, then tomorrow, I think it's about time I paid a courtesy call to our DI Fairbanks and find out how his investigation is coming

alone."

CHAPTER NINETEEN.

It was coincidental that Jaya Bahn and Brian Saunders arrived back at Maryhill incident room just moments after Larry Considine had spoken with the supervisor at the Technical Branch.
The two DC's and Considine, now seated in front of Eddie Fairbanks in the DI's room, began recounting their visit to Andrew Collins workplace.
"So," Fairbanks, stared from one to the other, "not a well-liked man?"
"Apparently not, no," Bahn shook her head.
"And what did you discover about this man who called in twice yesterday, looking for Collins."
"The young girl who took both calls described him as well-spoken with a Weegie accent and she reckons he sounds to be middle-aged, but being the age *she* is," Bahn sighed, "that could mean anything from thirty to sixty."
"And you said the company records all incoming calls in case there's a complaint. So, have you got the call information?"
"The manager, Mrs Cready, she had a CD of both calls made for us," Bahn lifted it from her handbag and handed it Considine. "We've got the calls and his voice, however," she frowned, "the mobile number from the call related data is the same number that the Techie's got from Collins unlocked phone."
"If I might," Considine interrupted. "The Techie supervisor tells me he'll do his utmost to try and find out which company are the number's service provider, but we've not to hold out any hope. In his experience, we're likely looking at a burner phone, a pay as you go, so it won't be registered to any individual."
Slowly nodding that he understood, Fairbanks smiled when he asked Bahn, "Collins hadn't any pals at the company who are Celtic supporters?"
"No pals anywhere, if you'd believe his team," she shrugged.
He continued smiling when he addressed Bahn and Saunders, "Thanks guys, so grab a coffee before you continue with whatever

else Larry has for you."

When they had left the room, he turned to Considine to tell him, "I think it's about time you slipped off to meet with my Ronnie and remember, she's having a friend over too, someone for you to chat with."

"Are you certain about this, Eddie?" he slowly exhaled. "I mean, not me slipping off; Duke Smythe is going to take over my desk and hold the fort for when I'm away and he's right up to speed with what's happening. What I'm talking about is putting Ronnie in the position of what, counselling me?"

"Larry," he locked eyes with the older man, "I've only known you since I've been at Maryhill, but I consider you to be a friend, as does Bobby Heggerty, so yes, I'm absolutely certain that with Bobby's blessing, I'm doing the right thing. Now get your arse away and hopefully, Ronnie or her pal will be able to put you in touch with some people she knows who can help you. You said it yourself," he grimaced, "if you don't get help, you're going to lose more than just your job and your pension. You're going to lose your wife and family."

He didn't immediately respond to Fairbanks reminder of what his addiction could cost him, but then licking at his dry lips, said, "I haven't had a drink in two days and for what it's worth, it's killing me."

But then he held up his palm towards Fairbanks and continued, "Before you think about congratulating me, Eddie, let me tell you this; my throats as dry as sand, my guts are twisting in agony, my chest is tight, my legs are shaking and my nerves are shredded and I'm barely holding it together. To be brutally frank, I want nothing more than to leave here right now and hit a pub."

"But you won't?"

He watched Considine take a deep breath, then slowly shake his head when he replied, "No, I won't, but that's not to say I won't be tempted to hit the bottle tonight."

"Well," he forced a smile, "let my Ronnie speak to you and if nothing else, Larry, hear what she's got to say."

"And you, I understand you're meeting Bobby at one this afternoon, for a chat?"

"You know about that?"

Considine smiled when he replied, "Bobby phoned me last night as he does every other evening to make sure I'm okay. Needless to say, he's also curious as to how you're coping with everything that's going on, but don't worry," he grinned as he rose to his feet, "I told him you're a wreck and I found you greeting like a baby at your desk."

"Thanks for that," he wryly smiled then waved Considine from the room.

He'd thought that he'd take the twenty minutes he had before leaving to meet Bobby Heggerty by catching up with the paperwork that never seemed to end, but glanced up to see his acting DS, Jackie Wilson, striding through the door.

"Got a minute, boss?"

He swallowed his sigh and waved her through the door to the chair in front of his desk.

"What can I do for you, Jackie?"

"I'm just off the phone to Barlinnie prison. They've got me down as their contact officer for the case against John Cooper."

"Problem?" he asked, immediately interested.

"Seems Cooper, him being a former cop or will be when he's formally dismissed," she sighed her opinion of the slow process, "is to be moved to solitary confinement in the remand wing because he's been assaulted."

"How bad was the assault?"

"He's been taken an hour ago to the Royal Infirmary to have his face stitched back on. The culprit somehow got hold of a Stanley knife and sellotaped a matchstick between the blade and a second blade, then run the two blades down his cheeks."

"Jesus," Fairbanks was visibly shocked. "How the hell is a doctor going to be able to stitch parallel wounds that close together? How many times was he struck with the knife, do you know?"

"The senor prison officer I spoke with says at least two, maybe three times, so four wounds minimum."

"Bloody hell! Cooper must be in a right state."

"I'm inclined to say good enough for him, but it begs the question, boss, with him being a former cop, why wasn't he in solitary in the first place?"

Fairbanks exhaled when he replied, "God alone knows, but the prison service are always complaining about overcrowding, so there must be a good reason."

"It'll need to be a good reason if the bugger makes a formal complaint against the prison service," she retorted. "It irks me the thought of that sod getting a successful financial claim against them."

"Was the culprit identified?"

"Not yet,' she shook her head, "but they're calling in Baird Street CID to investigate the assault. Now, the reason I'm bringing it to your attention is, should I inform young Alice Redwood about him being assaulted?"

His brow narrowed as he gave it some thought, then replied, "When she returns to duty, she's bound to hear about it, so maybe pre-empt that by taking a turn out yourself and visiting her; let her know personally from you, rather than hearing it over a phone call."

"Okay," she rose from the chair, "I'll try to get that done today."

"Anything else I need to know about?"

He watched her frown as she considered his question, then shake her head when she replied, "Nothing definite yet, but I've put the word out amongst my guys to listen for any chat about this mob you're looking at, this new Loyalist group. If we hear anything, obviously I'll let you know."

"Thanks, Jackie," he nodded her dismissal.

Glancing at the wall clock, he stood up and fetching his jacket from the back of the chair, made his way to the door.

****

Cathy Heggerty stopped the car outside the Tea Room within the Botanic Gardens then turning to her husband, said, "Now, don't forget. A cream cake with strawberries and definitely not cherries."

"I know, I'm not daft," he retorted, but was sharply reminded, "Aye, you said that a couple of weeks ago when I asked you for a punnet of strawberry's from Tesco and you came back with cherries."

"Okay, strawberries *not* cherries," he frowned, then leaned across to peck her on the cheek.

"Phone me when you're ready to be picked up," she smiled at him.

"Will do," he nodded and tried not to display how uncomfortable he was getting out of the car.

Slowly making his way along the path to the Tea Room, he entered the building to find that Eddie Fairbanks had already secured a table and was waving him over.

"Good to see you, boss," Fairbanks greeted him, then handed him a menu. "As you said," he smiled, "my treat."

After they'd ordered their soup and sandwiches, Fairbanks spent the next twenty-five minutes speaking in a low voice recounting the circumstances of the murder investigation, the only interruption being the arrival of their food.

Heggerty asked some questions about the involvement of the Special Branch officers, then offered advice that Fairbanks should consider "Take everything they tell you as a lie or at best, their version of the truth and tell them nothing that you believe they don't already know."

A little taken aback that Heggerty should have such a low opinion of the SB, it was explained when he added, "I've worked alongside some of them when Maryhill was previously used as the city's terrorist detention station, so believe me when I tell you; they are not to be trusted. They're like a sponge, Eddie. They'll absorb everything you have to give, then rinse you out with nothing that you can show for dealing with them."

Accepting the advice, Fairbanks concluded with Jackie Wilson's information about Alice Redwood's imprisoned former neighbour, John Cooper.

"Ouch," Heggerty grimaced at the news of Cooper's injuries. "That must've hurt."

"I hope so, after what he put that young lassie through," an unsympathetic Fairbanks responded.

"What about Larry Considine? How are you getting on with him?" Heggerty peered at his DI.

"In confidence?"

"Of course."

"I arranged for him to meet with my Ronnie this afternoon when hopefully she might be able to talk him into seeking the help he so obviously needs."

"That decent of you and if he's got the good sense he was born with, maybe for once the bugger will listen because he's never listened to me," he ruefully shook his head.

"You're fond of him, aren't you?"

"I am, yes. Larry and I have been pals for a very long time now and that's part of the problem," he sighed.

"If it had been anyone else, I'd have had to bring it to the attention of the rubber heels before now. But a mate," he exhaled as he shook his head. "It's difficult to be put in that position, believe me."
Unexpectedly, he asked Fairbanks "And speaking of Ronnie, how are you guys getting along?"
"Great," he widely grinned, then said, "I haven't told anyone yet, but Ronnie's pregnant and this morning, I asked her to marry me."
If he was expecting a congratulatory pat on the back or even a handshake, then Fairbanks was to be disappointed, for all Heggerty said, was, "Oh."
"Oh?"
The older man licked nervously at his lips when he slowly replied, "First of all, don't be going off on one, okay?"
"I'm sorry boss, what do you…"
But Heggerty held up his hand to stop him, then asked, "You haven't told anyone at all?"
"No," he shook his head, "Nobody. Why?"
His face expressing his dismay, Heggerty said, "When it becomes known that you and Ronnie are getting married, Eddie, then you have a problem."
****

Nineteen year old, multi-tattooed Gary Campbell never thought of himself as a loner, yet his mother, Patsy, with whom he lived in the two-bedroom, semi-detached council property in Larkhall's Mason Street, constantly worried about her teenage son and his lack of real friends.
Admittedly, Campbell, known locally as not being the sharpest tool in the box, was a member of a local Loyalist flute band, yet whenever the band paraded through the fiercely Loyalist village, her son was either following on the pavement or doing some mundane task, like carrying the water bottles or jackets; never actually playing his flute.
Of course, Campbell would indignantly tell his concerned mother, "I'm a vital member of the band, whether I'm out there playing or not," then would commence a two, sometimes three-day petulant huff that usually ended when he needed more money from his indulgent mother.
Since the day the tosser that was his father had abandoned his then pregnant girlfriend and left for England, the shop assistant Patsy and

her parents had between them, brought up her only child to be the God fearing, proud and steadfast Protestant Loyalist young man he had become.

It was no secret among the staunchly Protestant village that Patsy was an unmarried mother, a fact that she was frequently reminded of by some of the more secular villagers who were prone to gossip. Her response to such gossip was for the thirty-seven-year-old to live her life to the full and so the dyed, blonde-haired, short-skirted Patsy provided plenty of salacious gossip as evidenced by a variety of local men who most weekends, slunk out of her front door in the morning.

And so, the only man who was actually permanently in her life now was her five foot eight-inch, acne ridden, shaven headed, multi tattooed and committed Loyalist son, who to this day had never held down a job for any longer than two months and who, because of his mother's devotion to him, wanted for nothing.

Whether it be a new Rangers top, the latest laptop or money to attend the band's parades in Belfast or simply to permit him to attend the Rangers football matches at Ibrox, Campbell was never left wanting. Once more currently unemployed, the shiftless young man with no male role model would, after the home games at Ibrox, usually attach himself to some group or other, then drifted with the group towards the pubs and clubs that abounded in the east end of the city. Not that he was ever really part of the crowd; the truth being he was usually found on the periphery of such a crowd.

It was within one such pub some three months earlier and while celebrating the kicking meted out to three young, unfortunate Aberdeen football supporters that Campbell and ten of his new mates had happened upon within the Queen Street railway station, that an older man had engaged him in conversation.

As the third pint became the fourth then the fifth pint, Campbell was persuaded to accompany the man outside of the pub where with teenage bravado, he drunkenly boasted that he would die for the Loyalist cause.

The following morning, he awoke in his bedroom in Larkhall to discover that jammed into a pocket of his jeans was a piece of paper upon which was written a mobile phone and just three handwritten words that read; *Call the Commandant.*

****

In her upstairs bedroom in Lindsay Street in Belfast, Arlene McCandlish opened the ivory coloured, wheeled suitcase lying on the bed and stared at the empty interior.

She had not used the suitcase since her last trip with her husband John, a three-night theatre break to London.

Slumping down to sit on the edge of the bed, she found herself smiling when she relived that brief and happy time in their lives. Upon their arrival at Gatwick Airport, they had as they expected, been stopped by detectives from the Special Branch Ports Coverage Unit, who forewarned of their arrival and recognising the two well-known members of the UDA from the listed Watchlist, had separately interviewed them, then after two hours detention, released them.

Those two hours, John had explained in the taxi to the hotel, gave the Met Police Special Branch time to organise a surveillance team. Though they had not spotted any surveillance tailing them during their stay, he was certain they had been followed throughout the three days by the Branch or the Security Service, perhaps both, who no doubt was suspicious that their trip was not in fact social, but to meet Loyalist supporters in London.

How wrong they were, she found herself smiling.

The show, she couldn't even recall what it was about, and the freedom to visit pubs and restaurants without hindrance during those three days, was a compete diversion from their lives in Belfast and that, she sighed, was what she wanted to once again experience in her home city.

Freedom from fear.

Sitting on the edge of the bed, she realised with a start that it was the last time she could recall ever being truly happy and relaxed. Though the IRA were then conducting their mainland bombing campaign and targeting London in particular, it was something she and John had become used to living with and while the majority of Londoners got on with their lives in that vibrant city, she and her husband, whether being surveilled or not, had a great time.

Those few days of sightseeing, eating and drinking and the nights of loving had been glorious; memories that would never fade.

Her brow creased when she considered what was coming within the next few days and the great responsibility that she had assumed.

The forthcoming clandestine meeting with the representatives of the Irish Republican movement and the opportunity to once and for all, end this stupid, hateful and murderous conflict.
She understood why the Republicans did not want the UK Government involved, not least because the one thing both parties had in common was that whether they be Protestant or Catholic, the future of Northern Ireland should be decided by the Northern Irish themselves and not by the suits in Whitehall, whose sole ambition was to win another term for their Party in Government.
And for the first time in her life, she smiled at the thought she was in total agreement with the Republicans.
Irelands future, both North and South, should emphatically and without intrusion, be decided by the Irish.
However, it still deeply concerned her that the few remaining hawks within the Inner Council viewed her mission if not with hostility, then certainly with serious doubt.
Yet her first, tentative approach to the Republicans was not, as she had feared, dismissed out of hand; neither by some of her fellow Inner Council members or the 'RA' themselves, but certainly viewed on both sides of the border with mistrust and suspicion.
The main problem, as she saw it, was maintaining a line of contact with the Republicans without the knowledge of the UK Government. Months had gone by as each side weighed up the possibility of being hoodwinked, then through various couriers that primarily included priests of the Catholic church and ministers of the Church of Ireland, came the long-awaited letter from Dublin; the letter from the Republican hierarchy and the suggestion of a face to face meeting. The first steps to real peace and more than she'd dared to hope for.
To her surprise, even the Republicans accepted there would always be the dissidents on both sides; those with the ingrained hatred that could never be appeased. But for the rest, those who were open to discussion, she fervently hoped a new dawn was on the horizon and once more, thought of the children who played across the road in the swing park and likely had never had a Catholic friend.
At least, not in their childhood, but hopefully, her brow furrowed in thought, as the years must pass…
How long she sat there, she couldn't say, but then found herself smiling when she recalled that first meeting when she proposed her idea and the initial surprise of her fellow Inner Council members.

She had outlined her plan as similar to the car seatbelt legislation, an explanation that at first caused some amusement and sarcastic comment.

Everyone hated the new seatbelt legislation when it was introduced, she had begun, but then, as the first year passed and it was statistically recorded that lives had been saved by the new legislation, the country as a whole accepted the logic when in a vehicle, the necessity of wearing a seatbelt. And now, when getting into a vehicle no one now gave a thought about slipping on the seatbelt.

Yes, she had admitted, there were still those who would protest against the legislation or ignore it, but as time passed, they would pass into obscurity as the next generation took seatbelt wearing to be a natural act when in a car.

And so, she passionately spoke, her peace plan, just like the seatbelt legislation, would work.

She had continued and wisely included her audience in the decision making, using the plural if *they* were successful, the next generation of Northern Irish children and those generations that followed, Catholic and Protestant, would no longer care or be suspicious of the religion of their neighbour, but see *only* neighbours.

Importantly though and to her relief, there were those in the UDA Inner Council who had listened and fortunately, those in the Republican movement who also had listened.

And so, the parallel tale of the seatbelt legislation and her plan to meet with the Republicans, finally took shape, though admittedly slow at first.

Still sitting on the edge of the bed, she took a deep breath, her thoughts turning again to the meeting that was to be held in Glasgow and remembered prayers that she had not thought of for some time; indeed, if she were honest, not since her John had been so brutally gunned down.

Minutes passed then she rose from the bed and opening the wardrobe, began to select her clothes to be packed.

CHAPTER TWENTY.

That early Sunday afternoon, Larry Considine was a little uncomfortable when he arrived outside the building in Watson Street, the address at where Ronnie and now Eddie Fairbanks shared her flat.

He'd met her just the once and like most if not all men who met Ronnie Masters, was not only impressed with, but also a little intimidated by her beauty.

Sorely tempted to take a swig from the opened half bottle of Glenfiddich that nestled in his glove compartment, before getting out of his car he popped a couple of mints from the plastic container in the side pocket of the driver's door, then locking the door, made his way to the building's secure entrance.

Minutes later, he was greeted at the front door of the flat by Ronnie who wearing her hair down and a loose, sky-blue coloured kaftan and was barefooted, ushered him through the door with a smile.

Leading him into the comfortable front room, he saw an attractive, blonde haired woman, her hair fashionably styled and smartly dressed in a grey tweed skirted suit and who was seated on the couch with her hands on her lap, her legs demurely crossed and a mug of black coffee on the table in front of her.

"Larry, this is Anne," Ronnie smiled at him. "I hope you don't mind her being here and by way of explanation, Anne is my sponsor and she'll explain what that is. Please," she waved a hand, "sit down."

Anne, who he judged to be in her late fifties or sixty, greeted him with a smile then said, "We know how daunting this is for you, Larry, and can I say, we *do* know because both Ronnie and I have been where you are now."

"Look," Ronnie raised her hand, "I'll let you and Anne have a quick word so can I get you a coffee or tea?"

He was surprised how nervous he felt and almost inappropriately joked he would have preferred a whisky, but instead forced a smile when he replied, "Coffee, please, milk only."

"Coffee it is," Ronnie left the room.

He turned to see Anne staring at him, who then quietly said, "Let me properly introduce myself, Larry. My name is Anne and I'm an alcoholic."

"Eh," his voice stalled, for he just didn't know how to respond to that.

She softly smiled when she said "Kind of takes you aback, someone coming out with that kind of statement, doesn't it? Yet," she shrugged, "it's true. I am an alcoholic, albeit I've been sober for a number of years now. But still, as I can see in you right now, the temptation is always there, isn't it, Larry?"

She sighed when she continued, "I'm not certain what Eddie might have told you, but there is no cure for alcoholism. What there is, though, is hope."

She paused to let that sink in then in the same, calm voice, said, "We are all capable of beating our addictions, no matter what that addiction is; but it depends on just how much we *want* to beat them. We have to look at our life and ask ourselves, who is being hurt by our addiction. Then the next question is, what's more important; our family, our health or our need to satisfy the urge to drink?"

The image of his wife's face flashed through his head and he thought, where's that coffee, anything to distract this woman from…

But before he could even compose the thought, Anne continued, "You're not alone, Larry. You don't need to fight this on your own. There are any number of people who know what you're going through and who are there and willing to help. All you have to do," she slowly nodded, "is take that first step."

She paused again when she explained, "There are twelve steps in the programme, if you're willing to consider them and the first step, that I'll share with you, is we must admit to ourselves that we are powerless over alcohol and that our lives are unmanageable. Can I ask you, is that how you feel?"

He almost choked, so tight was his throat, and so unable to verbally respond, he nodded.

She took a soft breath then continued, "Once we have admitted that first step, the remaining steps all follow in line, Larry."

He couldn't explain why, he that through his career, had faced down neds with knives, dealt with violent offenders and been in life-threatening situations, yet here he was, staring at this blonde-haired woman with the gentle voice and could feel the tears were running down his cheeks.

He never even saw from where she fetched it, but she was leaning across to hand him a paper tissue.

"A simple question," she stared at him. "Can I be of any help to you, Larry."

He was too emotional to speak, his chest heaving as he fought to breathe and his lips trembling. It was all he could do to nod, but then surprisingly heard himself say, "Please, yes. Please."

How long they sat there in silence, whether it be two, five or ten minutes, he couldn't say, but then Anne softly told him, "There's no shame in recognising that you need help, Larry. Look, there's a visitor's toilet in the hallway. Why don't you wash your face and take time to compose yourself and I'll fetch that coffee you were promised and then, when you're ready and if you are genuinely interested in seeking help, we can discuss you and I maybe going to a meeting."

She rose to her feet, but then stopped and smiled when she added, "And if you need a friend, a sponsor, no matter the time of the day or night, I'll always be just a phone call away."

****

Duke Smythe filling in for Larry Considine, issued two Action's before calling Susie Lauder over to quietly ask, "Any idea where the DI's away to?"

"Not a clue," she shook her head, but added, "If Eddie's not mentioned it, then it's certainly not something he wants to share."

"Aye, right," Smythe sighed, then holding up his hand said, "Not that there's any great need for him to be here right now and he did say he'd be on his mobile but…"

They both turned to see Fairbanks striding into the room, his face red but whether from pounding up the stairs or anger, they couldn't say.

"Anything doing?" he curtly asked Smythe, who cheerily replied, "All quiet, boss, and I take it I'm behind the desk for the rest of the day?"

"Yes please, Duke," Fairbanks nodded then left the room.

"Something or someone's annoyed him," Lauder quietly commented.

"Aye, not like him to be so abrupt," Smythe agreed.

****

Closing his office door behind him, Fairbanks head was in a quandary.

Bobby Heggerty's revelation had not even entered his thoughts and now that it had, what the hell was he going to do if the issue did crop up?

Should he discuss it with Ronnie, then almost immediately decided no.

She was in the early stages of pregnancy and the last thing she needed was to be stressed with worry and, heaven forbid…but the thought of her having a miscarriage was too painful to even imagine. He slowly exhaled and tried to clear his mind of Heggerty's news, damning the man for bringing it to his attention, yet grateful for the heads-up, particularly when the DCI reminded him that ACC Alex Gardener not only has it in for Heggerty, but was malevolent enough to include anyone he believed might be close to the DCI.

And all because Gardener's nose was out of joint over a broken engagement all those years ago.

He glanced up when his door was knocked, then pushed open by Susie Lauder who precariously balanced two china mugs on a clipboard.

"Bad time, boss, or are you up for a coffee?"

He slowly smiled, then waving her in, said, "Kick the door closed behind you."

Laying the clipboard on top of the desk, she handed him a mug, then though uninvited, sat down before she asked, "You okay?"

"No," he sighed, "not really."

"Anything you can share?"

He smiled, then realised that though he'd known the young woman for just those few months, he regarded her as a close friend and inwardly bursting to share his news, smiled, "Ronnie's pregnant and she's agreed to marry me."

The expression on Lauder's face was one of pure joy and for those few seconds, he forgot about his predicament, particularly when she rushed round the desk to hug him and give him a sloppy kiss on the cheek.

"Hey," he pretended to protest, "just as well the bloody door's closed, Susie, or me and you will be getting a reputation."

"Sod them," she waved a hand at the closed door, then resuming her seat, she frowned when she said, "You are *happy*, aren't you?"

He nodded, then said, "About the pregnancy and getting married, definitely. That said," he sighed, "I had a meeting this afternoon with Bobby Heggerty."

He waved a hand, then continued, "Just an update of the investigation, but I got a bit carried away and broke the news about

Ronnie and me."

"Wasn't he pleased for you?"

He took a deep breath then slowly exhaled when he explained, "I don't need to remind you about Ronnie's past, her conviction in New York for drugs and her short sentence there before she was deported back to London. Well, without going into a lengthy explanation, ACC Gardener is on the DCI's case, some feud from a long way back. Bobby is concerned that if it becomes public knowledge about Ronnie and I getting married, Gardener will make difficulties for me under the Police (Scotland) Act, the section that prohibits an officer from associating, let alone co-habiting, with any individual convicted of a serious crime."

Aghast, she stared at him before she replied, "But that was in America. Surely that won't apply here?"

"A conviction and particularly a drugs conviction, Susie, will apply no matter when or where it occurred."

"And you can hardly hide the fact that you're getting married," she blew through pursed lips.

"No, I most certainly won't."

"Is your job at risk?" she hesitantly asked.

He glowered before he replied, "If it comes to a decision about Ronnie or the police, then yes, it is."

The both sat in silence for a few seconds, then Lauder stared at him before she asked, "Are you going to tell Ronnie?"

"No way," he vigorously shook his head. "She's on a high because of the baby and it's still only," he paused, then his voice a little softer, continued, "Well, Ronnie thinks she is only about six or maybe seven weeks, so I don't want her stressed, okay?"

"Of course, Eddie, I wouldn't dream of telling her. But if Gardener finds out, have you any idea how you'll handle this?"

He didn't have the opportunity to reply, for again the door knocked and was pushed open by Chief Superintendent Liz Malone, who wearing a plaid jacket and black jeans with walking boots, smiled and said, "Good afternoon, DI Fairbanks. I hope I'm not disturbing you."

****

Lying in his bed reading a pornographic magazine that he kept hidden under his mattress in the naive belief his mother knew nothing of it, Gary Campbell pawed at his groin as he stared at the naked women and startled when his door was knocked, then pushed open by his mother, her dyed blonde hair dishevelled and who wore a knee length pink, fluffy dressing gown to cover her nakedness. Embarrassed, he shoved the magazine under the quilt cover while Patsy pretended not to have seen it, then said, "There's a phone call for you."

Confused, he glanced at the mobile sitting on the bedside cabinet, only for Patsy to tell him with a scowl, "No, it's on the house phone, so get rid of that hard-on and get yourself downstairs."

When she stepped out of the room, he cried, "Ma, that's mean!" then scrambled to pull on a pair of jogging trousers he picked up from the floor.

Hurrying to the hallway, he ignored the man stepping out of the bathroom who glanced guiltily at Campbell before returning to Patsy's bedroom, then made his way downstairs to the phone on the narrow table at the front door.

"Hello?"

"Volunteer Campbell," the voice of the man known to him as the Commandant, greeted him.

"Eh, sir," wide-eyed with surprise at the call, he found himself straightening up.

"We need to speak. Nine o'clock this evening at the usual venue."

"Yes, sir, I'll be…" but the line was dead for the caller had hung up. Staring at the phone, he briefly wondered what the call was about, then turning, replaced the phone into the cradle and shouted up the stairs to his mother's bedroom, "Ma, I'm going out tonight and I'll need a bung."

****

Acting DC Mickey Rooney was out with his assigned neighbour, DC Tommy Anderson, conducting follow-up visits to tenants at the locus of the murder, the high-rise flats in Wynford Road, when his mobile phone activated.

Excusing himself to his neighbour and the couple they were interviewing, he stepped out into the hallway to answer the call from a woman who had in the past, provided Rooney with some good information.

"Janet," he greeted her, "how's things?"

"Can you speak?" was her hushed response.

"Aye, I'm on my own at the minute. What's up, hen?"

There was a few seconds pause before she replied, "I know I owe you, Mickey, for what you did for my Nicky, so can I tell you something and you promise it won't get back to me?"

"Look, Janet, I told you at the time, you owe me nothing," he said, but that didn't mean he wouldn't take whatever information she was about to divulge, then continued, "You know me, Janet, so you also know anything you tell me is between us, okay?"

He listened to her breathing and guessed that whatever was troubling her, she needed to get it off her chest. Another short pause and Rooney was almost certain that Janet was crying when she said, "It's my Nicky, he's got himself involved in some sort of, I don't know what you'd call them. He says they're just friends with people over in the North, but after the last time," Rooney heard a definite sob.

His brow furrowed, he asked, "The North? Do you mean Northern Ireland?"

"Aye, there."

"Are you telling me he's got himself mixed up with a Loyalist group, Janet?"

"I think so, Mickey," she carefully replied, then continued, "He's started going back to that pub in the east end, even though I told him if he went near the place again, he was out on his ear. I'm that worried, so I am, that he'll end up in the jail and him not even twenty yet."

Yes, Rooney was now convinced, there were definitely tears and for Janet to call him meant she really was concerned for her son.

"These friends that he's mixing with, Janet, do you know any of them?"

"No," she quickly responded, "what I do know is that they meet in this pub and that as far as I know. I can't say for certain, but I don't think any of them are from the Milton."

Rooney almost smiled at the comment for like many of her neighbours, Janet Speirs was extremely parochial and anyone not originating from Milton was almost classing them as foreign.

He glanced at the closed door where his neighbour continued the interview, then said, "Where are you the now?"

"Eh, at home in my house."

"Eh," he rubbed at his brow, "Scalpay Street, isn't it?"

"Aye, still here," she sighed.

"Can you get out, maybe meet me in say an hour in the café in Tesco on the Maryhill Road? Coffee will be on me," he added.

"An hour, Mickey? Right, okay and will you be able to help me?"

"Only if I can and when I know the whole story. One hour, Janet."

****

Excusing herself, Susie Lauder nodded to Liz Malone when she left Fairbanks office, then closed the door behind her.

Before he could speak, Malone sat down in the chair vacated by Lauder, then raised a hand to say, "I know, I shouldn't be here, but anything to get out of the house and away from the ironing," she smiled.

Staring at him, she frowned when she continued, "To be honest Eddie, Bobby Heggerty phoned me at home to tell me you were a bit upset when he spoke with you about your Ronnie. And by the way," she broke into a soft smile, "I hear congratulations are in order."

"Thank you, Ma'am, but while the DCI was only warning me and I'm pleased he did give me a heads-up, it's a bitter pill to swallow."

She stared for several seconds at him before she said "I only met Ronnie that couple of times when she was visiting you at the hospital. She seems to be a decent enough woman and by all accounts, has overcome her addictions," then raising a hand to forestall any discussion, soberly continued, "But that's not the reason I'm here, DI Fairbanks, to massage your hurt feelings about how Strathclyde Police might react to you living with a woman who has a drug conviction."

It was her change of expression and attitude that confused him, then to his shock, pokerfaced, she brusquely continued, "In the absence of DCI Heggerty, you are my senior CID officer and so the Division and I rely upon you to be at the top of your game, particularly as you are currently investigating a murder. Is that *clearly* understood?"

Stunned, his eyes locked to hers, he watched her lean forward when she continued, "And must I remind you that like all officers employed by the Force, you are subject to the Conditions of Service as laid out under the Police (Scotland) Act and it's written into your contract when you joined the police that you will *not* associate with anyone who has a criminal record."

She paused, then leaned back in her chair to tell him, "Whether you accept it or not, you have already compromised yourself by having a relationship with Ronnie Masters and in a very public violation of your contract with the police. Oh, and believe me," she slowly nodded, "when ACC Gardener learns that one of his senior officers has such a relationship with a woman who has *very* publicly been identified as a drug abuser, as he undoubtedly will, we both know what his reaction will be and you could be looking at being brought up before the Chief Constable and your dismissal without a reference or even your accrued pension."

He could feel his face flush and the anger rising in his chest, but before he could respond, once more Malone held up her hand when she said, "Now, that's the reality of your situation, Eddie, and I suspect the way I spoke to you is the manner in which Gardener will launch his assault upon you. So, how do you propose that we circumvent your downfall?"

"Ma'am?" he stuttered.

"Calm down," she casually waved a hand at him, "with the time I have left to serve I really don't give a shit about what the police think of your relationship with Ronnie and if the truth be known, I'm happy that you have found someone to care about. Wish I could say the same," she muttered with a soft smile.

Then her face changed to a frown when she said, "But as I told you, Alex Gardener is not a forgiving man and I suspect he already has you tagged as a friend of Bobby Heggerty and *if* that is true, you'll be fair game to him. So, again, how can we defuse a potential career-ending for you?"

"Eh," suddenly deflated, he could only stare at her, then recognising how confused he must be, she visibly relaxed in her chair when she smiled and said, "Okay, let's put it this way. Tell me about Ronnie. Everything."

****

It was almost five-thirty when Liz Malone smiled at Mickey Rooney in the corridor, who gave her a curious, if polite nod when he passed her by, before he knocked on Eddie Fairbanks door.

Waved in, Fairbanks said, "Duke Smythe asked me to hang on till you arrived back, Mickey, so what's up?"

Licking nervously at his lips and uncertain if what he had was of any use to the investigation, he began, "About two years ago, give or take a month or so, I arrested a young guy for a breach of the peace and assault. Nicky Speirs, who was seventeen at the time, lives with his mother over in the Milton. Scalpay Street. Big lump of a lad he is too," he grimaced. "Long red hair and a little over six feet, as I recall, though maybe not the brightest bulb in the box."

"Who did he assault?"

"Eh, me, actually."

Fairbanks eyebrows rose when he asked, "What was the nature of the assault?"

"Well, my neighbour and I attended a domestic at his mother's house and the young lad, Nicky, he'd had a drink and was kicking off. Took a swing at me and punched me on the shoulder before I decked him. His mother was going off her nut at him because he'd a job interview the next morning and knew if we'd given him the jail, he'd lose the opportunity of an apprenticeship. It was a big deal for him, you know?"

"Go on."

"Well, boss," his face creased, "I didn't actually charge him, though I should have done. In fact, I let him go with a warning because his mother, Janet, she was dead grateful that I didn't give him the jail and besides," he took a sharp intake of breath, "she'd mentioned she worked in a pub down on Maryhill Road."

Fairbanks eyes narrowed, already presumed where this was going when he slowly said, "I'm thinking, her working in a pub, she hears things, so I'm guessing you made a deal with her?"

"Yes, boss," he sighed, pleased he didn't have to explain it further, then grimaced, "The thing is, I never registered her as a tout, just gave her my mobile number and if she heard anything that might interest me. Well, you know what I mean."

"You know the rules, Mickey, about registering touts and why the rules are in place."

"Yes, boss, but…"

"And was this a *productive* deal?" Fairbanks interrupted with a raised hand.

"I did get a few titbits now and then, but mostly stuff that I passed to the collator so that it didn't compromise Janet as the source."

He licked nervously at his lips when he continued, "The reason I'm flagging it up with you is she phoned me today to tell me she's worried, that her son has become involved with a Loyalist group and to ask if I can speak with him."

Fairbanks eyes narrowed when he said, "Now you're starting to interest me, Mickey. Go on."

"It seems that young Nicky travels after the football at Ibrox to a pub in the east end. She doesn't know its name, just that it's a Rangers pub and is on Duke Street."
"A Rangers pub on Duke Street," he smiled, then added, "There's a few possibility's there, Mickey."
"Yes, well, Janet told me this afternoon that he doesn't know it, but she has the code for Nicky's mobile phone and when she can, she checks it to make sure he's not getting into anything he shouldn't be."
"And there was something on the phone she wanted you to know?"
"Aye," Rooney nodded. "Nicky got a text message from a number that she gave me, a text from someone calling themselves the Commandant and telling Nicky he wants a meet on Monday evening."

****

He had timed it nicely and it was just three minutes to midnight when the two-year-old, black coloured Volvo estate vehicle pulled up a little under two hundred yards from the gated entrance to the Eastwood Old Cemetery on Thornliebank Road.
Switching off the engine, Arthur Denholm turned to the young man in the passenger seat and sensing his excitement, said, "You know what to do?"
"Yes, Commandant," the younger man, Gary Campbell, vigorously nodded.
"I walk up to the gate and I find a plastic bag behind the big bin that's on the left-hand side of the gate. Then I bring the bag back here."
"A simple task Volunteer Campbell, but one that is of vital importance to our cause. Quo Separabit (*Who Will Separate Us*)?" he smoothly added.
"Quo Separabit*"* Campbell repeated with a wide grin.
Across the road and just forty yards from the entrance to the cemetery, DS Norrie McCartney sat in the darkness of the navy-blue coloured SB vehicle, sipping a now lukewarm coffee from the plastic beaker and grimly smiled when he saw the young man, his head swivelling on his shoulders, nervously approach the large, square rubbish bin.

CHAPTER TWENTY-ONE: Monday 25 September 2006.

Though he'd insisted for that one night he'd sleep in the spare room to permit his wife, Cathy, to get a good night's rest, Bobby Heggerty hadn't been able to sleep and by her tired expression when she joined him in the kitchen, he saw that neither had she.

"How you feeling?" she asked as he waved her to a kitchen chair.

Turning, he laid a plate of buttered toast and a mug of tea in front of her before he replied, "Honestly like I've been hit by a tram, that then reversed back over me. We'll need to change that mattress in the spare room. It's a right bugger, so it is."

She smiled then said, "I had a text early this morning from our Gail, wanting to bring the wee lad over for a visit and lunch, but I texted her back to say I was going out with my pals."

She paused when she asked, "Do you really think it's a good idea, Bobby, not telling the kids what's going on?"

He sat in the chair opposite with his own mug of tea, then shaking his head, replied, "I'd rather wait till we get the result of the colonoscopy before we give them any news, sweetheart. There's no sense worrying them until there's definitely something to worry about."

"Okay, but be it on your own head," she gently rebuked him. "You know what Gail in particular is like if she thinks there's something going on and she's not in the loop."

They sat in silence for several minutes, each lost in their own thoughts before he took a breath to say, "If the worst comes to the worst, it's my intention to resign."

"Why?" her forehead creased. "Won't you consider working till you feel you can't go on? You know you love your job, even though sometimes I think it takes too much out of you."

"Simple mathematics," he shrugged. "If I should die *in* the job, you'll get nothing but my pension, but if I retire through ill health and because I've served over twenty-six and a half years, I'll walk away with both my pension and my full commutation, my lump sum," he explained.

Then with a soft smile, he added, "And I get to spend more time with you."

Tears sprang to her eyes and she bit at her lower lip to stop herself from crying.

Seeing her distress, her reached across the table to tightly hold her hand, then said, "But let's wait till we get the result today from the procedure before we make any definite plans, eh?"

****

So far, the sailing had been a nightmare for Arlene McCandlish, though she hadn't complained.

They had left early to catch their seven-thirty early morning, booked passage on the Stena Ferry from Belfast to Cairnryan and now with Axel, being the older minder at thirty-one and the designated driver of the hired Mondeo, they'd queued for forty minutes, waiting to board.

At the check-in, it was as Constance McKenzie had predicted; security so lapse as to being almost laughable with a cursory glance at their false identification and their forced joviality causing the female security officer to smile at their eagerness to attend the fictional wedding.

Once embarked and on the passenger deck enjoying their breakfast, McKenzie, who had insisted she was the only one with all the details of their trip, was then able to disclose further particulars and in a low voice, told them, "The Mondeo's Satnav will take us to a flat in Glasgow's east end where we will be met by a man, the boss of a newly formed group loyal to the UDA, who'll give us the keys to a three bedroom flat that we will use as a base. I have his phone number, so I'll call him when we're a half-hour away to give him a heads-up."

"And the meeting, where is that to be held?" Arlene McCandlish, dressed for the trip, as were there others in casual tops and jeans, had rubbed nervously at her forehead, unwilling to admit she never liked sailing and particularly when the Irish Sea was as choppy.

That and if the motion in her stomach was correct, her on-board breakfast had been a huge mistake and was now threatening to return with a vengeance.

"The Republicans insisted on a completely neutral venue, so I booked a first-floor meeting room in a hotel that's located in Cambridge Street; that's in Glasgow city centre," she added as she stared at them in turn.

"As far as the hotel is concerned it's expecting representatives from two companies at two o'clock on Wednesday afternoon, so we'll all be dressed in our business suits."

"Do we have details yet of who the Republicans will be sending to the meeting?" McCandlish asked.

"Yes," she hesitated, then said, "Gary McGuigan and one other, but I don't have their name, plus two minders who, they assured us, like Axel and Johnny here, will also be unarmed."

"McGuigan," McCandlish's face turned pale. "I always believed him to be one of their most rabid hawks. He's willing to meet with me?"

"Apparently," McKenzie nodded, "and according to the information that came in the last correspondence, he *asked* to be the one to meet with you and also inquired if you'd agree to meet with him. I took it upon myself to agree on your behalf. Is that okay with you, Arlene?" she hesitantly stared at her.

"Well," McCandlish took a deep breath to fight her nausea, then slowly smiled when she said, "If nothing else comes of this, it should at least be very interesting."

"Now," she stood up and feeling a wave of nausea coming on, waved the two minders back down into their chairs, "if you'll excuse me, I think I'll pay a visit to the loo because I have a feeling I'm about to speak with God on the big white telephone."

****

Seated at his office manager's desk in the prestigious estate agency's office in West Nile Street, Arthur Denholm glanced nervously at the wall clock in his office, realising that if things were going according to the schedule, the four representatives would now be on the ferry and soon be docking at Cairnryan within the next hour.

According to his AA AutoRoute, the journey to the flat he had organised for them in Lamlash Crescent in the Cranhill area of the city would, assuming there were no hiccups, take no more than two hours.

"Mr Denholm?" he startled at the young woman's voice, seeing her fair-haired head popped in through the door that she held open with one hand, then quickly smiled to hide his surprise.

"Penny?"

"That was a phone call about the first floor flat for sale in Lamlash Crescent over in Cranhill. Someone wanting a viewing."

"Lamlash Crescent?" his heart almost stopped.

He felt his body tense, then as casually as he dared, said, "Remind me again. What flat is that?"

"Ah, it's a first floor, two-bedroom ex-authority flat. The owner has advertised it as a furnished rental and is asking for offers of three-twenty a month."

"Is that the only flat we have on our books for Lamlash Crescent?" he asked, knowing his hopes were about to be dashed.

Her brow furrowed as she stepped into the room then nodding, slowly replied, "As far as I'm aware, yes it is."

A cold hand gripped at his bowels as continuing with his forced smile, he said, "Yes, well, go ahead and make the arrangement then let me know what the details are. If you please," he added almost as an afterthought, his mind racing that the flat he had thought suitable, at least for the time the party of four intended occupying it, had just become a no-goer.

Now, with just a few hours before the arrival of the representatives, he had little option but to search for another flat, somewhere in the city; a flat that must be furnished and like the Lamlash Crescent flat he had visited the day before, he had to make time to purchase provisions and stock the fridge.

Shit!

Trying to calm himself, he turned to his desk computer to hastily begin his search.

****

Gary McGuigan was, according to the hated Brits, a convicted murderer.

However, to his fellow soldiers in the 'RA,' the republican army, and their supporters, he was a famed freedom fighter with numerous British soldiers and members of the RUC, as well as some noted Loyalists, all killed by him in the Cause to free Northern Ireland from British oppression and to unite his home country under the one flag.

A former member of a four-man Active Service Unit, an ASU, in nineteen-ninety-four on the Armagh border, McGuigan had been wounded in the leg, then captured by a Royal Marine patrol while returning to his home in Dundalk. The irony of the wounding was, as his comrades made good their escape, that the marine who shot him roughly tended to McGuigan's first aid and as the doctor later told him, likely saved the lower half of his leg from being amputated.

Tried and sentenced by the Brit court to life imprisonment for his actions, he had been one of the many freed under the terms of the Good Friday Peace Agreement, though at the time and as far as McGuigan was concerned, the Cause had to go on.
But that was then.
Returning after his liberty was granted to his mid-terraced bungalow home in Dundalk's Culhane Street, the slightly built and thinning grey-haired McGuigan had been welcomed by his wife and three daughters as the hero to the Cause he undoubtedly believed himself to be, but it had not been long thereafter, when disillusionment began to settle in.
The first time the Special Branch of the Garda Síochána visited him at home, he knew then he was a marked man, that the Guards who themselves through the years had lost members of their Department to the 'RA' and who were complicit with the Brit's, would watch his every move.
Finding a job with his reputation had been more than difficult until at last, an old friend with some reluctance gave him a job as a navvy on a building site, carrying the hod for the brickie's. However, it wasn't the back-breaking work that troubled him, but the lack of communication and support for his service from the senior figures in the Movement; the men and women who had trained and armed him to fight and who it seemed to him, no longer recognised the sacrifices he had made for the unification of his country.
But the final thing that decided Gary McGuigan was some months after his return home, when his wife, working at the local supermarket and he, earning a minimum wage and struggling to pay their mortgage and help their two elder daughters through college and university, was shocked to learn his youngest girl, then turned just eighteen years, had in a fit of naive patriotism, joined the Republican youth organisation, Na Fianna Éireann.
An Irish nationalist organisation that originated in nineteen-o-nine, it had survived to the present day as a fiercely Republican group committed to supporting Republican Sinn Fein and the newly raised Continuity IRA, who were dedicated to continuing the war against the British oppression in the north.
No matter that McGuigan and his wife had argued against their daughter's involvement in the group, she had declared her life was now committed to serving the Cause.

So, fearing for her future as well as her life, McGuigan had hesitantly turned to some former colleagues who, as disenchanted as was he, had come to accept that perhaps the real way forward for peace was discussion and negotiation, though not with the UK Government, but with their old nemesis; the Ulster Defence Association and its paramilitary groups.

As the months then the years passed, McGuigan, now in his mid-fifties, watched his daughter become more militant, then finally leave the family home to live with her boyfriend, a like-minded individual who McGuigan not only disliked, but suspected was already being targeted by the Guards for his outspoken belief in a continuation of violence in the north and mostly perpetuated by the Continuity IRA.

When the early months of two-thousand and six arrived, McGuigan's covert meeting with his former colleagues had by then agreed with many of the senior Republican figures, who had themselves been involved in the armed Cause, that discussion must be employed if they were to initiate a peaceful settlement with the Loyalists.

It was then through intermediaries, most notably a Northern Irish Catholic priest and a pair of Church of Ireland ministers, that the first tentative contact had been made with the UDA's Inner Council. Though he later learned that he was not the Republican's first choice to meet with the UDA's representative, McGuigan's new found passion for peace had finally convinced some of the doubters and so, with an advisor, a young graduate in politics called Donal O'Hara, and two minders, he was instructed to meet on Tuesday with the UDA's Inner Council member, Arlene McCandlish, in the agreed neutral venue.

Glasgow.

Fortunately, not only was young O'Hara travelling as an advisor, but it was he who had knowledge of all the arrangements, not only for their accommodation, but their transport and for the minders, their evening entertainment too.

McGuigan smiled when he recalled his visits to the Scottish city during those halcyon days gone by, when feted by the Glasgow Republican supporters and, he found himself blushing, particularly the women who had always been known for their hospitality for the men who fought for the Cause, though of course the minders were too young to have known of those times.

Of course, he had to remind himself, this was most definitely not a social visit and it wasn't quite as simple as being sent over the water to Scotland to shake hands and agree a deal.

Preliminary arrangements that were made included a delivery to McGuigan of a thick intelligence file that told him most of what he needed to know about the woman with whom he was to meet; Arlene McCandlish.

He read of her personal tragedies, the murders of her father Thomas, her brothers then finally her husband, John, while she herself had been targeted by the 'RA' on at least two occasions, but escaped unscathed.

He had exhaled with some relief when he realised that he had not participated in any of these actions.

However, it was the reference to the murder of her husband that interested McGuigan most; the responsibility for his murder was claimed by the local Belfast Brigade of the 'RA', though the file stated this had not been verified, that it was instead suspected an unknown Loyalist faction who were in fact responsible.

Reading on, he had learned that though she had never actually been an active member of any assault teams, McCandlish was a shrewd and intuitive individual who had organised a number of successful operations against the 'RA' and some of its leading figures that had resulted in the deaths of many Republicans, some of whom, he had grimaced, were well known to him and who he considered to be friends.

He had grimly smiled when reading that paragraph, for it seemed he was not the only one with blood on his hands.

And now here he was.

O'Hara and the two minders, as far as the 'RA's intelligence department knew, were 'clean skins' who were neither known to either the Garda Síochána's Special Branch nor to the British Security Service and it was therefore surmised they would not be on any ports Watchlist.

The trio, acting as business travellers, had been instructed to make their separate ways by ferry or plane to Glasgow where they would reunite within a well-known Irish Republican supporting pub in the city's Gallowgate area. From there, they would be directed to their accommodation within the local area and looked after by local and vetted sympathisers.

McGuigan's travel plans, however, was a different matter, for he was till the day he died, on a permanent Watchlist on both the Irish border area and either side of the Irish Sea.

His left leg, never quite right since a Royal Marines 7.62 round shattered the patella and leaving him with a permanent limp, was aching in the claustrophobic confined space where he now lay; the hidden compartment at the back of the driver's seat in a heavy goods vehicle tractor unit, that was to tow a freezer trailer filled with Irish meat and destined for the Glasgow meat market.

Just as Arlene McCandlish's personal assistant, Constance McKenzie had assured her boss, security at the ferry and airports had lessened in the preceding years, and so it was between the Dublin docks and the ferry's destination, the Holyhead Port.

After an uncomfortable confinement of just over three hours in the secret compartment, the HGV pulled into a layby some distance from Holyhead where the driver operated the catch that released a relieved McGuigan, who now thankfully was clear to continue the remainder of the journey in the cab's passenger seat.

****

Bobby Heggerty, like everyone who attended hospital as a patient, left his dignity at the entrance doors and was now wearing just his underwear and a hospital issued gown and non-slip socks.

Nervously clutching at his wife Cathy's hand, he waited to be called forward to the small consultation room.

Though he had been expecting it, he still jumped when he heard the young Staff Nurse call his name, then rising to his feet, as did Cathy, they embraced before he inhaled, then forcing a smile, said, "No matter what, I'm definitely for a curry tonight. What about you?"

Her eyes bright with unshed tears, she nodded when she replied, "Sounds like a plan," then with a heavy heart, watched him walk through the door that closed behind him.

****

It was fortunate that the Detective Inspector in charge of the Serious Crime Squad's surveillance unit, Willie Healy, was a former neighbour of Eddie Fairbanks when both had been DC's, for it made it that much easier for Fairbanks to call in a favour.

Now sitting sipping at his coffee, Healy stared at Fairbanks before he cautiously asked, "Isn't this *really* the remit of the Branch?"

"It should be, but you know them as well as I do, Willie. They'll want everything and give nothing back and this *is* related to my murder investigation, so as far as I'm concerned, I'm prioritising my murder over any interest they might have in this Loyalist mob."

He didn't bother explaining that the murder suspect, Andrew Collins, had been identified and was himself dead, that he needed Mickey Rooney's new suspect, nineteen-year-old Richard 'Ricky' Spiers, followed to try and identify the man known as the Commandant.

Healy slowly exhaled, then placing his china mug onto the desktop, slowly shook his head when he said, "You're putting me in an awkward position, here, Eddie. We both know I can't just target a suspect without proper authorisation, that there should be a warrant signed for the surveillance operation before my team can take him on. So, can you get a warrant before this afternoon?"

"The short answer is no, I can't. I really don't think I've enough to crave a warrant, Willie, and unless the procedure has changed, my understanding is that the details of any surveillance warrant is recorded on the PNC so that there won't be any overlap by two surveillance teams on the same target. That said, if the Branch hear that you guys are taking him on to meet with this guy they call the Commandant? Well," he shrugged, "frankly, my arse will be hanging out of the window."

Healy couldn't help but smile at Fairbanks analogy, then again exhaled when his eyebrows knitted and his mouth twisting, at last he said, "You know, I think my guys have been getting a bit rusty these days."

"Eh, what? Rusty?" Fairbanks was confused.

"Yeah," he shrugged, "letting things slip a little, not quite getting it right, so I'm thinking I should give them a bit of on the job training this evening, just some vehicular and foot following practise. And," he wheezed, "If it's a training evening, there's absolutely no requirement for a warrant."

Sensing where this was going, Fairbanks mildly asked, "And how would you go about this training evening?"

"Well," Healy slowly drawled, "what we usually do is pick some random guy or woman and just follow them about for a while, see where they go, who they meet and we'll note descriptions, that sort of thing. All to sharpen our surveillance, administration and observational skills, you understand?"

"Of course," Fairbanks nodded, then said, "And when you say you'll pick some random subject to practise this surveillance, I don't suppose you might *randomly* consider a young guy about nineteen with long red hair and who's over six feet tall, built like a rugby scrum-half and lives over in Scalpay Street, in the Milton?"

"Could do," he shrugged again then said, "The Milton you say? Well, it just so happens that the Milton area is where the local worthies in that neck of the woods can usually spot a strange vehicle hanging around, so that *would* be excellent practise for my team. We could maybe spend a few hours practising up around there and if we picked up a subject, say someone like you described, we could see where that subject takes us on a training surveillance."

Fairbanks smiled when he replied, "I'm grateful, Willie, and I hope your training evening goes well."

CHAPTER TWENTY-TWO.

DI Healy had been gone just twenty minutes when Fairbanks door was knocked by DI Sadie McGhee, who smiled and said, "Got a minute?"

"Do I have a choice," he coldly replied, then watched as she entered his office and closed the door behind her, seeing that she wore a fawn coloured two-piece skirted suit and had quite obviously taken some time that morning with her hair and make-up. In fact, though he was loathe to admit it even to himself, she was a *very* attractive woman.

"No gorilla trailing behind you?" he couldn't keep the sarcasm from his voice.

"That's really unkind," she pouted, then added, "Now, now, Eddie, let's not fall out."

Sitting in the chair opposite, then though he couldn't see them, she slowly crossed one leg over the other while she continued to smile as though at a petulant child, she continued, "I mean, we're all in the same job, trying to keep the peace and jail the bad guys, are we not?"

"The difference being," he scowled when he dropped his pen onto his desk, "is that I am doing it lawfully while you, DI McGhee, I am *not* so sure about. In fact," his eyes narrowed as he stared at her, "to be honest, I do not trust you, so what the hell do you want?"

"My goodness, we are in a grumpy mood this morning," she teased him. "What, hasn't your Ronnie been giving you, well, I'm sure you can guess what I mean?" she again pouted at him.

Then apparently hoping to surprise him, changed her tact when she said, "I hear your murder suspect has been identified, that Andrew Collins has died. So, that concludes your murder investigation, does it not?"

"And where did you hear that?" he inwardly raged, but whether at her reference to knowing about Ronnie or that somehow, she had learned of Collins death, he wasn't himself quite certain.

"What, that Collins is dead or that your murder investigation is concluded?" she goaded him.

"Either."

"Well, we in the Branch have our sources, Eddie; so, I assume you have closed your investigation and we will not be bothering you again."

"Assume what you want, DI McGhee, but…"

He got no further, for the door was knocked then pushed open by DS Larry Considine, who said, "Sorry to bother you, boss, but you're needed in the incident room."

Then, as if noticing McGhee for the first time, Considine smiled pleasantly at her when he said, "I'll accompany you downstairs, Ma'am, to see you don't get lost on your way out."

Rising to her feet, her face flushed at her abrupt dismissal, she sniffed, "There will be no need for an escort, Detective Sergeant!"

"Oh, my pleasure, Ma'am," he gushed like a schoolboy as he continued to smile at her, even theatrically slightly bowing from the waist as she passed him by, then turning to Fairbanks, outrageously winked at him before following McGhee along the corridor.

A minute later and as he expected, Fairbanks learned from Duke Smythe in the incident room, "What. Someone looking for you, boss? Not that I heard," the big man shook his head.

****

To his immense relief, Arthur Denholm happened upon a new rental contract that had arrived that very morning, but was not yet published on the company's website; a furnished, three-bedroom duplex flat in Lancefield Quay whose balcony overlooked the River Clyde and came with its own dedicated parking bay.

"Bloody hell," he absentmindedly muttered as he glanced at the advertising photographs then unconsciously wondered at his luck in finding the beautifully maintained property.

Now all he had to do was get the keys from the front desk, then go out and collect some shopping that would see the group of four through the next few days.

Calling his young assistant, Penny, through to his office, he explained he had a personal task to attend to and would be gone for some hours; however, he assured her with a tight smile, he would be on his mobile should she or any of his five staff require him.

"Oh," he turned as though having a sudden thought, "that property that is coming on to the rental market. The flat over in Lancefield Quay."

"Yes, Mr Denholm?"

"Hold off advertising it on our website for a couple of days. I might be able to pre-empt the advertising for I have someone in mind, but I won't be able to speak with them for a few days."

"Of course, Mr Denholm," she smiled.

Pleased to be trusted with the responsibility of looking after the office while he was gone, Penny was just pleased to be left in charge of the office and had no misgivings as to why her boss should be taking off nor why he was rummaging in the drawer where the property keys were stored.

****

Following his Commandant's instructions, Volunteer Gary Campbell, as he liked to think of himself, caught the bus that took him directly into Buchanan Street bus station, then walked the short distance to Sauchiehall Street where in the pedestrian precinct, he stared pokerfaced at the Celtic FC retail shop across the way.

The money borrowed from his mother burning a hole in his pocket, he finally strode across the precinct and pushed open the door to the interior of the shop, surprised to see the young male and female staff all similarly dressed in Celtic football tops or tracksuit tops, each bearing the Celtic logo and curiously thought of himself as being in enemy territory.

A young woman, about his own age, he thought, smiled then said, "Can I help you?"

He choked back his sarcastic response and fought not to scowl, but instead forced a smile when he replied, "I'd like a Celtic top, my size, please."

"No bother, the girl smiled at him and led him to a rack with the enemy's green and white hooped tops, then selecting one, he almost backed off when she held it against him then said, "There you are that should be a perfect fit."

Minutes later, the purchase made and carried in a white plastic bag with the Celtic logo predominant on the front, he crossed the precinct to enter the Primark store where he bought a black coloured, three holes-balaclava, then stuffed it in with the football top.

Back out into the precinct, he took a deep breath then began to make his way back to the bus station.

At the bus station, Campbell removed a folded, Cooperative plastic shopping bag from his anorak pocket, then transferring the football top and balaclava to the Co-op bag, discarded the Celtic shopping bag into a nearby bin.

Waiting the fifteen minutes for the bus that would return him home, Campbell's thoughts turned to the small, old handgun with the chipped enamel that exposed the silver underneath, that lay hidden on the springs and under the mattress of his bed, alongside his favourite issue of Playboy and idly fantasised about what he intended doing with the gun.

****

In a bedroom within a semi-detached house on the other side of the city and sixteen months into his apprenticeship as a painter and decorator, Nicky Speirs mind wandered, as it was apt to do when slapping emulsion onto a ceiling and to the constant consternation of his journeyman, who yelled, "Watch what you're doing! You're splashing it every-bloody-where!"

Once more, Geoff Ramsay, who ran his own one-man business, shook his head and wondered why he'd taken the useless bugger on.

Of course, Ramsay knew fine well why he'd taken Spiers on as his apprentice, for every Saturday night after her shift at the pub, Nicky's mother Janet would visit Geoff at his flat in Springburn's Galloway Street and express her gratitude in his bed; a gratitude that was well worth the small gratuity he usually slipped into her handbag the following morning before she left.

"To buy yourself something nice," he frequently reminded her with the assurance he wasn't paying for her services.

So far, he smiled to himself, he had evaded any suggestion of her being a permanent fixture in his life, for their agreed arrangement suited the older, widowed man just fine.

Yet turning to stare at her son who, because of his height, didn't need a ladder to emulsion a domestic ceiling, he often wondered how a petite and shapely woman like Janet could produce such a lump like him and privately reminded himself never to goad Nicky too far, for though he himself was no shrinking violet when it came to fisticuffs, Ramsay doubted if he'd be able to handle an enraged teenager Nicky's size.

What the journeyman could not know was that right at that moment, Speirs attention had drifted because he was anxious to know why the Commandant wanted to meet him that evening, and in his daydreaming, excitedly yearned that since his secret initiation into the Friends of Ulster Loyalists, he might be given his first mission.

****

Constance McKenzie, sitting in the rear of the vehicle with McCandlish by her side, pressed the green button on her mobile phone and said, "Yes?"

McCandlish watched as McKenzie nodded then heard her say, "Wait a second till I write that down."

Scrambling in her handbag for a pen and a small notebook, she nodded again when she said, "Yes, I've got that and you'll be there with the keys?"

"Okay," she replied to the caller then asked Johnny in the front passenger seat, "What does the Satnav say about our time of arrival at the destination?"

"Fifty-five minutes," he replied over his shoulder.

McKenzie repeated the time then, said, "That's approximate, if we're now going elsewhere."

"Okay then," she nodded once more then ended the call.

"What?" asked McCandlish.

But it was to Johnny that McKenzie replied when glancing at her written note, she said, "Change of destination for the Satnav."

****

Laura, Ronnie Masters deputy, smiled when she watched her boss dealing with a grateful customer for like Ronnie, she could hardly contain her excitement knowing that the Life & Fashion Management magazine was to be on the shop counters the following day.

Several times she had calmed the equally excited Ronnie, whose emotions ranged from childlike enthusiasm to a wary and cautious gloominess that the photoshoot might not be received as well as they both hoped.

That and Laura had a sneaking suspicion that Ronnie was holding out on her and so, when the customer left the shop, she approached and said, "Miss Masters, might I have a quiet word?"

Leaving their two assistants to tend to any customers who might enter, the two women retired to the small office in the stock room where a curious Ronnie asked, "Everything okay, Laura?"

"I might ask that of you" she dryly replied, then with a soft smile said, "I can't help but notice that every now and then, you pat at your stomach and seem to either be suffering a tummy ache or, dare I ask?" one eyebrow raised.

She watched Ronnie's shoulders slump, then she broke into a wide smile when she replied, "Is it that obvious?"

"And you're happy?" Laura hesitantly asked.

"Very."

"Then," to Ronnie's surprise, the usually undemonstrative Laura threw her arms around her boss and hugging her to her, she whispered, "I'm so pleased for you and Mr Fairbanks. So *very* pleased."

Releasing Ronnie from her hug, her eyes glistening, she stepped back and smoothing down her blouse, once more adopted her formal expression and sniffing to fight the tears that threatened to spill from her, said, "Sit down and take five minutes and I'll have one of the girls bring you a nice cup of tea."

Without waiting for a response, she turned and was through the door. Taken aback, it was all that Ronnie could do not to reply, so with a sigh, sat at her desk and idly patted at her still flat stomach.

****

Calling Larry Considine through to his room, Eddie Fairbanks related the conversation with DI Willie Healy, only for Considine to frown and tell irritably him, "You both know you're kicking the arse out of it, boss, that if any of the management find out about your ruse, you'll both be for the high jump?"

"And that's why we're keeping it between us, Larry," he quietly responded.

"Willie will let me know anything they discover that might be of use to us as unattributable information. However, what I need to know from you is if there *is* anything we can use, will you be able to feed it into the HOLMES system without any reference as to where it originated from?"

Considine's face creased when he slowly exhaled through pursed lips, then replied, "I've no need to remind you that every investigation that is recorded on HOLMES is subject to scrutiny for any number of reasons and so the provenance of such information is important."

He grimaced when he shook his head to add, "If the information should later be valuable as evidence in any subsequent trial and we *do* use the information without identifying its origin, we leave ourselves open to an outside Force inquiry. That and we could lose not just the opportunity to use the info as evidence, but as the SIO, you leave yourself open to a disciplinary hearing."

He shrugged when he said, "That said and if you still want to go ahead with this, give me some time to think about it and I'll get back to you."

"Okay, and Larry, I'm sorry to put you on the spot like this, but if I didn't think that it was necessary…"

Considine raised a hand when he interrupted with, "Look, I know you're doing your best and I agree with your thinking, but like I said, I don't like the thought of you putting yourself out there like that."

Fairbanks wryly smiled when he replied, "I'm guessing you've been there and back?"

He had to smile at that when Considine replied, "Maybe a couple of times."

"On other issues, let me say at the outset, Larry, that while I know you visited Ronnie yesterday, she definitely would not discuss with me what happened, but I'd be lying if I said I wasn't curious. So, was it worth your while?"

Considine gave a brief thought to the visit and how he had become emotional and instinctively believed Fairbanks knew nothing of what had occurred, but then nodding, said, "Yes, it was and I'm attending my first meeting this evening with Ronnie's friend, Anne."

"Good, I hope it works out for you. Now," he rose from his chair, "let's find out how the team are getting on."
****

Deputy Chief Constable Charlie Miller glanced up when his door was knocked then pushed open by his secretary, Ellen, who he had brought with him along the Command Suite corridor when he had been promoted to his current rank.

Her expression questioning, she said, "Sorry to interrupt, sir, but I have Chief Superintendent Malone in my office, asking if you're free to have a word?"

"Of course," he smiled, pleased for any excuse to avoid another minute reading a budget report.

When Ellen re-opened the door to admit Liz Malone, he said, "What's the chance of a couple of coffee's, Ellen?"

"Of course, sir," she smiled then closed the door behind her.

Waving Malone to a chair, she said, "Sorry to drop in like this, Charlie, but I was at the Personnel Department making arrangements for my retiral."

"Wow," his eyes widened, "is it that close?"

"Weeks away, now," she sighed with a smile.

"How do you feel about it?"

"Truthfully? A little anxious, though of course the kids are looking forward to having a part-time child minder now on tap."

She wryly smiled when she added, "However, what they don't know is I haven't yet shared my plan to move abroad, to Spain."

"And is that going to happen?"

She widely smiled when she replied, "If the deal I've got planned for the flat on the Costa del Sol goes through, then yes. A place called Vilassar de Mar in Catalonia that overlooks the sea."

"Well, good luck with that," he nodded, then added, "I'm suspecting that your visit to the Personnel Department, then coming to see me isn't coincidental?"

"Correct," she nodded, but stopped when Ellen pushed open the door to carry in two mugs and a plate of Tunnocks caramel wafers.

When she had left the room, he shook his head before he sighed, "It's only when I have visitors who Ellen likes that I get the good biscuits. Any other time it's the plain digestive."

She smiled, then slowly exhaled, her expression changing to one of concern when she asked, "In confidence?"

His frown indicated she didn't need to ask that question of him.
"Alex Gardener."
He pursed his lips then thoughtfully exhaled when he said, "Good at his job as ACC (Crime), if a little overzealous, sometimes. Abrupt manner that alienates him from his CID subordinates, but all in all, he's smart, very presentable and there's a real likelihood that one day, he might replace me."
She slowly nodded as she took in his opinion and realised, that no matter of her opinion of Gardener, Miller was correct.
"You know about Bobby Heggerty?"
He nodded when he explained, "Bobby shared with me what he and his wife, Cathy, are going through at the minute. In fact, before I leave today, it's my intention to phone him at home to find out how he got on."
"You're also aware then, that Gardener has had it in for Bobby for some time?"
"I *think* I'd just left Stewart Street at the time, but I do recall the rumours about Cathy throwing Gardener over for Bobby and yes," he grimaced, "I'm aware that Alex is an unforgiving man. There's only black and white where he's concerned. No shades of grey."
"Well, what you may not know is that Gardener has been sniffing about my Divisional headquarters, trying to find out why Bobby is off duty and so far, I've managed to deflect him and his aide from finding anything out."
"Because you think Alex will use Bobby's illness to force him to retire?"
"They say revenge is a dish best served cold," she shrugged.
His lips tightened when he slowly nodded, then said, "But that's not the real reason you're here, because we both know that Bobby is more than capable of defending himself."
Her brow knitted when she slowly replied, "I'm concerned that if Gardener can't get at Bobby, he'll go after his DI, Eddie Fairbanks."
Miller's eyes narrowed when he asked, "Why would he do that?"
"Because not only does Bobby think highly of Eddie, but he likes him too and believes Eddie will one day maybe even sit in your chair," she softly smiled.
"For what it's worth and in strict confidence, I'm impressed by Fairbanks too and would it surprise you to know, Liz, that I also think that he could be steered towards senior rank?"

"So, neither of us want to see Fairbanks fall because of Gardener's intense dislike of Bobby Heggerty?"

"Correct. Now," he stared at her, his hands clenched on his desktop, "what makes you believe that Eddie Fairbanks is so vulnerable?"

Sipping at her coffee, the biscuits ignored, she recounted her conversation with Fairbanks, his short-lived joy at discovering his partner, Ronnie Masters, was pregnant and his intention to marry her.

But then she recounted his anger when she reminded Fairbanks of Ronnie's American conviction and her scandalised drug and alcohol abuse, then heard him say and saw it in his eyes that Ronnie, not the police, would always come first.

"As is right and proper, because after all, when it comes down to it, the police is a job, not a life commitment as is a relationship," Miller admitted and agreed with Fairbanks commitment to his partner. Then, his face creasing, he asked, "But all that's in her past now, I believe?"

"Completely," she nodded. "Ronnie is now a sober and successful businesswoman and if what my friends tell me and from what I hear is correct, she's completely turned her life around. Eddie even let it slip that she's planning to host a charity sale of the bespoke clothes she modelled last week for a fashion magazine, clothes from her own boutique that I can assure you," she smiled, "must be worth a pretty penny or two."

"Really?" his mind was racing when he asked, "Do you happen to know what charities she intends donating to?"

"Eh, no, I don't. Why?"

"Just the semblance of an idea," he smiled, then sitting back in his chair, he reached for a caramel wafer, then smiled when he added, "Tell me more about your Spanish flat."

****

When he finished work that afternoon and returned home to his mother's house in Scalpay Street, Nicky Spiers quickly changed from his paint splattered overalls into a clean, grey coloured sweater, blue jeans and Doc Marten boots.

With his mother, Janet, gone from the house and already at work in the pub, he glanced at the clock in the kitchen and decided he didn't have time to cook a meal, so made himself a jam sandwich and grabbed a can of Irn-Bru from the fridge.

In the hallway, he donned a blue coloured three-quarter length anorak, then pulling open the door, stepped out into the path to make his way towards Liddesdale Road to catch a Glasgow city centre bound bus.
Had he not been hurrying, he might have noticed the old and battered Transit van that was parked fifty yards from his front gate, but could not have suspected that the surveillance officer concealed inside was on the radio and issuing the warning, "Stand-by, stand-by. Tango One out of the house and now walking east, over."

CHAPTER TWENTY-THREE: Tuesday 26 September 2006.

Eddie Fairbanks slowly came to, to hear Ronnie in the en-suite and throwing up.
Jumping from the bed, he hurried through to find her again on her knees, her head bent over the bowl.
Rubbing gently at her back while he held her hair back from her face, he reached for a facecloth that he handed to her.
"Hope this wee bugger is worth it," she managed to gasp between her bouts of nausea.
He couldn't help but smile when he replied, "I know I'm half of the blame, but I really am sorry it's you who is experiencing all the physical problems that comes with pregnancy."
She turned to sit with her back against the tiled wall and stared curiously at him before she said, "You think there's some sort of blame, me being pregnant?"
He held up an apologetic hand, then grimaced, "Wrong choice of words. "I'm just feeling guilty that it's you that's suffering."
"And so you should be," she scowled at him, then with a final burp, added, "I think it's over for the minute, so let me get cleaned up a bit and go and make me some dry toast and a nice cup of calamine tea."
Bending to kiss the top of her head, he left the en-suite then used the bathroom before heading into the kitchen.
A little over five minutes later, a pale-faced Ronnie, wearing her dressing gown and her hair tied back with a ribbon, collapsed onto a kitchen chair, then said, "I'm beginning to feel fat."

Standing at the sink, he turned to grin at her before he replied, "You're not fat and there's hardly even a bump to show you're pregnant, which reminds me. When is your appointment with your GP?"

"This evening at six-thirty. Fortunately, she knows me so she's going to hang on after the surgery closes to see me. Will you make it, do you think?"

"You know the old saying about wild horses, so yes, I'll make it. Just text me the address."

"I know you don't like talking about your work, but how is your investigation coming along? I sense that you're a bit stressed at the minute."

He hadn't changed his mind, having decided to avoid telling her about Liz Malone's warning about the Force's policy of their officers cohabiting with individuals who have been convicted of crime or offences, and so with a smile, sat down opposite her when he replied, "We've identified our killer, but that's not the end of the investigation. We think that someone was pulling his strings and so we're endeavouring to identify that individual."

"But you," he hurriedly changed the subject, "you've got the magazine coming out today. How do you feel about that?"

She frowned, her brow knitting when she said, "Truthfully, a little anxious that I'll be seen as an over the hill model. I mean," she shrugged, "look at the young women these days; they're young, slim and not just beautiful, but neither are they carrying the baggage of a history like I have. I'm nervous that…well, that I'll be compared to them as their older auntie or even their granny."

"Maybe, but you've got something not all of them have," he smoothly countered, then added, "a lasting beauty."

That did make her genuinely smile and shaking her head, she softly asked, "What did I do to deserve you, Eddie Fairbanks?"

"Let me think about that one," he stood up from the table, then quipped, "Time I was getting away. Things to do, people to jail."

"And as for you," he bent down to kiss her, "do not be stressing yourself. You've our child to think about and I'm told a mother's emotions carry through to the womb."

"How the hell did you find that out?" she laughed.

At the kitchen door, he stopped and turned when he replied, "On the way home, yesterday, I stopped off at Tesco to buy some maternity

magazines. They're on the couch waiting for you."
****

Arthur Denholm's mouth was dry as he dialled the number of the man he was to contact, the man with the rough Glasgow accent, then when the call was answered, he breathlessly said, "They're here. They arrived yesterday and I put them in a flat in Lancefield Quay, down on the River Clyde."

"And have you arranged for the hit and someone to deal with the shooter?"

'Yes," he croaked. "All arranged, now I was wondering…"

"Don't be wondering, Arthur," the man said, sending a chill through his body that the man knew his name. "Simply do what you're being told to do."

"But…"

However, line was dead for the man had ended the call.

Staring at his mobile, Denholm felt the familiar fear race through his body, then almost hyperventilating, for the first time realised exactly what he had got himself into.
****

Removing the SIM card from the burner phone, DS Norrie McCartney turned to DI Sadie McGhee to inform her, "It seems it's all set."

Nodding, she lifted the desk phone then dialled the London number.
****

Their cooked breakfast over, McCandlish and her three colleagues sat around the kitchen table discussing the arrangements for travelling to the meeting in the Cambridge Street hotel.

Axel, the senior of her minders, recounted his reconnaissance visit the previous evening and
commenced the briefing.

"The hotel itself is a four star and was busy when I arrived. The bar and dining room on the ground floor in particular seem to be a popular venue and the front door has a uniformed concierge there to direct guests. There are eight floors in the hotel and the meeting rooms are located on the first floor, where the ballroom is too. The floors are accessed by elevators from the reception area and stairs to the left side of the elevators."

He paused, then continued, "There is parking at the hotel, for a small fee, that I recommend we use; however, the bad news is the car park is covered by CCTV cameras as it appears is the reception desk too. There are also cameras monitoring the two entrance doors, one that leads to the bar and a canopied entrance that leads to the large foyer, reception and the lifts."

He paused again, then continued "My recommendation is that Johnny drops us three off at the canopied entrance, parks the car then joins us in the foyer area and we travel together to the first-floor venue. Questions?" he glanced at them in turn.

"Well, you're the protection," McCandlish shrugged, "so we'll go with your advice."

"Okay, then. The meeting is at two and it's a five-minute journey, ten at the most," Axel reminded them, then suggested, "So I suggest we depart from here no later than one-thirty and Johnny," he turned to the younger man and smiled, "make sure you've got cash to pay for the parking. Don't be using a debit card."

"Got it," Johnny added.

To McCandlish's surprise, Axel then asked her, "Him that got us this place and gave us the keys. What's your opinion?"

Her eyes narrowed with suspicion when she replied, "Why are you asking?"

He nodded around the flat and said, "I can't complain about the accommodation, the place is right smart and it was good of him to leave us a fridge of food."

"But him?" he grimaced, "I don't know him and I've never heard of him before yesterday. That and calling himself the Commandant?"

He shrugged when he explained, "I just got the wrong vibes from him and couldn't help but see that he was really nervous."

Though she had never really attributed her minders with overthinking, she had come to trust Axel's instinct in matters of her personal security and so calmly replied, "What's got your itch going?"

"I can't really explain it, Arlene," he frowned, "and maybe I'm being oversensitive, but like I said, he's not someone I've dealt with before. So, Constance," he turned to her, "you made the arrangements. What do we know about him?"

She shrugged when she replied, "Only that he's set up a new support group called the Friends of Ulster Loyalists and he's been sworn in by the Inner Council, so doesn't that vet him in some way?"

"Who in the Inner Council?" McCandlish turned to her.

"Ah, I don't know. I only know when I asked for details of a contact here to provide accommodation, he was the man recommended to me."

"Recommended by who?" Axel pressed.

Slowly shaking her head, she replied, "I'm not sure. I got the e-mail on the secure account so I don't know who sent it."

"Look," McCandlish interrupted, "maybe we're getting a little paranoid here. Axel," she turned to him.

"You know I trust your instinct and that you and Johnny have served me well, but this is a huge opportunity for us as an organisation. Let's not get distracted by looking for threats that aren't there. Like Constance told us before we set out, she's the only one who knows all the details, so if there *was* any kind of threat, I'd expect it to come from the Republicans, not our people. Now," she smiled reassuringly to indicate the subject was closed, "I want us to go over the plan for the meeting, one more time."

His head bowed as he listened to McCandlish, Axel's mind was drifting elsewhere.

Though his boss had outwardly dismissed his concerns, he still had that gut feeling that there was more to the skinny guy who pompously called himself the Commandant and vowed that if there was some kind of betrayal, he'd find the bugger and do him in.

****

Across the city in a tenement flat located in the Shettleston area, Gary McGuigan and his advisor, Donal O'Hara, finished their tea and thanked the elderly woman, who leaving them in the front room, closed the door as she returned to the kitchen.

"She's a good one, that," McGuigan smiled at the closed door. "Not the first time she's had me looked after. Now, how are the lads doing?"

"If I know that pair," O'Hara scowled, "they'll have been out on the ran dan last night, pretending they're the heroes that sent the Brit's packing, but they'll be sober this morning or I'll know why not."

"You're too hard on them," O'Hara smiled. "They're just kids. They can't be any older than their mid-twenties."

"Kids or not, Gary, they're here to protect you, so you have to know they were not my first choice coming over here."

"Well," McGuigan calmly replied, "if today's meeting goes as planned, there shouldn't be any need for them to protect anyone, Donal, and I've a favour to ask of you."

"And that is?"

"When we're at the meeting, I want us to be seen to be amicable and definitely open-minded, not confrontational. Not at all," he shook his head.

"From what we know about her, Arlene McCandlish has put a lot of effort into persuading her hawks in the UDA to speak with us, so I do not envisage her wanting this meeting to be anything but a success. Are you with me on this?"

"Yes, Gary, I am, but why do you need me to confirm that?"

"I have no wish to offend you, Donal," he took an apologetic breath, "but you didn't bear arms against the Brit's and the RUC, so being an academic, for which I truly *do* appreciate your value and advice, you have a different attitude to someone like myself who's known the fear of operating against them."

"You think I'm any less determined to seek peace?" O'Hara's brow furrowed with just the hint of anger on his face.

McGuigan paused before he replied, wanting to calm the younger man down, "As a young man at your age, Donal, you have never really known peace with the Brit's and the Loyalists, so you have no yardstick with which to judge peace. Me? I remember the days before the Civil Rights movement kicked off in '68, and now I'm at *my* age, I long for those days to return."

He grimaced when he added, "I don't know if I'm making any sense, but…"

However, O'Hara interrupted when in a low voice, he said, "Gary, you're correct. I didn't carry a rifle and yes, I want a united Ireland. *And* like you," he stressed, "I do genuinely desire peace and for what it's worth, I will support you in these negotiations. Completely. You have my word."

"Then that's settled, McGuigan smiled with some relief, then added, "Now, let's have another look at who we're meeting this afternoon."

Stepping over to his briefcase, O'Hara fetched the file produced by the Republican intelligence officers that contained every known detail of Arlene McCandlish.

"You'll have your work cut out for you, Gary, dealing with this woman," O'Hara shook his head. "She'll be looking for a complete disarmament and likely, to be supervised by a joint party of us and them."

McGuigan smiled when he replied, "It'll be the same old story, Donal, they'll take us to a couple of arms dumps where they've hidden a few rifles and handguns and we'll do the same, but not everything will be disclosed. Then, when we're mutually satisfied how honest both sides are, we'll announce to the world that the cease-fire has begun, that the 'RA' and the UDA have finally laid down their weapons and we're both at peace."

"And the dissidents who'll disagree, ours and theirs? O'Hara's eyes narrowed.

"That'll be up to us and them to deal with our own and we both know," a vision of his daughter's face appeared in his mind, "there will be problems there. Perhaps even some violence to make them see it our way, the way it has to be if we're to finally unite Ireland," he wearily sighed.

He continued, "However, the *political* struggle to unite our twenty-six counties with the six up north will continue and I believe the Unionists up North will understand that, but the ultimate goal today is to ensure that in Northern Ireland, no-one else dies by an act of violence."

O'Hara stared hard at him when he sighed, "I can't imagine the pressure you must be under; you being the sole representative of the movement. After all those years fighting for the Cause, you now carry everything on your shoulders. Too many of our people, Gary, you'll for evermore be a hero."

"But equally, Donal, if I fuck it up," McGuigan softly smiled, "I'll be vilified as the man who *betrayed* the Cause."

****

Learning there was nothing new in their search for the man called the Commandant, Fairbanks was just leaving the incident room when he happened upon DI Willie Healy sloping along the corridor. Nodding that Healy follow him to the DI's room, Fairbanks rounded on him when he asked, "Anything?"

"Nothing," he shook his head.

"We took him from his address to a pub in the east end over in Duke Street, a Rangers pub located across the road from the junction with Paton Street, but there's no way I was having any of my guys go in there. All it would need was for someone to recognise my footman as a stranger or worse, as a cop, and he'd be getting a glass in the face."

"No, I understand," Fairbanks held up his hand.

"Anyway, we hung about for a while, but it got to the time I had to send my guys home, Eddie."

"Here," he handed Fairbanks a buff coloured cardboard folder. "We took a note of the registration numbers of the vehicles that were parked outside or within a short walking distance from the pub's doors. For obvious reasons, I haven't had them PNC'd in case one of my bosses wants to know why I'm putting all these numbers through the system when I wasn't officially on an operation."

"Thanks, Willie," he took the folder. "I'm grateful to you and your lads and I'll have one of my guys drop you off a crate of Tennents for your help."

"That *will* be appreciated," Healy smiled, then turning, waved cheerio.

He glanced up when Larry Considine appeared at the door to ask, "That the DI from the surveillance unit, eh...?"

"Willie Healey, yes, and he's dropped off a list of vehicles that he thought might interest us. Will you be able to put them through the PNC as part of our investigation?"

"As far as anyone is concerned, if they even check, they'll be vehicles parked at the murder locus we're finally catching up with," Considine nodded, though didn't admit he was relieved that he did not have to compromise the HOLMES system with unattributed information.

"Good. Now, anything else doing at the minute?"

"Right now," Considine took a short breath, "no, but the team are getting restless. Because they know that this is turning into some sort of terrorist related incident, they're wondering why the Branch aren't knocking on our doors."

Fairbanks brow creased when he replied, "Get them together, Larry, and I'll come through. Let's consider shaking the tree a bit."

"What you thinking?"

"This young guy Mickey Rooney turned up, the lad Speirs. Let's go and fetch him in and see what he knows about this man called the Commandant."

****

In the office in the rear stock room, each with their copy of the Life

& Fashion Management magazine, Ronnie and Laura pored over the six page feature for several minutes before Ronnie turned to hesitantly ask, "What do you think?"

Laura stared pokerfaced at her, then her expression changed to one of pure joy when she replied, "I think it's *fabulous* and you are an unqualified success!"

"Really?"

"Really," Laura nodded with a huge grin and just as Ronnie's mobile phone chirruped.

Staring at the caller ID, she said, "It's Tony Harper from the magazine," then pressing the green button, hesitantly greeted him with "Hello, Tony. I've Laura here with me and I'm just putting you on speaker."

"Have you seen today's issue?" he hurriedly asked.

"Yes, we've got a copy here in front of us. It seems to be very well done, the photos and that, I mean."

"Well done? Ronnie! The phones in the office here are ringing off the wall! Charity asked me to call you because right now because she's onto a London agency who want to follow-up with your photo shoot! Darling, you are an outstanding success!" he raved at her.

She didn't realise she was crying until Laura handed her a box of tissues, then after Harper promised he'd have Charity Dawson phone her, he ended the call.

They stared at each other before Laura suggested, "I'm putting the kettle on. This calls for a cuppa."

It was then that one of the two young assistants arrived in the stock room to say, "Sorry to interrupt, ladies, but we've suddenly been invaded by a large number of customers, most of whom are carrying that magazine," she pointed at it.

Then with a wide grin, she added, "And they all want to meet Miss Masters."

****

In the privacy of his locked bedroom, he had spent most of the previous evening playing with the gun; loading the chamber with the six, dulled brass bullets, then practised holding and pointing it, unloading it again and going through the process several times until he was satisfied he was as competent as any of his heroes in the Loyalist movement.

His mother off to work earlier that morning, Gary Campbell stared at his reflection in the mirror and wryly smiled that he should be wearing the hated colours of his team's greatest rivals.

Yet, as the Commandant explained, it was necessary that the operation should be seen to be conducted by Irish Republicans. Pulling on the black balaclava with just the three holes for his eyes and mouth, he involuntarily gasped at the almost claustrophobic sense as the knitted material tightened on his skin.

Grinning with surprise, he again stared at his reflection and recalled the Commandant explaining that, security for this type of operation being paramount, this was the reason Volunteer Campbell had never met any of his fellow members of the FUL.

The Commandant had at length further explained that the Volunteers isolation from each other was to guarantee their safety. If one Volunteer should be compromised or arrested, Campbell and the others would be safe.

Accepting the explanation as good, common sense, Campbell has no reason to question his mission.

Holding the Smith & Weston revolver two-handed as he had seen handguns held in countless films and shows, he uttered the words he never thought he would ever use.

Teeth gritted he pointed the weapon at his reflection and loudly cried out, "Up the IRA."

Feeling a little foolish at what he'd done, and with a final glance at the bedside clock, he saw he was on time for the Buchanan Street bus and grabbing at his nylon jacket with the deep pockets, shoved the handgun into a Co-op plastic bag alongside the small battery-operated torch, the photograph and the piece of paper given to him by the Commandant, then excitedly made his way downstairs.

****

In the north of Glasgow and though neither he nor Campbell were known to each other nor his fellow member of the Friends of Ulster Loyalists, Nicky Spiers, again went over in his head exactly what his instructions were.

In his room and seated on his bed, Spiers was dressed in black clothing, a large bladed kitchen knife from the cutlery drawer lying on the bed beside him.

Slowly rocking back and forth, he considered the enormity of what was required of him.

No stranger to violence and particularly when at the football matches with a group of like-minded pals, he was more used to using his feet and his fists, but never before had he used a knife.

However, when in the pub the previous evening, the Commandant had reminded him of his sworn oath to Queen and Country and the defence of the realm against all, including the hated Irish Republicans who had murdered so many good and innocent Protestants.

"Now, Volunteer Spiers," the Commandant had placed a reassuring hand on his shoulder, "here is your opportunity to hit back at the terrorists who have caused so much mayhem and bloodshed in our land."

Last night, Spiers recalled, it had all seemed so simple; go to where the Republican bastard was expected to be found, then a couple of thrusts to the chest, then get out of there and return home, not forgetting to leave the knife at the scene of the killing.

He squirmed with embarrassment at the memory of the end of the evening when he had drunkenly boasted to the Commandant that he'd do his duty and that he wasn't afraid, that he'd kill anyone who got in the way of his mission, that he'd die for his country.

It was when he'd wakened that morning, his head aching; he'd recalled his instructions.

His mission completed, he'd to return home immediately where he was to wash all his clothes and his footwear too and at a very hot wash.

There must be nothing, no blood and no witnesses who might connect him to the operation.

Until he had been contacted by the Commandant himself, the older man had emphasised, Spiers was neither to discuss his mission nor attempt to make any contact with any member of the group.

Buoyed by the importance of his mission, he had willingly agreed. But that was last night and after he'd sunk more than a couple of pints.

He'd turned his head slightly to stare down at the knife with the long, shiny serrated blade and inwardly shivered, yet he had no choice, for he had made the commitment.

He was a soldier of the FUL and must do his duty.

****

Conscious that Mickey Rooney had said that he was a big lad, Eddie

Fairbanks tasked Rooney, Duke Smythe and, just in case the mother was at home, Susie Lauder too, to bring Nicky Spiers in for interview; hopefully voluntarily rather than detaining him.
With luck, he and Considine agreed, Speirs might disclose the identity of the elusive Commandant.
It was simply by chance that when Lauder drove the CID car into Scalpay Street, Rooney identified the hulking figure of Spiers ambling along the road towards Scalpay Place, which in turn led to the busy Liddesdale Road.
"What do you think, Mickey?" Smythe, the senior officer in the vehicle, cast a glance over his shoulder to the back seat.
Rooney's eyes narrowed when staring along the road and just as Spiers turned the corner into Scalpay Place, he then said, "If it was me, I'd be curious to know where he's going, particularly as he's not at his work, today."
"Agreed," Smythe thoughtfully replied, then said, "Susie?"
She stopped the car and turning to him, said, "I've no radio, but I've my mobile so I'll stick with him. He doesn't know me, so I'll see how far I get."
Seconds later she was out of vehicle and when Rooney replaced her in the driver's seat, Smythe used his mobile phone to inform Larry Considine of Spiers being out and about and their agreed suspicions he could be going for a meet.
****
Deputy Chief Constable Charlie Miller rang the doorbell, then greeted by Cathy Heggerty, he said, "You're sure he's up for a visit?"
"I guarantee you, he'll be pleased to see you," she smiled widely.
Picking up on her relaxed manner, Miller followed her into the spacious living room where seeing Bobby Heggerty wearing a plaid dressing gown and pyjamas, he hesitantly asked, "Is there good news then?"
Heggerty frowned at his wife, who holding up her hands, grinned, "I never said a word. Must I remind you, Bobby, he *is* a detective."
Motioning that Miller sit down, she cheerfully added, "I'll just go and pop the kettle on."
When they were alone, Heggerty tiredly smiled when he said, "You know I had the colonoscopy, yesterday?"
"Yes," Miller nodded.

"Well, likely you will know it was suspected from the symptoms that I might have colon cancer. However, when they did the procedure, it seems that I had a number of things called polyps that the surgeon removed during the procedure. The short story is that while I was still on the surgical bed, the polyps were sent for a biopsy to check if they were cancerous, but thank God, they weren't," he sighed.
"And so," Miller stared at him, "just to be clear, Bobby, you've *not* got cancer?"
"No, boss, I don't," his eyes glassed over.
"Well, that's a bloody relief," Miller sprung up from his chair to vigorously shake Heggerty's hand.
The door opened to admit Cathy Heggerty who carrying a tray, glanced at them in turn, then smiled when she said, "Give me a week, Mr Miller, and I'll have him back at work."
****
Larry Considine hurried into Eddie Fairbanks room to tell him, "Nicky Speirs, boss, he's on the move."
"Eh?"
"When the guys got to Scalpay Street, he was out and walking off, so Duke made the decision not to detain him, but to follow him. Well, what I mean is, he sent Susie after him."
"Where are they now?"
"Spiers is on a bus and Susie got on behind him. As of two minutes ago, the bus is heading for the city centre with Duke and Mickey Rooney following in the car."

CHAPTER TWENTY-FOUR.

Considine phoned Smythe, then with the big man still on the line, then stood watching as seated at his desk, Eddie Fairbanks phoned Susie Lauder's mobile.
When the phones connected, Fairbanks put his mobile on speaker and watched Considine place his mobile against the DI's phone, thereby permitting Smythe to hear the call.
Fairbanks greeted her with, "Susie, I hear you're on a bus with Spiers."
"Oh, hello, Mary," she replied, "yes love, I'm just heading into town

now and should be there in about five minutes at Buchannan Street, unless I decide to get off first."

Glancing at Considine, he smiled at her quick thinking, then said, "I take it he's close by, so has he met anyone on the bus?"

"Aye, close by and like me on my own, but I'm thinking my two pals might be at Buchanan Street to meet me so hopefully, I should have company."

He glanced up to see Considine giving him a thumbs up, then with his own mobile in his hand, he stepped back into the corridor.

"And are you okay, I mean are you safe?" Fairbanks asked.

"Right as rain for the moment, but no idea where I might end up."

"Okay, Larry's contacting Duke to pass your message, so...."

"I'll hang up now, Mary, because I'm just getting off in Cowcaddens Road, so keep in touch, eh?"

"Roger," he ended the call, then rising from his desk, shouted through to Considine standing in the corridor by the open door, "He's getting off, Larry! Cowcaddens Road!"

Considine gave him a thumbs up, then spoke into his mobile.

****

It was as they'd agreed.

Jimmy, driving the Mondeo, dropped McCandlish and her two colleagues off under the canopied entrance at the front of the hotel, then as they made their way inside, he drove the car to the underground car park.

Stepping into the large foyer area, McCandlish immediately hesitated, for there at the reception desk side-on to her, stood the man she had come to meet, a man wearing a navy-blue business suit and carrying a briefcase and who she recognised from a photograph in her own intelligence file.

Gary McGuigan.

****

He had come a little early and now, his jacket stuffed into the Co-op bag and the handgun in his waistband beneath the Celtic top, Gary Campbell stood nervously shivering in the small cleaning cupboard located on the deserted staff corridor on the first floor; a corridor in the stairway the hotel guests had no reason to access or use.

Once more he switched on the torch to glance again at the photograph and the small hand drawn diagram that indicated the room where he would find his target.

****

So focused on his mission, it never occurred to Nicky Spiers that anyone might be paying attention to him and so thirty yards behind him, like so many passing her by with her mobile phone to her ear, Susie Lauder now had direct contact with Duke Smythe and said, "He's just meandering along and keeps glancing at his phone, either because he's waiting on a call or maybe," her brow creased, "he's checking the time."

It was Smythe who suggested, "If he is waiting on a call, he's no need to keep looking at his phone, so I'd suggest he's keeping an eye on the time. But why?"

"He's stopped at the traffic lights at Cambridge Street, waiting to cross the road, Duke," she glanced behind her, but there was nowhere to go nor anything she could do other than pass him by as he waited for the green man.

Adopting a cheery expression, she continued talking when she said, "Aye, that's right. I'm just heading to the bus station."

Resisting the urge to glance back to see if he was watching her, she sighed with relief when Smythe said in her ear, "We see him. Keep walking, Susie."

****

Her body tensed as McGuigan turned, then seeing her standing there just ten metres away, raised his hand to the three men with him and said something as he walked alone towards her, his eyes meeting hers.

She too raised a hand to prevent Axel from instinctively stepping in front of her, telling him, "Let's stay calm here, okay?"

McGuigan stopped in front of her, then to her surprise, smiled first at McKenzie then extended a hand to McCandlish when he quietly said, "If we're about to trust each other, Mrs McCandlish, how would you feel about telling our minders to go and grab a coffee at the bar there."

Her hand clasped in his, he reached across with his left hand to cover hers and gently squeezed, telling her, "Then you and me, with your friend here," he nodded at McKenzie, "and my young man, Donal; we can go and have a chat without any tension in the room."

"I don't think that's a good idea, Arlene," McKenzie interrupted, her eyes shooting across the room to where Axel and Jimmy stood. "I don't like leaving them down here and us alone upstairs."

McCandlish glanced from McKenzie to McGuigan, then she replied, "If there's to be trust, then it starts here."
****

Campbell checked his mobile phone.
The Commandant's instructions had been quite explicit.
"Remember, one of our supporters who works there will leave the door in the lane unlocked, so your entry will be no problem. Then, after you've hidden yourself in the cupboard marked in the diagram and at ten minutes past two, no later mind, you go for the target alone; at least four rounds in the body and you know what to shout out. Do you understand, Volunteer Campbell?" he'd stared into the younger man's eyes.
"The target *alone*. If anyone should try to interfere before you shoot the target, you have permission to shoot them too. Is that *clearly* understood?"
It was his adrenalin bravado that had him agree, but now, standing in the freezing cold cleaners' cupboard with boxes of toilet rolls stacked on shelves against one wall, mops and buckets against another and plastic bags filled with who knew what, the mission didn't seem to be as glamorous and exciting as he had imagined it would.
Checking the time again, he saw it to be just two minutes after two and his legs unaccountably shaking, he fetched the balaclava from the Co-op bag then pulled it on.
****

"It's only on the first floor," McGuigan had reassuringly smiled, "so why don't the four of us just take the stairs."
She agreed with a nod, but could see that his companion, the pokerfaced young man he'd introduced as Donal O'Hara, wasn't happy about leaving the minders behind and from her expression, neither was Constance.
****

Watching Speirs head bob down every half minute, Smythe whispered to Mickey Rooney, "Aye, he's definitely checking the time, but for what, God alone knows."
"It's just gone five past two," Rooney responded then when his phone beeped, Smythe heard him say, "We're on the first floor of the car park on the corner, Susie. Speirs is standing in Cambridge Street

across from the big hotel, there. Looks like he might be waiting on someone."

"Right," she replied, "if he's seen me on the bus, I'll hang back in case you need me."

"Roger," he ended the call.

****

In the incident room, Fairbanks and Considine waited frustratingly for an update, but as the three watching Spiers had no personal radios with them and were using their mobiles to communicate, they daren't interrupt.

****

Because the room had been booked in her pseudo name, Constance McKenzie turned to hand the key provided by the reception desk to Donal O'Hara, then watched him unlock the door.

Both men stood to one side as Gary McGuigan politely indicated both women enter first.

Glancing around the conference room with its highly polished oak table surrounded by a dozen straight backed, padded chairs, Arlene McCandlish strode into the room then nodded her approval when she smiled at McKenzie.

"Perhaps these four chairs here," she pointed towards two on each side at the top of the table where on the table between them, was a wooden tray with eight cups and saucers, two thermos flasks with tea and coffee and a plastic container containing an assortment of biscuits.

"That's our second agreement then," McGuigan smiled, before he joked, "I hope those four downstairs are still on speaking terms when we get through here."

Her eyes narrowed when McCandlish replied, "And here's also hoping that we are too."

****

Fetching the handgun from the back waistband of his jeans, Gary Campbell glanced once more at the hand drawn diagram, then taking a deep breath, opened the cupboard door.

****

Spiers glanced again at his watch then glancing left and right at the traffic, hurried across the road in the direction of the hotel.

****

Though she had been waiting to receive more phone calls, Susie Lauder startled when her phone rung to hear Mickey Rooney telling her, "He's on the move down the street next to the hotel, Susie," then heard Smythe's voice in the background saying, "He's away into…wait. It's like a wide lane, but there's a sign that says its Hill Street."
****

The two detectives began to race down the concrete stairway that led to the car park exit on Cambridge Street in an effort to catch sight of Nicky Speirs, then their eyes narrowing as they emerged from the car park into the bright sunlight, hurried to the corner of Hill Street, where a confused Smythe irately muttered, "Where's the bugger gone?"
****

The service corridor remained empty as gun in hand, Campbell nervously made his way to the door marked on the diagram; the door that the Commandant told him was a mere ten metres from the door to the room where the target was located.

It was then he realised he badly needed to pee and his left leg shaking, fumbled at the zip on his jeans before returning to the cupboard where he peed into a mop bucket.
****

"There!" Rooney pointed to a door on the left that was another entrance/exit to the car park. "Maybe he's away in there."

Rushing to the door, they almost collided with an elderly couple whose expressions gave voice to their feelings about nearly being knocked over.

"Sorry," Smythe gasped, then eyes narrowing, he said, "No, not the car park, Mickey. He looked like he was watching the hotel, wasn't he? Over there."

Rooney turned to see him pointing at a door opposite that according to the sign above, read, 'Hotel Staff Only.'

As one, the two men began to run across the narrow road to the door.
****

The negotiations had begun amicably, with McGuigan pouring coffee for all four and while handing out cups and saucers, politely telling McCandlish that while he was in no doubt she knew of his background, he assured her that he was convinced that her peace initiative was the right way to end the conflict and save lives.

As he continued speaking, she found any doubts or questions or reservation she previously had about McGuigan were slowly fading; then to her surprise, was beginning to believe that he too sought peace and unconsciously began to relax.
****

The carpeted corridor with the papered walls and paintings hung at intervals was a complete contrast, Campbell saw, to the service corridor, with its whitewashed walls and concrete stairs and from where he peeked out. As the diagram had indicated, he could see the door indicated on the diagram by an X, no more than several strides away.

Bracing himself, he glanced back and forth, but the corridor was empty, so stepped out and towards the door, his mouth suddenly dry yet inwardly reminding himself what the Commandant had told him. Once through the door he was too loudly shout, 'Up the IRA.'
****

Cautiously opening the staff door in Hill Street, Smythe was about to enter when he heard the sound of a man shuffling his feet and stopped dead, for the sounds seemed to be coming from the half landing directly above where Smythe silently stood.

As quietly as he dared, he turned to place his forefinger to his lips to warn Rooney to be quiet while pointing with the other forefinger directly above their heads.

Both now standing just inside the door in the square space beneath the bottom of the concrete stairs, it was Smythe who made the decision when he softly whispered, "I'll stop here in case he comes back down. You nip out and tell Susie to join us, then phone the boss and let him know what we're doing."

"What if he goes out the front entrance?" Rooney whispered back.

Shaking his head, Smythe replied, "He obviously doesn't want anyone to know he's in the hotel, so I'm certain he'll come back this way and when he does, we'll detain him."

"Right," Rooney nodded, then stepped back out the door into the street, his mobile phone already in his hand.
****

Readying himself Campbell placed his left hand on the door handle then taking a deep breath, shoved it open, the gun held out in his shaking right hand and prepared to fire it.

****

In the room, the four delegates were seated with McCandlish and McKenzie facing McGuigan and O'Hara, who sat with their backs to the door and who, when it crashed open, turned to see a male figure burst in and who wore both a Celtic football top and a full-face balaclava, his mouth open and a gun held in his right hand that he waved as though looking for someone to shoot.

****

Firearms, no matter what their size or calibre, are simply pieces of equipment and like all equipment require to be serviced and maintained to operate at their maximum efficiency.

However, Gary Campbell who other than toys and who had never in his life handled any kind of firearm, was not to know that the nineteen-twenty-eight manufactured Smith & Weston revolver he held with the six rounds in the chamber, had lain in a country house cabinet for many years before being stolen, some fifty years previously.

Following its theft, the gun passed through several hands before turning up in a terrorist related seizure by the police, then was misappropriated by DS Norrie McCartney of the Special Branch, who in turn passed it within a plastic bag to the man known as the Commandant.

And so, the handgun now wavering in Campbell's nervous hands had not been serviced for all those decades and thus was not in good working order.

In the two or three heart stopping seconds that followed after Campbell barged through the door, the stunned men and both women stared in open fear at the crazed man with the handgun, who then recognising Arlene McCandlish from her photograph, suddenly turned to deliberately point the handgun at her.

To everyone's surprise and not least his own, it was Donal O'Hara who reacted by jumping from his chair with the intention of tackling the gunman, but knowing that as he did so he was too late, that the gun was already firing.

Campbell his mouth too dry to shout out what he had been instructed, had pulled the trigger and that's when it all went wrong. The Smith & Weston, never maintained nor serviced since its theft all those years before, reacted as it was designed to do.

The brass cartridges in the chamber, all six more like the weapon, more than fifty years old, had also not weathered well, so when the firing pin struck the base of the cartridge, instead of the powder contained in the cartridge exploding in the chamber and sending the lead .38 bullet out through the barrel, it was the metal chamber itself that loudly exploded in a puff of smoke.

O'Hara, stunned, fell backwards onto the carpeted floor as the agonising scream that followed came not from any of the four occupants of the room, but from the gunman himself, who staring at the shattered, smoking revolver saw that part of his right thumb and most of his right forefinger was missing, while the rest of his hand was nothing but a bloodied mess.

With a shriek of agonising pain, he dropped the burning hot handgun, then stumbled back through the door, weeping and holding his injured hand to his chest, then dripping blood, staggered towards the door that led down into the service corridor.

In the meeting room, the shaken occupants stared from one to the other, but it was McGuigan, who gathering his thoughts, then instinctively said, "Arlene! We need to get out of here before the Guards come. Now!"

Grabbing at their jackets and files, the four rushed from the room with McGuigan steering them towards the stairs, then hissing at McCandlish, he cried, "It wasn't us, Arlene! We had no part in this!"

****

On the half landing in the service corridor, Nicky Speirs had heard the loud bang and readied himself, drawing the large knife from the poacher pocket inside his heavy jacket and stared narrow-eyed up to the door on the landing above.

****

Duke Smythe, standing quietly on the ground floor too had heard the bang, though the sound was muffled because of the closed door that led from the first-floor hallway into the service corridor.

But then he heard the door above opening and the stamp of someone's feet running down the stairs.

****

In the small seating area opposite the reception desk in the foyer, the four minders, seated around a table together and oblivious to what had occurred in the meeting room, had found a mutual, if rival interest in football and were engaged in a good-humoured slanging match about their respective teams, Celtic and Rangers.

Startled, the four men turned when the door to the upper floor's stairwell was thrown open and saw McCandlish being hurriedly escorted by McGuigan, his arm protectively around her shoulders, burst into the foyer and followed by O'Hara helping a shocked McKenzie.

Axel was the first to react and jumping up from his seat, advanced towards McGuigan who quickly held up his free hand to breathlessly gasp, "There's been an attempt on her life, but I swear, it wasn't us!" Glancing behind him, he added, "You need to get her out of here and now!"

Aware that guests and staff were staring open mouthed at them, Axel grabbed McCandlish, who clutched her file to her, then snapped at Jimmy, "The car to the front door, now!"

As one, McGuigan's minders hustled him and O'Hara away as McCandlish called after him, "I believe you!" then saw him nodding as he was unceremoniously pulled through the front door and out of her sight.

****

Up in the first floor, Campbell shouldered open the door to the service stairwell, then sobbing in agonising pain, lurched through the door to bounce off the whitewashed wall, then used his uninjured hand to tear the suffocating balaclava off before dropping it onto the stairs he was now staring down at.

His legs shaking and clasping his bloodied hand to his chest, he ignored the cleaning cupboard where his jacket lay within the plastic bag and weeping, instead began to stumble down the stairs, intent only on getting as far away from the hotel as quickly as he possibly could.

Twelve steps down on the half landing, his body shaking in anticipation, Nicky Spiers silently waited as he stared up at the figure who wore a Celtic top, coming down towards him.

Engrossed in his own agonising pain, too late Campbell saw a large man dressed in dark clothing, who snarled, "Fenian bastard!" then lunged forward to drive the knife into his chest, once, twice, then a third time at which discovered he could not withdraw if from his victim's body, that the blade had lodged between two ribs.

Shocked, the knife firmly wedged in his body, Campbell pushed back with both his uninjured and bloodied hands against his assailant, but to no avail, then fell back onto the concrete stairs, his weight pulling the knife from Spiers bloodstained grasp.
****
Downstairs, Smythe's eyes narrowed and he cocked his head when he heard what sounded like a brief scuffle, then an almost imperceptible gasp for breath.
****
Blinking rapidly and pale faced, as though suddenly realising what he had done, a horrified Spiers stood for several seconds staring down at the man he had just stabbed and who spluttered blood from his mouth, the knife wounds having pierced his lungs.
Turning, Spiers raced down the stairs to the door that led out onto Hill Street.
However, large though the young man was, he didn't expect to be met by Duke Smythe, who timing the sound of the footsteps racing down the stairs, stepped out from the space beneath the stairs and grabbed him around the neck.
Taken by surprise, Spiers cried out and tried to struggle free, but Smythe, a veteran of more than a few street brawls, forced him to the ground where he adeptly handcuffed his wrists to the rear, then turned him over on to his back.
"Now, now, son, calm down," Smythe growled into the face of the stunned Spiers, his nose wrinkling when he saw the younger man had peed himself.
Unaware of what had just occurred upstairs, Smythe's eyes narrowed when he saw fresh blood on Spiers jacket and so he calmly asked, "Right, son, tell me, what are you running away from?"

CHAPTER TWENTY-FIVE.

Two hours had passed since Nicky Spiers, now languishing in a detention room at Stewart Street Police Office, the A Divisional headquarters, had been grabbed by Duke Smythe.
Two hours in which minutes after Spiers was detained, Susie Lauder and Mickey Rooney discovered the corpse on the half landing; a

corpse wearing a Celtic top and whose right hand had been almost mutilated.

Minutes after that, it was Mickey Rooney who happened upon the balaclava lying on the ground by the door that led into the first-floor hallway. Cautiously following the trail of blood and ignoring an elderly couple who passed him by and stared curiously at him, Rooney discovered the remains of the handgun lying just inside the door of a meeting room where he also saw a chair had been knocked over.

By the time Rooney fetched his mobile phone from his pocket, two marked police vehicles had converged on the hotel in response to the receptionist's panicked call that some sort of incident had occurred on the first floor and was reported by several guests that it had sounded like a small explosion.

By the time Smythe and his two colleagues had liaised with the A Division officers and explained they had a male in custody as a suspect for a murder, the local CID were in attendance and Smythe, having handed Speirs over to be placed in the rear of a police vehicle, was on his mobile breathlessly updating Eddie Fairbanks.

"Okay, Duke," a confused Fairbanks, wondering at this unexpected development, breathed anxiously into the phone.

"I'll come down and join you at the hotel. Who's the senior CID officer on site from the Stewart Street office?"

Smythe, stood outside the staff door in Hill Street, glanced across at the brunette with her hair tied back into a tight ponytail and who was in the middle of briefing five of her detectives and a uniformed sergeant, before he replied, "DCI Elaine Fitzsimmons. Do you know her?"

"Only by reputation," Fairbanks nodded into his mobile before he added, "Tell her I'll be there in twenty minutes for a meeting."

"Roger, boss," Smythe ended the call.

In the Maryhill incident room, Fairbanks turned to Considine to ask, "Fancy a wee trip down to Cambridge Street?"

****

Axel, in the front passenger seat, had to lay his hand upon the younger man's shoulder to calm him when he said, "Slow down, Jimmy. As far as I can tell there's nobody following us, so the last thing we need is the peelers stopping us for speeding."

In the back seat, both McCandlish and McKenzie sat quietly, each lost in their own thoughts as Jimmy drove them back towards the riverside apartment.

McKenzie hesitantly turned towards McCandlish when, her voice shaking, she said, "It was them, wasn't it? If not McGuigan, it was definitely the 'RA' wasn't it?"

McCandlish, still deep in thought as she stared at the back of Axel's head, didn't immediately respond, then half a minute later, she dully muttered, "Who really knows."

Pulling into an empty parking bay, Axel turned to the two women and told them, "Wait here. Jimmy and I are going to check out the flat to ensure there's no surprises waiting there for us, then we'll throw our things into the bags and be back as quick as we can."

"Arlene," he stared meaningfully at her, "take the driver's seat and if anything spooks you, drive off and find a peelers station. Forget any thoughts of staying incognito now; there was CCTV cameras in the foyer, so the peelers will know soon enough who it was that hired the meeting room, then bugged out after that guy tried to kill you."

She balked when she said, "You're certain then it was me that was the target then, not McGuigan?"

"Oh, aye, no doubt," he nodded, then, as if angry or uncertain of what he was about to say, he added, "From what you told us and what McGuigan's man did, it seems not all the 'RA' support your peace initiative."

"Right," he suddenly opened the passenger door, "Jimmy, get out and let Arlene into the driver's seat and remember," he turned again to grimly instruct McCandlish, "anything you see that you're not happy with, get the fuck out of here and sharpish."

****

McGuigan's minders had speedily returned him to the safe house in Shettleston then giving him the minimum time to collect his things, he and O'Hara were driven on the M8 through to Edinburgh airport, where McGuigan was to catch a flight to London.

Handing him a stolen Irish driving licence and an Irish passport that had been altered to exhibit his own photograph and with details that matched the licence, his senior minder explained, "These were prepared as a back-up in case things went sideways. I've already booked you on a late afternoon flight and there will be minimum security if you're travelling within the UK, than over to Éire or the North. When you land at Heathrow, head to the McDonald's and wait there, we'll send your photo to our contact on her phone and she'll introduce herself as Siobhan. You'll receive travel arrangements from her. Got it?"

"Got it," he agreed with a nod, then turning to O'Hara, who sat with him in the rear seat of the Vauxhall Vectra, he quietly asked, "Was it us, do you think?"

Tight-lipped, O'Hara shrugged before he turned to reply, "You know as well as I do, Gary, there are those amongst us who will never settle any agreement with the Unionists. All I can tell you is this; I had no idea that we might have been compromised like that because as far as I am aware, everything was tight with a need to know caveat on the meeting. The time, the location and who we were meeting with."

McGuigan's eyes narrowed when he thoughtfully said, "There will be repercussions Donal, if it was us."

"And if I'm being honest, Gary, that's what worries me," the younger man thoughtfully replied.

****

Ronnie Masters wrist ached and her face felt as though it was now fixed with a permanent smile after attending to the dozens of customers who insisted she sign their copies of the Life & Fashion Management magazine or wanted their photographs taken stood beside her.

Still smiling, she backed into Laura to quietly say, "It's all very well having so many customers in today, but are we selling any gowns?"

Just as subtly, Laura smiled when she softly replied, "We've taken twice as many orders today than any *week* I can recall, so yes, we're doing rather well, Miss Masters."

"Good gracious," she took a breath as another pair of grinning women approached to have her autograph their magazines.

It was then that Laura intuitively said with a bright smile and loud enough for everyone close by to hear, "Miss Masters, you have a telephone call in your office."

Signing both women's magazines, she followed Laura through to the stockroom where she sighed, then with some feeling, said, "Thank you, thank you, thank you! My feet are *killing* me."

"I thought you were looking a bit pale, so sit yourself down and I'll have one of the girls bring you through a cup of tea, but I'll be staying out front."

When Laura had gone back to the front shop, Ronnie slowly exhaled and unconsciously rubbed at her stomach when she thought, happy as I am to be a success again, I think I'm getting a little past that life. She glanced down at her midriff and smiled, wondering at the evening's appointment and what her GP would make of her being pregnant at her age.

****

On the way to Cambridge Street with Fairbanks driving, Considine asked, "You had any previous dealings with DCI Fitzsimmons?"

"No, though I've heard of her, of course."

Considine took a slow breath, then sighing, smiled when he said, "I know her because she was a DS in Govan CID, for a while when I was doing my aide there, working for a DCI called Mary Wells. Wells," he nodded, "she was a good yin too."

He paused as he reflected on that time in his life, then his brow creased when he continued, "She's gone past her thirty years so she must have about thirty-four, thirty-five years in, but I did hear she's due to retire soon."

"Wonder why she stayed on after her thirty?" Fairbanks risked a glance at him.

Considine face expressed his interest when he said, "Unless she's changed any and I doubt she has, the people who work for her will have been pleased she did stay on. Elaine Fitzsimmons is a right good boss and smart too. As for her staying on, if I recall correctly, she's got twin daughters and was married to a cop; Eric, I think his name was, a Sergeant in L Division. Again, if I'm right, a heart attack took him a few years back. Probably being widowed and as a DCI, likely Elaine just decided to take the option of doing the extra five years permitted her because of her rank."

His face wrinkled when he added, "Age wise, I don't think she's any older than her mid-fifties and if she hasn't changed," he grinned, "a bit of a looker in her day, was our Elaine."

"So, apart from your one-track mind," Fairbanks pretended to chide him, "you're of the opinion that she'll be cooperative, that she won't be pissed our guys stumbled onto her murder?"

"Not at all," Considine shook his head. "Like I said, unless she's changed, she'll listen to what you have to say, then give you her take on it."

"Well," Fairbanks nodded forward, "we're here now and so it seems are most of the cavalry."
The uniformed cop who was standing behind the yellow tape spread across the entrance to the canopied entrance of the hotel recognised the vehicle to be a CID car and approached to tell Fairbanks, "We're a bit jammed up here at the minute, so can you turn around and use the multi-storey car park, please?"
Considine was about to explain to the cop he was speaking with a DI, but Fairbanks laid a hand on his arm, then replied to the cop, "No problem and can you tell me where I'll find DCI Fitzsimmons?"
It was then the cop guessed the driver must be a boss, so politely said, "Eh, she's in the side street there, sir. Hill Street," he pointed behind the car, then added, "I understand that's where the body was discovered."
Thanking the cop, Fairbanks did a U-turn in the street then drove to the entrance of the car park.
Minutes later, both he and Considine exited the car park side door onto Hill Street where Fairbanks saw a woman conversing with Duke Smythe, who seeing his DI, beckoned both men to them.
"Boss, this is DCI Fitzsimmons," he introduced her, but she first grinned, then held out her hand and said, "Larry Considine, you old reprobate. I thought you'd either be dead or in jail by now."
"And nice to see you again, boss," he smiled in return.
She turned her attention to Fairbanks and squinting at him, greeted him with a handshake and said, "It's Eddie, isn't it?"
"That's me, Ma'am."
"DC Smythe here has been giving me a summarised account of why your guys are in my Division finding dead bodies, so let's you and I head into the hotel, find a seat and you can give me the full story."
****
A little over twenty minutes later, seated in a quiet corner of the foyer that had been cleared of guests, Fitzsimmons slowly nodded when she said, "And this man, the Commandant. You think he's orchestrated the attempted murder of whoever was in the meeting room, then had his assassin killed, presumably to silence him?"
"It's just a working theory, Ma'am, but right now given the few facts that we have, yes, that's what I think."
Staring at him, Fitzsimmons slowly exhaled through pursed lips before she said, "Now, let me get this straight. You're also of the

opinion that our Special Branch are somehow involved? That they provided the original weapon that was recovered at your original murder locus, this man, eh…"

"James Crawford. I'm satisfied that his killer, Andrew Collins, who himself has died as a consequence of Crawford's dog biting him, was to be the real assassin, He'd purchased a Celtic top and balaclava, just as the murdered man in the stairwell was wearing."

"And he was what, a replacement for Collins?"

"I believe so, yes," but inwardly wondered at the tall story he had just related and could see the doubt in her eyes.

"And the suspect that DC Smythe detained. He was sent to kill the assassin?"

"Again, it seems likely, yes."

She continued to stare at Fairbanks for several seconds before she shook her head, then said, "Honest to God, Eddie, you couldn't make this up, could you? Either you and your team have stumbled onto some kind of serious plot or you're putting two and two together and coming up with five. The thing is at the minute," she frowned, "I'm not sure which it is."

A DC approached to glance at Fairbanks, then told Fitzsimmons, "That's the SOCO almost finished, boss. Do you need anything else done here?"

"What I need is a gin and diet tonic, but as I'm on duty, see if you can charm a pot of coffee out of the staff for me and DI Fairbanks when we come back downstairs? Oh, and if there's any choccy biscuits?" her eyebrows raised in hope.

"Boss," the young DC laughed, then left.

The short exchange between Fitzsimmon's and her young DC impressed Fairbanks and he realised Larry Considine had been correct.

His first impression was that the DCI did seem to be a good boss.

"Right then, Eddie, now the SOCO are almost finished their bit, you and I can take a tour upstairs to the meeting room where the four individuals who were in the room have since fled and visit the stairwell where the murder was committed."

"Have the four been identified?"

"No," she shook her head, but according to the reception staff, there were a further four men downstairs who helped them get away, so as far as we know, eight in total. However," she wryly smiled, "we have them caught on CCTV as they entered then exited the hotel, so that's a starter for ten for identifying them. That and I'm told it looks like the four upstairs used some crockery in the meeting room, as did the four seated at that table over there," she pointed at a table with four chairs where police tape had cordoned the table off, "so we might be looking at fingerprints."

"We know who the killer is, Nicky Speirs, but what about the dead man? Anything to identify him?"

She shook her head when she replied, "Nothing to *identify* him, but we discovered a plastic bag with a jacket lying in a cleaner's cupboard that we presume to be his, and there was a bus ticket issued earlier today to Buchanan Street bus station. The ticket's stamped with the time and date, but not where it originated. Oh," she grimaced, then to his surprise, heartily laughed when she added, "and we think he was hiding in the cupboard for a while because it seems he peed in a bucket."

Then she sighed when her eyes narrowed and further added, "As you know he was wearing a Celtic top; however, and curiously, when the casualty surgeon examined his body to pronounce life extinct, he discovered the deceased's arms to be covered in tattoos that declared his affection for King Billy and the Rangers football team."

Her brow furrowed when she stared at Fairbanks to sigh, "Rangers, King Billy and wearing a Celtic top. Quite a contradiction, isn't it?"

****

While at that time Fitzsimmons was conducting her tour of the murder locus with Eddie Fairbanks, seated at his desk within the Command Suite at police headquarters, ACC (Crime) Alex Gardener stared at his aide then said, "I've just had my wife on the phone, DI Cameron. It seems her morning paper delivery included one of those women's fashion magazines that she seems to favour and she has asked that I speak with one of my officers to request a signed copy of the magazine."

Confused, Cameron stared at him when he replied, "Sir?"

His face reddening, Gardener continued, "My wife has within the last ten minutes informed me that upon reading her magazine, she learned that one of my officers, Detective Inspector Edward Fairbanks of Maryhill CID, is named in the storyline and is in fact the partner of a former model, who features in the bloody magazine! A woman called," he glanced at his handwritten note then his voice raising, he continued, "Ronnie Masters, who according to the article, is apparently a rehabilitated former drug addict, but has served a sentence in an American prison!"

Cameron could see that Gardener's rage was not one of anger or disappointment, but that he seemed to revel in the fact that at last, if he were unable to pin down the boss of Maryhill CID, for whatever personal reason he had it in for the man, Gardener now had good reason to go after Heggerty's DI, Eddie Fairbanks.

Though he could feel his throat tightening, in as calm a voice as he could muster, Cameron replied, "As it happens, sir, I recall the stories a few years ago in the media about Ronnie Masters, who as you say, was a famous international model, but her life took a disastrous turn and she was vilified by the press. However, as I recall being told by a former girlfriend, Masters has turned her life around and…"

But he got no further when Gardener slapped a hand down onto his desk and hissed, "Enough! There is no excuse for one of my officers associating with such a woman! A convicted drug addict no less! And, as I am certain you are *aware*, DI Cameron," he stared steely eyed at the younger man, "Fairbanks association with this woman completely undermines the judicial system and is *contrary* to the Police (Scotland) Act in that apparently, according to the magazine article, he also cohabits with her!"

Oh shit, thought Cameron, and just when he'd thought the pompous bastard had calmed down about Heggerty.

"You will contact DI Fairbanks," Gardener continued, "and have him attend forthwith at my office. Is that clear!"

"Yes, sir, of course," he replied, knowing that anything else he said would be a waste of breath.

Leaving Gardener and entering the outer office, in a low voice, Cameron asked the ACC's secretary, "Did you hear all that?"

The middle-aged woman, upon leaving college all those years before, had worked first for the City of Glasgow Police, then after the amalgamation, graduated from a clerical position to serve as the secretary for a few Chief Superintendents before being promoted to personal secretary to a number of Assistant Chief Constables.

Though she would never openly admit it, working daily for ACC Gardener was a trial and he definitely was not her favourite person.

The young DI, however, though he had been in the job for a short time, was always courteous and treated her with a respect due both her age and experience and for that, she was grateful.
Shaking her head in disgust, she glanced at the dividing wall between the inner and the outer offices, then quietly replied, "There are things that I turn a blind eye to, DI Cameron; things that I hear, but would never repeat. On this occasion, seen as you have asked," she pointedly stared at him, "I heard every word."
"Well," in the same low voice, he said, "I'm not one to condone gossip, but I understand you to be friendly with the Deputy Chief's secretary, Ellen, aren't you?"
Smiling at the inference in his voice, she replied, "Indeed I am."

CHAPTER TWENTY-SIX.

The sat almost knee to knee closeted in the small room in Stewart Street Police Office that accommodated the CCTV unit, whose primary job was to monitor the strategically placed cameras located at the flashpoints in the city centre; both traffic and public areas where disorder might be expected.
In the tight little room, DCI Elaine Fitzsimmons and Eddie Fairbanks patiently watched and waited while in the duty operator's chair, occupied by the CCTV supervisor, he pored over the console. John Fields, now in his mid-fifties, slim with dyed blonde shoulder length hair and overtly gay, was known and widely respected throughout the Division and beyond for both his expertise and good humour and during his service had earned a plethora of commendations for his technical skills, many of which had resulted in convictions at the low and high courts.
Fairbanks immediately warmed to Fields when he outrageously winked at him, then said, "Call me Gracie. Everyone does."
Then he turned from the bank of screens in front of him to ask Fitzsimmons, "And these are the original DVD's the hotel provided, Ma'am?"
Nodding, she replied, "Yes. I told them we'd retain these and return them copies for their own security issues."

"I'll see that gets done," Fields eyes narrowed as he inserted a disc into the DVD player, then pointing at one screen, asked what the relevant times were that he was looking for.

"We're told sometime prior to two pm this afternoon, the four principal individuals we're concerned with, two men and two women, all respectably dressed in business suits, entered the foyer area with another four men who we suspect might have been bodyguards."

"Bodyguards?" wide-eyed, Fields turned towards her.

"Actually," Fairbanks intervened, "they didn't all arrive together. One of the witnesses recalls that two women and a man arrived together and that was shortly after four men, who'd arrived together some minutes previously."

He added, "And lastly, a man who joined the first three and all within a very short time, around one-fifty to two o'clock."

He glanced at Fitzsimmons, who nodded he continue, then said, "Our problem is from our initial inquiries, we've learned the meeting room where they planned to use was booked using a bogus company name."

He paused then continued again, "One of the women collected the key to the meeting room from the reception desk. After she collected the key, two men and both women used the guest's stairs to leave the foyer and walk upstairs to the first-floor meeting room, but we're told there's no cameras in that hallway or rather, none that record the short distance from the stairwell to the door of the meeting room."

"Okay, and the other four men?"

"They remained downstairs. They ordered coffee and sandwiches and sat together in the small seating area in the corner of the foyer."

"Right then," Fields began to press buttons, "Now I have a time frame, let's see what we've got."

It was then that Fairbanks received a text message on his mobile phone.

Opening the phone, he saw the message was from Larry Considine, that reads, *'ACC Gardener's aide, DI Cameron phoned looking for you. Says you're wanted by the ACC at HQ. Cameron suggests you phone him prior to going.'*

The text included a mobile phone number.

"Problem?" Fitzsimmons saw his face fall.

"Not certain, Ma'am. It seems I'm wanted by Mr Gardener at Pitt

Street, but I've no idea why."
But that wasn't strictly true, for Liz Malone's warning came rushing back and he wondered if today, of all days, his career might come to a crashing halt.
However, he was not prepared for Fitzsimmons response when in a voice filled with sarcasm, she said, "Well, Mr Gardener will have to wait, DI Fairbanks, for I have an on-going murder investigation to deal with and you and your own investigation parallel mine. So, for the time being, you're mine and if he wants to complain, he can come and see me."
He stared at her, then slowly smiled, realising that Elaine Fitzsimmons was definitely not a woman to trifle with.
"I don't want you getting into bother over me, Ma'am."
Conscious that Gracie Fields was earwigging, she sighed when she said, "While I've not previously met you, Eddie, I know of you and from what my good pal, Bobby Heggerty, tells me, you're a fine detective, both loyal and unusually in this bloody job, not afraid to upset the senior management. As for me and getting into bother, I'll assume that bugger Larry Considine has already told you, I'm past my sell-by date in this job, so there's nothing a man like Alex Gardener can do to me. Now, Gracie," she turned to Fields, "how are we doing?"
"There," he sat back and pointed at the screen. "Your two women and their male escort entering the hotel and fortunately the hotel has invested in quality cameras, because I'm about to print you out some excellent photographs. Give me another few minutes and I'll have photos of the rest of your suspects, too."
"Hold on," he suddenly leaned into the screen and stared at it, before he muttered, "So, where's the second guy?"
Turning his attention to the DVD discs from the envelope, he sighed, "Ah, here we are."
Ejecting the foyer disc, he inserted a second disc then explained, "Just a thought, but perhaps the fourth member of your quartet might be parking a car."
And that, Fitzsimmons thought with a smile, is why Gracie Fields is so respected at his job.
Pressing a button, the DVD activated onto the screen, then pushing some buttons, Fields arrived at the approximate time the three arrived in the foyer then wound back slightly and smiled, "There we

go. What you're seeing is a split screen, the entrance and the exit to the underground car park. The cameras are activated by a beam so when a vehicle entering or exiting crosses the beam, the barrier rises and permits the vehicle to pass through and for the purpose of payment, also records the vehicles registration number, as well as the time of entry to and exiting from the car park."

His eyes narrowed when he stared at the screen and winding the picture back a forth a few times, added, "It seems only one vehicle entered the car park about that time, Ma'am and what's curious is, the registration plate is three letter and four digits."

He turned to stare at Fitzsimmons before he calmly said, "Unless I'm mistaken, your vehicle is a black coloured Ford Mondeo with a Northern Irish registration plate."

****

With printed photographs of the eight individuals and particularly, the four who apparently were within the meeting room when it was attacked by the unidentified dead man, they left Gracie Fields to continue searching the other DVD for any trace of the vehicle used by the other four men who also remained unidentified.

Making their way to Fitzsimmons office on the first floor, she pushed open the door to find Larry Considine already seated in one of the three chairs in front of her desk. Occupying a second chair was a well-built man in his mid-forties, Fairbanks guessed, who completely bald sported a bushy dark beard and who rose to his feet when then entered.

"Eddie," she motioned a hand towards the man, "this is my DI, Alan Hamilton, who keeps following me around the city each time I get promoted," she grinned at him, then added, "Alan and I started off as neighbours in sunny Govan under Mary Wells, just about the time Larry was there too."

"That's right. While we've been waiting for you, Alan and I have been chewing the fat," he grinned, with a nod as Fairbanks shook Hamilton's hand.

Seating herself down at her desk while Fairbanks occupied the third chair, she addressed Considine when she asked, "You bring Alan up to date?"

"As much as I know, yes, boss," he nodded again.

"Okay, then before we start, let's set up some ground rules. Eddie," she turned to him, "as the investigations seem to overlap and in the current absence of Bobby Heggerty, do you have any objection to me being the SIO for a joint A and C Division investigation, with you acting as my deputy SIO?"

"None at all, Ma'am," he shook his head, "and in fact, as we already have a HOLMES up and running at Maryhill, can I suggest we use my incident room as the collation centre and if you agree, Larry here continues as the incident manager."

"Seems practical," she nodded then addressing Hamilton, said, "Alan, you are in charge here will I decamp with some of the team to Maryhill. We'll sort out later who I'm taking with me."

"Right, now that's settled," she frowned, "thanks to Gracie Fields downstairs, there seems to be a bit of a development."

Handing over the eight photographs for Considine and Hamilton to peruse, she continued, "It seems likely our suspects either are from or have a connection to the Province over the water."

To Fairbanks surprise, it was Hamilton who muttered, "Oh, shit, we're talking about the bloody Branch here, aren't we?"

"Your thoughts on it, Alan?" Fitzsimmons could barely suppress her smile.

Idly tossing the photos onto her desk, he replied, "What's the odds that the Branch are somehow involved in this, Elaine? I'm betting my pension if we took these up to them right now, they'd hum and haw, but there would be no doubt they'd recognise who these people are *and* I suspect, unless you want to differ, they'd tell us nothing, even though it's a murder investigation."

His eyes narrowing, it was Fairbanks who interjected when he said, "I *might* have an idea about that."

"And that is?" Fitzsimmons stared at him.

"Let's cut the Branch out of it for the minute. Why don't we contact the PSNI ourselves and ask them to do a PNC check for us."

"I like it," Fitzsimons grinned, but was interrupted by Hamilton who said, "As I understand it, the Northern Irish registration numbers are on the PNC, UK wide. Why do we need to contact the PSNI when we can do that ourselves?"

"Eddie," she turned to him with a questioning glance.

"Yes, we could do our own check," he agreed, "but it would only give us the bare essentials; owner's name and address. Whereas if *we* speak with the PSNI, we can request they not only PNC it for us, but also request they provide us with any intelligence about the vehicle's keeper. I'm guessing that if the Mondeo is somehow related to any of the organisations over there, it'll be recorded on their system and the PSNI's own Special Branch will be informed of our inquiry. If I'm correct, the PSNI Branch will in turn, contact our Branch here to find out what *we* know about the Mondeo and that," he smiled, "will have our Branch knocking on our door, rather than us knocking on theirs."

"Good one," Hamilton suddenly grinned.

Rising from her chair, Fitzsimmons added, "You and Larry will want to head back to Maryhill Eddie, so I'll finish up collating what we know from the locus and that'll give me time to sort out who I'm bringing with me."

The three men had hardly risen from the chairs when her desk phone rang and identifying herself, held up her hand to stop them leaving. They watched her lift a pen from her desk and write on her pad, then end the call with, "Thanks, Gracie. You're a star."

Replacing the handset, she thoughtfully said, "That was Gracie Fields. He trawled the CCTV cameras around Cambridge Street and about the material time the suspects fled the hotel, he has four men running east in Renfrew Street towards a parked car, a silver coloured Vauxhall Vectra that when they got in, took off at speed."

"Tell me he got a registration number," breathed Fairbanks and saw her nod.

"Yes, GB plates this time. That and he captured the car on a succession of cameras heading towards Milton Street, which if you don't know it," she glanced at Fairbanks, "runs adjacent to the motorway, where it turned left at the lights…"

"And didn't appear the other side of the underbridge, where there's an on-ramp to the M8," Hamilton finished for her.

"Yes, and he's currently talking to the ANPR people to try and determine where the Vectra went thereafter. However," she suddenly smiled, "Gracie had the duty officer downstairs PNC the registration number and guess what?"

It was Fairbanks again who suggested, "For any checks on that number, the purpose and details of the inquirer of the search to be forwarded to Special Branch?"

"Exactly," she grinned again.

****

Now late afternoon, Ronnie Masters was feeling the effect of a long and tiring day and with an apologetic grimace, left Laura to close up the shop while she returned home to prepare for her early evening appointment with her GP.

Though she didn't want to pester Eddie at work, she fervently hoped that he would make it to the Radnor Street surgery.

Though her GP was located in the Kelvinhaugh area of the city, Ronnie had known then come to trust Ella Harris after her breakthrough in the modelling profession.

Then, as the years passed and when the drugs and alcohol took over her life, sought Harris's help when with the assistance of Ronnie's friend, Anne, and the Fellowship, she fought to beat her additions.

Entering the flat, she decided on a shower rather than a bath, which would give her that extra time to lie on top of the bed and relax.

Kicking off her shoes, she lay down and unconsciously stroked at her belly, her thoughts turning to the life growing within her.

Quite unexpectedly, she felt the tears running down her cheeks and used the back of her hand to wipe them away.

She sighed, recognising that her hormones must be playing havoc with her emotions.

When ten minutes had passed and knowing that if she didn't move herself, she'd likely nod off and miss her appointment, she rose from the bed and made her way to the en-suite.

Stripping off her clothes, she stood naked in front of the full-length mirror and critically examined her figure, smiling softly when she imagined she saw a slight curve to her belly, yet even Ronnie knew that was too soon and more to do with her imagination.

Needing to pee, she squatted on the bowl, then rising, turned to flush, but stopped almost immediately as a cold fear gripped at her, for there, on the side of the white bowl, were some small, yet definite spots of fresh blood.

****

After handing over Nicky Speirs to the Stewart Street CID, Duke Smythe, Susie Lauder and Mickey Rooney returned to Maryhill Police Office where with the temporary absence of Larry Considine, Smythe resumed the role of incident room manager.

"Right you two," he beckoned Lauder and Rooney to him, "Find yourselves a quiet space and start your witness statements from the minute we saw Spiers walking in Scalpay Street to handing him over to the A Division guys. Oh, and Susie," he addressed her with a

pretend frown, then grinned, "That was a good bit of work, hen, taking him onto the bus and using your mobile to update us."
She flushed when she nodded, then replied, "Team effort, Duke. I think we all deserve a pat on the back."
He smiled when he nodded, "All the same, you did okay, lass, and I know you've not had any lunch, so why don't you and Mickey nip down to the café of Maryhill Road and grab a couple of rolls. There's a real chance," he sighed, "we might be here past finishing time tonight."
"Okay, I'll bring you back something, too."
In the corridor outside the incident room, Lauder and Rooney met with Fairbanks and Considine, who both greeted them with their own congratulations in a job well done; catching and detaining Spiers for murdering the as yet unidentified man.
"We were just nipping out for some rolls," Rooney stared from one to the other, "can we bring you something in?"
Before either could respond, the door to the incident room was opened by one of the civilian HOLMES operators, who seeing Fairbanks, said, "Ah, good, sir, you're back. That was ACC Gardener's secretary on the phone. Apparently you were expected at his office some time ago?"
"Oh, right, thank you," he frowned, then glancing at Considine said, "If you're looking for me I'll be in my office."
When the door closed behind him, he slowly walked to his desk to compose his thoughts.
He had no doubt why the ACC wanted to see him, correctly guessing that Gardener must have learned about Ronnie's past.
His hands balling into fists on his desktop, he'd already decided that regardless of what else was happening in his world; if Gardener went after him because of their relationship then *sod* the bastard!
He was out and to hell with the job!
A cold anger filled him that in the middle of a serious investigation, all the ACC could think of was how to use the Police Code of Conduct to gain some sort of spiteful revenge against Bobby Heggerty, using him and Ronnie as the pawns in Gardeners twisted vengeance.
Bastard!
He slumped down into his chair, but whether from tiredness or the

knowledge that no matter what he said or did, he could not fight a set-in stone regulation for ultimately, there was no choice to make. Like it or not, the decision was out of his hands and already made for him.

Ronnie and their unborn baby, *they* were his life now and the police? Well, he felt himself inwardly sneer it was after all just a *fucking* job. He glanced up when the door was knocked, then pushed open by Gardener's aide, DI what's his bloody name.

"Yes?" he snarled at Cameron.

"Before you go off on one," Cameron stared steadily at him, then asked, "what's the likelihood of me and you having a little chat?"

"Why? Have you been sent by your boss to collect me?"

"Actually," Cameron drew out the chair in front of the desk, then sitting down, calmly said, "he thinks I'm out of the office carrying out another task for him that's *not* related to you, but I wanted to speak with you before you went to see him."

Fairbanks was in no mood for office politics, so snapped at him, "See me about what?"

"First of all, Eddie," Cameron raised a hand, then softly smiled when he continued, "Can I call you Eddie? Well, you may not know me, but I'm nobody's lapdog and I consider what Gardener is doing is not only reprehensible, but to use me as some sort of fetch and carry; that's just not on," his lips puckered when he slowly shook his head. "What I'm trying to say is that I don't know why he has it in for Bobby Heggerty, but it's plainly clear to me that if he can't get Heggerty, he's going after you because he seems to think he can hurt Heggerty by bringing you down."

Interested now, Fairbanks eyes narrowed when he said, "Go on."

"Well," Cameron drawled, "I don't know you that well, Eddie; in fact, not at all, but I've spoken to a few people who do know you and you seem to be well regarded amongst your peers; our peers, I should say," he smiled.

"Anyway, and I trust you will keep their confidence when I tell you this, since I've been working for him, I've learned that in the Command Suite there's a network that operates between the secretaries who work for the senior officers; probably the best way to describe it is, you might say it's a kind of unofficial information service."

He slowly smiled when he continued, "By way of explanation, some if not most of these women, who I should add are in a position of trust because of the nature of their job, have worked for the police for a hell of a lot longer than you and I."

He sat forward and stared keenly at Fairbanks.

"These secretaries, they use this kind of network to pass info to their bosses when they think that boss should know something."

"Why are you telling me this?"

Fairbanks watched Cameron take a slow breath before he replied, "Gardener's wife, a nice lady I have to admit and unlike him, I don't think she's got a bad bone in her body. Anyway, she spoke this morning to him and asked him to get you to obtain a signed copy of that fashion magazine your partner featured in. Apparently, his wife had read the full article. Mrs Gardener also told him that the feature contained a short summary of Ronnie Masters past and current life and of course, how she's at last found happiness with her current partner."

He smiled when he added, "You. Detective Inspector Eddie Fairbanks of Strathclyde Police."

Fairbanks slowly exhaled, but Cameron continued when he shrugged, "I have it on good authority that Gardener's secretary, you don't need to know her name, has fed his intention to some of her friends in the Command Suite; his intention to have you in front of him, to force you to either comply with the code of conduct regulations or, well, you know the rest."

"Like that's going to happen," Fairbanks shook his head.

They sat in awkward silence for several seconds before Cameron stared inquiringly at him to ask, "I know it's a very personal question, Eddie, but with your career in the balance, is she worth it?"

He stared pokerfaced at the younger man before he abruptly replied, "Absolutely."

Slowly nodding at Fairbanks sharp response, Cameron seemed to be deeply thoughtful before he said, "One further thing, Eddie, my boss isn't one for staying late at the office so there's little point in heading to Pitt Street at this time of the day. He is, however, an early bird into the office in the morning. Needless to say, he'll be fuming that though you were summoned, you never appeared this afternoon. Of course," he wryly smiled, "first thing tomorrow morning he'll take out his petulant anger on me that I didn't, ah," he grimaced, "*persuade* you to hotfoot it to his office. It's my intention to tell him you were unavoidably detained because of your on-going murder investigation. Are we on the same page if he asks *you* why you didn't show up?"

"Yes," Fairbanks replied with a nod, then asked, "Why exactly are you sticking your neck out for me, DI Cameron?"

He smiled as though a little surprised, then he repeated the question, "Why am I helping you? Hmm," his eyes narrowed as though in thought.

"Two reasons, Eddie. Like I said, I don't like being used as Gardener's gopher like I'm some sort of rookie to the CID. We both know I'm young to be a DI, but I've worked hard to get my promotions and I believe. I not only consider myself to be quite a bright guy, but to be frank, I'm pissed at not working at a Divisional CID; at my real job that I reckon I'm good at."

He sighed, then said, "Secondly, from what I've learned about you, you seem to be just as smart and it's mooted you're being marked for great things in the police, so there's no doubt our career paths will at some point merge and that all said, I'd rather be your friend than your enemy."

"Fair enough," Fairbanks again nodded as he watched Cameron rise from his chair, but who then stopped and stared down at him when he said, "One last thing. Before you visit ACC Gardener tomorrow morning and might I suggest as early as possible, you should know this."

CHAPTER TWENTY-SEVEN.

With almost thirty-five years under her belt, the majority as an operational CID officer, Elaine Fitzsimons was no stranger to pressure and from behind her desk, issued instructions to her deputy, DI Alan Hamilton, before selecting the half dozen detective officers who would accompany her in two vehicles to Maryhill Police Office.

"And," she stared at those selected who stood before her, "remember we are guests of the Maryhill CID, so whether you know some of the staff there or not, you will conduct yourselves as I would wish because you represent me. Understood?"

The nods and "Yes, Ma'am," responses indicated they did, for good boss that Fitzsimmons was, all six knew too, not to step on her toes. "Right, I'll see you guys there because I'm taking my own car," she arose from behind her desk to dismiss them.

A little under twenty minutes later, Fitzsimmons pulled into the rear yard at Maryhill then getting out of her car, heard her name called. Turning, she smiled when she recognised the uniformed woman who strode towards her, then said, "Liz Malone. I thought you were supposed to be away?"

"Another couple of weeks, Elaine, then it's a sunnier climate for me. How you getting on?"

"Oh, so, so. You know how it is. We live in the West of Scotland so we're all subject to the damp climate and that means…"

"Arthritis. Aye, I know. My knees are buggered too," Malone smiled.

"I feel your pain," Fitzsimmons returned the smile, then asked, "Finished for the day?"

"Yes and no. I'm away to visit Bobby Heggerty. You know him, don't you?"

"Yes, I do. Him and Cathy. Nice people, them both."

Her eyes narrowed when she said, "I heard a whisper he's off right now on the pat and mick. Nothing serious, I trust?"

"A cancer scare that fortunately turned out to be polyps."

"Oh, right," her forehead creased and she grimaced when she replied, "I suffered those in the bowel after I delivered my second. They still don't know how they arrived there," she sighed. "Nasty buggers, too. I was shitting blood for a fortnight before I got them dealt with."

"But you're okay now?"

"Right as rain. Speaking of which," she glanced up.

"And you're going upstairs to see Eddie Fairbanks?"

"I am, yes. We've agreed I'll be the SIO in the joint investigation. You know what's going on in the investigation?"

"Not totally up to speed, but I've a fair idea, yes. And while we're talking about young Fairbanks," she grimaced.

Almost ten minutes passed before Fitzsimmons thoughtfully said, "Thanks for the heads-up. Well, Liz, I'd better let you get into your car before the two of us get soaked. I'll see you tomorrow?"

"Most definitely and Elaine, Eddie Fairbanks. I just want to add that he's a good one and a rising star. One to watch."

"For the time I've got left anyway," she laughed, then waved cheerio as she headed for the back door.

****

Across the city and citing a headache, Arthur Denholm left his assistant Penny to lock up the office and tensely made his way downstairs to the private car park.

Once in the car, he took several gulps of breath in an effort to ease the pain in his chest as he glanced at his wristwatch, knowing the operation must have by now, succeeded.

It was almost on the hour, so switching on the car radio, his hands clenched into fists and his right foot beating a tattoo on the cars rubber mat, he impatiently listened for the start of Smooth Radio broadcast, the station that delivered the local news.

At last the news summary began, the first item frustratingly reported that afternoon, Tony Blair made his final speech as Prime Minister at the Labour Party Conference.

"Come on, come on," Denholm muttered through gritted teeth.

His eyes widened when the second item reported that the police in Glasgow had sealed off Cambridge Street due to an on-going incident at the hotel located there and while there were no further details, some guests spoken to by the station reported the large police presence seemed to indicate there had been a murder within the hotel.

"Yes! Yes!" he hissed as he slapped both hands at the steering wheel, a feeling of exhilaration replaced the doubt, confident now that his volunteers had done as instructed; Volunteer Campbell had killed the traitorous bitch while Volunteer Spiers had cut off any connection that Campbell, an unfortunate but necessary sacrifice, had with the FUL and him in particular.

Starting the car engine, his thoughts were filled with the news that the group's first operation – *his* first operation – had been a success and already he was imagining the plaudits he would accept when he received the call to attend at the secret meeting in Belfast of those Inner Council members who still believed in victory.

****

On her way up the stairs to the CID suite, Fitzsimmons saw a well-dressed, handsome young man in his late twenties, maybe thirty, she thought, who politely nodded at her as he passed her by.

Sticking her head into the incident room, she nodded to Larry Considine, who seeing her, grimly smiled and waving a sheet of paper, then said, "The DI's in his room, Ma'am, and I've an update for you both."

"Okay, and what's the chance of a coffee?"

It was Susie Lauder who raised a hand to reply, "I'll see to that, Ma'am."

"Just milk, please," Fitzsimmons smiled at her then followed Considine to the DI's room.

When they were seated, it was Considine who opened the briefing. Turning to Fitzsimmons, he said, "I have a source in the Branch and I reached out to them about the Vectra."

She raised a hand when she drolly replied, "And I just know you won't divulge who this source is, Larry, so tell me; what did they disclose about the Vectra?"

Fairbanks smiled at Considine's subterfuge, that he didn't reveal the gender of his source, but who then replied, "The Vectra is registered to a woman who resides in the Shettleston area of the city. She's a known Irish republican sympathiser who has in the past, accommodated active service unit members, ASU's I think they're called, who have come over to spend some rest and recreation time here in Glasgow. You know, wine, women and song and all provided *gratis* for the heroes of the Cause," he couldn't help but inject some sarcasm into his voice.

"Unfortunately," he sighed, "since the Good Friday Agreement, the woman hasn't featured on the Branch's radar since and they've no idea to whom she might have loaned her car or indeed, gifted it to."

"And as it was four men who were using it, we can rule her out as being involved in the disturbance at the hotel," Fairbanks commented.

"That, boss, and to protect my source, we can't interview her with the knowledge that we know her to be an IRA supporter either."

"Right," Fairbanks conceded with a nod then said, "but it doesn't prevent us from asking who was using her car at the time of the incident."

However, his suggestion fell flat when Duke Smythe knocked on the door with a sheet of printed paper and his face told them it was bad news.

"Just PNC'd the car boss, the Vectra. It has now been reported stolen from outside the keeper's address in the Shettleston area. The registered keeper says she hadn't noticed it gone from its usual parking spot and last saw it two days ago."

"Fly bitch," Considine bitterly muttered. "They must have guessed we'd obtain the reggie number and that's them protecting her from any involvement."

Fitzsimmons loudly exhaled when she said, "But it does confirm the Irish Republican connection to the meeting in the hotel room. That in turn would suggest," she held up her hand, "and mind, it's only speculation, that the four in the Vectra were either meeting members of some *other* republican group or," her eyes narrowed, "am I way off course here when I wonder; maybe some Loyalists?"

The silence was broken when Fairbanks snapped out, "A false flag operation!"

"Eh, what?" Fitzsimmons said as they both stared at him.

"It was something that Susie Lauder said, some idea she had," his eyes beamed brightly when he glanced at them in turn.

"When we identified Andrew Collins as the killer of our first murder victim, James Crawford, the team turned Collins house where he lived with his mother and discovered a Celtic top and a balaclava. Well, when we learned of him to be a Rangers supporter and an apparent Loyalist, it was Susie's idea when she suggested that perhaps it was Collins intention to pretend to be a Republican when attacking some Loyalists."

"And the Republicans would get the blame," Fitzsimmons nodded in understanding.

"And if what we suspect, if it *was* a meeting between both sides of the divide, it now begs the question," Considine stared from one to the other.

"Why would Irish Republicans be having a meeting with Loyalists?"

****

Gingerly dressing and fearful that to active a movement might result in further bleeding, Ronnie Masters swithered whether to phone Eddie and tell him about the blood spotting or as previously agreed, simply meet him at her GP's surgery.

Finally, she decided that she wouldn't unnecessarily worry him, that she wouldn't risk driving either, so telephoned a black hackney cab to take her to the Radnor Street surgery, all the while anxiously worrying herself that what she had seen might be the start of a miscarriage.

Arriving early at the surgery for her six-thirty appointment, pale faced and drawn, the receptionist acknowledged her arrival and asked her to take a seat in the waiting room.

With hesitant smiles at the two other women who sat in the room, both noticeably pregnant, she glanced at her watch and saw it to be five minutes after six.

****

Though she thought he might be overly cautious, Arlene McCandlish's senior minder, Axel, had instructed Jimmy to avoid a direct route to Cairnryan that added almost an hour to the journey. However, no matter what she thought, she did not object for if as Axel suspected that along the route they would naturally take, there might be a back-up attempt on her life, someone lying in wait them, then any ambushers would be disappointed.

His alternative route that first took them south on the M74, then across country to travel on the A75 through Newton Stewart towards Glenluce, would bring them to Cairnryan from the opposite direction that an enemy might have assumed.

However, the extra time in the car had given McCandlish time to think and it was shortly after the vehicle passed the turning towards Portpatrick that McCandlish, peering ahead through the windscreen that was splattered with rain, told Jimmy, "When it's safe, pull over onto the hard shoulder."

Turning in his seat, Axel stared curiously at her when he asked, "You okay, Arlene?"

Pale-faced, she nodded as the car slowed, then stopped, with Jimmy first pressing the button for the four-way indicators, then switching off the engine.

The silence in the car lasted for several seconds before McKenzie asked, "What's wrong, Arlene? Are you not well? Car sickness?"

She turned to stare at McKenzie before she stonily replied, "No, Constance, just a touch of clarity."

"Clarity?"

She took a breath and locking eyes with McKenzie, said, "You were the one who arranged the hired car, the ferry, and the meeting at the hotel and more importantly, the accommodation with what you said was the Glasgow contact. In fact, Constance, you went to great

lengths to keep all those details to yourself, for weren't Axel, Jimmy and me told by you it was a need to know, for *security* reasons?" she calmly added.
She watched McKenzie's face turn chalk-white, who then stuttered, "What are you implying, Arlene, that I was somehow involved in that Fenian madman trying to kill you?"
"Yes, Constance, that's exactly what I'm implying. Trying - to - kill - me," she locked eyes with McKenzie.
"Not anyone else in the room," she quietly continued.
"Me. The driving force behind the peace initiative between the Republicans and us."
Slowly shaking her head, she scoffed, "A man wearing a Celtic top, a man who was *supposed* to look like a Fenian. How bloody ridiculous was that?"
She sighed when she continued, "I'm guessing the plan was for you and Axel and Jimmy to report back that it was a Republican assassination, that the 'RA' had changed their mind about any peace initiative and it must have shocked you to see McGuigan's young fella, O'Hara, jump to my defence."
Her eyes narrowed in thought when she added, "And that's why you were so annoyed Axel and Jimmy didn't accompany us upstairs to the meeting room. It was nothing to do with them protecting us, it was because you needed them to witness my murder by a man wearing a Celtic top."
"And him supposedly a *Fenian*," she stressed the word, then added with the same emphasis in her voice, "A *Republican*."
Again, she shook her head.
"Wait a minute, Arlene," Axel began to protest, but McCandlish, continuing to lock eyes with McKenzie, held up her hand to silence him and shaking her head, said, "No, Axel, you and Jimmy," she shook her head, "I'm satisfied that you didn't know about this."
She turned to glance at him when she continued, "You two were to be the patsy's who were to witness me being murdered and were bound to report back that a man in a Celtic top had shot me. A Republican," her voice oozed sarcasm, "simply because he was wearing a Celtic football top. But not being present in the room, Constance would instead tell you when she came down the stairs that's what happened. That *was* your plan, wasn't it, Constance, and you knew all the details of my assassination because it was you who

was involved in setting it up, wasn't it?"

McCandlish saw the three-inch scar on her cheek turn paler than the surrounding skin and realised McKenzie now knew she had worked it out, then watched the blood drain from the younger woman's face. McKenzie knew she had minutes, if not seconds before she was dead, but decided to spit out her vitriolic hatred before she was gone. Teeth gritted, she sneered, "Yes, it was me and the true Loyalists who hate what you have become; a traitor to your people! A Protestant apologist for fucking Republicans to gloat over! They murdered my family! They murdered your father, your brothers *and* your husband," she stabbed a forefinger at McCandlish and vehemently hissed, "yet still you want to make peace with the bastards!"

She drew breath, then sneered, "Have you no shame!"

Little balls of spittle formed at the corners of her mouth and her hands clenched into fists, yet McCandlish knew that McKenzie would not attack her, not with Axel, shocked though he was, ready and waiting to pounce and always prepared for such an assault.

She slowly exhaled, then almost wearily, said, "Axel, fetch Constance's bag from the boot please."

"What," McKenzie realised what was happening and said, "you're going kill me here in the middle of nowhere? Axel," she turned to him then watched when he stepped through the front passenger door to pull open the rear passenger door, "for fuck's sake! You can't possibly agree with her? Don't you know what she's proposing with the Republicans?"

Glancing past her to McCandlish, who he saw give a subtle shake of her head, he calmly replied, "You either step out, Constance, or I drag you out by the hair."

"Bastard!" she screamed at him, but realised resisting him was futile. Stepping out of the car, he stood to one side watching her closely, his hand still on the door and his other hand tightly gripping a shaking McKenzie by the arm.

In the driver's seat, a stunned Jimmy stared wordlessly at the road ahead, suddenly wanting no part of what was happening behind him. From the rear seat, McCandlish leaned forward to tell McKenzie in a low voice, "No, Axel's not going to kill you, Constance, though some might say it's what you deserve. You have been part of a plot to murder me and derail what might lead to an eventual peace between our people and the Republicans."

She took a short breath, then said, "So, while I might one day forgive, I will *never* forget."

She drew another breath to calm herself, hiding the fact that beneath her skirt her legs were shaking, before she added, "Consider yourself lucky you are being put out the car in Scotland, but if I should hear of you returning to Ulster," her teeth gritted when she added, "you're a dead woman."

The rain now falling heavily onto her shoulders and bareheaded, a shocked McKenzie watched the Mondeo disappear into the gloom, then her hands shaking, she clumsily fetched the mobile phone from her jacket pocket.

Dialling the number listed in her directory as auntie Sadie, when the call was answered, her voice faltered when she simply said, "It's me. We failed and she knows it was a set-up."

****

As the discussion in the DI's room continued, he glanced at the wall clock then his face paled.

"Shit!" he stammered.

Elaine Fitzsimmons stared at him when she asked, "Pardon?"

"Ma'am! Sorry," he rose from his chair, and almost leapt across the room to grab his coat from the peg on the wall, then gasped, "I'm meeting my partner at six-thirty for a doctor's appointment down in the west end!"

Then it was out before he realised when he added, "She's pregnant!"

"Well," Fitzsimmons choked back a laugh, "you'd better get your skates on, Eddie. You've ten minutes to get there, but don't kill yourself on the way," she called out, but by then he was running down the corridor.

Turning to Considine, she smiled when she asked, "Did you know?"

"Hadn't a clue," he shook his head, then smiling asked, "So, Elaine, digressing completely. How's life treating you these days?"

****

Ronnie's GP, Ella Harris, a slim, middle-aged woman with short, tight curly and prematurely greying hair and who wore a brilliantly white lab coat, asked, "Are you sure you don't want to wait for him?"

A little miffed, Ronnie shook her head when she replied, "No, I'm too agitated to wait. It's not like Eddie to forget this. If he's not here then something must've held him up."

It was then the door was knocked by the receptionist, who said, "Miss Masters' partner's here, doctor. Shall I send him in?"

Smiling at Ronnie, Harris nodded and said, "Please do."

Seconds later, the door opened again to admit a red-faced and breathless Fairbanks who striding over to Ronnie, kissed her on the cheek and said, "I'm sorry I'm late."

"Yes, you are," she chided him, then turning Harris, she said, "He doesn't know."

"Know what?" he turned from one to the other.

"Please, both of you," Harris indicated the two chairs in front of her desk, "sit down."

When all three were settled, she explained, "This afternoon, Ronnie saw some spots of blood in the toilet bowl. Now," she held up a hand to pre-empt Fairbanks panicked questions, "there might be a number of explanations for this, starting with the simplest which is that in the early stages of pregnancy and commonly up to about three months, bleeding is fairly common and may or may not be a sign of a problem. Is that clear?"

She watched them both nod they understood.

"The worst-case scenario, which I'm certain you will both be thinking, is miscarriage. So, before you worry yourselves to death, let me explain. There are a number of facts that can contribute to a miscarriage," she stared at Ronnie, "not least the age of the mother."

"Ronnie, are you happy with me asking you some very intimate questions in front of Eddie?"

She forced a smile when she sighed, "After my history, I have nothing more to hide, so yes; ask away."

"Have you previously conceived and had a live birth or lost a baby?"

"No never. I've *never* conceived," she stressed with a blush.

"Okay," Harris drawled, then asked, "Do you have any knowledge of a family genetic condition that might affect your ability to carry a child?"

She shook her head when she softly replied, "Not to my knowledge, no."

"And though I already know the answer, I need to ask. No more alcohol or substance abuse?"

"Not even over the counter medication since I became sober," she shook her head.

"For what it's worth, Ronnie, I thought not," Harris softly smiled.

"And you, Eddie," she turned to him.

"Me?"

"Well, you certainly seem young enough for your age not to be a problem, but any issues in your male family members re their sperm?"

"Eh, not that I know of," he found himself unexpectedly blushing.

"Do you have male siblings and if so, have these siblings sired children?"

"A brother yes, he's in Australia. He's married with two daughters."

"Good," Harris slowly replied, then said, "Well, I'm a GP, so all I can say is that in the darkest depths of your imagination and particularly at night, you will both imagine the worse. Try as you might, Ronnie, Eddie," she stared at them in turn, "your minds won't settle until an obstetrician examines you. The sad thing is," she frowned, "that there is a lengthy waiting list on the NHS, perhaps even three or four weeks. However," she again stared at them in turn, "if you are willing to go private, say to Ross Hall over in Crookston, I could arrange a friend of mine to see you a lot quicker."

"How quickly?" Fairbanks asked.

Her face creased when she suggested, "I won't promise, but perhaps as early as Friday or Saturday this week?"

"Do it, please," he nodded.

****

The desk phone in Eddie Fairbanks office rang and was answered by Larry Considine, who nodding, scribbled on the desk pad in front of him.

When the call ended, he told Fitsimmons, "That was your DI, Alan Hamilton. Says to tell you that the two guys you tasked to interview the suspect, Nicky Speirs, have reported that Speirs is now lawyered up and to report the interview was a washout. He says other than admitting his name, Speirs folded his arms and stared at a corner of the detention room and completely ignored every question that was put to him."

"Well," she grimly smiled, "if my former SB training is correct, that smacks of someone who has been told about how terrorists are told to respond when they are arrested, but we'll see just how resolute

Speirs is after a night in the cells, then a remand at Barlinnie. Anything else?"

"Yes," he grimaced, "the DNA sample from our deceased wearing the Celtic top has been matched to a Gary Campbell, with an address in Larkhall."

His brow furrowed when reading his notes, he added, "A PNC check indicates that Campbell has previous convictions for breach of the peace at football games and is recorded in his antecedent history as a member of a Larkhall Loyalist flute band. Alan asked if you want any of his team to inform the next of kin about Campbell's murder?"

Glancing at her watch, Fitzsimmons grinned when she said, "We're still Federated ranks, Larry, so unless you've a pressing need to get home, how's about me and you earning ourselves a spot of overtime?"

****

Because of the evening commuter traffic, with Considine driving, it took them a little over forty minutes to travel to the South Lanarkshire town of Larkhall, where the Satnav directed them to Campbell's home address, a mid-terraced house in Mason Street. Getting out of the car, it was Fitzsimmons who muttered, "Nearly thirty-five years in and no matter if it's a good guy or bad guy, I've never got used to delivering death messages."

Considine's knock on the door was answered by a blonde-haired woman who Fitzsimmons guessed to be in her mid to late-thirties, wearing a shops assistant's overall over jeans and training shoes and who might have been pretty, but for the make-up caked to her face. Staring suspiciously at them, her eyes narrowed when she said, "What?"

"Mrs Campbell? I'm…"

"Ms Campbell and you're the polis, aren't you," she sighed, then turning away from the door, snapped over her shoulder, "You'd better come in before the neighbours see you, as if I haven't got enough for them to gossip about."

They followed her into an untidy front room, where women's magazines lay scattered across a glass-topped coffee table and the couch and where the large and blaring television was switched on to a pop channel.

"Wait a minute," Patsy held up her hand to mute the sound, though the TV remained switched on.

Crossing her arms, she scowled when she said, "If you're here and he's not, he must be locked up somewhere, so what's he done now?"
"Just to confirm," Fitzsimmons calmly replied, "you are Gary Campbell's mother?"
"Aye," Patsy cocked her head to one side then forcing a smile when patting at her hair, she added, "Though I'm always getting taken for his big sister."
Aye, that'll be right, Considine unkindly thought, but took a deep breath when he heard Fitzsimmons, slowly, calmly, and with sympathy in her voice, break the news of Gary Campbell's murder. For several seconds, a stunned Pasty stared unbelievingly at them in turn then sinking to her knees, she began to tear at her hair and loudly wail.
****

He drove them back to the flat in silence, such was the fear that possessed him that he was unable to find the words of comfort that Ronnie so badly needed.

At last, arriving in Watson Street, he switched off the engine then turning to her, took her hand and said, "This changes nothing. I still want you to marry me."

"You're sure," she tried to smile, her expression one of surprise as though doubting his sincerity.

"Ronnie, I didn't ask you to marry me because you are pregnant. I want to marry you because I love you and need you in my life, so baby or not and please God, everything works out, then yes. I have never been so sure of anything in my life."

Her eyes suddenly moist and her voice a whisper, she said, "I'm sorry."

He froze, panicking that she was refusing his proposal, then gently asked, "Sorry for what?"

"About the baby," she sniffed, a trickle now running down her cheeks.

Awkward though it was in the front of the car, he pulled her close to him and tightly hugged her, his own eyes now moist too, then slowly repeated, "I want to marry you because I love you. Please say yes."

Her lips trembling, at first she was unable to speak so nodding into his shoulder, at last found her voice to mumble, "Yes, I'll marry you."

"And what if…" she couldn't bring herself to even speak of it.

"No matter what the outcome, we'll be together and that's what is important, Ronnie. Me and you; together."
The tears now freely flowing, again she couldn't trust herself to speak and simply nodded.
Together.

CHAPTER TWENTY-EIGHT: Wednesday 27 September 2006.

A sleepless night ensued for them both with him rising at three in the morning to make Ronnie a hot chocolate, her comfort food in times of crisis she had once told him, then saw him return to bed where they lay in each other's arms until to Fairbanks surprise, the digital clock alarm woke him.
Though they'd both had just a few hours, he felt remarkably refreshed.
After showering and dressing, he persuaded Ronnie that she remain and rest in the flat for the day, that she phone Laura her deputy and have her run the boutique, then decided his first port of call had to be attending at Alex Gardener's office for what he guessed would be a confrontational meeting with the Assistant Chief Constable (Crime).
Now driving towards police headquarters in Pitt Street, he again reflected on what Gardener's aide, DI Cameron, had told him, but was mistrustful enough to wonder; was he in fact being set up by Cameron who he suspected though clearly a smart individual, might be cunning enough to play Gardener against him.
His eyes narrowed as he recalled Cameron's admitted desire to return to a Divisional CID and wondered too; is he being set up to take a fall and thus create an opening at Maryhill CID for Cameron to slip into.
With a shrug, he knew he could only play as the dice fell and that no matter what was about to occur in Gardener's office, he was not giving up Ronnie.
****
Against his wife's advice that threatened, among other warnings, divorce, shunning him for a week as well as banning him from further marital expectations and to the spare bedroom, DCI Bobby Heggerty rose that morning with the intention of returning to work.

Now seated at the kitchen table with his breakfast of tea and toast and his sullen wife sitting with her arms crossed and glaring at him from across the table, he tried to explain he needed to do this, if for nothing more than his own morale.

Tight-lipped after refusing to even speak with him, Cathy Heggerty, wearing a dressing gown over her pyjamas, at last sighed, then rising from her chair, said, "If you're going to do this, then I will drive you to work, because so soon after your procedure, right now I don't think you're fit to be on the road."

"Really, I'll be…" he started, but shut up when raising her hand, she snarled, "I will not accept any argument, Bobby Heggerty, so eat your toast and wait here while I get dressed."

When the door behind her closed or rather, was slammed, he softly smiled for knowing Cathy as he did, she'd cool down later in the day.

Then grimly thought, I have to do is get through the next hour and a bit.

Of course, the doctor had told him not to return to work for at least a week, yet Heggerty felt guilty that Eddie Fairbanks was dealing with a murder that seemed to have grown arms and legs, much less knowing that prat Alex Gardener, unable to get at him, was going after Eddie because he had stolen Cathy from under his nose.

That, in Heggerty's book, just was not fair and so though he suspected Cathy had also realised that too, that was why he had to get back to Maryhill.

As the minutes passed, he was contemplating a top-up of tea when the door opened to admit Cathy, now dressed and wearing her overcoat and who said, "This is about your DI, isn't it?"

He sighed, "Yes. Eddie Fairbanks is a competent young guy, Cathy, and I trust him to be doing a good job. But Alex Gardener has set his sights on me and because he can't get me…"

"He's going after your man Fairbanks," she finished for him.

As they stared at each other, she shook her head when she softly said, "And you wonder, Bobby Heggerty, why at that time I gave him up for you?"

He began to smile, but stopped when she snapped, "But you're still an idiot who won't listen, so get your backside out and into the car."

****

That morning, Larry Considine met Elaine Fitzsimmons in the rear yard at Maryhill Police Office and told her, "I got a text from Eddie Fairbanks. He's been ordered to attend at ACC Gardener's office, so he'll get here whenever he's finished."

"Any idea what that's about?" she asked as she strolled through the back door he held open.

"Only that in the recent few days, Gardener's been looking for Bobby Heggerty, then when he couldn't contact him, turned his attention to Eddie. Whatever it's about, Elaine, I don't think it bodes any good for Eddie."

Her brow furrowed thoughtfully when she recalled her recent conversation with Liz Malone; the heads-up about Eddie Fairbanks and his relationship with his partner; Ronnie Masters.

Ronnie Masters, narrow-eyes, it was a name Fitzsimmons recalled from the tabloids some years ago and that led Fitzsimmons to guess at Gardener's reason for wanting to see the young DI.

Reaching the corridor where the CID suite was located and just as Considine pushed open the door to the incident room, Fitzsimmons was grumbling that these days, walking upstairs caused her knees to ache, then stopped and smiled, for sitting in the DS's chair reading the daily synopsis of the investigation, was DCI Bobby Heggerty.

"Now there's a sight for sore eyes,' she grinned at him and extended her hand as did Considine, who smiled, "I didn't expect to see you back so soon, boss."

"Neither did Cathy," he grimaced, "but I've already had my verbal doing, so don't either of you start."

"Right while you two catch up," Considine grinned, "I'll fetch us some coffees."

Sitting herself down, she and Heggerty chewed the fat for a few minutes before he said, "From what I've read, Elaine, I believe it's only right and proper that you and Eddie continue the investigation. My DC, Jackie Wilson, is doing a good job in the acting rank, running the general office, so I'm keeping her at the acting rank though I'll manage the day to day crime that comes in, unless you have any objection?"

"No," she nodded, "you're right, Bobby. Better Eddie and I keep the continuity going and besides," she smiled, "I think this will likely be my last major investigation, so I'm keen to go out with a winner."

"I'm up to speed as of last evening," he tapped a forefinger on the file, "the last thing being you and Larry heading out to break the bad news to the next of kin. How did that go?"

Fitzsimmons described how Gary Campbell's mother, Patsy, had completely broken down at the news of her son's death, then her hurt had turned to anger when she learned of how he had been killed, confused as to why he'd be wearing a Celtic top and a balaclava even more so that he'd had possession of a handgun.

"As far as she knows, he's only slightly affiliated to a Loyalist band and admitted that generally, he was friendless young man, that the band just string him along because he was always so eager to help them out. That said," she sighed, "While he was dead keen on supporting Rangers, she has no knowledge of him being involved in any militant group."

"And your opinion, you and Larry's, I mean," he added with a nod at Considine, who carrying three mugs, entered the room, "is that this meeting in the hotel, presumably from what little you've learned, you believe it was between Loyalists and Republicans and was a set-up to blame the Republicans for a murder? An assassination?"

She could see the doubt in his face when she said, "What?"

"Come on, Elaine, is it likely that the Republicans and the Unionists would meet without the UK Government being involved?"

She glanced at Considine when she replied, "I have no answer to that, Bobby, and remember, without any evidence to confirm it, it's only a theory, but we think so," then related Susie Lauder's assessment of a false flag operation.

"And the Special Branch. What are they saying about it?"

"Ah, now there's another story," her face creased.

****

Sitting in Gardener's outer office in the Command Suite, Eddie Fairbanks mind was reeling at what kind of hostile reception he might expect from the ACC.

Curiously, when he'd arrived some fifteen minutes earlier, DI Iain Cameron was already in the outer office chatting to the middle-aged secretary, then after greeting Fairbanks, excused himself to, as he'd said, "Fetch this lovely lady and I, a roll and bacon and mugs of tea." When he'd gone, the secretary, who had smiled at Fairbanks, had confided in a low voice, "Such a nice man, DI Cameron. Always very solicitous to us ladies," her shoulders shook when she gave a small giggle.

His thoughts returning to his pending meeting, he forced himself to calm down, knowing that if Gardener thought for one second that he might give up Ronnie for…

He didn't finish the thought for the door to the outer office opened to admit Gardener, who resplendent in a brilliantly white shirt, scarlet and navy blue striped tie and tailored navy blue three-piece suit, merely glanced at him before rudely addressing his secretary with, "Where is DI Cameron?"

To his surprise, she sneaked a glance at Fairbanks when she blatantly lied, "I believe he's attending to an issue at the personnel office, Mr Gardener."

"Oh, right. I have some paperwork to examine before I see DI Fairbanks. I'll let you know when to send him in."

"Yes, sir," she dutifully smiled then with another glance at Fairbanks, her eyebrows raised when she bent her head to use her computer.

He couldn't explain why, but that simple gesture seemed to relax him and he found to his surprise, he wasn't as tense as he'd previously been.

It was then he recalled Cameron's throwaway comment about the secretaries who worked for the senior management, about their 'unofficial information service,' was the words Cameron had used, that they knew more about what was going on and how they passed information to their bosses.

With a sly glance, he studied the middle-aged secretary and wondered; just what information had she passed on about him?

Minutes became a quarter of an hour before the secretary's phone rang, then he heard her say, "Yes, sir, I'll ask him to go in."

The call finished, but the phone still in her hand, she smiled at Fairbanks, then said, "He's ready for you."

Rising to his feet he strode to the door then opening it, entered the inner office, though unaware the secretary, with a worried glance at the closed door to the inner office, was now dialling an internal number.

****

Returned to her home in Belfast's Lindsay Street, Arlene McCandlish called a meeting of the five most senior members of the Inner Council to relate the circumstances of the attempted assassination in the Glasgow hotel.

In the roadway outside, a number of cars not usually seen in the quiet street were parked. Each vehicle had arrived with not just their principal, but with an additional two or three men who now either stood outside the cars in small groups, smoking or quietly chatting or sitting within their vehicles. However, wherever they stood or sat, their eyes and posture were fully alert to any danger or suspicious movement towards them or the house where McCandlish's meeting was being held.

Within the extended kitchen downstairs, at a crowded gate leg table now fully extended and upon which lay three ashtrays and empty coffee mugs, sat five men all staring at Arlene McCandlish.

Among the five was prominent one of her most circumspect supporters, a man known as Richard 'Dicky' Porter and popular with the Northern Irish Unionists, though equally infamous among the Republican community, who asked, "You are entirely convinced it was not the Republicans?"

"Yes, I am convinced it was *not* them," she sighed and waved a hand through the fug of cigarette smoke that drifted to the ceiling.

"I'm sorry to admit that if the attack was not actually conceived by Constance McKenzie, who," she held up her hand in dismay, "I also regretfully admit, a woman that I implicitly trusted, then she was certainly complicit in organising the murder attempt and though I've no proof, she did so probably in partnership with the man who runs the Glasgow group, this new Friends of Ulster Loyalists mob."

Then spat out the name, "Arthur Denholm."

"And you say McKenzie actually admitted this to you? That she colluded with others to kill you?" asked another sceptic.

"She did," McCandlish grimly nodded, then added, "And she did so in front of Axel and Jimmy. If you need proof of what I'm telling you, I can call them into the room."

"There's no need for that," a third man raised a hand. "Did she name any accomplices?"

"No," McCandlish stared keenly around the table at the five men. "Only to say that her *accomplices* are the true Loyalists."

She paused then continued with a wry smile, "Now, I have to ask, do those true Loyalist accomplices include any of you gentlemen?"

A tense silence followed, broken when Porter asked, "Why didn't you bring McKenzie back with you, Arlene? I'm certain with the," he hesitated, then said, "the *right* inducement, we could have had the information out of her as to who else was involved."

"Well," she slowly scoffed, "for one, knowing why we were bringing her back here, that she would be brutally interrogated and maybe even executed for her treason, there might have been some difficulty getting her through the security at the ferry if she was not willing to go. And two, albeit the attempt on my life was a failure, what we did learn from it is that the Republicans *do* want to talk to us. In fact, so much so when the gunman entered the room, it was a Republican who threw himself in front of me; McGuigan's advisor, a young guy who would have taken the bullet. Then, when we were running from the hotel, Gary McGuigan himself actually called out to me that the attempt was *not* them, that they had nothing to do with it."

"And," the third speaker interjected, his voice betraying his cynicism, "because of that, you believe the word of a *Republican*" he sneered the word, "that they will still want to speak with us about a peace initiative?"

"I do," she confidently replied.

Porter glanced around the table at his fellow members then sighed, "Let's return to the attempt on your life, Arlene. You're suggesting that someone, maybe more than one," he irritably sighed again, "and presumably a member or members of the Inner Council, is not only responsible for the attempt on your life, but what we can reasonably assume to be an attempt to disrupt the peace initiative that you are driving forward?"

"Yes," she cautiously nodded, wondering where this was going.

"Then," he shrugged, "as your life is so obviously in danger, I suggest that you take a step back and permit a named successor to carry on what you have so far achieved."

She stared hard at him before she replied, "Is this a genuine concern for my welfare Dicky, or am I simply being side-lined in a veiled attempt to kill off the chance of real peace with the Republicans?"

Locking eyes with her, Porter replied, "Arlene, you should know that I am the man who suggested that this new Glasgow group, the FUL, be the unit who met with you and accommodated you and…"

"Are you telling me that *you* are responsible for the attempt on my life," she snarled, her hands clenched like fists on the table and her legs shaking as she prepared to launch herself at him.

"Not at all," he defensively raised both hands when he calmly replied.

"What I'm saying," he forced his voice to remain calm, "is that our security is not as tight as we had believed, that whoever was aware of what arrangements I had made, whoever that person or those individuals might be, has obviously hijacked those arrangements to their own end. However," he quickly continued, "we must assume that you are no longer safe to deal with the Republicans and *that* is why I suggest you take a backseat, that now we know we have a leak in the Council we can take the necessary precautions to protect our new representative."

She felt herself choking and her mouth suddenly dry, but managed to ask, "And would you be considering yourself as this new representative, Dicky?"

He smiled when he said, "Arlene, I certainly don't want the job. I'm certain the Republicans have a lengthy file on my activities during the war and I'm not putting myself up there as a target for revenge. No," he slowly shook his head, "I think a representative should be chosen by the Council and it should be someone who perhaps is not a reviled by the Taigs as I know I am."

She stared at him, knowing of his past history, the awful deeds he had done and of the Catholics he had either personally or ordered murdered.

A freed man under the terms of the Good Friday Agreement, Richard Porter had carried a death sentence since the 'RA' had discovered him to be one of the chief torturers of Catholic's simply snatched off the street, whether the victims had been involved in acts of terror or not.

She took a slow breath, then, her throat tight, exhaled and stared into his eyes before she said in a low voice, "I agree with Council Member Porter's suggestion for a replacement representative; however, I have one request."

She knew the others were staring at her when she said, "Find me the man or woman or whoever was involved in trying to kill me."

****

ACC Gardener didn't invite Eddie Fairbanks to sit, but instead thundered, "It has come to my attention that you are currently co-habiting with some woman who has accrued a criminal conviction and indeed, has served time in prison. I trust you understand the position this places you in, that you are currently contravening the Police (Scotland) Act and our own Force's disciplinary regulations." Staring down at him, Fairbanks resisted the urge to lean across his desk, grab him by the tie, pull him back across the desk then smack him around the head, so instead replied in a calm and neutral voice, "If you are referring to my fiancé, Miss Ronnie Masters, sir, then I will be obliged if you refer to her by name rather than you calling her, some woman."

He watched the ACC's eyes narrow and his face redden, but before Gardener could respond, the door behind Fairbanks was knocked then pushed open and a familiar voice said, "Ah, good. You're here. Sorry to intrude, Alex, and I hope you don't mind me interrupting you, but I'm keen to speak with DI Fairbanks."

Turning, his eyes widened when he saw the Deputy Chief Constable, Charlie Miller, standing in the open doorway and smiling in turn at him and Gardener.

Flummoxed, Gardener stuttered, "And how might I help you, Mr Miller?"

Stepping into the room, Miller closed the door, then cheerfully said, "My wife, Sadie, she brought an article to my attention in one of her magazine's and lo a behold," he widely grinned, "it turns out it was about DI Fairbanks fiancé, Ronnie Masters. Well," he stepped further into the room to stare down at Gardener, "having met Ronnie, who I consider to be an *outstanding* young woman who I'm sure, Alex, you're probably not aware, was a former and very famous international model who not only beat her admitted addictions, but has become a successful businesswoman."

Without hesitation, Miller continued, "And, if I might be so bold, DI Fairbanks, you're certainly punching above your weight with your fiancée," he grinned again.

"Anyway, I was delighted to read in the magazine that she is currently organising a function in the Merchant City's Fruit Market, selling off what Sadie tells me are the *very* expensive gowns that Ronnie wore in the magazine's article and giving the proceeds to charity. I mean," he nodded at a stunned ACC, "how decent that is of her, eh?"

Before Gardener, his mouth now gaping, could comment, Miller continued, "And do you know," he unexpectedly clapped Fairbanks on the shoulder, "because of her relationship with this fine young officer, I've also learned that Ronnie has decided that part of the proceeds of the charity sale will be donated to our very own Strathclyde Police Benevolent Fund. Well," his face creased when he drawled, "I was so impressed that I have decided to offer Ronnie the services on the night of the event of our very own Strathclyde Police Choir to participate in the show. What do you think, Alex? Great idea of mine. Good publicity for the Force and so *generous* of this young man's fiancée to organise such an event, eh?"

Fairbanks, astounded and whose attention had been completely taken by Miller's boisterous enthusiasm, turned to see that Gardener's face had turned from strawberry red to chalk white and who could only nod at Miller's question.

"Right then, well, don't let me disturb you any further, so again," he smiled at Fairbanks, "please thank Ronnie on behalf of both myself and Strathclyde Police."

When the door had closed behind Miller, Gardener, his hands clenched and his knuckles as white as his face, stared up at Fairbanks, then simply said, "Get out."

CHAPTER TWENTY-NINE.

Arthur Denholm was a worried man.

A very worried man indeed.

Not only did the newspapers report that following the discovery of a man's body in a prestigious hotel in Glasgow's Cambridge Street, there was no mention of a woman being killed; simply that the police were now engaged in a murder inquiry.

His first thoughts were that a D-notice had been served on the media; that the nature of McCandlish's murder had caused the Security Services to advise that any media publishing of the death of a prominent Northern Irish Loyalist was not in the interest of national security.

But he quickly dispelled that theory, facing the awful truth that his operative, Volunteer Campbell, had failed.

And yet a body *had* been discovered.

That *could* mean that Volunteer Speirs had succeeded in silencing Campbell, who it now seemed certain had botched his mission.

And yet he feared contacting Speirs to confirm the operation was unsuccessful, worried the police might have arrested him and therefore would be in possession of his phone.

A sudden cold chill overtook him when the paranoia set in.

Though there was no mention of anyone being taken into custody; so, did the lack of contact from Speirs mean…dear God, that he *had* been caught?

But in the event he had been arrested, would he would adopt the procedure that all the Volunteers had practised and maintain his silence?

Then of course, his mind raced as he grasped at the one hope that remained to him; he'd instructed Speirs not to make any contact with him or other members of the FUL, so perhaps Speirs was simply obeying his instruction to maintain strict silence.

He glanced at the door, his eyes widening as he imagined helmeted, black suited police officers with machine guns bursting into his office to arrest him.

His hands shaking, he reached into the desk drawer for the cheap, disposable mobile phone, his burner as he'd heard them called, then lifting it, stared suspiciously at it for several seconds as though the very device would somehow lead the police directly to him.

His mouth dry and the realisation that if he needed information about what had occurred or his next move should be, there was little point in again calling Volunteer Speirs.

He knew there was only one option, like it or not, he had to call the number of the local contact.

Taking a breath to calm himself, he scrolled own the few numbers in the directory, then tightly closing his eyes as he composed in his head what he would say, pressed the green button.

****

Through the wonder of technology, Denholm's call arrived at DS Norrie McCartney's own mobile burner phone less than twenty seconds later; unfortunately, McCartney was unable to respond to the call for just at that minute, he was following his boss, DI Sadie McGhee, through the door into the DCI's office, where Bobby Heggerty sat behind the desk with Elaine Fitzsimmons sitting in the chair in front.

Glancing at the caller ID, McCartney pressed the red button and returned the phone to his pocket.

Heggerty, eyes narrowing at the vaguely familiar face of the burly man and his face registering his curiosity as to who they were, asked, "Can I help you?"

"DI McGhee from Special Branch," she smoothly replied, then said, "I was looking for DI Fairbanks, the SIO of the on-going James Crawford murder investigation."

Before Heggerty could respond, Fitsimmons said in a voice oozing sarcasm, "Well, well, DC Norrie McCartney. Still punching the shite out of handcuffed suspects?"

"Actually, Elaine," he smirked, "its DS McCartney now."

A tense few seconds followed, broken when Fitzsimmons coolly replied, "*Actually*, DS McCartney, it's *DCI* Fitzsimmons now, but you can call me Ma'am."

"Right then," she turned towards McGhee, "DI Fairbanks is not currently available, but I am now the SIO of the on-going investigation into the murder of James Crawford and other issues related to that murder. So, how may I help you, DI McGhee?"

Both she and Heggerty watched as McGhee's face turned bright red and it was clear this must have been a surprise to her, but collecting her thoughts, she quickly replied, "We at the Branch have learned there was an incident at the Cambridge Street hotel, Ma'am, and wonder if we might be of some assistance?"

Fitzsimmons took a lengthy breath, then turning towards Heggerty, asked, "What do you think, Bobby, after what we learned about this pair, do you want them involved in this investigation?"

"Really, Ma'am…" McGhee began, but stopped when Fitzsimmons held up her hand and her brow furrowing, responded with, "Let me be clear, DI McGhee. If I require any assistance from the Branch, I'll contact them, but I am curious to know why you've suddenly turned up here at this office and so recently after my team has been in touch with the PSNI about a certain vehicle registration number. I suspect that you have something to share with us, DI McGhee, so be as so kind to tell us what you know?"

"Eh," she blushed again, "I have no idea what you believe we might know, Ma'am, but I assure you…"

But McGhee was interrupted by Bobby Heggerty, who turning to her said, "Perhaps it might be an idea, DCI Fitzsimmons, to have a word with the Head of Special Branch to confirm that he is aware of his DI and her sidekick visiting us about an investigation that they are supposed to know nothing about?"

McGhee could feel the blood drain from her face as McCartney brushed past her to sneer, "You might think you pair are on top of what's going on…"

"Norrie!" she hissed at him, but he ignored her and carried on.

"…but this is *way* out of your fucking league, so go ahead and contact the HSB, but…"

"DS McCartney!" McGhee grabbed at his arm.

Turning towards her, his face expressing his vehemence, Fitzsimons and Heggerty thought in that heartbeat that McCartney was not just going to shrug her off, but also…what?

Strike her?

It was Heggerty, who slowly rising to his feet, stared at McCartney, then calmly said, "You will *immediately* remove yourself from my office; in fact, from this building and should you fail to do so, I will place you under arrest! Do-you-understand!"

"Arrest me for what?" McCartney sneered, but turned and bullishly strode from the room.

McGhee, her eyes widening and caught like the proverbial rabbit in the headlights, wordlessly followed him from the room.

Turning to stare down at a stunned Fitzsimmons, Heggerty asked, "Now, what the *hell* was that all about?"

Staring at the open door, her eyes full of suspicion, Fitzsimmons finally muttered, "I really don't know, Bobby, but what I *do* know is that I won't be letting those two come here and regardless of their denial, I truly suspect they have some knowledge about that debacle at the hotel that they obviously will not share."

****

It was only when he had returned to collect his car from the underground car park at police headquarters and still a little dazed from what had occurred, that Fairbanks realised the Deputy had referred to Ronnie as his fiancée.

How the hell did he know about our engagement, he wondered?

Feeling like he had somehow stepped back from the edge, Fairbanks drove out of the exit onto West George Street, almost immediately parked in an empty bay to catch his breath.

His first thought was to phone Ronnie, for though he had not wished to worry her by divulging the threat he had been under, his curiosity was roused by Charlie Miller's confident statement that he and she must have been in conversation about her plans for the charity event.

"First things first," he greeted her, "how are you feeling?"

"Good news and bad news," she sighed. "The good news is that there hasn't been any more blood spotting."

"And the bad news?"

"I've been vomiting for Scotland, peed myself twice while doing so and feel like I've been run over by a bus."

He fought the relieved grin at the good news, then sympathised at how she was feeling before he asked, "You haven't been speaking recently to my boss, Mr Miller, have you?"

"Curious you should ask," she replied. "He must have kept my number from that time you were in the hospital, because he phoned me about, oh, maybe three-quarters of an hour ago to inquire about my plans for a charity event; told me that if I was willing to donate a small sum to the police charity, the, eh…"

"The Benevolent Fund, yeah?"

"Yes, that. Anyway, he said if I did so, he'd arrange for the police choir to sing at the event, a kind of *pro quid pro*, he called it. Told me they were very good."

Fairbanks smiled, recalling how swiftly Miller had come to his rescue and realising DI Cameron's information about the unofficial information service between the secretaries must after all, be a real thing.

"And you agreed?"

"Course I did. I remember when you were injured and how he visited you and was, well, he seemed really worried about you. I like him, Eddie, and he strikes me as being a really nice man."

More than you can imagine, he thought, but Ronnie hurried on, "I have other news. Dr Harris phoned to inform me that her friend, the obstetrician, conducts an evening surgery on Friday at Ross Hall Hospital in Crookston and has made an appointment for us at seven-forty-five."

"Good," he felt yet another sense of relief, then said, "Look, I'm heading back to Maryhill now, so try and rest up today, okay? And anything you need, sweetheart, anything at all, you'll get me on my mobile."

The call ended, he took a few seconds to compose himself, much relieved that Ronnie sounded in better spirits.

Yes, he was also thankful that there had been no more blood spotting, but that didn't mean their concern was over. Friday would hopefully bring them good news, yet there was still that nerve-wracking worry till then.

Then of course, as far as his career was concerned, he had dodged the bullet, but he wasn't so naïve and knew that Alex Gardener, who because he had harboured a grudge for all those years against Bobby Heggerty, was unlikely to forget today.

He had to accept that he had made a dangerous enemy; one who held sway over his career and was in an influential position to disrupt or worst-case scenario, even end it.

****

In their car in the rear yard at Maryhill, an angry DI McGhee, sitting in the passenger seat, turned on her neighbour, Norrie McCartney, and bellowed, "What the fuck were you thinking? You won't get away speaking to two DCI's like that! And not only that," she hissed at him, "if they phone the HSB before we get the opportunity to explain to him…"

"Shut the fuck up and let me think," he snarled while staring thoughtfully through the windscreen.

Stunned, her eyes widening, she continued to stare at him when she slowly replied, "What did you just say to me?"

He turned threateningly towards her and for the first time since they had been neighboured, she felt real fear.

Then, his yellowing teeth gritted, he calmly told her, "Listen, pretty girl, you're nothing but a mouthpiece for the cousins down south, so don't overestimate your value to them or to me. I've been at this game since you were at primary school, dealing with both sides; the Loyalists *and* the Republicans and I know where more than a few bodies are buried and no," he sneered, "I'm not speaking literarily."

She felt herself shrink back into the seat when he continued, "I have a good idea how much money the cousins down south have invested in the war between the Loyalists and the 'RA' and I can hazard a reasonable guess just how much of their budget would be slashed if those two gangs of thugs make peace; hundreds of staff would be affected and the layoff's from Thames House alone would likely cause the sodding place to close down."

He paused, then taking a breath, turned his head to again stare through the windscreen when he quietly said, "I also know why you were sent over the water to join Strathclyde and don't dare think that because you're sitting at the DI rank, you are anywhere near as connected as me. I have contacts in Thames House who would scare the shit out of you and who, because I have all those years of serving our political masters, owe me more than a few favours. So," he again turned to face her and in the same quiet voice, said, "As from now, do not forget who is running this show."

He paused again, then calmer, said, "Our first priority is meeting with the woman McKenzie and ensuring she doesn't run off at the mouth and name names to save her own skin. Is that *clearly* understood?"

Up to this point, she quickly realised, it had all seemed so simple; all they'd had to do was follow the instructions from down south, not get their own hands dirty, just let the Loyalists kill each other and place the blame on the Republicans.

But the man tasked by Arthur Denholm to kill Arlene McCandlish had so deplorably failed and that failure completely changed the game plan.

And with McCandlish having identified Constance McKenzie as a key player in the attempted assassination, those Inner Council members who were known to McKenzie and who opposed the peace initiative were now at risk of being themselves exposed and who in turn, to save their own skins, might publicly point the finger at the Security Services.

Now, her stomach churning, she knew exactly what McCartney's intention was, that they were going to have to get their hands dirty after all.

They'd meet with McKenzie in some secluded spot and dealing with her meant only one thing.

****

Pleased to see Bobby Heggerty seated at his own desk, Eddie Fairbanks agreed with both him and Elaine Fitzsimmons that the mutual investigation continue to be run as previously agreed.

"So," Fitzsimmons smiled at him, "if you're okay with it, Eddie, I'll use the DI's office as my office while you, Bobby, continue to run your Department. Okay all round?" she glanced at them in turn and saw them both nod.

"Right then, Eddie, let's get into the incident room and we'll brief the team on what we know."

In the corridor outside Heggerty's office, she laid a hand on Fairbanks arm to stop him then quietly asked, "Your fiancée. Everything okay?"

She watched his face crease when in the same low voice, he replied, "Ronnie had some blood spotting, boss, and we're seeing an obstetrician on Friday evening, at Ross Hall Hospital in Crookston. We'll know then if there's an issue with the pregnancy."

To his surprise, he saw her eyes glisten, but could not know that her mind had been cast back all those years when her husband Eric, who for several days ignored a stabbing pain in his chest in the belief it was heartburn, then finally succumbed to a catastrophic heart attack.

He saw her take a deep breath as she stared at him, then squeezing his arm, she muttered, "There's nothing more important than family, Eddie, so if your Ronnie has any kind of warning signs like that again and she needs you at *any* time, no matter what the hell is going on here, you go to her. Is that agreed?"

"Eh, yes, boss, of course," he nodded at her.

"Right," she released his arm and cleared her throat, "let's brief the troops."

****

In his home in Culhane Street in the suburb of Dundalk, Gary McGuigan, having taken the day off work to attend the meeting with his former ASU colleague, donned a heavy coat against the biting wind and pulled on a navy-blue woollen tammy.

Calling his eight-year-old dog Thatcher to him, he left his mid-terraced bungalow, his thoughts filled with the incident at the Glasgow hotel and the questions he needed answered.

Thatcher, an ill-kept mongrel rescue dog that refused to be groomed and with a dubious temper and who was cynically named after the former Brit Prime Minister, wagged his tail with excitement at being taken out.

Stepping out into the cold and with an apparent indifferent glance, McGuigan's eyes scanned both left and right, but other than some cars or vans that belonged to neighbours, he did not see any vehicles in the narrow road that shouldn't be there.

However, while he was not so conceited to believe himself to be worthy of a twenty-four-hour, seven-day week, surveillance by the Garda Síochána's Special Branch, that didn't mean he wasn't still of interest to them.

Past experience had taught him that with certainty, every now and then the Guards routinely took a look at him; whether that be when leaving his home or arriving at work or on occasion, seeing the strange face in his local pub sitting alone and nursing a pint while studiously avoiding glancing his way.

And so, because there was never any fixed day, time or reason for them to be watching him, he remained constantly vigilant whenever he left the house.

If they ever found out, the Guards would have been surprised to know that he didn't really mind them following him, at least when he knew they were there, for he had come to recognise faces and sometimes even their individual posturing or body language.

His one frustration was that just when he'd logged their vehicles reggie plates, makes and models in his head because it was bad practice to write anything down, they changed their vehicles.

McGuigan also went to great effort to pretend to not to see them or be aware of their presence and this worked to his advantage, for as the time passed, the surveillance became more relaxed in the belief he was not an alert target.

When on occasion he was obliged to contact his colleagues in the Cause, he reverted to his tradecraft and use the dead letter boxes to plan ahead for such covert meetings, a trick he'd been taught from his days clandestinely operating in the North; just as he had done for today.

Conversely, it was when he didn't clock the surveillance that McGuigan was most concerned, though never, ever dropped his guard and so it was when he did not see the regular faces or any vehicles he recognised, his counter-surveillance radar was at a high pitch.

With a resigned sigh, his nerves on edge and Thatcher on the rope lead pulling eagerly to be walked, he began the short walk to the road bridge over the Castletown River that to any watcher, would recognise as his usual route when walking the dog to the Moorland on the other side of the river.

Arriving at the bridge, he crossed through the light traffic to the other side of the Newry Road, then stopped in the middle of the bridge and peering over the stone wall into the water below, would seem to any observer to be just taking a breather, the reality being he wanted to determine if he were being followed.

As much as he dared without actually staring at the passing vehicles, he turned and twisted as though playing with the leashed dog, but used his peripheral vision to examine the traffic, yet none slowed nor it seemed did any drivers nor their passengers pay him particular attention.

As satisfied as he could be and with Thatcher continuing to pull eagerly at his lead, McGuigan continued his walk and reaching the other side of the bridge, turned right into the open parkland.

Walking from the pavement onto the tarmacadam cycle track, he was passed by two teenage girls on bicycles, cheerfully egging each other on to increase speed and could see that apart from several women walking in the park, some with prams or children or both, there was nothing to alert him to the Guards being there.

Walking on, he reached the spot where he believed Thatcher would not run back to the busy road and so let the dog off the lead, then watched as it raced around the park, pursuing some birds who flew off.

As arranged, almost immediately the dog stopped and sniffed the air, attracted to a woman sitting alone on a wooden bench located in the grassed area some twenty metres away and some five metres from the edge of the track, who held an open paper bag that exuded the pungent smell of cooked chicken.

The dog's nose lifted and McGuigan watched as Thatcher made a beeline for the woman.

As though he were simply fetching his dog, he approached the woman, his hands outstretched as though in apology and saw it to be her, his former colleague, muffled in a long navy-blue coat and wearing thick, black framed glasses, her shoulder length red hair now cut to her collar and dyed black and who, even at this close distance, was almost unrecognisable as the former IRA explosives expert she once was.

"Don't sit, just stand as though we're chatting," she smiled amiably at him.

"Long time no see," he greeted her with his own smile.

Feeding Thatcher some chicken, she dipped her head, then ruffling the chewing dog under his chin as though speaking with Thatcher, she said, "What went wrong?"

"I need to know, was it us?"

"Was what us? What do you mean?" she continued staring at the dog.

"Was it us who tried to murder McCandlish?"

Her head snapped up as she stared at him and he instinctively realised that either she was an Oscar winning actress or what was more likely, she had no idea what he was talking about.

At least, he hoped that.

"Jesus! You mean there was an attempt on her life?"

"Young guy, wearing a Glasgow Celtic football top. The bloody gun exploded in his hand otherwise McCandlish would have been stitched up in the chest."

He stared narrow-eyed at her when he asked, "It wasn't us you're telling me?"

She slowly exhaled then resisting the urge to shake her head, replied, "I'll see that some local inquiries are made in Glasgow, but no; as far as I'm aware, it was not us."

Maybe not her, he exhaled, but that didn't mean that someone in the Cause hadn't gone rogue.

However, it was her phrase, 'as far as I'm aware,' that repeated in his head and in those few seconds, it caused him to wonder that though he was certain *she* was telling the truth and denying any knowledge of the attempted assassination, it wasn't the first time that both had been lied to.

In those few seconds, he recalled with some clarity an incident many years before in South Armagh and just north of the border, when he and his colleague had machine-gunned a min-bus supposedly carrying members of the RUC, but later discovered to have been members of a teenage rugby team, Protestants all.

Five dead and eight seriously wounded.

The following day, when safely returned to the south and he'd discovered they were just kids and of course, unarmed, he had vomited with shame.

"Jesus, Gary," he saw her startle, "are we being set up by our own boys or…"

She stopped, causing him to ask, "What?"

She didn't respond for several seconds, then slowly suggested, "Maybe some of the Prod's aren't as keen on the peace as is Arlene McCandlish."

Curiously, for all his experience, it was something he hadn't considered, for he had unwittingly swallowed the lie; the Celtic top and the balaclava suggesting the would-be assassin was a Republican and particularly as the man had definitely aimed at McCandlish.
Bending down on one knee to attach Thatcher's lead, he stared at the dog, then patted it when he said, "I'll be hearing from you, then."
"When I've made the inquiry, I'll get back to you, via a note under the bench," she smiled and politely nodded to him that to any watcher, was a woman simply admiring McGuigan's dog, then casually waved a cheerio as he continued his walk in the park.

CHAPTER THIRTY.

Elaine Fitzsimmons and Eddie Fairbanks agreed that she would remain in charge at Maryhill Police Office he would take charge of the investigation outdoors.
"However," she added, "Before I do anything, I need to pay a visit to ACC Gardener at headquarters."
Seeing his face fall, she shook her head when she further added, "Nothing to do with you, Eddie, but I want a meeting with him and the Head of Special Branch (HSB), Callum Fraser. If that bastard, Norrie McCartney, and his sidekick think they can come into Maryhill office here and interfere with our investigation, then I'll be demanding an explanation from their boss. That and if I find out they're withholding information relevant to our investigation, I'll charge the pair of them with perverting the course of justice."
Though he hadn't known her long, Fairbanks had no doubt that when provoked, Fitzsimons could be a force of nature, but said anyway, "He's a Chief Super, boss. What if he just tells you to bugger off or comes that old chestnut," he waved his forefingers in the air like italics, when he said, "National Security. How will you handle that?"
"I've known Callum Fraser since he was a DC, before he was recruited into the Branch where he's spent most of his career. When I knew him, he was nothing but honest and straight as a die, so unless he's changed, I don't expect an argument from him. He'll either tell me what I want to know or," she shrugged, "that he can't

discuss that pair. As for Gardener," she sighed, "much as I don't particularly like him these days, there was a time when he was a good operational detective and I'm sure he will not dismiss my complaint without hearing me out. Yes," her brow creased when she slowly nodded, "I'm certain of that."

"I know it's me, that I'm probably prejudiced about our ACC," he grimaced, "but good luck anyway and I'll hear later how you get on."

****

Calling Mickey Rooney to him, Fairbanks told the acting DC that their first port of call would be interviewing Nicky Speirs mother, Janet, then instructed Rooney to phone her to ensure she was at home.

Minutes later, with Rooney driving, they were on their way to Janet Speirs home in Scalpay Street.

After she admitted them to the council owned, three-bedroom mid-terraced house that was located opposite the extensive parkland, Fairbanks saw the property to be extremely well appointed and guessed the single parent had ploughed a lot of money into the furnishings.

Now sitting opposite them in an armchair in the front room, Janet, an attractive and youthful looking forty-eight-year-old divorcee, clearly still distraught at the news her only child was in custody charged with murder, wiped at her eyes with a handkerchief, then asked, "Will he get bail? I mean does he have to stay in the jail till the trial?"

It was Fairbanks who replied, "In my experience, Mrs Speirs, and while I accept courts can be unpredictable, I think it's highly unlikely your son will be bailed; not for a charge of murder. It doesn't help his case either that he has completely refused to cooperate with us, not even to provide any form of defence. Yes," he nodded, "he's perfectly within his rights not to speak with us, but we suspect he's been influenced by a third party not to assist us in any way."

"A third party?" her brow ceased as she stared at Mickey Rooney. "What kind of a third party? Who are you talking about here?"

With a glance at Fairbanks, Rooney said, "That's just the thing, Janet, we have no idea. We suspect that Micky thought he was murdering a Celtic supporter…"

"Wait," she held up her hand. "You're certain he actually did this? That he killed somebody?"

Having encountered it so many times before, both Fairbanks and Rooney recognised the disbelieving parent, immediately reacting by questioning their child's guilt because they were unable to comprehend that their son or daughter could be capable of murdering another human being.

"We have overwhelming evidence, Janet," Rooney softly said. "Nicky was caught trying to flee from the scene and there is Forensic evidence that frankly, is undisputable. Trust me when I tell you that yes, he did kill the young guy and as you already know, we have the knife that was shown to you and that you identified, which he took from your cutlery drawer in the kitchen. The young guy he murdered," he turned towards Fairbanks who slightly nodded he continue, "his blood was on Nicky's jacket too."

Her hand rose slowly to cover her mouth as more tears rolled down her cheeks for since receiving the bad news, she had clung to some hope that there had been a dreadful mistake, that her Nicky wouldn't, no *couldn't* murder anyone.

Not her boy.

Fairbanks broke into her thoughts when he asked, "Is there anyone who you know that Nicky has recently been hanging around with, Mrs Speirs? Anyone you might not have approved of?"

Through her tears, she slowly shook her head and sobbed, "No, I told all this to your detectives when they were here, when they were searching his room. He's a quiet boy normally, is my Nicky. Just keeps himself to himself, other than going to watch the Rangers and maybe having a pint or two after the game."

"Does he have a local pub? I mean does he use your pub, where you work?"

"No," her lips trembling, she tried to smile when she explained, "that's an old man's pub, he tells me. No, Nicky, he prefers the pubs in the east end where the other Rangers supporters go."

"Any pub in particular?"

"Eh, I'm not sure. I don't really know that end of the city."

They all turned to the door when it was pushed open by a man wearing a bunnet and paint stained overalls, who glancing uncertainly at the two detectives, said, "It's me, hen. I've just heard about your Nicky being arrested. Is it true?"

Nodding, she turned to Fairbanks, then said, "This is my friend, Geoff. It's him that employs Nicky as an apprentice. These gentlemen," she waved at hand at them, "are police detectives here about Nicky."

"Oh, right, if I'm disturbing you…" he began to walk backwards to the door, but at a subtle glance from Fairbanks, Rooney stood up and with an open smile, said, "I'll maybe have a wee word with you in the hallway, Geoff."

"Eh? Aye, okay then," and was followed by Rooney from the room, who closed the door behind him.

Fairbanks turned to Janet to say, "Do you know if Nicky was part of any group or organisation, Mrs Speirs? I mean, would he tell you if he was?"

"Do you have kids, Mr Fairbanks?"

"Eh, no," he grimly smiled, "I've never been blessed with children."

"Well, if you ever have kids," she sighed, her lips again trembling, "they turn into teenage monsters who think they know the world a whole lot better than you do and believe me," she said with some venom in her voice, "they're good at keeping secrets. So, if my Nicky was in a group or part of something, he bloody *didn't* tell me about it!" she snorted, though whether her anger was directed at her son or at him, Fairbanks wasn't certain.

It was then he decided that there was nothing more to learn from Janet Speirs and so rising from the couch, suggested if she visited her son on the remand wing, she should tell Nicky it might do his defence some good if he considered cooperating with the police. Leaving her in the front room, he stepped out into the hallway to see that Rooney and Geoff were now in the kitchen.

Catching sight of his boss, Rooney closed his notebook, then thanking Geoff, joined Fairbanks in leaving the house.

When they were in the car and Rooney was about to drive off, Fairbanks asked, "Anything?"

"Well," Rooney exhaled, "Geoff is shagging Janet and part of the deal is he puts her son through an apprenticeship, but thinks Nicky is not just a lazy, idle bugger who needs watching, but is as thick as two planks of wood."

"However," he paused, then swore while negotiating around a delivery van that suddenly stopped in front of the car, "last week sometime, though he can't recall the day, he said he walked in on

Nicky, who was supposed to be splashing paint on a wall to find him on his mobile phone. When Geoff chinned him and told him to get off the phone, Nicky said to whoever was on the line, something like, 'Sorry, Commander, I have to go.'"

"Commander? Maybe what he actually heard was Commandant," Fairbanks turned to stare at him.

"Commander? Commandant? Yeah, Commandant. That's more likely," Rooney glanced at him when he nodded.

****

DS Norrie McCartney, sitting in the driver's seat of the CID car parked outside the cafeteria at the Bothwell service station and just off the M74, turned to an ashen-faced DI Sadie McGhee and said, "Call her. Find out where she is. We need to deal with her before she opens her mouth."

"What? Don't be ridiculous," she hissed at him. "We're already in enough shit without you…"

She wasn't prepared when without warning, he swiftly turned and with his right hand, seized her by the throat and pushed her head back to bang against the headrest, then sneered, "I told you once, you are *not* in charge; I am! Now," he leaned close to her, his spittle spraying onto her face when he said "Unless you want to find yourself in jail, you'll listen to me and think about it! A good-looking woman like you," he sneered, "you'll be the eye candy for every lesbo in the place! So, if you can't or *won't* do as I say, then we're both going down for complicity in the murders of that wee Proddy toe rag in the hotel! Do you *fucking* understand!"

Terrified and fighting for breath, her hands clawing at his powerful grip, it was all she could do to nod, then when he released her, he turned back to stare again through the windscreen and calmly told her, "Catch your breath, then make the call. She's to give us a location that's easy found, but away from any houses or roads. Got that?"

"Yes," she fearfully gasped, now too shocked and too scared to argue, as well as the thought of going to prison scaring her out of her mind.

Fumbling with shaking hands in her handbag for her mobile phone, she could not know McCartney had already decided that if he were to survive the disastrous operation that the Thames House mob had dreamed up, he would need to clear his feet of anyone who could associate him with the murders, starting with Constance McKenzie and, with a sideways glance at McGhee; if it come down to it, her too.

****

After phoning ahead to request her meeting with ACC Alex Gardener and her second request, that the HSB, Chief Superintendent Callum Fraser also be present, Elaine Fitzsimmons was dropped at the front door of police headquarters, then after she'd parked the car, told her driver, DC Jaya Bahn, to take herself up to the canteen for food and from where Fitzsimmons would collect her later.

Admitted into Gardener's office by his secretary, Fitzsimmons saw that Fraser, a tall, fair-haired man in his mid-forties, was already seated there and with a nod to each man, thanked Gardener for taking the time to see her.

"I'm curious why you've called this meeting, DCI Fitzsimmons and requested the presence of Mr Fraser, but must assume it's something to do with your ongoing murder investigation in the city centre. Am I correct?" Gardener politely asked, always formal and with his elbows resting on the arms of his chair and his fingers making an arch.

With a glance at Fraser, she replied, "As you will be aware, sir, and to bring Mr Fraser up to speed, I am currently the SIO in an on-going joint murder investigation that involves both the Maryhill Division and my own Division. Maryhill's murder investigation of James Crawford has ramifications that in turn resulted in the murder of a nineteen-year-old youth, Gary Campbell, within the Cambridge Street hotel."

Allowing this information to sink in, she continued, "Our inquiries so far has discovered that minutes prior to Campbell's murder, a meeting was being conducted in a room hired under a fake company name, on the first floor of the hotel and attended by two women and two men, with a further four men downstairs who we assess to be minders for the four in the meeting room."

Again she paused, seeing Gardener's eyes had flitter with undisguised surprise, then said, "The meeting was interrupted by what we again assess to be an attempted assassination of one of the individuals in the room."

She watched Gardener's eyes widen as he slowly said, "DCI

Fitzsimmons, none of this was in the Chief Constable's Daily Briefing Summary. Why is that?"

"To be frank, sir, most of what we know is up till *very* recently a fractured assessment, but we are slowly piecing together a picture that as the hours pass is becoming clearer. For example," she risked a brief glance at Fraser, "might I inquire if the HSB is aware that two of his officers either have knowledge of or are maybe even complicit in providing a handgun to the first victim, the man murdered in Maryhill, James Crawford?"

She watched as Gardener's head snapped around to stare at a pale faced Fraser, before he grittily asked, "Mr Fraser?"

Turning, she saw Fraser's lips tighten before he calmly replied, "Firstly, I have no knowledge of what DC Fitzsimmons is suggesting," then turning to meet her stare, he asked, "Can I assume these two officers you refer to are DI McGhee and DS McCartney?"

"That's correct, yes," she nodded.

He softy exhaled then turning towards Gardener, said in a weary voice, "Well, that explains it. Those two have been a thorn in my side since I assumed the position of HSB. Though of course I have known McCartney since I joined the Department," he added with a voice full of contempt.

"Kindly explain that, please," Gardener stared narrow-eyed at him. Fraser grimaced and his brow knitted before he replied, "I know that DCI Fitzsimmons…" he paused, "Elaine, has some idea of how the Branch works, sir, while I'm aware you yourself have not served in the Department."

He paused for several seconds, then began, "Though you might have an idea of how my Department does work, please bear with me if I give what is really a simplistic overview of the Special Branch. First and foremost, throughout the United Kingdom, each Force or Constabulary Special Branch's loyalty is to their respective Chief Constable, not as others might assume, MI5, or as we know them, the Security Service. That said, the Branch are what might be called the operational wing of the Security Service, simply because we as police officers have the power of arrest while under normal circumstances, the Security Service do not have such power."

He paused again, then continued, "With respect and forgive me if I relate what you might know, but it's easier to explain it when I explain it as the Branch have a number of tasks, such as providing assistance and intelligence collected from within their respective Force areas. Intelligence that we forward to the Security Service, as well as such local issues as monitoring disruptive groups, close protection for visiting dignitaries and advising our Divisional colleagues to be aware of matters that might affect our own national or UK security. As I say," he apologetically spread his hands, "a simple description of what sometimes can be a complex job."

"While I *am* aware of most of those tasks, Mr Fraser," Gardener interrupted, "please get to the point."

Glancing at him, Fitzsimmons saw Fraser's throat tighten when he said, "Of course, sir. Within my Department, we have equipment that is provided by the Security Service; what you might call state of the art surveillance equipment. This equipment is not recorded as being purchased or owned by Strathclyde Police nor is it budgeted for and thus, in essence, does not exist. While it is of great assistance to us, it comes at a price. That price is permitting us…" he shook his head, then corrected himself, "*me* to assign and permit some of our officers to both assist with and work closely with the Security Service in local counter-terrorist operations."

He paused, then licking at his suddenly dry lips, he said, "Frankly, those officers assigned to these duties frequently operate outwith my authority and thus I am not party to whatever counter-terrorist operations they are involved in. I should add," he quickly said to Gardener, "and believe me, sir, when I inform you this is not a defence for me, but this arrangement precedes my appointment as the HSB and it is an agreement that I am neither entirely satisfied nor comfortable with."

Again he licked at his dry lips.

"However, if my Department is to continue to provide the high-quality intelligence that we currently send to the Security Service, then like it or not, the arrangement must stand."

Seeing the shock on Gardener's face at this revelation, it was Fitzsimmons who asked, "Am I correct in assuming those assigned officers are McGhee and McCartney?"

"That's them," he sighed.

"Mrs Fitzsimmons…Elaine," Gardener almost smiled, "please update Mr Fraser and I about your suspicions and how you believe these two officers are involved in your joint investigation."

She began slowly, describing first the murder of James Crawford and how the handgun discovered at Eddie Fairbanks murder location was bugged, the belief that Crawford was holding the handgun for a third party, then the arrival of McGhee and McCartney at Maryhill Police Office and the resulting break-in to Fairbanks desk where the device discovered in the handgun was stolen.

Stunned, his mouth dropping open at the revelation a CID office had been subject to a break-in, Gardener wordlessly glanced at Fraser then back at Fitzsimmons and nodded she should continue.

Warming to her story, she related the time line of the discovery of James Crawford's killer, Andrew Collins and his death brought on by the dog bite. The subsequent discovery of the Celtic top and balaclava in Collins bedroom.

She stressed the growing suspicion that McGhee and McCartney were somehow involved with James Crawford, then the discovery by one of Fairbanks detectives, DC Bahn, of a Loyalist group called the Friends of Ulster that was run by a mysterious figure called the Commandant.

She paused before she stared at Gardener and said, "It was due to DI Fairbanks' persistence that though Crawford's killer had been identified, he decided to keep the investigation running because he suspected there was more to the old man's murder. It was then again, thanks to Fairbanks tenacious diligence, a loose surveillance was conducted on a young man who had come to their attention, Nicholas Speirs, and while being followed by three of Fairbanks detectives, they apprehended Speirs in the Cambridge Street hotel and just after he murdered Gary Campbell, who at the time of his death was wearing a Celtic top and had just discarded a balaclava. Coincidence?" she stared at them in turn, then with her bottom lip pursed, added, "But we as the CID don't believe in coincidences, gentlemen, do we."

Before either man could remark, she continued, "It was at the time of Campbell's murder that it emerged a covert meeting had occurred in the hotel and from CCTV footage, it was discovered that of the four participants at the meeting and their four associates, the two women and two men fled in a Northern Irish registered vehicle that DI Fairbanks discovered to be hired in a false name from a sympathetic Loyalist garage in Belfast."

"How did he come by this information?" Fraser interrupted.

"He didn't say and I didn't question," she stared challengingly back at him, the implication being that it was better he didn't know and that ended the query.

Turning to Gardener, she then said, "The other vehicle, a Vauxhall Vectra, was identified as departing Renfrew Street and transporting the remaining four men. It was PNC'd to an individual who resides here in the city, but on this occasion," she sighed, "registered to a woman who is logged on *our* system as being of interest to our Special Branch. A simple check with the collator at E Divisional Headquarters identified the woman as an Irish Republican supporter."

"And that," Gardener, nodded, "is how you came to believe the meeting was between these two groups?"

"Yes, sir," she nodded.

"And this young man Campbell?" he asked.

"He was there to assassinate someone, maybe more than one individual at the meeting, but who, we don't yet know. Fortunately for his suspected target, the gun blew up in his hand. Ballistics preliminary examination of the weapon suggests it was old, not maintained and far deadlier to the shooter than anyone else."

"Do you know why he was murdered?"

"Our opinion, sir, is that whoever is behind these two young men, Campbell and Speirs, is cleaning his feet."

"This individual, the Commandant, presumably?"

She was pleased that arse though he might currently be, Alex Gardner still thought like a working detective.

"Yes, sir. He's obviously worried that if Campbell were arrested, he'd identify the Commandant and the easy way to deal with that is have Campbell killed."

"What's Speirs saying to all this?"

"He's closed mouth and obviously been trained or watched interviews with terrorists, for he simply stares at the corner of the room and says nothing. Needless to say, he's been remanded. DI Fairbanks is currently interviewing his mother and trying to persuade Mrs Speirs to speak with her son and for his own sake, cooperate with us."

"Well, Elaine," Gardener wheezed and slowly shaking his head and to their surprise humourlessly laughed when he said, "it seems there was quite a lot missing from the Chief's Daily Briefing."

Staring at Fitzsimmons he continued, "That's quite a story and not that I disbelieve you, but the Loyalists and the Republicans? Sitting down together in a Glasgow hotel?"

He shook his head when he sighed, "I realise that it's only conjecture that you believe they were meeting, but for what purpose?"

Turning to Fraser, he asked, "Have you any knowledge of these two Irish groups speaking with each other?"

"None, sir, through the, ah, *official* channels," Fraser cautiously said.

Both Gardener and Fitzsimmons, staring at him, wordlessly urged him to continue.

"My counterpart over in Brooklyn House, the headquarters of the PSNI. She's intimated there have been rumours, but I have to stress it's rumours only, of the hierarchy of both the IRA and the UDA seeking some sort of agreement; a peace initiative, if you will."

"And now you bring it up?" Gardener's expression was one of displeasure.

It was clear to Fitzsimmons that Fraser was extremely uncomfortable when he continued, "There has been nothing from the Security Service about this…"

"But you did raise it with them?" Gardener continued to frown.

"Yes, sir, I did, but the reality is while we share everything, our colleagues in Thames House share what they want us to know."

Gardener glanced at Fitzsimmon's when he softly asked Fraser, "While the general public and the long-suffering people of Northern Ireland, I'm certain would welcome such a peace initiative, am I to understand from your reticence, Mr Fraser, that you don't believe the Security Service would be like-minded?"

He stared his ACC in the eye when he quietly replied, "Sir, I am of the opinion the Security Service would find it extremely difficult to reconcile with the idea of a peaceful Province."

"And why do you think that is?"

To both their surprise, it was Fitzsimmon's who drily interjected with, "Budget cuts. Redundancies. Loss of favour with the Government if the Troubles actually ended without the Party in power being involved to take credit and worse of all, senior management within the Security Service suddenly finding their usefulness at an end."

They stared at her when she exhaled through pursed lips, then said, "At this time there might not be an actual shooting war, but the

Troubles do continue to fester under a very thin blanket of peace and if my reading of the news and other sources is correct, it could kick-off at anytime, anywhere."

"Particularly if it were given some assistance," Gardener thoughtfully nodded.

"Tell me about these two officers," his voice, suddenly dangerously quiet, he stared at Fraser.

"DS Norman McCartney," Fraser shook his head. "He'll be in his late-forties now and with, I'm guessing, twenty-five years or more service, most of which is within the Special Branch. A brute of a man, extremely pugnacious…"

"Oh," Fitzsimmons interrupted with a sigh and drew a sharp glance from Gardener when she said, "I can corroborate that."

Fraser permitted himself a small smile at her comment, then continued, "I believe my predecessors used McCartney for what is informally termed, 'black bag jobs.' If ever a man should have been dismissed long ago from the Force," he sighed again, "it's McCartney. I wouldn't trust him to tell me the time of day, but no matter that even though I am a Detective Chief Superintendent, I have tried time and time again to have him removed from the Department."

His eyes narrowed when he sombrely added, "Each application to have him removed has been rejected and because," he held up his hand, "it seems that someone, somewhere, and no prize for where that someone works from, exerts influence within the Personnel Department and my application goes nowhere."

"Oh, is that right," Gardener bent his head to make a note on his desk pad. "Well, we'll see if an Assistant Chief Constable can do better. Go on, Mr Fraser."

"DI Sadie McGhee," his face creased, "Late twenties and joined my Department or rather, was transferred to my Department from the PSNI Special Branch earlier this year."

His brow creased in thought when he continued, "My brief about her was that she had a source running with access to the Inner Council of the UDA, a woman I believe though I never learned the name, but somehow or other McGhee had been seen in the sources company and identified as a police officer and so, for her own personal safety, was transferred to Strathclyde Police."

He slowly shook his head when he added, "It was suggested by my opposite number in Thames House that I neighbour her with McCartney in the small unit that until then, McCartney had been running. Needless to say McGhee outranked McCartney, so took over the unit. I should add that at the time he took over the unit and again, some years preceding my promotion to HSB," he once more made the point, "McCartney reports directly to Thames House and while I receive a copy of his reports, I am confident I am not fully in the loop, as it were."

"Yet you *are* the Head of Special Branch," Gardener's eyes angrily narrowed.

"With a staff of over one hundred and thirty police and civilian personnel, yes sir," he nodded with gritted teeth, a faint anger creeping into his voice, "but if I am to successfully run my Department on the budget permitted me by Strathclyde Police, then I will fail. Therefore, I find though it irks me to do so, I have to cooperate with Thames House on whom I rely on both extra funding as well as intelligence issues, so there are certain concessions I must make and those two *buggers* are part of those concessions."

Gardener didn't immediately respond, but then tiredly said, "I believe that is a matter for further discussion at a later date, Mr Fraser. Now, I will be grateful if you can find those two buggers, as you call them, and bring them here to my office. As soon as possible, yes?"

"Yes, sir," Fraser replied in a voice that indicated he was relieved to be leaving.

Fitzsimmons too rose from her chair, only to be gruffly told, "DCI Fitzsimmons, stay behind for a word, please."

CHAPTER THIRTY-ONE.

Ronnie Masters had so far, had a lazy day, something that she hadn't had for some years and though she knew she should be relaxing, restlessly paced about the flat.

The kitchen was now spotless, the bed quilt and sheet changed, the bathroom scrubbed from top to bottom and little else left for her weekly cleaning ladies, Debbie and Kaitlyn, to deal with.

Now wearing a lime green loose tracksuit with a coffee cooling on the table by the couch and one leg tucked under her, she had collected her large sketchpad and pencil set from the top of her wardrobe and stared thoughtfully at the blank page.

As a schoolgirl, Ronnie had always enjoyed art class then, as a younger woman carried her hobby on and into the world of fashion. It had once been her desire not just to wear the fashionable gowns but also to contribute to their design, but then work and life had caught up with her and the idea faded away.

Now with time on her hands as it were, she had in the recent days given thought to again taking up drawing.

As a model, she had often complained about dresses or trousers that were either too tight, buttons inappropriately placed or designs that cared more about the fashionable look than the comfort for the wearer and had frequently pointed out it wasn't all size eight figures who should look good.

A thought struck her then and she glanced down at her stomach, then gently stroking at it, slowly smiled.

Maternity wear.

Fashionable maternity wear for the blossoming mother, she smiled, for why shouldn't pregnant women look good too?

Inwardly excited, she began to sketch a smock like dress then frowned.

My God, she thought, I'm drawing a bell tent.

Tearing out the page, she was about to begin again when her mobile phone rung and recognising the calling number, greeted her deputy with, "Laura."

"Miss Masters," her deputy manager responded abruptly, causing Ronnie to wonder at her gruffness.

"I have a lady, ah, here in your office who is looking for you. She'd come to the shop to find you, but I explained you are, eh, elsewhere at the minute."

Her eyes narrowing with suspicion, Ronnie asked, "Can she hear you?"

"No, the girls are out in the front, Miss Masters," Laura shrewdly responded.

"So, you didn't tell her I was at home?"

"That's correct. A young lady, Miss Masters," Laura again was discreet.

"Did she give you her name?"
"Yes, Miss Masters," Laura replied, then after a hesitant couple of seconds, she said, "It's Gill Masters, your sister."
****
"What do you think, boss," Mickey Rooney, driving, risked a glance at Fairbanks. "Do you think she'll try to persuade her son to speak to us?"
"You've known her for a while now, Mickey," he turned the question around. "What do you think?"
Rooney's face creased when he slowly replied, "The boyfriend, Geoff. He says she's keen to move in with him, that him and her are quite good together, but the son? As far as he's concerned, Nicky's the sticking point."
He shook his head when he continued, "Between us, he told me he'd like to see the boy gone and if that means jail time for murder, then so be it. Says that young Nicky's a waste of space, takes his mother for a mug and half of her earnings are spent on him and what Nicky wants. That said, she'll not hear a word against her son, really dotes on him. So," his brow wrinkled in thought as he repeated Fairbanks question "will she try to persuade him to talk to us?"
He exhaled when he said, "Yes, I think so."
Then he explained, "While she probably accepts he is going to the jail for murder and there's no way round that, I think you've dangled a wee carrot that if he does cooperate with us, the Crown Office might take it into consideration when he's being sentenced."
Fairbanks stared at him then slowly smiled when he replied, "That's quite an assessment, Mickey. You're not as daft as you look."
Rooney again glanced at him when he asked, "Am I to take that as a compliment or a criticism?"
"Put it this way, I'm so impressed if you find us a café, I'll treat you to a cuppa and a roll and sausage."
****
Nodding that Elaine Fitzsimmons again sit, ACC Alex Gardener said, "I couldn't help but note that during your summary of the murder investigations, Elaine, you seem to be impressed by DI Fairbanks. Have you known him for a while?"
She didn't fail to notice the use of her forename and with a shrug, replied, "I only met him yesterday, though of course through the rumour mill I'd heard about him being knocked down and badly

injured prior to his promotion to DI."

He stared blankly at her before he asked, "Can I also presume you heard a *rumour* that I had a bee in my bonnet about him?"

"That too," she slowly smiled.

"I'm guessing you rate him quite highly?"

"Too soon to give you a full appraisal of him, but in the short time I've seen him in action and watched how he handles his team, I'd say," she pursed her lips when she cocked her head at him, "based on my own experience of course, that Eddie Fairbanks might one day be sitting in your chair. He's one to watch," she parodied Liz Malone's earlier assessment.

She watched him wearily rub a hand across his face when he took a breath, then replied, "It might just be that I have misjudged DI Fairbanks."

With the short period of time she had left to serve as a police office, Elaine Fitzsimmons was not one to hold back on her thoughts, so calmly said, "You were a fine operational Divisional detective, Alex, and on the occasions I worked with you, I really admired how you got the job done. However…"

He was about to interrupt, but she quickly held up her hand and continued, "*However*, since you achieved your exalted rank, there's a change came over you."

She paused as she stared at him then continued, "Yes, you were sometimes a bit stand-offish, and always very dapper, but most people who interacted with you could see past that because you were a good man and a good detective."

She paused again and took a sharp breath, wondering perhaps if she was going too far, but then realised she had committed herself and continued, "Based on my own personal experience both as a police officer and a woman of, let's say, mature years, if I was ever to offer you any advice," she exhaled, "it would be that you do not retire from this job as the ACC your staff dislike and fear."

She saw his eyes widen, but again, before he could respond, she continued.

"Don't let all the good will and admiration you built up through your career end like that with your legacy being the mean spirited-man you seem to have become."

Stunned as he stared at her, he finally stuttered, "Is that how you see me, Elaine? A man who is disliked and feared?"

"Not by me, Alex," she smiled, "because I'm too long in the tooth, but there's a whole generation of hardworking detectives following you and me and those young detectives look to you to be their guide in the job. You are the Assistant Chief Constable in charge of the Force's CID and currently in the role that many of them aspire to achieve. So, if you are honest with yourself, would you want them to end up as bitter and as removed from their staff and as you seem to have become from yours?"

She rose to her feet, then staring down at him, softly said, "You still have time to turn things around, Alex. You don't need to be every young detectives' friend, but you do need to be their role model and if you treat them with dignity and respect, *that* is what you will be remembered for."

She smiled again when she formally said, "Now, sir, if you will excuse me, I have some bad guys to catch and an on-going murder investigation that seems to have grown arms and legs."

After she had left the room, he sat for several minutes literally catching his breath for no-one had spoken to him like that for a very long time.

Glancing at the photo of his wife on the corner of his desk, a horrified thought occurred when he wondered; have I been acting like…like that at home?

Moments passed as he reflected on what Elaine Fitzsimmons had said, then with a resigned sigh, he lifted the desk phone and told his secretary, "Please call DI Cameron and tell…"

He stopped and drawing a breath, then continued, "Please ask him to come to my office," then quickly drawing a breath, ended with, "Thank you."

****

Driving south on the M74 motorway, DS Norrie McCartney heard Sadie McGhee's phone chirrup, then scowled, "Is that her again?"

Glancing at the screen, she timidly replied, "No, it's the office."

"Don't answer," he hastily said, then added, "They'll be looking for us, wanting to ask what we know about Denholm's man that's been arrested."

"But we can't just ignore them, Norrie," her voice was now almost a plea for she had quickly come to realise that she was no match for this brute of a man, that any dissent on her part might provoke him into hurting her and with him planning to kill Constance McKenzie, she now had the horrible thought that there was no telling just how far he might go to cover his own back.

"We'll ignore them for as long as we can," he quietly replied. "When we get back to Pitt Street, all we have to tell them is that we were chasing down a lead, that we'd learned from a source that one of the women who had been in the hotel was staying in the caravan park in Newton Stewart and we went down there to confirm it with the intention of interviewing her."

He snatched a glance at her, then in a forceful voice, added, "Have you got that?"

"Yes," she snapped back, but he let that go, guessing how frightened of him she now was and as far as he was concerned, that was in his favour.

Minutes passed before she asked, "Thames House, will they help us if we are interviewed?"

"Of course," he confidently replied. "They'll tell HSB that we were acting on their behalf and that prick Fraser, he'll simply back off because he'll worry if he argues or presses them for details, they'll cut off his funding. They've no backbone when it comes down to the crunch, some of these bosses," he sneered.

She stared out at the thick trees and foliage when passing Galloway Forest Park, though having no idea where they were, so asked, "How far away are we from Newton Stewart?"

"About another twenty or thirty minutes, I think. I'm not familiar with this area," he shrugged.

Seeing a sign for a hotel just six hundred metres ahead, she pointed then said, "Stop at that hotel, please. I need to pee."

He too needed to pee, so nodding, replied, "Okay, five minutes and no longer. If McKenzie's waiting for us, I don't want her getting spooked and making a run for it."

His answer chilled her to the bone and she fought the panic that threatened to overcome her.

Pulling into the deserted car park of the old coach house that appeared to have been recently modernised, he stopped the car then when the engine was switched off, he leaned across her to open the glove compartment.

To her horror, she saw a black enamelled handgun within the compartment.

He grinned at her when he reminded her, "The raid in Ayrshire where I got the gun I gave to Denholm. It wasn't the only gun I forgot to log in the productions register. But this one," he fetched it out and balancing it low on his knee, stared down with approval at it when he added, "This is a *real* good one; a Glock G32 with a full magazine, so more than enough to do the job, eh?"

Staring mean faced at her, he snarled, "We don't want to be doing anything silly when we're in this place now, Sadie, do we?"

She watched him place the gun into his jacket pocket, then reminded her, "Five minutes, no more or I'll have to come and find you."

Passing through the door into the restaurant, McGhee forced an inquisitive smile at the curious young woman behind the bar, whose expression changed to one of understanding when returning the smile, she pointed towards the Ladies toilet.

Seconds behind her, McCartney too made his way to the Gents.

A little under five minutes later, she hesitantly returned to the parked CID car to see McCartney already at the rear of the vehicle, one hand on the boot lid.

Glancing into the boot, she saw he had taken an old, much used dirt-ingrained spade from a nearby wheelbarrow then told her, "It might come in handy."

It was then she realised she should have remained in the hotel and called to the staff for help, but now with him standing so close to her and too frightened to run, she simply did nothing when he ushered her into the front passenger seat, then closed the door.

"Seatbelt on, please," he casually smiled at her, then with a grin, he added, "Can't be too careful now, Sadie, can we?"

So scared she couldn't speak, when he started the engine, she stared out through the windscreen, her terrified thoughts filled with the handgun he carried in his jacket pocket and the spade in the boot of the car.

****

Pulling open her front door, Ronnie, still wearing the lime green tracksuit, but now with slippers on her feet and her hair tied back, stared at her sister, who with her the palm of her right hand raised, greeted her with, "I'm not here to steal back my ex-boyfriend, if that's what you're thinking."

She forced a smile then wordlessly stood to one side to permit Gill to pass her by, who then carried on walking through to the front room.

Following her, Ronnie's professional eyes couldn't help but admire the pencil, bottle green skirted suit Gill wore nor did it escape her notice her blonde hair had recently been cut and she looked as attractive as she ever had.

In the front room and turning to face her, she sensed that no matter her initial statement, Gill was clearly nervous as was she and said "Sit down. Can I get you a coffee or tea?"

"Coffee, please, and you know how I like it. In fact, why don't I come through to the kitchen and we can talk there?"

A minute later, Gill seated at the kitchen table while Ronnie brewed the coffee, she turned to ask, "I really didn't expect to see you again, Gill, and you never answered my calls or my text messages. So, if you're not here as you say, to steal Eddie back, then why are you here?"

Before Gill could respond, she quickly added, "You know he's asked me to marry him?"

She watched Gill's face pale and take a deep breath before she shook her head to reply, "No, I didn't know that. I assume you said yes?"

It was when she unconsciously stroked at her stomach that Gill's eyes widened when she sighed, "You're pregnant."

"Just over six weeks, yes."

"Is that why he's marrying you? Because you're pregnant?" she nastily snapped at Ronnie.

Ronnie stared at her sister and a sudden calm overcome her when she found to her surprise that Gill's spiteful retort had no effect on her, that again to her own amazement, she actually felt sorry for her. She slowly smiled and exhaled with sudden relief at her new-found confidence when at last she replied, "No, Eddie's marrying me because he loves me as I love him. It just so happens that I'm pregnant and he's keen to marry me before our child is born."

She watched tears glisten in Gill's eyes and wondered; is she reflecting on what might have been had she been honest with Eddie and treated him better?

She turned when the boiled kettle switched off and poured the water into both mugs, then handing Gill a mug, asked again, "Why have you come to see me, Ronnie?"

Seconds passed before Gill replied, "I came to say goodbye."

"Goodbye?"

"There's whispers that our parent company, the National Australia

Group, are thinking about divesting the Clydesdale Bank, though probably not for a few years; however, it's likely it could mean early redundancies here in the UK. My boss, he's moving out to join the Bank of Australia and suggested that I go with him; start a new life out there."

"*With* him?"

"Maybe, probably…" she shrugged, then, sighed, "Yes, *with* him." She couldn't meet Ronnie's eyes, for it has always been a constant argument between them, that Gill treated every man she met as a challenge, even when she had been with Eddie; a succession of men who in due course, recognised her for the unfaithful woman she was, then inevitably dumped her.

"When do you leave?"

"In three days, from Heathrow to Singapore for a five-day stopover, then on to Melbourne."

She paused then added, "I won't be coming back, no matter what."

"Then this is it?" Ronnie slumped down into the chair opposite.

They sat in silence for several minutes, neither looking at each other, then Ronnie asked, "This boss of yours. Married?"

"Separated."

"Older?"

Gill nodded before she self-consciously replied, "Just eleven years though."

"He has family?"

"Yes. Two daughters and a son," she cleared her throat, "but why does that matter?"

"And he's leaving them behind?"

"He wants to be with me, so yes, he's leaving them behind," she scowled.

"And his marriage, it's definitely over?"

"Yes," she quickly replied, but Ronnie thought with a little too much determination.

"And how long have you been together, you and your boss."

"I didn't come here to be cross-examined, Ronnie," she tartly replied.

"But you did come to say goodbye," Ronnie said with some force in her voice, "and to tell me that once more, you've involved yourself with a married man who you're *also* telling me that, regardless of his relationship with his wife, is prepared to leave his children and travel hallway around the world with you."

"Oh, Gill," unhappily, she slowly shook her head when she stared at her sister and said, "When will you finally learn that you can't keep running away from responsibility? How many men have you…"

"Enough!" Gill jumped to her feet, tears of shame smarting at her eyes, "I wanted to see you before I left, but clearly this is a mistake."

"Gill," she called after her, but the kitchen door was already closing and no matter that Ronnie run to the front door after her, she was too late and only heard the clatter of running feet going down the stairs.

****

Larry Considine, seated at his desk in the incident room, picked up the desk phone then called across the room to DCI Elaine Fitzsimmons, "Boss, telephone call. Chief Superintendent Fraser from Special Branch."

Glancing at Eddie Fairbanks, she nodded that he follow her to Considine's desk, then answered, "DCI Fitzsimmons."

"Elaine, Callum Fraser," he breathlessly greeted her. "I've just taken a phone call from DI Sadie McGhee and it sounds like she might be in trouble."

"Go on."

"She was on for just a minute, says that she and McCartney are in the Dumfries and Galloway area they'd stopped briefly at a hotel on the road to Newton Stewart for a comfort break."

Fitzsimmons smiled and her eyes narrowed as she wrote on Considine's desk pad and wondered why Fraser couldn't just say they'd stopped to pee.

"Newton Stewart?"

"Yes. They're en-route to a caravan park in Newton Stewart where they've learned one of the women who fled from the Cambridge Street hotel, a Constance McKenzie, is lodged there."

A definite pause ended when Fraser said in a monotone voice, "McGhee claims that McCartney intends murdering this woman and McGhee too is in fear of her life."

Shocked, Fitzsimmons indicated to Fairbanks what she'd written, she then pressed the desk phones speaker button and her eyes on Fairbanks, said, "So, McGhee claims McCartney intends murdering this woman, Constance McKenzie. Have you contacted the local police about this?"

"My Deputy is doing so as we speak, but there's something else."
She heard a sharp intake of breath before he said, "McGhee also claims that McCartney is armed with a handgun."

CHAPTER THIRTY-TWO.

Travelling on the A714, it was when they arrived on the outskirts of Newton Stewart that Sadie McGhee's phone activated with an incoming text message.
"Is that her," McCartney gruffly asked and risked a glance at McGhee.
"Yes, she says she'll meet us at the Aroma Café on Victoria Street."
"The what?" he angrily burst out. "I *told* you to tell her," he seethed, "we were to meet somewhere quiet."
"Well, evidently she doesn't trust us," she snapped back, then flinched when without warning, he viciously backhanded her across the face with his left hand, causing her nose to burst and a fine spray of blood to stream out across the dashboard.
Yelping, she raised both hands protectively across her face, but his hands were back on the wheel and he quietly growled, "Do not talk back to me or I swear, I'll do more than fucking slap you!"
Her hands shaking, she fetched a handkerchief from her jacket pocket and dabbed at her rapidly swelling nose to stem the flow as her tears mixed with her blood and began to drip down her cheeks onto the collar of her blouse.
"Clean yourself up," he hissed at her. "You can't go into a café looking like that."
"Now," he continued in a calmer voice, "keep your eyes open for this Victoria Road and the café."
****
DI Iain Cameron reported to ACC Gardener's office, then knocking on the inner door, heard him call out, "Come in."
Bracing himself for another bout of sarcasm, Cameron politely greeted Gardener with, "You're looking for me, sir."
"Ahem, yes, Iain, come in.
Iain?

What the hell, Cameron wondered and was even more confused when Gardener waved at a chair and said, "Sit down."

The ACC, his fingers arched in front of his nose, sat staring for several seconds at the young DI, then said, "I understand that you would prefer to be working at a Divisional CID than working as my aide. Is that correct?"

"Yes, sir, it is," Cameron returned his stare.

Again, several seconds passed before Gardener said, "How does Coatbridge suit you? For travelling, I mean."

Cameron's eyes narrowed when he asked, "Are you telling me I am to be transferred to N Division, sir? To Coatbridge CID?"

"You worked that one out yourself, did you?" Gardener slowly smiled.

"That would suit me just fine, yes sir," a relieved Cameron smiled back.

"Well, you start there this forthcoming Monday, Iain, and it only remains for me to wish you good luck and ask one thing of you before you depart."

"Sir?"

Gardener's brow furrowed when he said, "Give some thought on who you think might be suitable and where I can find such an individual to replace you."

Then peering studiously at the younger man, he added with a sigh, "Someone who is as capable as you so obviously are."

****

Arlene McCandlish sat at her kitchen table cradling her mug and staring at her minder, Axel, who sitting opposite, sipped at his tea. Then she asked, "You're certain about this? That Constance was touting to the PSNI?"

"As certain as I can be," he sighed, though his face betrayed his rage at McKenzie's alleged betrayal.

"But how certain *is* that when you say, as certain as you can be and by the way, who is your man?"

"We did a few jobs together when the war was on going," he grimaced, "and I pulled his arse out of the frying pan once, so he owes me big time."

She smiled at that, but before she could respond, he continued.

"Look, Arlene," he leaned across the table as though to emphasis his words, "In light of what occurred in Glasgow, I've serious doubts about who we can really trust anymore. Now, my man tells me that McKenzie was seen with a woman on a number of occasions in different parts of the city and he was ordered by that two-faced bastard Dicky Porter to follow the woman and when he did, he saw her going into the peelers station in Knock Road. And that time," he sat back again, "was directly after she'd met with McKenzie in a café on the Shankill."

A doubtful McCandlish replied with a shrug, "Doesn't mean she's a peeler though, this woman. She might work there and be, say, a secretary or a cleaner. Anything."

"Do you really believe that?" he squinted at her.

"No," she sighed with a shake of her head, "you're probably right and completely confirms what we now know about Constance."

"But the bigger picture," he continued, "is that Porter must have known about McKenzie before we travelled over to Glasgow. So, doesn't that put him in the frame for setting you up to be murdered?"

"Let's think about this," her face creased. "If Constance was touting to the peelers, then it follows they knew of my plan to travel to Glasgow to meet with Gary McGuigan. If *that* is true, then does it also mean that the PSNI were aware there was to be an attempt to murder me?"

"Unless" he quietly said.

"Unless?" she stared curiously at him.

"We've always known the RUC…" he stopped and wryly smiled before correcting himself "the PSNI intelligence departments are being run by the British Security Service, so what if this woman McKenzie was touting to is *not* the peelers. What if she's MI5?"

McCandlish had never really credited Axel with more than a basic intelligence, but now she stared hard at him, then softly asked, "What are you thinking?"

Licking at his suddenly dry lips, he exhaled when he said, "Both us and the 'RA', we agreed to cut the British Government out of the talks because simply put, neither side trusts them, so what if through McKenzie, they learned of the meeting in Glasgow and orchestrated the hit on you, with the blame to lie at the feet of the 'RA'?"

A cold chill swept through her when shivering, her eyes narrowed and she curiously found herself asking, "Is it me or has it suddenly become cold here in the kitchen?"

As if realising it was an odd thing to say, she then added, "You think the Security Service might be responsible for the attack, but why?"
He shrugged when he replied, "I know it sounds pretty simplistic, Arlene, but the only reason I can think of is that if there *is* peace between us and the 'RA', what the hell are spooks going to be doing with their time? I mean…"
But he got no further, for though Axel would never know that his suggestion not only mirrored the thoughts of Elaine Fitzsimmons, a soon to be retired Detective Chief Inspector of Strathclyde Police, but it caused Arlene McCandlish to gasp when she stuttered, "MI5, they'll have lost control over here. They'll not be needed and…my God, Axel! You're right!" Outraged, she jumped up from her chair, her eyes blazing in anger.
"Some *bastard* in the British Government has been told by MI5 of the Glasgow meeting and decided that if they were to continue to influence policies here in the Province, they were to thwart any attempt at peace between us and the 'RA' and that meant, me being the driving force behind the initiative, that I be killed and for what!" She took a deep breath when she screamed loudly, "And all so they don't lose control?"
Seconds later, responding to the scream, the kitchen door burst open to admit Johnny, the younger of the two bodyguards and his gun in his hand who stared bewilderingly from one to the other before being waved from the room by Axel.
Shaking her head, she stared down at Axel, seeing his face pale at her vehemence.
Then forcing herself to be calm, her teeth gritted, she said, "I know Dicky isn't supporting the peace initiative with the 'RA', but I would have drawn the line about him colluding with the Security Services or whatever name they're using these days! It's all been down to Constance and the *bitch* she was touting too. I didn't believe it at first," she shook her head, "that Constance would have been involved orchestrating the attempt on my life. But now," she seethed.
Then quietly added, "Now I've changed mind and to *think* I let her escape with her life!"
****

Eddie Fairbanks didn't believe it could all happen within just twenty-five minutes, but here he was, Duke Smythe by his side and standing on the tarmac at the Glasgow Heliport by the River Clyde, watching and waiting for a marked police Transit van to arrive. Upon stopping nearby, the back doors of the van opened to disclose five heavily armed police officers, all members of the Tactical Response Team and similarly dressed in black coveralls and armed with Heckler & Koch carbine's and Glock 17 pistols in holsters strapped to their legs.

Emerging from the van, the two detectives saw each of the four men and one woman carried ballistic helmets in their hands. As they approached Fairbanks and Smythe, the two detectives also saw two of the men carried a spare bulletproof vest, one each for the two detectives.

The sergeant, who identified himself as Liam McGregor, then pointed at the Eurocopter EC135 with its engines were idling, and said, "If we're in a rush, boss, can I suggest that you brief us while we're travelling via the headphones on-board?"

Within two minutes, the five police officers with the two detectives aboard, being the choppers maximum passenger payload, was off the ground and en-route to Newton Stewart.

Seeing that all five uniformed colleagues were now wearing headsets, Fairbanks raised a smile when he began with, "Thanks, guys, for coming along. Now, here's what I know."

****

When Norrie McCartney and Sadie McGhee, embarrassed by her swollen nose and bloodstained collar of her blouse, entered the Aroma Café on Victoria Street in the small town of Newton Stewart, there were just five occupants at the tables. Two elderly ladies who sitting together, glanced towards the door when the strangers entered and another elderly couple, so engaged in conversation they hardly heard the bell above the door chime.

The fifth occupant was a woman sitting alone at a table at the back of the café, an empty white mug in front of her, her hair tousled and wearing a short denim skirt with her blue anorak zipped to the neck and raised her head from her iPad to stare curiously at McGhee.

Striding towards McKenzie, it was McCartney who greeted her with, "Is this what you call a quiet place?"

"No," she replied in a low, Belfast brogue, "this is what I call a safe place because I don't know you and that means I don't trust you. Who the hell *is* he, Sadie," McKenzie turned her attention to her.

It was as they sat down that McCartney calmly replied for her, "I'm Norrie, your new handler. Sadie brought me down from the city to meet you and debrief you."

"Debrief me?" McKenzie's eyes opened wide, then she sneered, "Debrief me about what?"

She turned to address McGhee then leaning towards her, she hissed, "McCandlish knows about me, Sadie, and right now I'm lucky I'm not rotting in some hole in the ground! What kind of balls-up happened back there in Glasgow? Your man had one job to do, shoot McCandlish then run! That's all there was to do, but no!"

Her face registering her disgust, she vigorously shook her head.

"The bloody gun *exploded* in his hand! And now?" she sat back and hissed, "Now McCandlish knows I'm involved in trying to have her murdered and I'm out in the cold and you," she turned towards McCartney, "you want to *debrief* me? Who are you kidding!"

McGhee watched his face turn pale and it was then that McKenzie took notice of her swollen nose and collar and suspiciously said, "What the hell happened to you?"

"My fault," McCartney easily interrupted with a grim smile. "I stamped on the brakes when a bloody sheep crossed the road and Sadie here; well, she wasn't expecting it and when I threw up my arm to prevent her bouncing off the windscreen, she banged her nose. Isn't that right, boss," he stared at her, the warning in his voice chilling McGhee to the bone.

"Can I get you guys anything," the ginger-headed young waitress smiled down at them, pencil and notepad ready in her hands.

"Coffee's all round," McCartney smiled back at her, then his eyes appraising her, watched her walk off before he turned back to face McKenzie and said, "When we're done here, we'll head back to your caravan, Constance…"

His eyebrows knitted when he asked, "Can I call you Constance or do you prefer Connie?"

"I'd prefer it that you call me Miss McKenzie, because like I told you," she jeered, "I'm out. I've nowhere to go and the money your mob was supposed to pay me? Well, I don't suppose that's going to happen now. So, tell me, Norrie, now that your lot have buggered up my life, where exactly do I go from here?"

"Ah, but we have a surprise for you, Constance," he smiled, then turning to McGhee, his eyes again warning her to play along, he said, "We've a present in the boot of the car. A package that contains a passport and driving licence in a new name and TSB bank cards in the same name with a sizeable amount of cash in the account for the service rendered. Yes," he pursed his lips and shrugged, "the operation went south, but that doesn't mean it was your fault and my mob, as you call them, they're grateful for your part in it and they always pay their way."

He was interrupted by the return of the waitress who with the same, broad smile, delivered the three coffees, then glanced up as the elderly ladies waved cheerio at the door.

"Anything else you need, I'll be in the back," the waitress told them, "so just give me a shout."

On the pavement outside, the two elderly women stopped chattering when they were distracted and looking up at the loud noise, saw a low flying helicopter that seemed to be skimming the rooftops.

Alone again at their table, a suspicious McKenzie asked, "Why didn't you just bring this package in with you?"

"Oh, you'll have the package," he assured her, "but only after I debrief you. We know *what* happened in the meeting room, but not what was said before that. So," he smiled, "a short briefing, then the package."

McKenzie turned towards McGhee with her eyes narrowing in suspicion and said, "You're being very quiet here, Sadie. Why is that?"

But she didn't get the opportunity to respond because McCartney, impatient now with McKenzie's obstinacy, interrupted with a loud sigh, "I didn't want it to come to this, but here's what you should know. Right now I have my right hand on a gun in my pocket, so you and Sadie and me are going to walk out of here towards our car, that's parked right outside."

Staring at a shocked McKenzie, he continued, "If you make a fuss or in any way try to scream or alert anyone, I'll kill you and that wee couple sitting at the table behind me, then that young darling waitress with the red hair, too. This is a one-horse town, sweetheart, and I doubt if there's any more than a couple of cops on duty, so there won't be any cavalry coming to rescue you. Now," he smiled warmly at her, "is that clearly understood, *Miss McKenzie*?"

Staring at him, McGhee, shaking with fear, could not help but wonder; how did she come to be associated with this man who she

realised now to be a complete sociopath?
****

The Dumfries & Galloway Constabulary, the territorial Force responsible for policing the south of Scotland at the border with England, covered a largely rural area and is overseen by no more than five hundred officers.

The two D&G officers on duty that day at Newton Stewart, a female Sergeant and her male Constable, now stood with the blonde-haired woman in a field adjacent to the caravan park, watching the Strathclyde Police helicopter circle before it set down. Parked behind them on the grass verge next to the road was a black coloured Volvo estate vehicle and a marked police Transit van.

Then, as the helicopter came down to rest with its rotors still spinning, they saw the two detectives, who soon introduced themselves as Eddie Fairbanks and Duke Smythe and accompanied by five armed officers, emerge from the rear two doors, then heads bent, run towards them.

As soon as the officers were clear, the helicopter revved its engine, then took off and within seconds, was almost out of sight.

Surrounded by his team and greeting the sergeant, Fairbanks was in turn introduced to the blonde-haired woman, the owner of the caravan park, who shook her head then said, "No, there's no Constance McKenzie staying here, Mr Fairbanks."

They then saw her eyes narrow when holding up her hand, she added, "Wait. A woman did check in yesterday, a Mrs Quigley, but she is Irish."

Fairbanks glanced at Smythe before he replied, "That's likely her. Do you know if she's in her caravan at the minute?"

"She's not there, no," the owner shook her head.

"She came to the office about an hour ago, maybe slightly longer than that, and asked about somewhere in town to have a coffee. I told her about the Aroma Café on Victoria Street and I don't think she's returned yet."

Glancing at the local sergeant, Fairbanks saw her nod when she said, "We'll take a wee turn past the cafe, Inspector, and find out if she's still there. If she is, we won't approach, but we'll call you on this," she handed him a police radio.

Half turning to point behind her, she added, "We brought my own car for us two and the van is in case you need to move. You'll find the keys in the ignition."

Smart thinking, he thought, then mentally promised he'd bring her actions to the attention of her boss.

"Okay," he acknowledged with a nod, "two of my guys can accompany you just in case things kick off and while you're checking out the café, we'll try the caravan for her."

"I'll show you where it is," the owner interjected, who now conscious that if this turned out to be newsworthy, there was a real possibility of some local gossip and free advertising for the site and who smiled with excitement.

"Okay, let's get it done," he waved two of the armed cops to accompany the sergeant and her constable.

****

McCartney had managed to get them out of the café and into the car without having to shoot anyone and as far as he was concerned, he was now halfway home.

A short drive to the Galloway Forest, find a path into the Forest then park somewhere remote, have them take turns at digging a nice deep hole, then do the two of them.

Sitting in the back of the car, the Glock nestling on his knee, he ordered that there be no talking, that they do not turn around and sat staring at the back of their heads, knowing that McKenzie was now as terrified as was McGhee, who was driving.

The feeling of power that he had over the two women was electrifying and curiously, he felt himself become aroused.

It was then a thought occurred and he wondered; he'd always had a fancy for the stuck-up bitch that was McGhee. Maybe he'd have a bit of fun with her before dumping her in into the ground with McKenzie.

His imagination took over and glancing at them in turn, his thoughts turned to having fun with them both, one after the other.

After all, he found himself grinning, he was going to kill them both anyway, so why not be in for a penny, in for a pound.

"They'll find the letter I've written," McKenzie broke into his thoughts.

He was about to tap her on the back of the head with the butt of the Glock, but stopped, then said, "What are you talking about. What letter?"

She didn't turn, but her voice faltering, she replied, "Last night, after I booked the caravan, I wrote a letter to Arlene McCandlish, apologising for my part in trying to kill her and telling her everything."

"You're lying," he sneered, guessing she was playing for time.

He watched her nod, then needing time to think and seeing a layby ahead, snapped at "McGhee, Pull in and stop the car, but if either of you try to run for it, I'll kill you both. Understood?"

He saw them both nod, then hissed, "I want to hear it! Is that understood!"

"Yes," they both replied, their quivering voices betraying their fear and entirely believing what he told them.

His eyes narrowed when he thought, if there was a letter the bosses at Thames House would not be happy chappies if it turned up and implicated the Security Service in the attempted murder of a member of the Inner Council.

That and no prizes for guessing who they'd blame.

And, if that happened, there was little doubt in his mind he himself would become expendable and nothing would save him from being prosecuted…or worse.

No, if the bitch has written a letter, he inwardly sighed, it had to be dealt with now.

When the car was parked in the layby, he softly exhaled, then used the barrel of the Glock to lightly tap McKenzie on the head before he said, "Turn around and tell me more about this supposed letter."

Her breath coming in spurts, she turned in her seat, then replied, "It was to be my insurance because even if the plan to kill McCandlish had worked, I thought Sadie was going to betray me. That her or someone from MI5 would kill me because of what I know."

"My, my," he sneered at her, his voice full of false sympathy, "what a suspicious and twisted life you have led. Is the letter posted?"

She knew then that she had him hooked and continued with the lie, but knowing if she said yes, she'd posted the letter, he'd kill them because there was nothing he could do about it.

Hoping to buy herself more time, she said, "Not yet. I was planning to buy stamps after I met with you."

She could see the doubt in his eyes when he stared at her and said, "Even though you thought someone might kill you at the café or soon afterwards, you hadn't yet posted the letter? So, what," his eyes widened and she guessed he was enjoying himself, the power over them that he had, "I just kill the two of you, then fetch it from the caravan? Now, that wasn't very bright, was it, *Miss McKenzie*."

She realised she'd made a mistake, so quickly stuttered, "But when I don't return to the caravan, they'll search it and then they'll find the letter."

McGhee, almost too scared to even breathe, gently undid her seatbelt, but held the belt at the buckle and inwardly prayed that he would become so distracted by McKenzie, she might be able to make a dash from the car.

He took a deep breath as he stared at McKenzie then barked, "Your handbag. Hand it over."

She reached down to the footwell and grabbing at the bag, handed it to him.

The gun held levelled at her with his left hand, he rummaged in the bag with his right hand then hissed, "Where's the caravan key?"

The key was in her jacket pocket, but she lied, "I...I didn't bring it. There was a deposit of thirty quid for the key and I'm short of funds, so I couldn't risk losing it and I hid it near to the caravan door."

"Where?" he stared keenly at her.

She took a sharp breath before she replied, "I'm not telling you."

Seconds passed as he stared at her, then to her shock and without warning, he raised the Glock and smashed the butt sharply down onto the top of her head.

Stunned, her body shaking, she slumped in her seat and instinctively reached up to feel blood oozing through her fingers.

Now was her chance, thought McGhee and opening the driver's door, leapt from the car.

Racing to the front of the vehicle, she saw a barred metal gate in the hedgerow that hid the field running alongside the layby and beyond the gate, a rutted track.

Pulling up her skirt, she ran for the gate, but unaware that McCartney had leisurely got out of the rear door on the hedgerow side.

Her terror spurring her on, she didn't see him casually walk towards the gate that McGhee had clumsily climbed, then fallen over and heard her scream in pain.

She'd twisted her ankle when she'd fell and turning her head, saw him approach the gate with the gun pointed at her.

Limping as quickly as her injured ankle would permit, only seven or eight metres separated them and with a quick glance to ensure there was no traffic on the B listed road, McCartney stood at the gate and balanced both hands holding the Glock, on the top bar of the gate. Turning to face him, she realised she could not escape him, but continued to back away, her face streaked with tears and both arms stretched forward as though in an attempt to ward off what she knew was about to happen.

Weeping now, she begged, "Please, Norrie, I'll not tell anyone! Please! Don't shoot me! Please!"

But all to no avail.

A police trained and authorised firearms officer, McCartney couldn't miss at that short range and fired twice in rapid succession, just as he'd been taught.

The double-tap.

He watched and smiled with satisfaction, as the two crimson spots appeared dead centre on her chest as she was flung back into some tall grass where she lay, eyes and mouth wide open and splayed like a broken and abandoned doll.

Pity, he thought, he was really looking forward to have some fun with her.

With a resigned sigh and knowing now he'd have to come back later to retrieve the body that fortunately lay out of sight of the passing traffic, he returned to the car.

Getting into the driver's seat, he saw that McKenzie was still dazed from the blow to her head and jokingly told her, "We'll collect Sadie later. She's having a bit of a lie-down at the minute."

With his left hand, he started at her knee, then working his hand up under her skirt began to gently stroke her bare inner thigh, his fingers moving up to her crotch and ignored her shaking hand that tried to push him away.

Leaning towards her and now fully aroused, he whispered, "Just me and you now, sweetheart, so don't be saying or doing anything to make me angry, okay?"

Switching on the engine and tyres screeching, he did a swift U-turn and began the return journey to Newton Stewart.

CHAPTER THIRTY-THREE.

"No trace of anyone fitting the description of any of your suspects, Inspector," the radio blared in Fairbanks ear, "so I had a word with the lassie on duty. She says an Irish woman was in and was joined later by a man and another woman, all three left some twenty minutes ago."

"Roger," he sighed, then added, "Nobody returned to the caravan, though there is evidence she's been here and might come back, if the suitcase and discarded clothing on the bed means anything. That and she's booked the caravan for a second night. Right," he rubbed at his forehead, "return here and we'll reassess our plan. At the minute because of our limited resources, all we can do is remain at the site and hope that she or our other suspects show up."

"Roger," the sergeant acknowledged and ended the transmission.

He turned when Duke Smythe said, "The tactical boys are secreting themselves about the caravan, boss, just in case either the woman McKenzie or McGhee and her headcase neighbour do show up here. In the meantime," he flashed a smile, "I'm away to charm that big darling in the office out of two cups of coffee, so I'll get you back here."

"Don't forget to see if she's any biscuits," Fairbanks grinned at him then when Smythe left, sat down on the built-in couch that doubled as a bed.

Fetching his phone from his pocket, he dialled Ronnie's mobile number, then greeted her with, "How are you feeling?"

"Calmer now and nothing to report physically," she glumly replied.

It was an inner sense rather than her voice that made him ask "Something going on?"

It was seconds later before she replied with, "Gill showed up at our door."

He felt his body tense when he asked, "Is she still there?"

"No, she's gone to Australia."

"Eh, what?"

"Sorry," he heard her softly laugh, "I mean she's away, but she came to say goodbye. She's a new man in her life and they're moving to Australia."

"Oh, right," he was suddenly elated that if it were true, Gill and her wayward behaviour would no longer be a concern hanging over them both, but forcing himself to be calm, asked, "How do you feel about that?"

"Truthfully?" he heard her sigh, "I don't really know how I feel, but look; you're at work, so I won't keep you. I'll tell you whole story when you get home this evening."

"Eh, about that," he grimaced.

"Eddie. What's going on? Where are you?"

"Actually, I'm sitting in a caravan," he glanced about him, "in Newton Stewart down in the Dumfries and Galloway area."

"Newton Stewart? Where is that?"

"I'm told we're about fifty miles from Dumfries, towards the Scottish west coast, I think. I'm not too familiar with this area."

The door opened to admit Smythe who balancing in one hand a plastic tray with two white enamel mugs on it and in the other hand, a plate of chocolate biscuits.

"Sorry, love, don't know what time I'll get home this evening, but if it's late, do not wait up. Love you," he added with an embarrassed glance at Smythe.

Laying the tray down onto the table in front of Fairbanks, the big man ignored Fairbanks sentiment when he said, "The owner, Julie's her name, she's seeing that the others are getting coffee as well, boss."

"So, no movement so far then," Smythe slumped down onto the bench seat opposite, then asked, "I take it we're here till we get a result?"

"Probably, but I'd better get onto Elaine Fitzsimmons to update her anyway," Fairbanks first sipped at the scalding coffee then dialled the number for the DCI.

The door opened again to admit the local sergeant, who said, "Your guys are being briefed by their own sergeant, sir, so me and my neighbour will return to our office and take the Transit van to get it out of sight in case your suspects show. If you're not needing it, I'll take my car away, but leave radio for you to contact us, if we're needed."

"Thank you," Fairbanks smiled as she nodded cheerio, then closed the door behind her.

"Smart lassie that," Smythe nodded at the closed door.

"Seems to be, yes," Fairbanks agreed, then dialled Fitzsimmons number.

****

Elaine Fitzsimmons ended the call, then turning to Larry Considine, said, "Eddie Fairbanks and his team have missed the suspect, this woman Constance McKenzie, but there seems an indication she might be returning to the caravan, so they're remaining there for now."

"What about that pair, McGhee and McCartney? Any sighting of them?"

"Nothing so far, though a waitress in a café down there reported two people fitting their descriptions met with a woman in the café who was Irish and is likely, McKenzie" she shook her head.

"Boss?"

She turned to see one of Fairbanks DC's at her side and said, "Mickey, isn't it?"

"Yes boss, Mickey Rooney. I'm the CID aide," he nodded then continued, "I've just had Nicky Spiers mother, Janet, on the phone. She's been to visit him on remand and tells me that she's convinced him to speak with us, but she insists if he speaks with us that it has to count when he goes to trial."

Fitzsimmons eyes widened when she said, "Good work, Mickey. I understand she's been your source, so well done. Right then," she turned, then spying Jaya Bahn, called her over and said, "You two, get yourselves up to Barlinnie and while you're en-route, I'll contact the PF and have him arrange that you interview Speirs. If he's volunteering information, I want it officially recorded in your notebooks and we'll see if we can contact his lawyer to have him present too. Got that?"

"Yes, Ma'am," they replied in unison.

When they'd left the room, Considine asked, "What you hoping he'll tell us, boss?"

Her brow creased when she quietly replied, "I'm hoping he'll be able to give us the name of the individual who sent him to murder the Larkhall lad, Gary Campbell. If we can get that name, Larry, we might be able to trace back who gave this so-called Commandant *his* orders."

He stared intensely at her before he quietly said, "You're thinking this goes too far back for us to be able to arrest the real culprits, don't you?"

"Unfortunately," she grimaced, "you're correct. I'm thinking that at some point, someone who is a whole lot higher than us on the pay grade will stick their oar in and we'll be left prosecuting the puppets and not the puppet masters who are really pulling the strings."

"We can only do what we can, boss," he shook his head.

"Indeed," she grimly agreed.

She turned when a young civilian HOLMES operator called out to her to say, "That's the Fingerprints Department at headquarters wanting a word with the SIO, Ma'am."

Taking the telephone Fitzsimmons identified herself then listening carefully, replaced the receiver before she re-joined Larry Considine."

He could see she was troubled and asked, "What?"

"The sets of prints SOCO lifted from the meeting room at the hotel and the coffee table downstairs? It seems five of the sets are not on the UK Database; that's three from downstairs and two sets from the meeting room. However, the other three sets *are* recorded on the database, but if we want further details, there's a warning on the system we are to contact our local Special Branch office."

"Let me guess," he sighed, "there's some sort of security level for those prints?"

"Which to me, Larry, suggests the sets belong to individuals recorded after being arrested under the Prevention of Terrorism legislation."

He couldn't help himself when he rolled his eyes, then muttered, "Here we go again."

****

Approaching the entrance to the caravan, McCartney slowed down to permit a marked police Transit van, closely followed by a black coloured Volvo, cross the road in front of him.

Both drivers acknowledged his courtesy with a wave.

The van, he'd seen through slitted eyes, had just the driver in the cab and it seemed to be a female wearing a police tunic who was driving the Volvo.

To avoid the driver's suspicion if she glanced in the Volvo's rear-view mirror, he was decided to follow them a short distance, then turned off into a street on the right that led into an industrial estate, then parking outside a large hanger type building, switched off the engine.

McKenzie had by now recovered from her daze and staring through the passenger window, recalled with disgust his hand groping at her, but now fearful of again being struck with the gun, was too terrified to complain.

Suspicious of the police van exiting the caravan site, his mind raced as he wondered; was it related to her, he turned to stare at McKenzie, or was it simply a call to the caravan park that had nothing to do with anything?

With a sigh, McKenzie tentatively probed at the wound on her head and felt the congealed blood was beginning to scab over, but then thought, why did it matter, for he intended killing her anyway. It was then a cold chill run through her when she thought of what he intended for her before he shot her; the vile things he said and what he promised he would do to her.

"You'd better not be lying about this letter or the key you've hidden," he hissed at her, then without warning he leaned against her, his fingers reaching under her skirt to grip the inside of her thigh that he painfully squeezed while his nails dig into the soft skin.

She took a sharp intake of breath at the incredible pain and with both her hands, tried to remove his claw-like grip.

It was all she could do not to scream loudly, but guessed if she did, he'd hurt her more.

As suddenly as he had gripped her thigh, he removed his hand and then, as if nothing untoward had occurred, he calmly said, "Right here's what's going to happen. I'm going to drive us to the caravan park where you will direct me to the one you've hired. When we stop, I will switch off the engine and get out of the car. I will walk around the car and like the gentleman I am," he smiled benignly at her, "I will open your door to help you out of the car."

He paused as he stared at her then said, "Now, tell me, where have you hidden the key?"

She stared back at him, fatalistically accepting she was not going to survive this, yet the urge to live for that extra few minutes was so precious she was willing to continue the lie about the fictitious letter. And so, she softly replied, "If I tell you here and now, you have no further use for me and you'd just kill me, then go and fetch the letter yourself."

Turning her head to stare through the windscreen, she added, "I'll tell you when we get to the caravan."

It was then, staring at her bosom and seeing how the skirt had risen up to her thighs, he decided, why have his fun with her in a damp forest when they had the luxury of the caravan?
Nodding, he smiled when he replied "We'll do it your way then."
****
Arriving at HMP Barlinnie, Mickey Rooney parked in the staff car park, then accompanied by Jaya Bahn, was admitted through the prison to an interview room, usually reserved for prisoners and their lawyers, to find a Nicky Speirs, his head down and sitting at a steel table with a prison officer standing just behind the door.
"He's all yours," the PO told them, then shaking his head, he added, "His lawyer phoned to say that he won't be attending, that if he's volunteering information that isn't about the case against him, he's no interest in being here."
Leaving the room, he told them he'd be sitting outside if they needed him.
Sitting himself down in one of the two chairs in front of Speirs, Rooney greeted him with, "This is DC Bahn, so how are they treating you in here, Nicky?"
When he raised his head, it was clear the young man had been crying when shrugging, he replied, "I hate it in here. And the place stinks of piss and fried food and it's never quiet with people shouting all the time and the prison officers, they're always bossing me about. I just want to go home."
"You killed a young man, Nicky. Stabbed him to death. What did you think would happen to you after doing that?" Rooney asked.
They watched him shrug before he muttered, "My Ma, she says I've to tell you what you want to know and it will help me get out of here."
Rooney glanced at Bahn, who notebook in hand, wordlessly raised her eyebrows in what he took to be a signal that he put Speirs straight regarding that comment.
"Nicky," he stared at him, "your mum made a mistake, son. You are not getting out of here. You are going to be in jail for a very long time, but how long that will be might depend on what you tell us. Do you understand that?"
They saw his forehead creasing as he tried to comprehend that what his mother told him was wrong, that he couldn't go home after all, that he might be in jail for a long time, then said, "The Commandant.

He told me that after I killed the Fenian, I'd be okay, that he'd look after me, but he's not going to do that, is he?"

Was this a breakthrough, Bahn wondered, just as Rooney seized upon it and asked, "You think he's lied to you, Nicky, this man, the Commandant?"

"I don't know," clearly confused, Speirs shook his head.

"The young man you stabbed, Nicky, did the Commandant tell you he was a Fenian?"

"Aye," he nodded, "and he was wearing a Celtic top, just like the Commandant told me he would be."

"Nicky, look at me, son," Rooney said when he saw Speirs head droop.

"The man you stabbed, his name was Gary Campbell and we think he was wearing a Celtic top because that's what the Commandant told him to wear. But he wasn't a Fenian, Nicky, not even a Celtic supporter. In fact, he was a young Protestant lad from Larkhall and a member of a Loyalist flute band and we believe he was acting on the Commandant's order that he wear the Celtic top because of something *he* had just done."

"No," Speirs sat upright and vigorously shook his head, "that's not right. The Commandant, he *told* me the guy coming down the stairs was a Fenian! That's why I stabbed him!"

Rooney waited for several seconds till the younger man composed himself, then said, "I haven't lied to you before have I?"

With obvious reluctance, Speirs raised his head to stare at Rooney before he shook his head. "Then believe me now, Nicky, when I tell you, this man, the Commandant, *he* lied to you, didn't he?"

"He said I'd be a hero," Speirs muttered, the tears falling from his eyes, as did the realisation he'd been used. "But I'm not a hero, am I?"

He let several seconds pass to permit the sobbing Speirs to compose himself, then leaning forward, Rooney softly asked, "Nicky, this is important and it's to help *you*. Can you tell us where we can we find this man, the Commandant?"

****

The Tactical Response Team Sergeant poked his head into the caravan door, then said, "That's my guys deployed, Inspector. If this goes tits up, we'll deal with it before the suspects get the opportunity to enter the caravan. I've also deployed one of my team in the bushes at the road into the caravan park to alert us if the Branch car turns up or she sees any female matching the description the park's owner has given us, so we'll have at least thirty seconds warning."

"Thank you," Fairbanks acknowledged with a nod then watched as the sergeant reached to his ear and listening, then hurriedly said, "God's truth, that's the car coming now; it's turning into the caravan park, sir. One male driving and a female in the front passenger seat." The sergeant didn't wait for a response, but slamming the door closed, he was gone and hurrying across the small decking area that bordered one side of the rectangular gravelled parking bay allotted to the caravan.

Glancing at Smythe, Fairbanks saw the big man had instinctively ducked down onto one knee then turned to watch the DI do likewise. Then Smythe grinned, "What's the odds it's those two Branch sods and they've got this woman, McKenzie, with them?"

Fairbanks eyes narrowed when he softly replied, "If it is them, then they've taken a hell of a long time getting here, Duke. I'd have thought by now they had found her and be on their way back to Glasgow with some sort of alibi."

It was then they both heard the noise of a car stopping on the gravel outside and both unconsciously found themselves holding their breaths.

****

Glancing at the caravan, McCartney asked, "So we're here now. Where's the key?"

"That plant pot there," she nodded towards a potted Fuchsia placed by the caravan door.

"It's underneath," she held her breath, willing him to believe the lie, knowing her one chance of escaping him was when he took her from the car and inwardly prayed he was unlikely to fire the gun where others might hear or see him doing so.

The Tactical Response Team's Sergeant McGregor and one man watched the arrival of the car from behind nearby caravans, with the other two male officers a little closer, hidden beneath decking; all three with their carbines nestled in their shoulder and the sights trained on the car's occupants, tensely awaiting their supervisors signal.

"Stand by, stand by," the sergeant murmured in their earpieces while their female colleague, tasked with preventing the vehicle from escaping the park, hurried through the bushes bordering the entrance road, to join them.

Getting out of the car, McKenzie watched him walk around the front to her door that he pulled open, the Glock held in his right hand down by his side and unseen by any casual passer-by.

But not unseen by the armed officers, all four who listened intently as the sergeant hissed, "Male suspect armed. Handgun, right hand. Wait one, wait one."

McKenzie had unwittingly convinced herself that he would take her by the arm and pull her from the car and her plan was to push against him, to kick, to punch, to bite, anything to distract him for those precious few seconds that would break his hold and permit her to run.

What she did not expect was for McCartney to painfully wrap his meaty fist in her shoulder length hair, then drag her from the seat. Gasping in pain, she involuntarily reached up to grab at his hand, anything to ease the agony of being dragged by the hair and all thought of her escape now gone from her mind.

"Come on, sweetheart," she heard his sneer, "time me and you got a little bit more acquainted, eh?"

"Go! Go! Go!"

****

Inside the caravan, Fairbanks and Smythe both listened to the Tactical Response Team officers outside, screaming, "Armed Police! Don't move! Drop the gun!" and though both detectives were unarmed, instinctively jumped to their feet, unconsciously jostling each other to stare through the window that faced out onto the decking and seeing the four male officers either stepping out from behind the nearby caravans or sliding out from under the decking, their weapons trained on the two figures by the decking's steps.

It was Smythe, seeing the man and woman close together stood at the car's front passenger door, who unconsciously muttered, "That's not McGhee!"

****

Taken completely by surprise, McCartney quick-wittedly raised the Glock to place the barrel against the side of McKenzie's head, then screamed in response, "I am a police officer and I have a dangerous prisoner! Stand down! Stand down, now!"

But to no avail, for the four armed officers, now joined by their female colleague, slowly walked towards McCartney and McKenzie, their Heckler & Koch carbines threateningly aimed at the Special Branch detective and each, careful step taking them closer to the man threatening the woman.

Behind McCartney, Fairbanks rushed to open the caravan door and loudly called to him, "Drop the gun, McCartney! It's over!"

The female member of the Tactical Response Team, who also trained as a sniper and considered to be the best shot in her team, was now just twenty metres from McCartney, but had never before used live rounds to shoot anything other than paper targets and mannequins dressed in camouflage.

Her stomach churning, she saw from her peripheral vision that the rest of the team had halted their advance towards the suspect, all four men realising that tactically, she had the best opportunity to take the shot.

And so, her feet almost sliding along the tarmacadamed roadway to avoid tripping, she continued her advance towards McCartney to cut down the distance between them.

Her tongue rattling in her mouth and almost afraid to blink, she levelled her weapon's telescopic sight on McCartney's forehead and during those heartbeat seconds, heard Sergeant McGregor in her ear and calmly telling her, "I assess danger to life, Lizzie, so if you have the shot, then you are authorised."

Yet unconsciously, she inwardly prayed, please God, let him give up.

"No good will come of this, DS McCartney," Fairbanks, his hands raised and now standing on the decking by the open caravan door and just three metres from McCartney and the woman, worked hard at remaining calm, guessing that the McCartney was as tense as a violin string and at the slightest provocation, might kill the woman; guessing too she was Constance McKenzie.

"I'm telling you," McCartney, his face red with anger, slightly turned his head to stare at Fairbanks, but all the while, pressing the gun barrel painfully into the side of McKenzie's head, "tell those *bastards* to stand down or so help me, I'll kill her!"

In the same calm voice, Fairbanks replied, "So, she's not a dangerous prisoner, then; she's your hostage?"

His nerves shredded, Fairbanks guessed there was only going to be one resolution to the stand-off and inwardly thought, why the hell does it have to be me?

Trusting that the young fair-haired Tactical officer, who with her carbine raised to her shoulder and her head cocked to one side as she squinted through the sight, was now working her way even closer to McCartney, he fervently hoped she would react as she had been trained.

His heart thumping in his chest, he made his decision for he'd guessed the big DS would not surrender, that he must verbally provoke McCartney into turning the gun away from his hostage. Taking a short breath, his mouth unaccountably dry, he told McCartney, "It's all over, Norrie. You've been found out and you've nobody in your corner now. My boss has been in touch with MI5 and they've seen you as a liability and washed their hands of you. You are going to jail for a very long time."

Fairbanks could not know that in his arrogant and misplaced allegiance, McCartney had always believed himself immune to Scottish justice, that his trust in his true bosses at the Security Service was paramount to anything Strathclyde Police or the Scottish Crown Office could do to him.

And so, he sneered, "You can't touch me, you prick! I'll never see the inside of a jail, no matter what I do! I *know* too much!"

In those heart stopping few seconds that his anger and his conceit overtook his rational thinking, McCartney turned the Glock from the side of McKenzie's head to point it towards Fairbanks and it was then that the twenty-nine-year old, highly trained female member of the Tactical Response Team, took the shot for which she had spent fifteen months training.

CHAPTER THIRTY-FOUR.

In the hours and the aftermath of the shooting that occurred at the caravan park in Newton Stewart, the limited resources of the Dumfries & Galloway Constabulary were supplemented by members of Strathclyde Police Serious Crime Squad and Scenes of Crime specialists, as well as a number of senior management that included DCI Elaine Fitzsimmons and the Head of Special Branch, Chief

Superintendent Callum Fraser, who was there primarily to liaise with the senior CID officers of the D&G.

Due to the distance from Glasgow to Newton Stewart, the Force helicopter was kept busy making several trips to quickly convey all the personnel to the locus.

The shocked owner of the site was gracious enough to offer an empty caravan as a temporary base and some distance from where the body of DS Norman McCartney lay spread-eagled on the ground, while being examined by SOCO officers.

Initially distraught, but now calmed, Constance McKenzie, wrapped in a large blanket after having her bloodstained clothing seized as productions, was first treated for a wound to her head by a local paramedic, then interviewed by DI Fairbanks and DC Smythe.

It was the paramedic who had suggested, "She's in a bit of shock at the minute, Inspector, so maybe you might consider interviewing her at a later time?"

But Fairbanks, taking the advice with a smile, had bid the woman thank you when Smythe showed the paramedic the door.

However, he had no intention of letting McKenzie have the time to both recover from her ordeal and fabricate a story when he knew from experience the best time to get the truth of an incident was as soon as possible after it had occurred and was fresh in the mind of those involved.

Now sipping at his own mug of tea, he watched as McKenzie, with Duke Smythe hovering on the bench seat beside her, cupped her hands around her own mug and sipped at the beverage.

Then he said, "You do know he was going to kill you, Constance, that if we hadn't been here to save you, you'd be dead."

She stared into his eyes then sullenly replied, "So, you think because you'd offer yourself as a target that I owe you, is that it?"

"Oh, I think you owe us big time," he grimly smiled. "In fact, I think you owe us a statement regarding why you were in the hotel in Glasgow and who the guy wearing the Celtic top intended killing that day, when you met with the Republicans."

It was the tiniest flicker in her eyes that gave her away and he knew she must have been wondering how he had come by that information.

"Am I under arrest?" she suddenly asked.

"That's debateable at the minute," he smoothly replied, then explained, "You could be arrested as being complicit in the murder of a young man at the Cambridge Street hotel or instead," he shrugged, "we can detain you under the terms of the Prevention of Terrorism Act, that we now know from your fingerprints we obtained at the hotel, you are *very* familiar with."

He paused to let that information sink in, then continued, "We already have a printout of your history and are aware you are a former member of a proscribed organisation, that you served time and were discharged to be of good behaviour under the terms of the Good Friday Agreement."

He paused, then again continued, "However, your recent conduct and involvement in what we now believe to be a terrorist related incident in Glasgow, could quite possible mean your discharge being revoked and you being returned to prison in the Province."

Her expression changed to one of fear and he knew then he was on the right track, that just another little push might mean the full story from her, and so he carefully added, "Your detention under the POT Act could mean we'd need to hand you over to the Security Service."

He saw the veiled threat caused her eyes again to flicker at the prospect on being handed to the very people McCartney worked for.

"Or," he shrugged again when he offered her a lifeline, "you could be a witness who willingly provides us with a full and comprehensive statement regarding anything that we want to know, then unless any evidence arises that forces us to arrest you, you'd be free to go."

He stared meaningfully at her, then glancing out of the caravan's window to where he could see the two Force's senior officers in a heated discussion, he suggested, "Your choice, Constance, and eh, can I suggest that you really don't have time to think about it because truthfully, I have no idea what's going on out there, but my guess is after a shooting in their area, the local police will want you handed to them and arrested for something."

He watched as she mulled this over, then with a sigh, she said, "Okay, I'll tell you what you want to know, but I want an assurance that I will not be subject to any prosecution."

"What, no demand for witness protection?" he expressed surprise.

Pokerfaced, she stared at him when she quietly replied, "Don't be so naïve, Inspector. You can't protect me against them that are running the country, that run your police service too."

"And who are *they*, exactly?" though he already knew the answer.

She wryly smiled when in her strong Irish brogue, she replied, "Maybe let's just get on with my statement, eh?"

****

Seated behind his desk with Larry Considine stood beside the two detectives, DCI Bobby Heggerty stared in turn at Jaya Bahn and Mickey Rooney when he said, "In the absence of DCI Fitzsimons, I suppose that leaves me to make a decision because frankly, I don't want to bother her when she's enough going on with this shooting down in Newton Stewart. So," he sighed, "this murder suspect, Speirs, he's given us information that might identify his boss, the man, this so-called Commandant, who sent him out to murder the young lad Campbell?"

"Well," Rooney slowly drawled, before he added, "not his name, boss, but he's given us the Commandant's motor's registration number. Said he saw him leaving that Rangers pub in the east end one night and happened to take a note of the number."

"Why did he take the number?" Heggerty's brow furrowed.

"Even he doesn't know, just said it stuck in his mind because part of the plate is G-E-R, as in a GER, a Rangers supporter."

Heggerty exhaled then asked, "Have you PNC'd the number for the registered keeper?"

"No need, boss," Considine interjected. "The Serious Crime Squad's surveillance unit previously provided us with a list of vehicle numbers parked outside the pub and we'd already PNC'd them, though we'd no idea at the time if the cars might have been connected to this Commandant guy."

Heggerty's face creased when he casually asked, "So, Eddie had a surveillance authorised for the pub?"

Considine rolled his eyes when he replied, "Maybe you'll not want to ask that question, boss. Let's just say we've struck lucky, eh?"

Heggerty was long enough in the tooth to know when not to proceed with a question and so sighed "Who is the registered keeper for that number plate?"

Glancing at the notebook in his hand, Considine replied, "Arthur Denholm with an address over in Southlea Avenue," then raised his

head to add, "that's in Orchard Park over in G Division's area." Several seconds passed while Heggerty gave thought to what his old friend, Elaine Fitzsimmons might do with the information, then slowly nodding, addressed Considine when he said, "Larry, you're getting an away day. As far as I'm concerned, this is now a terrorist situation and given our recent experience with the Branch, I'm deciding that we're taking it on ourselves. Contact the Tactical Response Team and offer my apologies, but we need them to further assist us with some armed officers. Explain the situation, then put a plan together and go and get this bugger, Denholm."
****
A little over an hour and a half later, having learned from Arthur Denholm's shocked and tearful wife that no, her husband was not at home, but at his work in the estate agency's office in West Nile Street, he was seated behind his desk when the door was pushed open by two men, dressed all in black and wearing ballistic helmets who screamed at him, "Armed police! Place your hands on the desk, palms down! Now!"
Stunned and more than a little afraid, Denholm immediately complied as more armed officers rushed into his office and who were accompanied by two men and a woman, who dressed in civilian clothes, declared themselves to be CID.
It was the female detective who handcuffed him and with the younger male detective, then bodily lifted him from his chair before frogmarching him from the room.
His body shaking with fright, he didn't hear himself being formally cautioned by the older male detective nor as they walked into the large, general office, the same detective formally telling him, "You are under arrest for collusion in the murder of Gary Campbell."
His staff of five, that included a shocked Penny, slowly rose wide-eyed from behind their desks where the armed officers had instructed them to hide while they arrested their boss.
He'd didn't realise he had peed himself either, not until the female detective was placing him into the rear passenger seat of a car parked outside the main door of the red coloured sandstone Victorian building.
It was then he noticed other police vans parked in front and to the rear of the CID car and that armed officers were directing pedestrians away from the building entrance, while even more

officers were standing in the road, stopping the traffic from passing by.

When two of the detectives got into the car with the female sitting beside him, he heard the male detective in the driving seat, say, "Larry's staying here for the minute to conduct some preliminary interviews with the staff, but he's phoned the DCI to tell him the prisoner is en-route to Maryhill and to request a lawyer to be present."

The detective then turned to ask him, "Unless you'd prefer to have your own lawyer to be present?"

It had never occurred to him that he would find himself to be in this position and therefore had no previous need for a lawyer, so numbly, his mouth too dry to respond, he shook his head.

His main concern right at that minute was that after peeing himself, he worried his bowels might begin to move too.

It was then he began to weep for he knew then that he was caught, that his dream of becoming a senior figure in the Unionist struggle against the Republicans was over, that he was going to prison for a very long time.

****

In the late evening of that day and acting on information provided by Constance McKenzie, who from what she recalled though admittedly dazed at the time after being struck on the head by McCartney's handgun, was sketchy.

However, an extensive search by D&G officers, assisted by that Force's Dog Branch, culminated in the discovery of the body of DI Sadie McGhee within a farmer's field, just a short distance from Newton Stewart.

The subsequent post mortem and the resulting ballistics examination of the illegally held Glock handgun discovered in the possession of DS Norrie McCartney and corroborated by McKenzie's statement of the incident, conclusively identified McCartney as McGhee's killer.

****

As the evening settled in across the skies over Newton Stewart, Eddie Fairbanks phoned Ronnie to tell her, "Sorry, love, it seems I'm going to be pulling an overnighter down here, so you get yourself to bed and I'll phone you first thing in the morning."

"Are you okay? You're not hurt, are you?"

"No," he smiled at the concern in her voice, "I'm fine. It's just that we're a little short of transport right now and the pilot for the Force helicopter has almost exceeded his flying hours for a twenty-four-hour period, so it'll be morning before a car's sent to collect us, then me and my colleague, Duke, can return to Glasgow."

"Helicopter? My, you do live an exciting life, Eddie Fairbanks," she smiled at her mobile phone.

"I should have asked first, how are you feeling," he rubbed his forehead at the developing headache.

"Better now that I know you're okay," then she asked, "The evening STV news. It reported a shooting down in Newton Stewart. I'm guessing that's why you're there?"

"Yes, but it's all over now. In fact, Duke and I are being accommodated in a caravan for the night, so we're off to the local pub for our supper and a pint."

"Then I'll see you tomorrow," she replied, then almost shyly, added, "I love you, Eddie."

He didn't care that Smythe was seated nearby when he replied, "I love you, too."

The call ended, he turned when Smythe grinned expressively at him, then said, "Okay, boss, me and you to the pub and let's hammer the expenses."

****

After returning late that evening by helicopter to Glasgow, then on to Maryhill police office were she received from Larry Considine a summarised account of the arrest of Arthur Denholm, an almost exhausted Elaine Fitzsimmons discovered her day was not yet finished.

Waiting for her with Bobby Heggerty in the DCI's room at Maryhill Police Office was ACC Alex Gardener, who as the Chief Detective Officer in the Force, first formally commended DCI Fitzsimmons in her management of what was proving to be a serious terrorist situation, then offered her all the support that was available.

"Your suspect, Arthur Denholm, has made an extensive voluntary statement, Elaine, naming accomplices and his part in two murders," he handed her a photostat copy of a voluntary statement.

"And," he continued, "I'm staying here with Bobby and we'll run the incident room while you take yourself off to the DI's room and set out your plan for what you're needing done and by whom."

As she nodded then turned, he added with a smile, "I've sent out for fish suppers, Elaine, so Bobby and I will join you when they arrive." Walking in the corridor to the DI's room with a caffeine loaded coffee in her hand, she suspiciously wondered at Gardener's apparent cheeriness, then decided that no doubt she'd learn in due course what was up with him.

However, right now she'd people to arrest and a complicated arrest report to complete for both the Procurator Fiscal, as well as a copy for the Chief Constable.

****

In the privacy of the DI's room and now with a grasp of the investigation and complemented by Arthur Denholm's voluntary statement, Fitzsimmons called for assistance from the late shift Serious Crime Squad and with some inner reluctance, detectives from the Special Branch.

Accompanied by her own Divisional detectives and those of Maryhill CID, Fitzsimmons sent composite squads of detectives to attend throughout the city and the suburbs beyond to detain eight named men and two women.

These individuals, Denholm had freely admitted were recruited by him as members of the Friends of Ulster Loyalists.

In an attempt to curry favour and ingratiate himself by betraying his group, Denholm further admitted that the FUL were an offshoot of the Ulster Defence Association, already a proscribed organisation.

Of those sought, seven men and both women were arrested under the Prevention of Terrorism Act, while the eighth man was discovered to be holidaying abroad, but upon his arrival home some days later, would be arrested by the Ports Coverage Unit at Glasgow Airport.

Charges of membership of a proscribed were libelled against all those arrested and who were detained in custody pending their appearance the following day at Glasgow Sheriff Court.

Needless to say, throughout the following days, there followed a media frenzy that linked the shooting in Newton Stewart with the multiple arrests in the Greater Glasgow area.

****

Friday 29 September 2006.

Though the briefest joint statement by Strathclyde Police and D&G Constabulary was delivered to the media, leaks in both Forces provided information that suggested some sort of terrorist operation had resulted in several deaths of which at least three were murders. It was a shrewd, investigative journalist with an unnamed source in Strathclyde Police, who tied in the POT arrests with the previous murders of the Maryhill pensioner, James Crawford, the Larkhall teenager, Gary Campbell, and the deaths of two police detectives whose names initially were withheld, but soon leaked as DI Sarah 'Sadie' McGhee and DS Norman McCartney.

Initially assumed to be D&G detectives, simply because of the location of their deaths, further speculation arose when it was leaked that both officers were in fact members of Strathclyde Police Special Branch, with the assumption in many of the tabloids that the officers had been murdered while heroically working under cover.

****

That Friday evening, excusing himself from what continued to be an on-going and complex multiple murder investigation, DI Eddie Fairbanks drove with his partner, Ronnie Masters, to meet with the obstetrician at Ross Hall Hospital in Crookston, on the south side of Glasgow.

The obstetrician, a middle-aged woman who almost immediately recognised Ronnie as the famous model she once had been, was so enthralled to have Ronnie as her patient that almost without realising the obstetrician was examining her, twenty minutes passed before the woman told Ronnie, "I really don't think you have too much to worry about. It's what we call hormonal bleeding and can occur any time between four to eight or even nine weeks during the early stage of pregnancy. That said," she sighed, then turned to include Fairbanks in the conversation, "I will suggest that you take it easy for the next month and should there be any recurrence of the bleeding, do not hesitate to call me and we'll have you in for a bit of bed rest. Now," she stared meaningfully at Ronnie, "will you do as the doctor tells you or shall I have this handsome man tie you down to your bed?"

Before she could respond, Fairbanks firmly replied, "I guarantee you, doctor, Ronnie will be taking it easy. She has a very capable deputy who can run her boutique, though of course she'll likely be popping in now and again to check up on things."

"And I've a charity event to organise," she reminded him.
"Well, can this event wait four weeks before you commence your organising it?"
"Yes, I suppose it can," she sighed, then added, "because this baby is too precious to risk, isn't it?" she turned towards Fairbanks.
"It is," he agreed with a happy nod.

Saturday 30 September 2006.

The extraordinary conference to be held in the smaller of the two meeting rooms located on the fourth floor of Police Headquarters in Pitt Street was arranged for midday, to permit the two representatives of the Security Service to arrive from London.
At their request, a Detective Inspector representing Special Branch met them upon their arrival at Glasgow Airport, then ushered them through the concourse to the Branch car that was illegally parked in the taxi rank immediately outside the main entrance.
Swiftly conveyed to Pitt Street, the DI accompanied the man and woman through the West Regent Street entrance, then in the elevator to the fourth floor where he left them at the door to the meeting room.
Entering the room, those already present stopped speaking and turned to view the two representatives.
None of the police officers, except perhaps the Deputy Chief Constable, Charlie Miller, had a clue as to how the meeting would be conducted and there was a quiet tension in the room when both representatives took their seats.
There was no courteous handshaking that to DI Eddie Fairbanks, seemed to indicate the way the meeting was to follow.
It was Miller, who first politely introduced himself, then his colleagues, ACC Alex Gardener, Chief Superintendent Callum Fraser, who was known to the woman and politely nodded in greeting; then DCI Elaine Fitzsimmons and DI Fairbanks.
Finally, Miller turned to introduce Detective Superintendent Trevor Barton, representing the Dumfries & Galloway Constabulary.
The young woman seated at a hastily introduced desk at the side of the room, Miller introduced as DC Jaya Bahn, then explained Bahn was proficient in shorthand and would record the minutes of the meeting.

The female, an ill-kept looking woman in her mid-fifties, thought Miller, with brown, greasy looking, shoulder length hair streaked with grey and bad skin and who was dressed in a green blouse and a well-worn, tweed skirted suit, slapped her stressed, black leather briefcase on the varnished table, then sitting down with her colleague beside her, introduced herself as Catherine Jones, a Departmental Head, before introducing her younger colleague, Jason Smith, a handsome, fair-haired and smartly dressed man in his early thirties with dazzling white teeth.

As Fitzsimmons later snidely commented, "Unlike his boss, Smith looked like he'd stepped out of a Vogue magazine."

None of the police officers believed the couple's names to truly be Smith and Jones, that they were pseudo names and agreed later, obviously a play on the comedy duo made famous during the mid-eighties and the late nineties.

"Before we commence the meeting, Mr Miller," said Jones with a soft southern counties lilt and what she obviously believed was a winning smile, "I'd like to voice my opposition to notes being taken. It's not usually the rule when we meet with our police colleagues."

Miller returned her smile when he replied, "That may be the rule by which you conduct your business with the English Forces, Ms Jones, but you're in Scotland now and up here, we play by our rules."

His eyes narrowed, then he added, "Which brings me nicely to the reason you've been summoned today."

Watching her, Fairbanks thought she seemed to bristle at the suggestion she had been summoned, but wisely didn't respond.

He was also puzzled at the lack of the usual courtesy coffee or tea and wondered if this was a deliberate ploy by Miller to make the pair feel even more uncomfortable.

In a clear and concise voice, Miller, who hardly referred to the notes in front of him, summarised the operation that was carried out in Glasgow whereby a senior female member of the UDA, Arlene McCandlish, who at that time was meeting with a known member of the IRA and a man on the Ports Watchlist, Gary McGuigan, to discuss a peace initiative, but instead McCandlish found herself targeted by a gunman who not only botched the job, but immediately thereafter, was himself murdered.

"And why should a local criminal issue be of interest to we at the Security Service, Mr Miller?" she casually asked, but *too* casually, thought Fairbanks.
His expression was one of disbelief when he replied, "Absolutely correct when you refer to what occurred as a criminal issue, Ms Jones, but are you *seriously* telling me and my officers that the Security Service would have no interest in both these proscribed organisations discussing a peace settlement?"
It was as if she realised she'd made a faux pas when she stammered in reply, "Well, if we'd known about it, most certainly..."
But she was quickly interrupted by Miller who pokerfaced startled all those present when he loudly slapped his hand down onto the table, then hissed, "I see little point in beating about the bush. Your organisation concocted a plan to assassinate McCandlish and blame the IRA, thereby continuing the feud between both organisations. As to the reasoning behind this criminal intention, we as mere police officers can only speculate at the Machiavellian manner in which *you* people conduct your business! However, I do *not* believe we've got it wrong when we assess what occurred on Tuesday last in the Cambridge Street hotel, was not any kind of political strategy, but a Security Services operation to further your control and maintain your presence in Northern Ireland."
His anger obvious, he stared at her face as it paled when he continued with a snarl, "Your organisation's mistake, however, was conducting your operation here in Glasgow and but for the tenacity and professionalism of my CID and their uniformed colleagues, your *moles* in the Special Branch might have succeeded in carrying out *your* conspiracy."
"As it is," he quickly held up his hand to stymie her protest, "both your moles are now dead and your operation has not only cost the lives of a pensioner and an impressionable young teenager who had been recruited to carry out the grisly task of murder, but will also ensure a second extremely impressionable teenager will spend a goodly part of his life in prison!"
The tense silence that followed was broken when Jones tried to bluster, "I...we have no idea what you're talking about and I must protest..."
But she got no further when taking a deep breath, Miller calmly told her, "Don't bother trying to deny your organisation's involvement,

Ms Jones. My officers have sufficient proof of the Security Service's participation in the conspiracy and a report will be submitted to the Scottish Crown Office."

He stared at her, then slowly taking a breath, he shook his head when he quietly added, "That all said, none of us around the table here are so naive to believe that anyone from your organisation will be found culpable for their part in *your* fiasco."

He paused for several seconds before he continued, "I also have little doubt that pressure from your embarrassed colleagues in Whitehall will be applied to the Scottish Parliament for both Strathclyde Police and D&G Constabulary to cease investigating these crimes, for like all your colleagues and if experience serves me well, you and your organisation will slip away from facing the courts and the justice you so richly deserve."

He paused again for breath as with a nod to her stunned colleague, she angrily grabbed at her briefcase then rose from her chair, but stopped when Miller said, "Please inform your bosses, Ms Jones, that your organisation is served notice by both Strathclyde Police and Dumfries & Galloway Constabulary, that any future cooperation will come at a price and that the Special Branch, who I will remind you, serve *our* respective Chief Constables, will be returning any equipment you might have previously permitted them the use of. That, and if we discover any officer who is unlawfully liaising with your organisation, that officer will be put before the courts and I will *personally* ensure the court case is widely publicised."

"That might be a mistake you will come to regret, Mr Miller," she huffily replied.

He didn't respond to the veiled threat, other than to turn towards her and say, "DC Bahn, will you kindly escort these people to the West Regent Street door and by the way," he stared deadpan at Jones, "you'll find a taxi rank further along the street. Good day to you both."

****

After Jones, Smith and DC Bahn had left the room, almost a full minute passed before Alex Gardener broke the silence to ask, "You think Elaine's report to the Crown Office will get anywhere, sir?"

Miller shook his head before he replied, "Not a snowballs chance in hell, Alex."

They watched as he gently stroked the scar on his right cheek, then sighed, "A long time ago, I had some dealings with that mob when they were working covertly up here in Glasgow and frankly, back then they operated without any legal accountability. So, to answer your question, I don't believe that regardless of what laws are currently supposed to be in place to regulate their activities, they'll do exactly what they believe they can get away with."

He turned towards Barton, then said, "Trevor, I'm grateful you took the time to attend today. Needless to say, the joint investigation will continue with such support from us that you require. I know we didn't get the opportunity to speak before you arrived, so how are things proceeding down in Newton Stewart?"

Barton, a gruff Yorkshireman, replied, "It's been a busy few days, sir, and it's myself who will be reporting the circumstances of the murder of DI McGhee and the death of DS McCartney to Crown Office."

He glanced at Fairbanks before turning back to Miller, then said, "I'd like to say at this juncture, from the statements provided by your Tactical Response Team, DI Fairbanks there," he nodded at him, "and his colleague, DC Smythe, I will be recommending to Crown Office that the young lass who fired the fatal shot that killed McCartney should be fully exonerated. Indeed, I will be commending her actions to my Chief Constable, for its plainly clear from those who were watching that McCartney was turning the gun to shoot DI Fairbanks and thus, she saved his life," he smiled at Fairbanks.

"Well, that's a huge relief and no less so for Eddie," Miller grinned at Fairbanks.

"And on that point," he added, "Elaine, while I know you still have a massive clear-up job on the investigation, please convey my grateful thanks to your joint team and I'm certain Mr Gardener will *not* be quibbling about their overtime claims, for we are both aware that your team have been working round the clock."

With a deadpan expression, Gardener turned to stare at Fitzsimmons, then slowly smiled when he simply said, "Agreed."

"And so," Miller rose to his feet as the others courteously did so too, "it's Saturday, so I'll let you get on with the rest of your day. Thank you, all."

EPILOGUE

The media interest in the alleged terrorist incident that resulted in the death of a Larkhall teenager, Gary Campbell, at the Cambridge Street hotel and the alleged relationship between the murder in a Maryhill flat a week earlier of the pensioner, Jimmy Crawford, soon faded as conflicting stories circulated that the murder in the stairwell of the hotel was nothing to do at all with terrorism, but a drug gang hit gone wrong.
Needless to say, in common with their policy, Strathclyde Police said nothing to dispute that idea.
However, the deaths of the two police officers in the Newton Stewart area of Galloway, following the discovery by a local reporter that both were not as previously thought, local officers, but members of Strathclyde Police, raised further questions when it was also discovered McGhee was a Northern Irish born police officer. Conspiracists emerged from the woodwork and the story dragged on for some weeks until finally and to the relief of both Strathclyde Police Media Department and their D & G colleagues, there was nothing new to report in the press.
Though eventually interest in the story did die down, curiously, it faded to become local legend in the Newton Stewart area with a number of opposing versions of what had really occurred in the caravan park.
****
On the Thursday following the meeting at police headquarters in Pitt Street, Elaine Fitzsimmons, aware her final report to the Crown Office was a lengthy and convoluted story, decided to travel through to Edinburgh and personally deliver the report herself.
Arriving by appointment at the imposing Chambers Street building, Fitzsimmons, accompanied by DI Eddie Fairbanks, were led by a uniformed commissionaire to a private meeting room on the first floor, where within minutes and to both their surprise, they were joined by the Lord Advocate himself, Alexander 'Sandy' McKinnon. McKinnon, who as the senior law officer in Scotland, as well as being the longest serving Lord Advocate in the history of the Scottish legal establishment, had been in the role for almost twelve years and was a distinguished and much respected figure in the

Scottish Government, though had recently intimated his desire to retire from public life.

Greeting both Fitzsimmons and Fairbanks with a handshake, he called for an assistant to bring coffee, then invited both to sit with him at the highly polished meeting table while he took charge of, then speed-read Fitzsimmon's report.

Almost ten minutes passed during which coffee was served, though McKinnon notably did not touch his, so engrossed was he in the report.

At last he sighed and laying the report down flat onto the table, then explained, "As likely you'll have guessed, I was forewarned of your arrival today by Mr Miller, who is well known to me."

He took a slow breath before he continued, "Having read your report, DCI Fitzsimmons, I now understand why you wish to discuss this with Crown Office, rather than have it forwarded through dispatches by the Glasgow PF's office."

He paused before again continuing, "I am particularly troubled at your findings and your very serious allegation of the involvement of the Security Service in what your report seems to indicate was a conspiracy to murder this Northern Irish woman, allegedly a Loyalist activist."

He paused once more, staring in turn at them before he keenly asked, "So, now that you have my undivided attention, what's your suggestion about how I deal with this report?"

With a glance at Fairbanks, she began with, "It's our shared opinion that if what we have learned is true, the Northern Irish Loyalists and the IRA are resolved on agreeing a permanent ceasefire. Both organisations of course wish these meetings to be covert and without the involvement of the UK Government and indeed, the Government of Ireland."

She stopped, then tapping a forefinger on the report, said, "We believe a public trial for the named accused of murder," she nodded at the report, "could potentially bring future meetings between these two groups to the public's attention and seriously damage the opportunity for future negotiations. We would therefore respectfully request in the interest of National Security and in particular, for the benefit of our colleagues in the PSNI and the general public at large, that you consider authorising the accused's court appearances to be held *in camera*."

She paused for a few seconds, then continued, "Having brought our concerns to the attention of our ACC (Crime), Mr Gardener, he has agreed that the evidence against both Denholm and Speirs is frankly, overwhelming, Milord. However, while we anticipate there will be pleas of guilty by both Denholm and Speirs, it could be that their individual defence counsel might wish to change their pleas in an attempt to publicly highlight the purpose of their actions and thereby gain some leverage to plea bargain."

She paused again and found to her surprise, she was a little nervous. "If the evidence of their crimes," she continued, "should be divulged in open court and the general public learn that a terrorist plot and subsequent incident has occurred in Glasgow that resulted in four deaths, we fear that extensive media coverage might in turn provoke sectarian violence and disorder, not only in the Province itself, but also in Glasgow where as likely you are aware, there has always been an undercurrent of sectarianism, as evidenced by the support both the IRA and the UDA have in the past enjoyed from Scottish based supporters. That is why we humbly suggest a closed hearing."

She paused to raise a hand to declare, "I should add we do not include the death of the individual who committed the first murder, Thomas Collins. His death is down to his stupidity in not seeking medical assistance and cruel though it may sound, be it on his own head."

They watched his grey, bushy eyebrows knit and he sighed, "I understand your concern, of course I do; however, with regard to your report, I must inform you only three days ago, I received a delegation from the Security Service who, obviously aware of the arrest of these two men, categorically stated that the Security Service had no involvement in this matter."

"Bollocks," Fairbanks muttered then chalk-white and seeing the reproving expression on Fitzsimmons face, immediately added, "Sorry, Milord. I unreservedly apologise for that comment."

Neither Fitzsimmons nor he expected the response when McKinnon replied, "Bollocks indeed, DI Fairbanks," then with a soft smile, added, "While I might be getting on in age, I do not yet button up the back, as they say."

His lips pursed when he muttered, "That and the lady and her lackey, who had the cheek to arrive unannounced at my office, then had the audacity to remind me that I serve at the pleasure of Her Majesty. Damn cheek of her," he scowled.

His scowl turned to a frown when said, "Veiled threat though it was and no matter who they may be," his lip curled when he added, "*no-one* threaten*s* the Lord Advocate of Scotland."

Formally drawing himself up to stare at her, he said, "DCI Fitzsimmons, you have convinced me of the necessity to have the trial of these two accused, Denholm and Speirs, held *in camera* and I will also instruct there will be a media blackout of the trial. While a closed court trial also suits those who currently serve at Thames House and while I suspect it will do no real good, I intend poking the fire, as it were."

Glancing from one to the other, both Fitzsimons and Fairbanks were in no doubt of his resolve when he said, "On behalf of the Scottish Justiciary, I will be making an official complaint to the Intelligence and Security Committee that you may or may not be aware, provides an oversight of all UK operations involving National Security. With some luck," he shrugged, "the complaint may result in at best, dismissals or at worse, demotions within the Security Service, who so obviously have been caught red-handed, plying their dirty tricks in your fair city. Now," he smiled, "is there anything else I can assist you with?"

It was Fairbanks who asked, "Just one thing, Milord. Your recent Thames House visitor. Wouldn't happen to have been a Catherine Jones, in her mid-fifties, bad skin and greasy looking shoulder length brown hair and a young guy with fair hair and dazzling white teeth?"

They watched the Lord Advocate smile before he nodded, "Very perceptive of you, DI Fairbanks. That was indeed the names the woman gave me."

****

Axel stuck his head into the kitchen to tell her, "Arlene, that's Dicky Porter and two of his people turned up wanting to speak with you. Porter says it's important," he shrugged.

Wiping the flour from her hands onto her apron, McCandlish instinctively brushed back the loose lock of hair from her forehead, then replied, "Invite him through, Axel. I'll put the kettle on, so give it five minutes before you pop in to fetch your tea."

He smiled, knowing that was his cue; McCandlish telling him when

the five minutes was up, if she wanted Porter gone, he'd to bring Jimmy in too.
If not, she'd give him the nod that all was well.
Dicky Porter, looking as dapper as always in a knee length, charcoal grey coloured wool coat, greeted McCandlish with a kiss on her cheek, then said, "Sorry to come unannounced, Arlene, but I've had a wee word from over the water."
"And that is?" she gestured he sit at the table.
"We've a man in the jail over in Glasgow. A prison officer who used to work here at the Long Kesh, but now works over there in Glasgow, in the remand wing. It seems that Arthur Denholm and a number of his unit," he paused, then sighed "all of them, apparently, have been arrested. Denholm's in solitary with a young guy and they're both charged with murder. My man says that Denholm, he's tweeting like a budgie."
Her back to the sink and her arms folded, she stared narrow-eyed when she asked, "Your man, he didn't happen to get Denholm to confess who his contact is over here? The bastard who set me up and wanted me dead?"
"Yes, Arlene, unfortunately he did," Porter wearily sighed, then quickly pulling a small, Walther PPK semi-automatic pistol from his coat pocket, shot her three times in the chest.
McCandlish's body had not even fallen to the floor when the sound of the gunshots echoed through to the hallway outside the kitchen. Shocked, Axel was reaching for the handgun in the waistband of his trousers, but Porter's bodyguards, already aware of what to expect, speedily drew their own pistols from their anorak pockets, then turned when each man shot his target in the chest, though Axel had to be shot again in the head to finally kill him.
*****

Several weeks had passed since his safe return home from Glasgow. Arriving home from work that Friday evening, then calling his dog Thatcher to him, Gary McGuigan bent to put on the lead and as he had done in the previous weeks, led Thatcher out into Culhane Street, then toward the Moorland on the other side of the Castletown River.
Perhaps he was becoming lazy or no longer believed that the Garda Síochána had any interest in him, for his usual check for surveillance was at best, half-hearted.

The light was fading as he made his way through the entrance to the Moorland then bending, released Thatcher to run wild and chase the nesting birds.

Minutes later found him sitting at the bench then as casually as he dared, run his fingers under the wooden slats beneath him.

Countless time he had checked the DLB, the dead letter box, and always came away disappointed.

But that evening and to his surprise, he felt the slim envelope taped there and his heart beating, glanced around him, but saw nobody near and certainly, no-one apparently watching him.

Pulling the envelope free of its tape, he swithered whether to open the letter there or take it home.

Impatiently, he decided to read it while seated on the bench then fumbled in his pocket for his reading glasses before removing the single, typed sheet from the envelope.

His stomach tensed and his heart beating, he quickly read the typed text:

McCandlish assassinated by her own mob. Glasgow police arrested two men for trying to kill her. Theirs not ours. Talks are off.

He crumpled the paper in his hand then stuffing it and the envelope into his pocket, called Thatcher to him.

Clipping the lead to the dog's collar, the face of his eighteen-years-old daughter leaping into his mind, he sighed, "Let's go home, boy. There's nothing more we can do."

****

The murders of Arlene McCandlish and her two male associates, Axel and Jimmy, caused a furore in the hard-line Protestant areas of Belfast, resulting in cars, a couple of buses and street furniture set alight, bricks and petrol bombs thrown and riot police deployed to contain then disperse the troublemakers.

However, the more cynical members of the PSNI privately attributed the disorder to bored teenagers who likely had no real idea who McCandlish really was, but were encouraged by older hooligans' intent on having a good night out at the expense of the police.

Without evidence to disprove it, though the police intelligence suspected otherwise, the tabloids attributed the murders to a breakaway dissident Republican group and of course the media's so-called Loyalists sources predicted a harsh and vengeful response and so, for over a week, Belfast burned and there was a brief return to tit-for tat violence that resulted in four further deaths.

Of those who died, two were an innocent Protestant couple who while in their car and travelling on Crumlin Road, were attacked by bricks and bottles and in their haste to flee the angry mob, crashed into a building and suffered fatal injuries.

Of the two Catholics who died, one elderly woman, a Franciscan nun out collecting the state pensions for elderly members of her Order, suffered a fatal asthma attack when she was surrounded by an angry group of youths, who pushed and shoved at her.

The second death was of a teenager who during a skirmish with opposing Loyalist youths, was about the throw a petrol bomb, but misjudged the length of the ignited rag that caused the petrol filled bottle to prematurely explode, causing catastrophic burns on his right hand, arm, face and head and from which injuries he succumbed three days later.

At a rally held on a Sunday two weeks following the McCandlish murders and the ensuing rioting and deaths of the two innocent Protestants, in a field on the outskirts of Belfast and attended by close to ten thousand people, the elected spokesperson for the newly created Loyalist Coalition Group, Richard 'Dicky' Porter, addressed the solemn crowd.

"What is blatantly clear," he thumped the dais with his fist as he stared out at the admiring crowd, "is that so long as these Republicans' thugs can at will, enter the home of a good Protestant woman, then gun down her and her two friends in cold blood, there will be *NO* peace agreement between the true Loyalist people and the Irish Republican movement."

****

The pensioner, Jimmy Crawford, recruited by the former Detective Sergeant, Norrie McCartney, as the middle man to provide Arthur Denholm with a handgun, was buried six weeks after his murder. His daughter and her husband both attended the funeral, as did his son, Peter, also permitted to attend though handcuffed and escorted from HMP Barlinnie by two prison officers.

In a rare display of compassion and without informing her bosses of her intention, DC Jaya Bahn also attended the funeral where with the permission of the senior prison officer, Bahn handed the convicted murderer a small, wooden box and explained, "Your wee dog,

Baxter. He was cremated. I thought you'd want the ashes."
She didn't expect his reaction when the stoney-faced young man unexpectedly burst into tears and though handcuffed, leaned into her and with his head bowed, cried on her shoulder.
****

After her discharge from hospital and a convalescence period of six weeks, in discussion then agreement with her parents, Constable Alice Redwood resigned from Strathclyde Police.

It was some weeks later and just prior to her retirement, Chief Superintendent Liz Malone received a letter from the young woman, thanking Malone for her support during Redwood's sick leave and informing Malone that she had successfully obtained a place to train as a teacher at the Jordanhill Training College in Glasgow.

Redwood's assailant, the former Constable, John Cooper, appeared at the Glashow Sheriff and Jury Court accused of attempted murder, but continued to deny any knowledge of Redwood's assault.

However, the overwhelming Forensic evidence coupled with that of his estranged wife, Rose, who formally complained of his continuous domestic abuse, was sufficient to convince the jury of his guilt.

Cooper was sentenced to six years for the attempted murder of Alice Redwood and eighteen months, to run concurrently, on the charge of domestic abuse.

An attempt by Cooper, who at the time was in the care of the Scottish Prison Service, to claim compensation for the disfiguring serious assault that left him scarred, was dismissed by the Criminal Injury Compensation Board.

Because of his previous occupation and for his own safety, the SPS plan to segregate Cooper with prisoners at risk to violence from fellow inmates. Such prisoners include sex offenders and those who are imprisoned for crimes against children.

Rose Cooper, assisted by Woman's Aid (Glasgow), successfully divorced her husband and also, upon his release from prison, granted a restraining order without limit for herself and her children.

The divorce court also granted Rose full custody of her children and awarded her the marital home.
****

As the Lord Advocate had decreed, the appearance of Arthur

Denholm and Nicholas Speirs on the charges laid before them was held at the High Court of Justiciary in Giles Street, Edinburgh.
Both men pled guilty to the murder of Gary Campbell and related Terrorism charges.
A weeping Denholm was sentenced to life imprisonment for the charge of murder and twenty-five years on the Terrorism charges, both sentences to run consecutively.
Mindful of his age and the lengthy sentences she imposed, Her Ladyship presiding did not clarify any minimum term before he is permitted to apply for parole, but took a moment to remind Denholm it was likely he would die in prison.
Again, mindful of his youth and his apparent susceptibility to exploitation by the older Denholm, a befuddled Speirs was similarly sentenced to life imprisonment and an additional ten years on the Terrorism related charges to run concurrently, with the minimum term of eighteen years to be served whereupon dependent on his good behaviour, he can apply for parole.
The remaining eight men and two women, all of who without exception, pled guilty to being members of a proscribed organisation.
Dependent on the assistance provided by each accused to the investigating officers and any previous convictions they might have previously accrued, awarded sentences ranged from six months to five years.
As requested by Elaine Fitzsimmons, none of the foregoing sentencing appeared in the media.
****

In due course and subsequent to a post mortem, the body of the former Detective Inspector Sadie McGhee was returned to her family for burial in the County of Armagh.
Similarly, the body of Detective Sergeant Norman McCartney was returned to his family for cremation.
Strathclyde Police were not represented at either funeral service.
****

In the weeks following the conclusion of the joint investigation, several members of Strathclyde Police Special Branch were transferred throughout the Force to CID or uniformed posts and included the HSB, Detective Chief Superintendent Callum Fraser.

The day prior to his transfer, ACC Alex Gardener summoned Fraser to his office where the ACC bluntly told Fraser that he had lost control of his Department, reminding him that had Fraser questioned what was going on and why and also curtailed the influence the Security Service had on McGhee and McCartney, the circumstances that excluded Andrew Collins who succumbed to Sepsis, but led to the violent deaths of four other individuals, might not have occurred. A verbal deal was agreed and to his credit, Fraser accepted the formal rebuke that was not recorded on his record. It was also agreed that having neared his thirty years' service, he would accept the sideways uniform posting, then some months later, retire from the Force.

With his career unblemished and his lengthy service in Special Branch, Fraser was soon thereafter recruited by a prestigious security company.

****

The official complaint made by Scotland's Lord Advocate, Andrew McKinnon, to the Intelligence and Security Committee regarding the criminal activities of the Security Service in Glasgow, that resulted in a total of five deaths in Scotland, four of which were by violence, was acknowledged by the UK Government's Minister for such affairs; in essence, a state appointed Ombudsman.

Some weeks later, a summarised written response to McKinnon, simply concluded with the repetitive statement, 'lessons have been learned,' but with no indication of any individual being taken to task. As McKinnon later confided in a private telephone call to Deputy Chief Constable Charlie Miller, "It was as I feared, Charlie. The buggers have whitewashed their involvement. However, might I suggest that your CID and Special Branch keep their ears to the ground? I do believe our cousins down south will continue their nefarious activities, no matter what they may say."

****

Constance McKenzie did indeed provide a voluntary and self-incriminating statement that implicated her in the plot to assassinate Arlene McCandlish; however, Scottish criminal law requires corroboration of her statement and as at the material time, there was no such corroborative evidence and no other evidence against her of criminal wrongdoing that would substantiate a charge, she was released on her own cognisance to appear at any court date fixed thereafter, then permitted to leave Newton Stewart.

As DI Fairbanks later explained to DCI Fitzsimmons, "I believed that her information was more valuable than detaining her as a suspect and besides," he'd shrugged, "what would I have charged her with? Being a victim?"

Fortunately, Fitzsimmon's agreed with his decision.

It was some months later, in a wooded area just off the D4 rural road outside the small French town of Orbec in Normandy, the body of a strangled woman was discovered lying face down.

Called to the scene, the local Gendarmerie took charge of the body that they discovered was dressed in a flowery summer frock, but shoeless and had no coat, no identification, nor was any handbag or purse discovered.

A post mortem recorded the woman to have been dead for anything between two to three weeks and aged between forty and forty-five years. The only distinguishing feature about the woman was that she had dyed blonde hair with a visible two-inch scar on her right cheek. To date, though information has been sought by the Police Nationale throughout France, the woman remains unidentified.

****

As intimated by Detective Superintendent Barton of the Dumfries & Galloway Constabulary, the young Tactical Response Team member who fired the fatal shot, thereby saving DI Fairbanks life, was indeed exonerated and awarded a D&G Chief Constable's High Commendation for her action.

To his surprise, Eddie Fairbanks too was awarded the same High Commendation for bravely offering his life to save that of Constance McKenzie, though when his fiancée, Ronnie Masters, learned why he was to receive the award and proud though she was, he wondered if his split-second decision was worth the verbal scolding that later ensued.

****

DC Jackie Wilson, who stepped up to the role of acting Detective Sergeant and managed the Maryhill CID general office during the time of the joint investigation, some weeks after the conclusion to the investigation and to her surprise, was promoted to uniform sergeant at L Division's Helensburgh office.

Wilson's promotion created a DC vacancy that was later filled by acting DC Mickey Rooney.
****

DS Larry Considine has to date abstained from alcohol for eighty-two days and is a regular attendee at his local AA meetings. He continues to meet with his sponsor, Anne, and admits that while the struggle to stay sober continues, the craving is still with him.
On the plus side his relationship with his wife has greatly improved and who is already planning his retirement.
****

Now fully returned to work, DCI Bobby Heggerty was the principal speaker at the retiral function of DCI Elaine Fitzsimmons, who announced that having paid a deposit on a two-bedroom flat with a roof balcony overlooking the sea in the Spanish town of Vilassar de Mar in Catalonia, she would not be receiving visitors. However, she added with a broad wink and too much laughter and applause, she was hoping to catch herself a señor to instruct her in both Spanish and other local pleasures.
Other speakers included Deputy Chief Constable Charlie Miller and to Fitzsimmon's delight, ACC Alex Gardener, who arrived with his wife and who she saw spent some time engaged in amiable conversation with Bobby Heggerty.
****

The week following Gill Masters surprise visit to her sister, Ronnie attempted to contact Gill on the only number she had for her, only to soon discover the number was no longer receiving calls.
Letters to the Clydesdale bank addressed to Gill Masters via the Bank were returned unopened.
Disappointed, but now no longer fearing a miscarriage, she made the decision that during her pregnancy she would appoint her deputy, Laura, as manager of the boutique.
However, encouraged by her fiancé, Eddie, her latest project found her designing maternity wear for the mature mother and she is currently in talks with a local manufacturing company.
Ronnie now combines her busy day with coordinating the charity event that was planned for mid-November of that year.
Buoyed by the successful photo-shoot and granted the publishing rights to the event, Charity Dawson, the Editor of the fashion magazine, Life & Fashion Management, planned a full edition of the

magazine that would cover the entire event and so employed two much-needed assistants to support Ronnie with the administration of the event and a camera duo who recorded the lead-up.

Ronnie, whose expected delivery date is April 2007, and now blooming, signed a further contract with the magazine that intended a maternity fashion shoot as the pregnancy continued.

****

On Wednesday, twenty-fifth of October, 2006, within the luxury Victorian mansion in Glasgow's Park Circus that had formerly served as the Italian Consulate, Eddie Fairbanks married Ronnie Masters in a civil ceremony.

Attended by just thirty friends and family that included his brother, who had surprised him by flying in from Australia for the ceremony to be his Best Man, and while Ronnie was privately disappointed at the absence of her sister, Gill, she chose Susie Lauder as her bridesmaid.

The entire event, to Fairbanks embarrassment, was covered by the Life & Fashion Management magazine and featured a four-page special.

As Ronnie teasingly told him, "They're paying for it, including the champagne reception at the Central Hotel too, so just grin and bear it."

"Anything you say, Mrs Fairbanks," he shook his head in surrender.

****

A little over eleven weeks after the murder of Arlene McCandlish and her two bodyguards and with the PSNI struggling to find witnesses or evidence as to who was responsible, Richard 'Dicky' Porter, now having achieved some esteem within the Inner Council and widely regarded as the new leader of the recently formed Loyalist Coalition Group, stared at his reflection in the wardrobe mirror, then involuntarily nodded.

It had been a long and difficult struggle and now here he was, in his home in Belfast and on the cusp of being the most senior member of the Inner Council; in essence, the respected head of all true Loyalists in the Province.

But Porter's goal was not simply to be the head of the Coalition. No, his true ambition was to form his own Unionist Party and lead from the Northern Irish Parliament.

Stormont.

"Dicky, time to go," his minder called from downstairs.

Slowly exhaling as he continued to stare at his reflection, he smiled, then turning, lifted his written notes from the dresser and stuffed them into the inside pocket of his suit jacket.

The previous evening, the speech had taken him some hours to compose and summarised, it vilified not just the Republicans, but also the UK Government for their lack of backbone in dealing with the rise in Republican insurgency.

Porter's speech that he knew would cause outrage in the UK Parliament, proposed draconian measures, suggesting the Catholic minority be herded back into their own council estates and if necessary, just as the army had done in the Seventies, chain-link fences be built to keep them there, with gates at choke points and operated by the police and vetted security staff.

His proposal also called for identity cards for Catholics and he grimly smiled when he considered how *that* would go down with the politicians.

Such was his outrageous demands that, as he explained to his more conservative Inner Council members, "We ask for much more that they will willingly give, then after negotiation, we accept less, but that less will be what *we* want."

With a final glance at the mirror, he made his way downstairs to find his two minders, both loyal and true men he implicitly trusted; the men who had dealt with McCandlish's bodyguards.

Their coats on and waiting for him, he could sense them to be as excited as was he.

"This is it, boys," he grinned at them, then asked, "Any word from the City Hall?"

The older bodyguard replied, "Donegal Square is filling up with the vehicles of a number of camera crews, Dicky, and the word is the Hall itself is choked with reporters and not just from the UK."

"Good," he forced a smile and felt the first of a nervous twinge in his stomach.

He had accepted that he would be likened to a Hitleresque figure, that he would be accused of genocidal intent regarding his Republican minded neighbours, but he cared not, for his argument to the masses who crowded the halls and fields when he spoke was simply, "Those who criticise *us* do not have to live among *them*!"

Them of course, being the Catholic population of Northern Ireland.

"Right," he took a deep breath and prepared himself for the most significant event since he had taken up arms to protect his people, "let's go."

Their routine was as had always been, his senior bodyguard stepping out of his mid-terraced home in Riga Street, the bodyguards head swivelled left and right, then left and right again to identify any possible threat and where there was none, then getting down onto one knee to once more check the underside of the Range Rover for any sign of a possible IED.

In truth, he didn't expect to find anything anyway, for wasn't this predominantly Protestant area the safest in all of Belfast?

Seeing there was nothing, he stood back upright, then waved back towards the house to the second man, to bring Porter out and into the bright sunlit day.

Hurrying towards the lime coloured Range Rover parked in the layby just outside the house, the door was pulled open by the first man to permit Porter to enter the rear of the vehicle, while the second bodyguard stood guard, surveilling the road till his compatriot was in the driving seat before getting into the front passenger seat.

A little over one hundred and twenty metres down the road and seated in parked, dusty old-style Renault vehicle, the driver watched in his rear-view mirror as the three men entered the Range Rover, then lifting a mobile burner phone that was sitting on his knee, pressed the green 'send' button.

Through the night and while others acted as lookouts, the same man had unlocked the boot of the vehicle and left a holdall bag within that contained an improvised explosive device of eight pounds of Soviet-era, Czechoslovakian made Semtex explosive that wired to an electric detonator and powered by a small battery, was initiated by a call from the burner phone.

The Semtex, he inwardly smiled, was a nice touch, having been part of a seized shipment bound many years before for an IRA active service unit working in the County of Fermanagh.

Thus, when the Forensic laboratory of the PSNI examined the residue of the explosion, the cops would have someone to blame.

The resulting explosion completely shredded the Range Rover and tore the three occupants into dozens of pieces, as well as causing widespread structural damage to the houses and parked vehicles within a fifty-metre range.

The only other living casualty was a lone dog, who at a front door and whining to be admitted to a house thirty metres away, was struck by several large shards of glass and who also died instantly.

Driving off from Riga Street, the man switched to a second burner phone and again, pressing the single phone number in the phone's directory, simply muttered the codeword, "Breadcrumbs."

In an office within a grey coloured stone-faced building that sat on the Embankment of the River Thames, the woman with the greasy hair and bad skin and who called herself, Catherine Jones, softly smiled, for the final player in the conspiracy to murder Arlene McCandlish in a Glasgow hotel and who had he be so inclined, could implicate the Security Service, was now dealt with.

****

Printed in Great Britain
by Amazon

46339513R00215